APELLA'S TURN

Apella's Turn

Apella's Turn is a work of fiction. Names, characters, businesses, places, events, organizations and incidents are either the product of the author's imagination or are used fictionally. Any resemblance to actual persons, living or dead, is entirely coincidental. Reference to actual railroad lines is by permission of Montana Rail Link, Inc.

Cover design, back cover photograph, and water bear sketch
by Susan Rudd Mitchell

Cover photograph by Sindre Strøm

Interior design, typography and print-ready document by
Barbara Scott of Final Eyes

Published by Zāpus Fiction Group (ZFG)

Printed in the United States of America

ISBN: 978-0-578-72057-9

Apella's Turn

a mission turned on end
for a cause
worthy of your gifts

Larry G Mitchell

Acknowledgments

A bike shop guy named Methius put me on the road to Apella's Turn. Follow the rail line west to near the Idaho border, he said, and you'll find a wild corridor where cedars grow tall and the river keeps trying to be free — no better place to think and ride and see some bears.

This story took root under those tall cedars, and I have many to thank for their help and encouragement along the way. A short list includes Roy Anderson, Jean and Howard Arnott, Roberta and Mark Berger, Monty Clark, Michael Cunningham, Mike Edwards, Douglas Engle, Bill Gaut, Joan and Shane Goetz, Gayle Grant, Jay Huffine, Morad Koushan, Maryanne Martin, Paula and Paul Mitchell, Linda Morrison, Rita Morrison, Emily Reiser, Diane Rogers, Joseph and Peggy Rudd, Mark Smith, James Stephens, and Phillip Zapara.

Special thanks to my longtime friend Ernie Brown for setting Susan and me up in his riverside cabin and woods to complete the manuscript. And thank you Barbara Scott for converting the manuscript to bound book. It was a privilege and a pleasure to work with you.

Safety and Security Chief Pete Lawrenson, Locomotive Engineer Gerald Marshall, and others at Washington Companies' Montana Rail Link, provided virtually everything in this book about mountain railroading — except any errors, which are mine. Susan and I are proud we served as Chief Lawrenson's deputies in a section of Methius's wild corridor. Thank you MRL one and all, for sharing your time, knowledge, friendly waves, whistles, and rides of a lifetime.

I have priceless memories of mountain bike rides in the Rockies, alone and with my son Wes, and I am grateful to him for sharing his knowledge of bikes and zeal for the sport. He favors the fast downs, I prefer the long, slow climbs, and Wes is the rare companion who never chides about my pace.

One person, my chief editor and counsel, has been with this book and its characters as long as I have, but she values her anonymity. So I'll say this: I am grateful for your patience, insight, energy, and attention to every word and turn of phrase. Love forever.

For Lloyd, Virginia and Isabel,
who gave me music

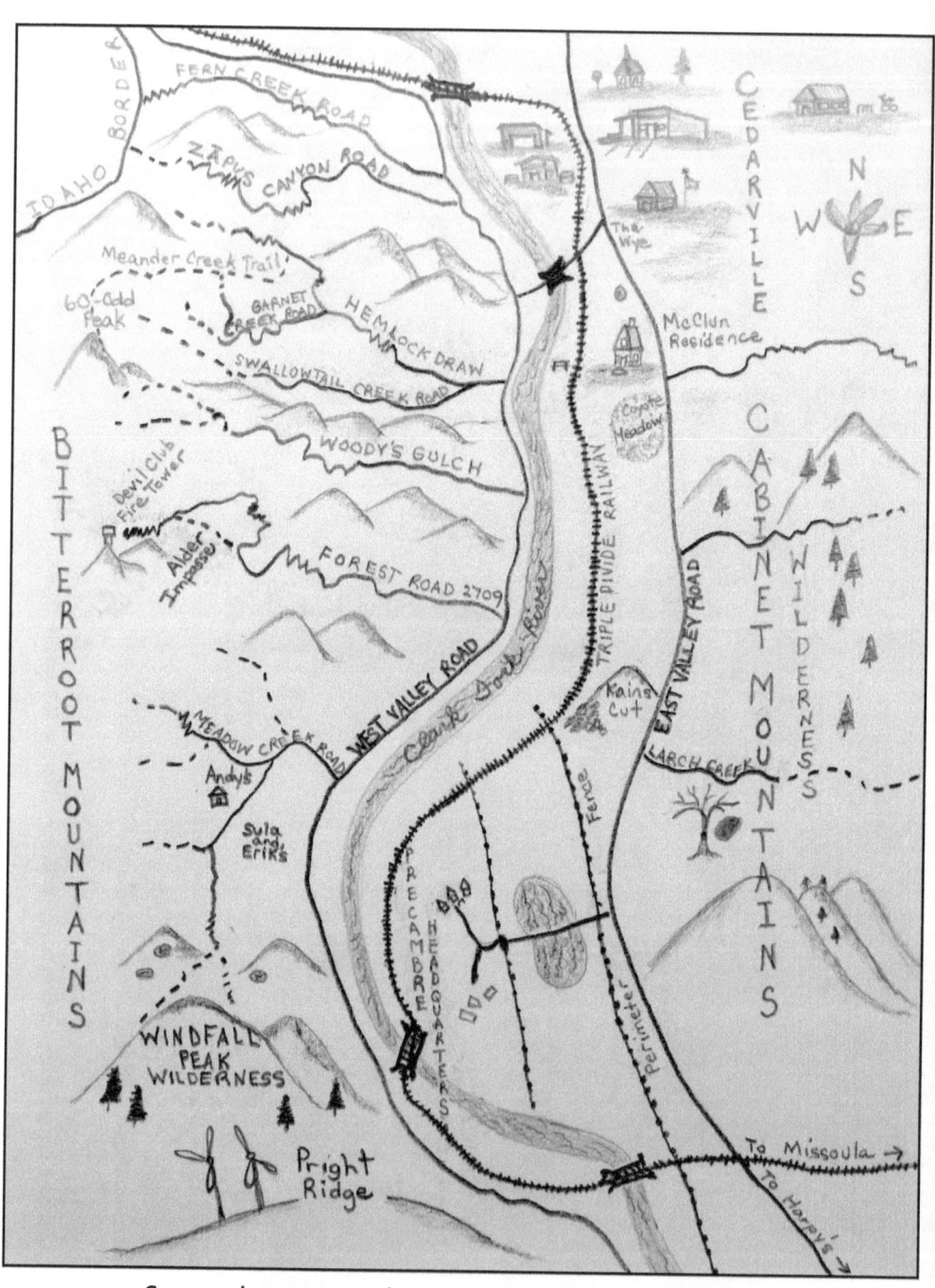

Somewhere west along the Triple Divide Rail Line

1

Yellowstone National Park USA

The big silvertip was down, trembling, then quiet in the melting snow. George lowered his binoculars, nodded reverently and said, "A timely meeting, Dan. Your last day in the park and there's the Patriarch, the oldest grizzly in the Northern Rockies. He won't be out long. Grab your bag. Let's get to him."

We hurried across the soggy meadow, eager and cautious as always. I unloaded gear, knelt close to the massive head and started into our routine. George talked quietly while checking footpads and claws. "This old guy's been with me since '87, and he's still young — need to keep him that way. Set your vitacorder on full, Dan, include a retinal scan. His nanotags are fine."

I'd been George Waterbear's assistant for bear research in Yellowstone Park for two years, never had a better job, a dream come true, and I didn't want it to end, ever. George is razor sharp and focused, demanding but patient. Every animal is special to him, and he made this clear to me on day one. Mr. Oyente, Dan, he said, working with me requires unconditional respect for the Great Bears. It also requires a singular ability to fix your mind on the task at hand. I believe you fit this position well. Don't disappoint me.

George and I became a finely tuned team, and now I have to leave for a very different job. Before I met George, I was immersed in a government program, training for low-level domestic surveillance missions. After years scraping by as a book rep, I wanted something beyond ordinary, preferably outdoor work with steady pay, and minimal-risk spy missions kind of pulled me in. My life changed when George walked into it, said he had a proposal. He could get my first mission deferred for two years if I went to work with him in Yellowstone.

So now, here we are. The deferment has expired, I'm scheduled for a mission and I'm running one last auditory test on the old bear George calls the Patriarch. As always, I waited for George to hold up his vitacorder and say, Good to go, before hustling back to the Park Service truck.

We were stowing gear when the Patriarch began to rouse, and we watched him roll to his feet, shake and lumber off, slowly at first then faster as he neared the trees…almost as though George staged it.

George reached into his truck's diamond-plate tool box, said he had a gift to commemorate our work together and handed me a watch. "The band is sterling silver, Dan, same size as your old one, and the inset is labradorite. It's the artistry of a close friend, his rendition of my namesake, the water bear."

The watch was custom fit and the water bear inset iridescent blue and brown. George waved off my thanks, adjusted his cap and said, "That watch will keep precise time and never stop. It will serve you well on your coming assignment, which we need to discuss. There's been a last-minute change of plans. They want you to begin with a train hop."

I snapped to attention. Did I hear him right? "What did you say, George? You can't be serious."

"You know I don't joke. Your orders are to hop a westbound freight on Bozeman Pass day after tomorrow."

All I could think was Bozeman Pass, great bouldering spot right off the highway, but hopping a train?

We climbed into the truck, George put on his wire frames and wrote some notes. "Your trip is set — in stone, so to speak," he said. "And you like trains so it shouldn't be a problem."

The Patriarch was gone, out of sight in the pines. He's the lucky one now, I thought, not me…far from it.

George gestured for quiet and whispered out the window, "Stay healthy, old friend. We'll give you more years next time. And for you, Dan, an important detail. You'll have to board the train with your mountain bike."

"With my bike? No way. I can't hop a train with a bike."

He shook his head. "They insist — not negotiable."

"That's insane, George. I was a young brat the last time I tried anything that stupid."

"I'm certain you can do it, and someone on the train will help. I printed a map to get you started…in the glove box."

He had highlighted Route 89 from Mammoth Hot Springs to Livingston and circled a railroad crossing on state land west of town. "That's the grade crossing where you need to be early Sunday morning," he said. "You'll want to stay out of sight on the inside berm and wait for a blue and yellow Triple Divide Railway locomotive with some old-style boxcars. Watch for a rough guy to lean out and give you a hand."

My mind raced. "Who's this guy? A train bum? What am I up against? What's his role in the mission?"

George put his pad and pencil on the dash and started the truck. "Take it easy, Dan. I'd expect the guy to be a surly train man who will test your patience and try to throw you off-guard with rough talk, but you're in the driver's seat. Keep in mind the people you'll be surveilling need you, want you to join. You just have to stay focused."

We were four miles from the barracks when he slowed around a curve and stopped for a bear, dripping wet, waiting for a toddling cub. "They've been in the river, George. Are they tagged?"

"Just mom," he said, jotting data, "and my clan considers a cinnamon black bear with a new cub a propitious sign."

We watched mom and cub amble to the side of the road, and George pulled slowly by. "A healthy clan of bears where you're going, Dan, likely some interesting people too."

"So you know where I'm headed?"

"Not precisely, though I'm sure the train man does. Riding with him will be a challenge, but I've arranged a brief respite for you. Your

3

professor-friend Dr. Jason Steller is expecting you in Missoula next week and like me he's been apprised of the mission."

"Dr. Steller? Really? Haven't seen him for half a century. He sent me an email about my son but didn't answer when I asked for more, not surprised he knows about the mission."

Old memories flashed through me—loud lectures, late-night politics, mountain roads and bike wrecks. "It should be a good reunion," said George. "You and the professor were close years ago, and he's still in the same northside house, living alone. Now, how about your gear and bike, everything in order?"

"Yeah sure, my bike's always dialed in. Hopping a train with it is the problem. I'll have to stay extra light with gear — stuff my pack with energy bars, two-liter hydrobladder with a sip tube, thermals and a few other essentials. One pair of padded pants will do, and I'll wear a down jacket and the yellow windbreak you gave me."

George drove into the barracks lot, forced a rare smile and said, "You sound ready despite your hesitance, and I'll drive you to Livingston tomorrow, late afternoon, set you up to bike the pass early Sunday morning."

I looked at my new watch, rubbed the water bear inset and thought out loud, "I don't know, thanks for the offer, George, but riding the whole way is probably a better option for me. If I'm really going to do this, I'll need those road miles to get in the mindset."

George pulled out his phone, adjusted his wire frames and tapped a quick message. "All right then," he said, "and how about your implant? Any problems there?"

"Nothing noticeable, doesn't seem to be active yet, just sitting in my brain I guess."

"As expected, and they informed me you're to check in via the device, Sunday at precisely 1800 hours. The water bear watch will help with that."

He reached over and gripped my shoulder. "I won't see you for a while, Dan, so I'll say this. The mission will be risky all the way. Don't lose yourself in it. Stay alert and don't be misled by anyone. They'll threaten one minute, engage the next. Take everything in stride and one step at a time. Concentrate first on getting to Livingston. Biking Highway 89 this time of year along the Yellowstone could be as hard as hopping that freight. Yankee Jim Canyon — black ice and gusts that could blow a biker down. Consider everything a test. And don't forget your map."

2

All Aboard

George was right about the ride to Livingston, and after seven hours dreading black ice on every curve, the drafty room on the west side of town felt just right. I propped my bike against the bed, kept my eyes on the time and spoke to my implant at six p.m. straight up. "Safe arrival in Livingston."

There was an immediate response.

Daniel, this is Apella. We have your position by way of the GPS in your implant.

"Apella? Really? I didn't expect — I mean it's been eleven hundred and nine days since our time in Baltimore. We said goodbye and nothing since."

You have a memory lapse, Daniel, but it is temporary. Things are different. I am here as your manager. We must put our past on hold and concentrate on the mission. I will brief you at four a.m. Get some rest.

"Hearing your voice, I want to keep talking."

A faint beep told me she was gone. She was always good at cutting off…saves time, not meant to hurt, she once said.

I slept through the night and was awake before dawn doing routine stretches when Apella made contact five minutes early.

Daniel, your implant picked up sounds around you during the night. All sounds and conversations transmitted by way of the device will be recorded in the course of the mission. Trust your training and experience for this assignment. The train man is aboard, ETA midmorning.

"Okay, guess I'm ready. Stay with me, Apella."

Two cups of motel coffee, a chocolate energy bar and an hour later I was pedaling to Bozeman Pass trying to stifle memories of our times. Short years together, long ones apart, trying others and none even close, and now all of a sudden she's my manager, Apella, my handler through an implant. Weird hearing her in my head, and she sounds different, must be the device. Damn — there's the grade crossing — hide!

I stashed my bike and helmet then sat behind trackside brush for nearly an hour before an eastbound freight, a Triple Divide Railway locomotive with a long string of flatcars and gondolas rolled by. A stack train followed, and I sat for another hour. My thoughts went back to Apella. How does this job fit her? We had a pact, total trust forever we promised. She wouldn't be part of anything that would put me in danger. But here she is managing me on a surveillance mission through a brain implant. How did she get involved? What does she know about the group I'm supposed to infiltrate, this dissident, possibly terrorist cell ensconced in the backwoods of northwestern Montana?

A raven touched down on the rail in front of me, and I could hear George's steady voice — one step at a time — then westbound whistles triggered a long-ago warning, If we catch you near one of our trains again you'll do some time! I put on my helmet, grabbed my bike and stood like I was waiting for a train to go by. Moments later a bright blue and yellow Triple Divide locomotive came around the bend, and the engineer gave me a friendly wave. A string of lumber racks passed, then intermodals, tank cars, two reefers. Where's the boxcar? And then there were three — and a fourth with an open door, an outstretched arm, and a strong voice over the screech of wheels, "Hand it up!" he bellowed.

No time to think — I tossed him the bike — leaped and pulled myself on. "I'm Dan, Dan Oyente," I said, steadying myself while he hoisted my bike to a pair of locking hooks spaced just right to hold the wheels. "Name's Thius," he said. "Where'd you ride from?"

"Mammoth to Livingston then here," I answered, trying to size him up — six two, broad shoulders, coal-dark eyes, bandana around his neck, big bushy red hair and about a week's growth on his face — not an old guy and almost too clean for a rail bum.

He looked me up and down and said, "Huh, nice outfit, just right for a train hop."

A sense of humor...didn't expect that. I took off my helmet, gloves and pack, braced against the wall and talked fast about my time in Yellowstone, how much I liked working with George Waterbear and the bears, and how George's nanotag invention ended the era of cumbersome collars, oversize implants and other tracking devices, all of which burdened animals and biased data.

Thius moved to the opposite sidewall and reached for a canvas bag hanging from a loose carriage bolt. "Yeah, that wiry little guy in Park Service greens, granny glasses and flannel cap has worked with a lotta people and a lotta bears over the years. We fussed at each other a few times back in the '80s when I thought he was taggin' every bear in western Montana. George Waterbear...always thought he'd freeze if he lost that cap."

He pulled a notepad and pencil out of the canvas bag, scrunched down against the sidewall, and asked if George ever said anything about his family name. I told him, "No, and I never asked, but he did show me some live water bears he collected from a hot spring north of Lone Star Geyser in Yellowstone Park."

The boxcar shuddered on some rough track, and I grabbed at the bike hook for support. Thius scribbled something in his notepad, squinted at me and asked what else I remember about water bears in Yellowstone.

Apella chimed in: *Let him hear your memory. Therein lies their interest in you.*

Okay. "The specimens George showed me were yellowish grey, partly transparent. They measured point-three to point-five millimeters long with four pairs of stumpy clawed legs and the gait of a lumbering bear." I paused. "You taking notes, Thius?"

Our eyes met and he said, "Mostly I'm watchin' time, milestones. I don't remember minutiae like you do, bike man."

I told him details stay with me because I'm hyperthymestic. "It means perfect or near-perfect recall."

"Yeah, big word for photographic memory, huh?"

"Think extremely. I can recall virtually everything about an experience. It's like I'm there again. When you asked about George, I started reliving a scene with him — rainbow colors, sounds, steam and scents of a Yellowstone hot spring, precise depths of bear and elk tracks in red and orange mud, the eyedropper George used to take a sample, the date and time of day, details of the microscope he set up on the scratched tailgate of his pickup, all that and more, even the inflections in George's voice and the lines on his face when he told me water bears are tougher than regular bears."

"Yeah right, regular bears can't dry up and come back to life after fifty years in a vacuum. Whadya do with all that crap? I mean if your brain won't filter it."

"It's a lot to process, but I have the storage capacity."

"Those dog tags around your neck? You in the service, a war? You bring a phone?"

I gripped the metal tags and said, "No, I don't have a phone, and these belonged to my son, Nathaniel…Nate. He died in Iraq, friendly fire, according to the official report."

Thius rubbed his beard. "Never understood how bullets that kill you can be friendly. So, you believe government conspiracy pap? You believe some radical Islamist Kalashnikofers assassinated Dolyle Pebre?"

I glanced out the door and said, "Maybe. How much longer on this side of the pass?"

"About twenty minutes, and these engines grind real slow, so take a seat, settle to the wheels and tell me why you think a Middle East terror group would spend that much effort on a loose-mouth Vice President."

I scrunched down like he did, hoped he'd settle to the wheels, and told him, "Maybe they knew something we didn't."

He lowered his voice, "Nope, Dolyle Pebre was an inside job. The alt-right made him VP, but his real handlers were covert, a power group I call the Malison — old name you rarely hear — means curse."

I told him I know the word and try not to clutter my memory with conspiracy theories.

Apella counseled, *Focus on your training, Daniel. Subtle interrogation. Calm persistence.*

Thius stretched out on the floor, put his notepad in his pocket and said, "Hell, the Malison terminated their loose-mouth VP a month after he went on a talk show and told the country it needed another 911."

I tried changing the subject. "It's been a long time since I hopped a freight. You do it a lot, Thius?"

He put the canvas bag under his head and asked, "Just why are you here, memory man?"

"I'm following a lead about my son. An email from an old friend raised doubts about the official report. It implied that someone in northwestern Montana survived the attack on Nate's platoon."

"And what if this northwest guy turns out to be your son's killer, friendly or otherwise?"

"I just want the truth."

"And what if rage takes over?"

"I'm prepared for whatever turns up and I have no violence in me."

"Yeah right, neither do we," Thius muttered to the ceiling, then nodded indifferently and appeared to doze.

Apella made contact. *Keep them thinking your only goal is to find out about Nathaniel. Our team is developing a profile on Thius. Now my director would like to speak.*

A deep male voice said, Hello Dan, you are doing commendable work. We see you as a strong asset and anticipate —

Thius jumped to his feet and ordered, "Set that rail spike in the door — gotta close up! A half-mile tunnel ahead. Heavy diesel!" He pulled off his bandana and tossed it at me. "Pour some water on that — hold it over your face or cough black for a week."

Apella said, *You'll get through and your implant will be fine,* but all I could think was black heat and roaring diesels thundering into darkness. *You'll get through and your implant will be fine,* she repeated.

"Thius! You ever pass out in a tunnel?" I shouted through the bandana.

"Yeah you can die in these old bores," he said in a low growl. "Straining diesels burn up air real fast. Crews carry oxygen in case they stall — hold on, point engine's almost out."

Moments later, light poured in as he pulled open the door and said, "Picture the choke in that rat hole in the steam era, and that's a short one. Try Cascade Tunnel east of Skykomish sometime. You ever read any hobo books?"

"A few when I was a kid, but right now I need to taste some cold clean air."

"Pay attention!" he yelled over the sudden squeal of brakes. "We're startin' down. Gotta sit face forward. Hold your feet against the front wall — like this!"

I braced in position and his talk got louder. "Lee Marvin, Ernest Borgnine! Remember that flick about hobos and train cops — cinder dicks hired to throw guys like us off freights? Depression years — half a million men, women, and kids stole rides. Lot of 'em died."

Daniel, don't respond. He's off the wall.

A loud bump shook the car. Thius rushed to close the door and announced, "Helper drop. They're leavin' two for the next eastbound."

"Helper engines?" I asked.

"Yep, that's what they called 'em 'til somebody invented the colorless term distributed power. You think Gaia is conscious?"

I wanted to yell, MAN, you're really out there, but Apella cautioned, *Don't let him get to you. This is his game.*

"Hmm…Gaia, interesting question," I said. "So, Thius, you've read Lovelock's books?"

"Yeah, all of 'em. Schneider and Margulis too but I learned about Gaia when I was a kid."

"When was that?"

"We're about the same. Somewhere between forty-five and seventy. I'm ageless the last ten. Survive this ride, you might be too — and for what it's worth, a conscious Gaia would've done more than warn us with viruses, earthquakes, fires, cyclones and whatnot. She would've cut us down to natural size a long time ago." He sliced his right hand through the air. "We'll be runnin' smooth awhile but pinched by towns and sandwiched by highways. Train cops like this stretch, hopin' to spot guys like us. Gotta keep shut 'til we swing northwest."

Was he trying to spook me? I pushed into a corner, felt the steady roll of steel and a flash of cold on a stainless table surrounded by masked figures in lab coats — where did that come from?

Thius was silent for over an hour, marching from side to side, squinting through cracks in the walls. I kept an eye on him and stayed out of his way.

Fresh air at last, I thought when he opened a door, leaned into the wind and announced, "Startin' down the Missouri. Next stop is Helena — pick up two helpers for Mullan Pass then grind slow to a tunnel near the top."

I cringed, "Really, another tunnel?"

"Yep, hotter and longer than Bozeman. Meantime, slide the other door and enjoy the ride. Not much snow on the peaks off east. Sun tempers winter and bears're out earlier most years. You ever hike the Meniscus Lake Trail with George Waterbear?"

I was surprised, tried not to show it. "Yes, George and I were there on a long weekend monitoring grizzlies and he showed me the water bear petroglyph."

"George tell you how the petroglyph got there?"

"No, he told me it was ancient and I didn't press him for more when he said It's a long story. Later, after thinking about it I figured maybe one of his ancestors chiseled the image."

Thius scratched his beard. "Really, let's see now. Given the size of water bears, George's ancestors would have needed a microscope to see 'em. George is Northern Ursavi — Uto-aztecan — so who knows, maybe an old Spanish microscope survived a trip from Central America to the Northern Rockies, say about three and a half centuries ago, and an enterprising Ursavi hunter-gatherer of the time found the scope, figured how to use it, discovered water bears, decided it was a fitting moniker for George's clan, and carved the petroglyph, I mean why not?"

"So you're saying the Waterbear family name is more recent or what?"

"Good question for our mutual friend George next time you see him. Canyon Ferry Lake's only forty miles but we won't make it much before dark. I like this stretch a rail…good sounds, so no more talk unless there's trouble."

We spent a talk-free hour looking out opposite doors, and I had a chance to update Apella when track noise got loud on a curve. "He's rough but tidy, two inches taller than me, thick red brows and beard, no facial lines, wide-set eyes, possibly one-eighty peripheral or better. Got a glimpse of an inch-long bear-paw tattoo underside of his left wrist. Maybe some Irish and Native American. Writes a lot of notes, probably about me. He's edgy — keeps me tense."

Useful material, Daniel.

The sun was down when we reached Canyon Ferry Lake. Thius pulled his collar up around his neck and sat against the opposite side-wall. "Missouri River Bridge comin' up," he mumbled. "Good time to rest. Helena Yard after that — lotta commotion there."

I grabbed a beanie and another thermal from my pack, tried to stay warm. How much can I trust him? Is it safe to sleep?

Apella came back. *Balance trust and caution. Thius's volatility belies his claim of nonviolence. Intel implies he is dangerous, but not to you, Daniel.*

I pictured her steady eyes, flawless face, wondered why she sounded so odd, then dozed to the cadence of wheels.

3

The Mouth of Bears

Three sharp whistles woke me the second day. The sun was up and Thius stood in the open door, backlit by morning rays. I heard him mumble, "New snow on the berm…lion tracks. Engineer probly saw 'em."

He turned around and yelled, "Get ready, bike man! We're on a high curve close to Mullan Tunnel."

I got up fast, helped him close the door and braced for another run through hell. "Keep your eyes shut and breathe shallow," he warned. "Scorched lungs suffocate. Where's that rag I gave you?"

"From ice to cremated alive," I yelled as we roared into another inferno. I pictured Nate in a crossfire then Apella in a heat wave on the ides of July. What's this insane train ride about?

You're strong and will get through this one too, said Apella, and light flooded in.

"How many more tunnels, Thius?"

"No more tunnels, memory man, and how'd you sleep through the whole night — the noise in Helena? Ahh, never mind. Get set for another downhill."

I braced my feet against the forewall, palms flat on the floor, and Thius ranted, "No more tunnels, no more caves — just a lotta heat waves and transparent crap when somebody needs a win — head shots and a quick dump at sea for none to see. John L woulda known."

"Man Oh Man," I said to myself.

I've never heard a more incriminating portrayal of a monster.

Thius stretched out on the floor and said, "No truth in obvious myths. And that's it for now. I'm sleepin' through the next helper drop. Don't wake me."

Streaks of light flickered on his flannel jacket and jeans. He started to snore, and I whispered to Apella, "He's tough and smart, a challenge, like George said." I checked my watch. "Where are we?"

Our Global Navigation Satellite System places you in the Little Blackfoot River Valley ten miles from the town of Garrison. When he wakes, try directing the conversation. Ask about his tattoo.

I thought, Garrison to Missoula, how far is that? And Thius roused. "Missoula's awhile yet, bike man — never know what could happen between here and there," and seconds later a loud crash brought him to his feet.

What was that, Daniel?

Thius shoved open the door, took a quick look outside. "Could be bad," he said. "Flatcars ahead of us hung up on a crossing — maybe ice or a broken rail. Be awhile 'fore they fix it."

I noticed a cluster of buildings in the distance. "Must be a ranch," I said. "Maybe we should go over there."

"Yeah, then what? Knock and show 'em two dirty bums. Hey, no need for the Pump-10."

"They might give us some food, let us use a shed for a night. We could hop another train tomorrow."

He waved out the door. "We're already on this train, but you go ahead, bike across that frozen stubble, savor the headwind."

"Guess not."

"Ahright then, pull the door shut, button up. Engine guys'll be checkin' damage."

We crouched against the forewall and quietly quizzed each other for what felt like hours. He asked what I did before the Yellowstone job. I told him I taught history in a small town in eastern Nebraska then sold textbooks for too many years.

"Textbooks, huh. Pedantic tomes widely sold and rarely read. How long in the Midwest?"

"Seventeen years, six months, and twenty-two days. I grew up in southern Iowa."

"You remember hemp crops?" he asked in a lighter tone.

I almost laughed. "Sort of, you ever try any?"

"Yeah me and my buddies would toke the flowers all day for a headache high. What was it like for an Oyente growin' up in the family farm belt?"

"I never really thought of it that way. My folks were born and raised in the Midwest and spent their careers there. We spoke English at home, and I took Spanish in high school."

"So, Latino in name only."

"I suppose. Where'd you grow up, Thius?"

"Out here mostly."

"You mean Montana, Idaho, Oregon?"

"Yep, intermountain."

I asked if his folks live around here.

"Mother, yeah. Dad's gone. Yours?"

"Both gone," I said. "They were musicians. Dad played cello, mom piano. They tried teaching me but it didn't take."

Thius dropped his guard and murmured, "Only one thing I'd choose to do long-term…play Sebastian Bach on big church organs."

"Really? You're trained?"

"Some yeah, mother's a keyboardist. Dad was a concert organist."

Do you judge this to be true, Daniel?

"So, Thius, something in common. Music is — "

"Listen!" He pressed his ear to the wall. "Hear those wheels — high-railer with a crane and crew."

"How can you tell?"

"From ridin' trains, and they'll work fast — just some simple welds. You think the government's still torturin' beagles to study crap like brain implants?"

Off the wall again, but was it a hint? Does he know about my implant?

Do not be concerned. Your security has not been breached. George Water-bear and Jason Steller are the only extramurals aware of your implant.

I shook it off and told Thius I love beagles and hate thinking about that kind of research. He took out his notepad and starting writing. The rail work got louder...a lot of pounding, and I talked over it. "I like your tattoo, Thius, rarely see any that cool."

He didn't look up. "Black bear saved my life when my dad died. I was six, and that's all I'm gonna say — they're just about done out there."

Minutes later the work noise stopped, and the crew boss shouted, "Early lunch, then we go."

The smell of torches mingled with coffee, mustard, cigarettes and muffled talk, then distant whistles, two long — one short — one long, and Thius stood up fast. "Comin' from the west, passin' a grade. Could be a hard joint."

I frowned, "A long way off, isn't it?"

He did a quick check on my bike, snugged it tight then braced himself in a corner. "Can't figure a mountain freight — ever. Curves'll fool you, specially when it's wet — here before you know it."

"What about the crane truck?"

"It's a high-railer. They're already off track. Too many questions. Get ready!"

I wasn't ready and a deafening crash slammed me to the forewall. When I woke up, Thius was standing over me, hands on his hips, voice loud and clear, "Book man. You concussed or what?"

"Where am I? Qué pasó?"

"Nice Spanish, Oyente. We're fifty miles east of Missoula rollin' along a peaceful stretch of the Clark Fork River."

He offered his hand and an odd parable, "A bird hits a window, it helps to set him up."

I checked for broken bones. "Guess I'm okay, just a sore shoulder and a head bump. Man, I hate to fall."

"Yeah, pays to prep for couplins' like that, give yourself time to brace. You fall much, book man?"

"Uh...no, can't afford to anymore."

"Peu de gens savent être vieux," he pronounced, and I rubbed my shoulder, countered, "Being old sucks no matter what."

"Yeah, whatever, but you took a hard hit, Oyente, and you were mutterin' some weird crap, somethin' about your son, hobo campsites, Devlinson and terror cells. What's that about?"

He's on to me and damn, what kind of rail bum quotes Francois de La Rochefoucauld in proper French?

You were disoriented but revealed nothing about the mission. Subdue his suspicions. Give him the source of your ramblings and we will pursue his.

I told Thius I must have been dreaming about a headline I saw in the Livingston Tribune. "It read, 'Echoing President Rodemont's concerns, Defense Secretary Devlinson confirms threat of homegrown terror cells throughout the US.'"

He stepped to the open door, sniffed the cold air, and thrust out his hand. "Headline, byline, myline, I prefer to read this scene. The river's high with snowmelt, the valley's full of spring, and we're way below speed even for these curves...must be pullin' off."

The train lurched to a stop, and I grabbed the side of the door to keep from falling. "Take a seat," Thius said. "You need it, and I'm thinkin' we'll be stopped awhile. This is the mouth of bears and foiled thieves. You been here before?"

"If you mean Bearmouth Hot Springs, yes, many years ago." I didn't tell him Apella and I once tried swimming here. It would have broken a pact she and I had to keep our times private.

"You ever try swimmin' or havin' sex in those steamy pools?" Thius asked.

I laughed, told him I remember a report about the pools being infested with leeches.

"Yeah, so what else you got in your memory banks about the mouth of bears?"

"Probably more than you would want to hear."

"Try me."

Yes, good opportunity. Fill his head with details of the place.

Thius leaned against the sidewall, and I said, "Okay, first to mind are heavy sulfur steam, near-vertical layers of orange and red mudstones, and sandy — "

"Good enough," he said, "and right over there used to be a Northern Pacific water tank. Steam engines would pull up for a fill, good place to hop a train, maybe rob it. That ring any Oyentean bells?"

"Yes, stories about a guy named George Hammond who did it twice — two westbound Northern Pacific trains."

"Yep. How much more you got in there, memory man?"

"I think more detail than anyone would want."

Do not waste this opportunity. Leave no doubt in his mind about the breadth and depth of your memory.

Thius said, "Gimme all the details you got."

"Okay, here goes. On October 25, 1902 at 12:35 a.m. Hammond jumped on with a 30-30 rifle and two .45-caliber Colt revolvers. He was early for Halloween but had a burlap bag over his head and a pair of leather sacks on his right shoulder. He held his 30-30 on forty-eight-year-old engineer Dan O'Neal and the fireman — told the fireman to step outside and turn off the headlight, then handed O'Neal a cigar."

I stopped talking while an eastbound freight roared by on the main line…did Thius know the stories well enough to test my memory?

"Ahright, what else?" he asked when the eastbound passed.

Yes, keep going.

I plowed on as our train pulled onto the main line. "O'Neal put up a fight, but Hammond gut-shot him, and he fell out of the engine and died…painfully, I'm sure. Hammond then forced his way into the express car and tried blowing the safe. He used eighteen sticks of dynamite and destroyed two railroad cars but the safe never opened."

"Yeah, Hammond got away with some watches and a few bucks, said he'd be back. When was that, memory man?"

I gave him a long answer. "At eleven p.m. on June 16, 1904, Hammond and John Christie jumped another freight out here, blew the safe and most of the express car, got away in a rowboat with close to fifty thousand dollars and about four hundred diamonds. These are estimates. I've seen conflicting reports of the amounts. Railroad detectives arrested Hammond in Spokane on July 13, 1904 and Christie on August 3, 1904 in Hope, North Dakota. Christie was sentenced to seven years, Hammond to fifteen."

Thius said, "Yeah, not much considerin' Hammond killed O'Neal, but they never pinned that murder on him. Two robberies at the mouth of bears. That was it."

"No," I said, "there was a third. On May 27, 1905, a train was inching through here — about like we are now — when Clarence P. Young stepped out on the track and waved it down."

"Right. Engineers would stop like that in those days. Some will today if you show 'em you're sober and they're goin' real slow. You ever try it?"

"No, but back to the robbery, Clarence Young climbed on, pulled pistols, and went for the safe. He tried three times, four sticks of dynamite, then six, then sixteen, which blew the safe to smithereens. He was contemplating his mess when railway expressman George Laub grabbed a board and swatted him in the face and back of the neck, knocked him cold. Mr. Young woke up in custody and received a fifty-year sentence then became a lifer after an attempted jail break."

Thius said, "Like I would if they found out I think bears are more important than humans."

I frowned and looked away, watched two ravens turn and tack with the train, whuh, whuh, aah, aah, aah, then a purple-black soar-away. Does Thius really think bears are more important than people?

He asked if I prefer raven or cuervo. "Hmm, no preference," I said, and he wanted to know if I remember a book that gave due respect to ravens, written by a woman about twenty-five years ago. I told him a man named Bernd Heinrich wrote a book like that in 1989.

"Right again, Oyente. So you remember names, dates, details of places, stories you read, classes you took? What else? You count cards?"

"Never been into cards. You have an interesting mind, Thius. What's your background?"

He fired back a question, "You're askin' if I'm credentialed? Got an honorary doctorate in quantum physics, tested out of advanced courses in Latin, French, Salishan and psychology."

"Really? Where?"

"Three U.S. schools, one in Quebec."

"And you're part Native American?"

"Yeah, I've got some Native genes, even some aliens," he chuckled, "you filin' this in your hypermemory, memory man?"

I told him I will remember some of what he says but details may fade depending on my focus at the time.

He didn't respond, and I heard Apella say, *Thius's role in the cell remains obscure. Some leads indicate he is their up-front filter, possibly an overt target set to draw attention and drain resources. Interesting his obviously inflated list of credentials and his multiple names for you, indicates developing comradery.*

More like sarcasm, I thought, and Thius asked, "What's on your mind now, memory man?"

"Actually, those foothills north of the river. When I was a young fool I hiked ten miles up one of the draws, shot a mule deer buck an hour before sundown."

He scoffed, "That was smart."

"Yeah, I quartered it, hung up the hams, hiked out in the dark. Cougar screams were close the last few miles. They can still make me shiver."

"You go back for the meat?"

"A day later with a friend and horses. The hams were there, a bear or lion must have taken the rest. The horses told us not to linger."

"Smart horses, and you're hoppin' toad in Missoula, right?"

"What?" I asked, wondering how he got from horses to toads.

He untied my bike, tossed me my helmet and said, "Derailing, getting off, it's train talk."

"Oh, okay. I did plan to spend a night or two with an old friend from the '60s."

"Better make it two if you wanna keep ridin' with me. I'll be on another westbound — day after tomorrow."

We need you to keep him close.

I put on my helmet and said, "I think my friend has plenty of room, and he used to be a great cook, probably still is."

"Naah, tempting but sounds messy. I'll walk town, see what turns up. Day after tomorrow first light, another TDR manifest with an open boxcar'll be idlin' west of the yard. Don't let anybody see you."

He tucked the rail spike in his bag and stood in the doorway. "Ahright, Oyente, Missoula's eastside — point engine's in the yard. Get ready, and take care of that sore shoulder — I'm gone."

I watched him hop off and land solidly on the ballast below. Moments later, I dropped my bike, jumped and hit the ground on all fours. Wary of being seen, I scrambled off the berm and heard Apella say, *Check in, Daniel. Where are you?*

"Hellgate Canyon and you should see my companion exit a moving train, definitely practiced. I'm heading to Jason Steller's."

And we have lost command of the target. Give the professor our best and make good use of your time there.

4

For What It's Worth

White shutters, blue door, cedar siding. Except for a metal roof, Jason's house fit my memories exactly. Fifty-five years and seventeen days had passed since I last saw him. Professor Jason Steller, once the brash young Turk in Garnet University's stodgy four-prof history department. I was his first graduate student, eager to learn, posing for approval. We quit corresponding six years before we had email, then suddenly the curt message about Nate. What's the professor like now? Retired, probably neat and trim as always. He's only five years my senior. Will we transcend our former relationship or should I still treat him like a mentor? Surely this will be easier than Thius and the boxcar.

I wheeled my bike to the professor's porch, and he opened the door, reached for my hand and exclaimed, "Welcome home, Dan! Expensive bike! You make a mint selling books?"

I didn't laugh. "No, I chose full suspension and a high-end platform instead of a mortgage."

"Well bring it in. This town ranks high as ever in bike theft. Pack and helmet hang on the coat rack as always."

He hefted my bike with two fingers. "Nice. A Specialized. What's it weigh?"

"Twenty-three point five with the tool bag. Not the ultimate climber but solid on the downs. A tolerable concession to age."

He set the bike upside down in the hallway, leaned against the wall and groaned, "Decades do fly, don't they? Remember those rigid

23

steel heavies I built?"

"You should have patented those frames, professor."

"I'm Jason to you now. And hell, except for the multiple gears, my heavies weren't much better than the junk the Bicycle Corps rode out of Fort Missoula."

"I remember that lecture, the Twenty-Fifth Infantry."

"All of it?" he asked, raising his barbered brows.

"Yes, every word, every student, the questions and more…and you pacing back and forth in your navy-blue blazer with chalk-dusted sleeves."

He stood tall as though appraising me, his six-three frame still strong, straight and taut, his face remarkably unchanged but clean-shaven now with wavy grey up top. "You still ride," I asked.

"Only on special occasions. Mostly I speed-walk, climb walls, pedal around town and use a rowing machine I keep upstairs. What's your story, Dan? You look great. I see you're still wrapped in high-end outdoor wear, gravity hasn't sagged your face much, and I do like your salt and pepper hair, very distinguished. I'm sure women fancy it." He laughed awkwardly and added, "But you cut the ponytail. If I didn't know better I'd think my fortunate old student was running for office."

I thought, David Crosby, John Fogerty, Fortunate student, Fortunate son, I'm neither, and I told the professor, "I mostly stay clear of politics these days and I try to stay in shape. My current employers require it. Twelve months of training included physical conditioning, and I've never let up on the biking. So how about a ride tomorrow, for old-time's sake?"

"Aah, I'm booked rather tight, otherwise I'd love to, and tell me something my youthful friend, how's your descent…as fast as ours when crashing was fun?"

"Oh Man, I try not to repeat any of that."

He motioned me to the kitchen and asked if I had a favorite memory from all the heated discussions we had there. I told him it was hard to pick from the fifty-eight times we faced off at his fine old wooden table, "and I see you've reset the stage for us, professor — I mean Jason."

"Yes, glad you remember. The open bottle is your favorite not-too-expensive Merlot, and no doubt the scents from the oven remind you of my culinary acumen. Pull up that chair of yours."

He poured two glasses of wine and toasted, "To times together and to George Waterbear. And how is our Yellowstone friend?"

I told him George is great and so was the job. "We were together in the field four or five days a week for two years. I learned a lot from him. He's an old-school, tech-driven scientist with a teacher's heart."

Jason leaned forward and locked his eyes on mine. "What do you think of a country that fails its teachers, Dan?"

I thought Here we go again.

"Hell!" he said and threw up his hands. "What do you think of a country that fails all but the wealthy and spends what's left on weapons and war?"

"Hmm." I took a sip of the red, maybe this won't be easier than Thius and the train.

Humor your professor, Apella said, and I told Jason I believe we need more teachers like George. "Man, the way he loves those bears. My last day I met the one he calls the Patriarch."

Jason's eyes lit up. "George has told me about that bear, a true survivor. His nanotags document how often he's roamed out of the park and gotten close to people including ranchers who wouldn't hesitate to shoot him. All his years, he has stayed out of trouble, even in towns at night. George envisions that old silvertip's genes factoring large in the future of Yellowstone."

He got up, walked to his restaurant-style oven and peered in. "Hope you're hungry, Dan. Dinner's on time and I'm eager to share a new piscine recipe with you."

I pushed back my chair and apologized for smelling like a rail bum in his spotless kitchen. He waved me off. "Don't worry about that. Just clean up and help yourself to a change of clothes. Upstairs room and bath are yours as always, washing machine is still in the basement."

"Twenty minutes max," I said, heading for the stairwell.

He had refinished the pinewood steps, but the second floor and eight-by-ten room I'd rented for three years looked pretty much the same. I washed up, borrowed a tie-dyed T-shirt and sweat pants from his closet then settled on a ladder-back chair and asked Apella to explain more about Jason's role in the mission.

George and Jason are intermediates, gantries to various groups. Fringe elements of cells, including the one you are surveilling, often contact them, rarely in person. George is a solid citizen whose technical knowledge and inventiveness make him one of our best agents of influence. Jason remains the same leftist academic you knew years ago but then he had no connections to us or any dissident group. He has been briefed on your assignment and need-to-know facts about the mission.

When I returned to the kitchen, Jason was the picture of past years — the affirmed bachelor professor in yoga pants and pressed Nehru-collar shirt, hustling around as he served dinner on vintage stoneware plates. With a confident nod, he asked, "So, how does basil-poached salmon with oyster mushrooms from the lower Bitterroot sound after two hundred miles in a boxcar?"

"It retrieves some heavenly scents and tastes from right here, long ago," I assured him.

Handing me another glass, he toasted, "To friends for life and causes worthy."

I tried to savor the dinner, told him his salmon is the best ever. "Wild Alaska King," he proclaimed with a wave of his fork, and I was reminded of being so impressed by his ability to talk and chew I paid little attention to anything else, including what I was eating.

He waved his fork again, "And about that memory of yours, Dan. Can you still recollect statements I made a half century ago?"

"Most likely yes."

"All right, governments are subsidiaries of corporate banks and energy conglomerates."

"You may have said that, Jason, but not to me. My lie detector is more acute than ever."

"Correct!" he said, leaning forward with his fists on the table. "I didn't see the whole picture until years later. Plutocrats and monster corporations hold sovereign power."

"Still testing," I said, thinking back to his oral exams, hot-tempered seminars, and rapid-fire question and answer sessions.

"Correct again!" he said and took care spreading a napkin over his empty plate. "Our university here granted me a life-time position, mostly to offer upper level seminars, and for what it's worth, I do remain the inveterate querist and ivory-cage radical, but unlike you, life hasn't dealt me any serious blows. How do you deal with losing your son to a war?"

"It's not easy, Jason, and your email brought it all up again. What have you been told about this mission?"

He stood up slowly, started humming a '60s tune and poured coffee from a French press. "Fresh extra-dark decaf," he said. "You'll like this, and let's see now, the email I sent contained everything I gleaned from a briefing regarding your son, and I'm sure you know the mission is government sponsored. I've also been informed about your implant situation, and your old flame Apella Inglason is your on-site manager, so to speak." He sat down, drummed his fingers on the table and asked, "What's it like wearing a walkie-talkie in your brain?"

"Weird as hell to put it mildly, and I'm not sure I would have followed through with this spy mission if you hadn't suggested there was more to learn about my son. I might still be in Yellowstone or out on my bike — a good hill to climb, that's all I really need. You always wanted or expected more from me, but I'm not that guy, never have been."

He started picking up dishes. "Pardon me, Dan, I could not disagree more. You're still a budding radical. I see it in your eyes, always did. And that memory. When will you really do something with it?" He reached for the coffee. "We'll have more decaf and my special recipe in the den. Grab our cups and that plate of brownies on the counter."

Not much had changed in his den, same turntable and rows of vinyls. He put on a Buffalo Springfield album, waved me to a chair, and I sank into worn leather that felt ancient a half century ago. Jason sat on his swivel desk chair, kicked off his Birkenstocks and proclaimed, "Music…it can take you back like a time machine, back to the '60s when I first realized how much I enjoy your mind, Dan. You were an exceptional academic who came to Garnet with a raw talent for critical thinking and refined it admirably — that memory coupled with your uncanny ability to pick arguments apart, none better over all my years teaching."

"Yes, the university scene suited me for a while, so did selling books, but here I am. And I may be out of line but I have to say, You are really lucky, Jason. You found a job that pays you to live by your wits and fill young minds with far-out thoughts."

He lowered his chair, crossed his legs and nodded proudly. "Yes, can't deny it. My academic façade continues to serve me, and here's an update for you, my gifted friend. Democracy is under siege. Too many elections hinge on fear, rage, gerrymandering and outright cheating. Racism continues to gain on pluralism. Without a persuasive global voice for peace, truth and serious economic reform — the militant right, religious fanatics and cyberganda could push most of this world to war."

"Hardly an update, Jason, except for cyberganda you said all that in a 1965 seminar."

"Aah, that memory again. I certainly hope that walkie-talkie hasn't affected it in any way."

I touched the faint scar on my forehead and told him, "I have 163 hours of memory loss…frequent flashbacks and this scar but no details about the operation or whatever they did to install the implant. Apella assures me everything will be okay, but I'm not convinced."

"I think you should believe her and move on. Trust my lead about Nate and play it out."

"How did you get involved in this, Jason? I can't see you teaming with a government agency, no matter what the situation."

He leaned toward me and said, "You think being leftist precludes helping a worthy cause?"

I nearly choked on a bite of brownie, took a sip of coffee. "A worthy cause, Jason? I'm supposed to be infiltrating a radical anti-government cell. You're against groups like that now?"

Dial it down, Daniel, the professor is on our side.

Jason shuffled papers on his desk, and his voice tightened, "I hesitate to say it, old student, but I believe you have much to learn about the people you're pursuing. Thius Terrene, for example, after two days with him, do you think you understand him, his politics?"

Don't overreact. It makes sense he is acquainted with some of these individuals.

I frowned, ran both hands through my hair, "So, Jason, you know Thius?"

"Yes I do. Young Mr. Terrene audited two of my seminars shortly after you left. The man is exceptionally bright, and I am not surprised they chose him to begin your evaluation. Sizing people up is his specialty. He's a tenacious game player, an uncompromising harrier."

"Definitely, you're right on that. Thius is a tough read, a talking contradiction, and there were times when he acted like he knew about my implant. I mean, if he did, and they could intercept my communications with Apella. What then?"

Jason slapped the arm of his chair. "Forget the implant. I want to hear about the train ride. Give me some highlights."

Make it interesting, we're all listening.

"Okay, there were miles of pretty scary stuff. Two oxygen-deprived tunnels, a derailment that slammed me to the floor, knocked me out cold — and Thius was major trouble the whole way."

He chuckled. "But Dan, you've always been up for high-risk adventure, probably liked most of that ride, and I don't believe these people want you hurt. They need you and your memory. And concerning the brain device, I am certain there is nothing like it outside the government."

"So I've been told."

And harbor no fears.

Jason went to the front door, locked the dead bolt and said he was obliged to call it a day. "And for tomorrow, Dan, I recommend you take that ride, start out early, maybe go up Rattlesnake Draw. It's overused, of course, but less beleaguered by developers than most canyons around here, and we'll talk more tomorrow evening. Look forward to another out-of-this-world dinner."

5

Loose Rocks Roll

I left Jason's house an hour before dawn and was pedaling hard along Rattlesnake Creek in early light. Jason loved mountain roads and trails like this and he was fun on the rides. In spring and fall we would climb to the snowline, hop off and push our bikes up through drift after drift, then race down laughing, slipping, legs out to balance in the white. Give your mind to the hill, he would preach before any major descent, and he didn't mean take it slow. I hate squeezing brakes, he liked to say. Risk is the essence of this fine sport. If you never crash you never feel the fullness of wild descent.

I agreed then but not so much today…sounds like immortal youth, Jason, and we've got too many old scars that say another fall will hurt forever or end it all. We were so lucky so often.

Starting up a straightaway, I thought of us racing down a forest road on a wet day back in June 1964. He was on the inside lane. I was a bike length ahead, edging a drop-off. Rounding a sharp curve, I saw a boulder too late and was set to hit it. TAKE A RIGHT! Jason shouted. I swerved in front of him, slammed my brakes and heard him crash. What a relief when I turned and saw him upright, brushing off. I'm okay, he said, had to ram the bank or backside you. I'll need a wheel true, and my helmet's cracked, guess it saved my brain. He picked up his bike and looked at the cliff above us. Loose rocks do tend to roll on wet spring days, he mused, or hell, maybe a bear kicked 'em down.

Man, thanks! I told him, I'd be in pieces or dead — you saved my life. I owe you, Jason. Nah, forget it, he said. Just some road rash and bruises and nothing shows so I don't have to tell students about it.

That day and others like it convinced me that no matter what happens between us, I will remain Jason Steller's loyal friend. I pedaled to the snowline, stopped to chew an energy bar then held a moderate pace on the downhill. Two bikers yelled, "On your left," and sped by as I slowed along the creek with thoughts of my last ride with Nate. There were new leaves in the wind, sun in the cottonwoods, catkins in our derailleurs. Nate nearly hit a deer one month before he went off to a fool's war.

Back in town, I stopped for more memories and a late lunch at Pete's Railyard Bar and Grille, a Missoula landmark and Jason's after-ride favorite. Seated at the counter, three camo-clad diners were glued to an oversize screen broadcasting last season's Montana Grizzly highlights. A newscast blared from another screen, but I was taken by a soulful baritone coming from a sidewall speaker. "Any chance you could turn him up and the screens down?" I asked a hip young waiter.

"Sure," he said, handing me a menu. "I'm Mike, part-time waiter, full-time philosophy major at Garnet U. Sit wherever you want."

"Good to meet you, Mike, I'm Dan, and this single table right here looks good for a listener. I've been a Richie Havens fan since he played the Woodstock Festival."

Mike crossed his arms and looked puzzled. "That name sounds familiar, but what festival was that?"

"Woodstock…guess you're not a classic rock fan, huh, Mike?"

"I like most of it," he said, "even some of the old stuff, but I don't know Woodstock."

I felt my years as I told him, "Mid–August, 1969. Three chance-of-a-lifetime days of great rock and folk on Mr. Max Yasgur's six hundred-acre dairy farm forty-three miles west of Woodstock, New York. Lucky I'd been visiting relatives in upstate New York and was camped at a state park west of Albany when a deputy sheriff walked over to me, eyed my long hair and asked if I was going to the hippy music festival. Sure don't get some of the names, he said, Grateful Dead, Sha Na Na, Ten Years After, The Who?"

I stopped talking for a second and asked Mike if he really wanted to hear more.

"Totally!" he said.

"Okay, I knew there were some rock concerts in the area but I had a feeling about this one and broke camp right away, made it to the festival on Thursday, a day early, couldn't believe the traffic and crowds. I sat on a hilltop, watched the twenty-by-fifteen-foot stage take shape and wondered how the word got out to so many people… easy to figure today but not then. It was Friday at 5:07 p.m. when Mr. Havens opened the festival. He played a full set, the audience kept calling for encores, and he finished with 'Freedom'. I stayed on that hilltop most of the time, night and day, tried to file every detail of the thirty-two acts and all the great musicians who played their hearts out. I'm sure you've seen pictures of the audience, a half million of us, mostly your age, Mike."

"Wow," he said, "that musta been way sweet."

"Sweet's a good word for it. Sweet peaceful ordered chaos, and the music — out of this world. I left Monday morning, exhausted and elated when Jimi Hendrix finished his two-hour set, my favorite probably being his screaming guitar rendition of the national anthem."

"Dig it! Good memories, man. My favorite music is a capella, my favorite group is Pentatonix. You know 'em?"

"Yes I do, and I think a couple of them went to the same high school in a glitzy entertainment city in Texas."

"Really? Watching them sing gives me major chills. What would you like?"

I ordered a grilled cheese sandwich and listened to Richie sing on. My mind drifted — first to handsome Nate marching to a foreign war then back to a big screen when one of the camo clads boosted the volume. A Billings newsman had been hospitalized. The anchor reported that longterm news analyst Adam Lockfoil collapsed at noon yesterday, allegedly poisoned by muscarine, a common mushroom toxin. The night before, Mr. Lockfoil had eaten a batch of chanterelles his wife purchased at a farmer's market.

I mumbled to myself, "Poisonous chanterelles? No. Muscarine?" I thought about Thius. He could have been in Billings at the time.

Daniel, our people were on this when Lockfoil was admitted to the hospital. And Thius's whereabouts unknown after he left you in Hellgate Canyon.

I mentioned the report to Jason that evening over decaf in the den. He shook his head and said, "Yes, I saw it. Ridiculous. Chanterelles are perfectly safe. Some amanitas can kill you, not chanterelles."

He glanced at his watch. "They've scheduled you to reconnect with Thius at first light tomorrow, and forget the yard. Bike west out of town and take the highway up Evaro Hill. I'm sure you can picture it — steep on this side with tracks close to the highway — local freights grinding slower than any pace we pedaled. On the right starting up, there's a two-hundred-foot-high span of steel. The last time I saw a train on that trestle, I thought the whole manifest would fit under a Christmas tree. You remember Marent Trestle, Dan?"

"Perfectly, plus Evaro Hill."

"Good, and you need to get up past the trestle before dawn and be patient. Freight delays do occur. How fast do you climb these days?"

"Never fast. Most days, somewhere between a slow walk and six miles an hour."

"How fast on the downs?"

"Rarely over thirty."

He raised a brow and said one of his favorite memories was pushing fifty on a ride down Skalkaho. "Insane, weren't we?"

"Whew, Jason. There was that ghost-white VW bus coming straight at us. If we'd met it on a curve, we'd have been hood ornaments, and you weren't so lucky that time up the Rattlesnake when you took a fall for me. You saved my life."

"You still cogitate that?"

"Yes, often. It was the first time I felt real fear. I owe you."

"Don't worry about it, nothing to it, and I'm certain I told you about the Chicago engineer who slipped off a flat car and fell from Marent Trestle…kind of puts bike spills in perspective."

Jason stood, took my cup and stacked it on his. "I'll see you early for breakfast, Dan, and help check your bike over."

Daniel, the director wishes to emphasize that we understand your loyalty to Professor Jason Steller. Keep in mind that he and George Waterbear are extramurals, working for us while maintaining the trust of our adversaries. There is inherent danger in their positions, and the director wishes to assure you Jason and George will be protected.

Man, she sounds bizarre, so formal, uptight, but it's good she's with me on this mission.

Two hours before dawn, Jason and I were on his porch doing a 13-point safety check on my bike. "Evaro Hill is nothing like your ride out of Yellowstone," he said, "but it could be slippery. I'd set the tires at 40 psi in the back and 30 in front."

"Sounds right, Jason. As you used to say, it pays to keep your machine custom-tuned to the road." He nodded, turned off the porch light and sat next to me on the step. Out on the street, a parked car's headlights blinked but Jason didn't seem to notice. "Now," he said, "I don't think this should concern you, but the latest news about the Billings media guy is not good. He's in a coma, probably won't make it. They're considering homicide. Maybe it's a warning in disguise, telling you not to get too confident."

I asked if he thought Thius might have been involved.

"Not likely at all," he said, "but hearing about a possible murder with ties to the Billings yard at that particular time compelled me to warn you to be extra cautious. I know you're fittingly trained and your cover is convincing — just keep your guard up."

Yes and practice fine focus, Daniel.

I slipped my helmet and gloves on, and Jason gave me a bag of chocolate-dipped espresso beans. "For an added boost up that first hill and beyond," he said. "You'll travel through some spectacular country today, Dan. The track runs close to the Flathead River on land hopefully held in perpetuity by the tribes. Minimal human clutter out there. No roads, docks or castles on the islands. Montana the way it should be and testament to the tribes holding their land and wits instead of staring at screens, clutching phones, and buying junk."

He handed me a brown envelope. "Here...some semi-literate scribblings when you have the time. Push hard, be free, safety third, as we used to say."

6

Dream Police

Evaro Hill was an easy climb, no headwind or traffic, and dawn was just breaking when I ducked off the highway, spotted an evergreen thicket close to the track and settled in for a wait that turned into hours. By midmorning a lone coyote had trotted along the berm but no trains, not even a whistle. Where are you, train man? I opened Jason's envelope and pulled out a typed letter.

16 Apr

Dear Old Friend,

As you noted, fifty-plus years in classrooms have not slowed me down. On the contrary, they have confirmed my love of working with young minds and watching them expand. History's great lesson is Survival Requires Change, and I am certain you realize constructive change should be the calling of our time.

The calling raises the question, Is this species, which Swedish botanist-creationist Carolus Linnaeus named Homo sapiens two and a half centuries ago, up for the challenge? I try to remain hopeful, but where is the evidence? We are still electing destructive fools, amassing wealth, squabbling, fighting. WAR? WHY?

WHAT FOR? How many times did you hear me say Thomas Mann referred to war as a cowardly escape from the problems of peace. Truly, if half the trillions wasted on weapons went to planet-saving, we would have full employment and a good chance to solve real problems. You asked about my role in the mission. Know this. I will continue raising my voice to oppose any group, tribe, cell, nation or individual who promotes armed conflict.

Dan, you gave me a lift when you quit your sales job. I'm glad you had a chance to work with George and the bears. We are hoping your current venture will help you decide what to do with the rest of your life, I mean besides biking the high country. Always take heart in your status as a thoughtful young senior.

Your friend and fellow rider (in spirit),
Jason

There was more to the letter, but a shrill flicka, flicka, flicka and a flash of scarlet orange swept by, then an engine horn blew in the distance — two long, a short and a long — a westbound at a grade crossing. I tucked the letter in my shirt. Just need another open boxcar with an outstretched arm. I can do this again — but why am I so eager?

Two engines thundered by then nineteen gondolas, twenty-three tank cars, ten autoracks, nine boxcars — all locked tight. Where's the old-timer with an open door? There, faded graffiti — no, shut tight. Two more — closed. Then a rusty red — open, and there he was, arm out, grabbing the bike. Miracle — sort of.

Great! Apella exclaimed as I leaped aboard.

Shaky and off balance, I yelled, "Yes!" and noticed another mountain bike fastened to the sidewall.

Thius locked my bike on a set of hooks and asked if I recognize this hill from an earlier life.

I caught my breath, said, "Yeah, and that's a cool bike, Thius, a Santa Cruz Heckler. You ride?"

"Transportin' it for a friend and no better'n yours, is it?"

"Personal preference, but all else equal, it might beat mine on steep slicks. How far we going?"

"Downriver all the way. Wait! Grab a hold! Drive wheels slippin'. Wet rails — they'll be pourin' sand."

"Whoa!" I shouted as the wheels caught and we surged forward. Thius said, "That's probly it, we're almost up, and you probly know Evaro's level on top. We'll slide through open meadow, then be on Salish, Pend Oreille and Kootenai land, aka the Flathead Reservation. We'll see a high peak they call N'tsuitsen. Snowmelt up there floods rivers earlier every spring. Every valley shall be exalted, and every mountain and hill made low."

The voice of him that crieth in the wilderness. Daniel, try for names, places, dates, anyone he knows on the Flathead Reservation. We are cross-checking tribal police records with railroad arrests.

Thius stood in the middle of the boxcar, loose and balanced, like he's got sea legs, I thought, and he mumbled, "Next time we slow on a wide curve, we'll be turnin' northwest — to Ursavus."

"Thius, did you say Ursavus? How do you spell that?"

"U–R–S–A–V–U–S, Latin for grandfather bear, the ancestor, lived about twenty million years ago. The spirit of Ursavus lives today in an international organization — antiwar and wealth, pro-survival, and dedicated to essential nonviolent action."

Don't react. We're on it!

I didn't ask any questions and Thius reached for his bag, squatted down and said he had some writing to catch up. I moved to a corner, pulled out Jason's letter and started reading again.

P.S. Dan, you recall our discussions about the military-industrial complex. What was Eisenhower thinking when he cautioned the country about it? He knew his administration was deeply involved.

Today the MI complex aka the GCC (Global Corporate Council) owns governments. People vote thinking they have ultimate control, but sorry folks the GCC holds the reins. With remarkably few exceptions, public service is a sham.

I leafed through the packet and Thius asked, "What's in there?"

"A letter from my Missoula friend. It's kind of boring to me but you might like it. You want to read it?"

"I caught the gist of it, heard you mutterin' about the Global Corporate Council. The GCC is a politically correct name for the Malison. Funny how many people tolerate government by felons and fools, but the populace wishes to be deceived, populus vult decipi — always been true — and we're on that big curve headin' northwest to Ursavus about now."

He opened both doors, and out the right side I recognized the grassy hills of the National Bison Range. I did a double take when I thought I saw a distant boulder move. "Nope," said Thius, "not a rock, just an old guy enjoyin' his cud and the mornin' rays."

The scenery held my attention for miles after that…budding cottonwoods and twisting currents of the Jocko River then the Flathead's glacial blues running fast and easy by stately ponderosa pines. Icons of the mountain west, I was thinking when Thius pointed to a treetop nest and said, "One time right out there, I saw a bald eagle lift a dead deer off the track, then drop it on a pine branch forty feet up. Another time downriver, I watched a locomotive plow through a herd of elk restin' on the rails, and I remember thinkin' they shoulda heeded the train before it was too late. You could say the same for humans."

Parables rooted in violent death. Unbefitting a pacifist, and we now posit his involvement in the shooting death of a mining crew foreman seventy miles downriver from your present position.

"Scary thoughts," I said to her and Thius. "They remind me of a recurring dream."

"About trains, future culls or what?" he asked.

"About seeing two passenger jets explode while I was biking on a plateau in the Crazy Mountains. I raced downhill to a hostel, dropped my bike in a snow bank and saw two reporters telling their headsets the government ordered the explosions to prevent planetary war. Three federal marshals stepped out of the trees, confiscated my bike and biometric card. I told them it's just the end of a cycle. One of them said, nice pun. Another told me my life would never be the same."

Thius swiped the air. "Your dream's about lies and fear. What are you afraid of?"

"Dying without knowing myself and how my son died."

"Pro salute animae, nosce te ipsum. For the health of the soul, know thyself. Let your son's fate rise on its own."

Daniel, you may have less than one hundred miles to gain full disclosure on this volatile transient. We predict they will have you detrain alone somewhere near the Montana and Idaho border. Thius will continue west to Washington. We still have no intel for an organization called Ursavus but will keep researching.

I glanced up when we passed under a highway bridge, and Thius said, "Keep your eyes on the geography. In a decade or less, this'll be the southern edge of North America's habitable land. South'll be mostly boilin' desert...lots of jobs at solar energy farms, that is for the lucky ones who can afford the water bills."

"Hmm, I've read just the opposite and I think you're talking, maybe end-of-century."

He frowned. "You'll soon meet people who believe otherwise."

"So you live somewhere out here, Thius?"

"I was born a close hitch, in the Kaniksu part of Kootenai National Forest."

"The Kaniksu," I repeated for Apella.

Thius almost purred, "No better place for me than the lower Clark Fork between the Bitterroot and Cabinet Mountains...home to big cedars, maroon-tinted bears, mountain valley mists and trains, and a river that keeps tryin' to be wild. Natale solum, native soil."

I offered him some of Jason's espresso beans and asked if they teach Latin in the Kaniksu. "Latin, French and Ursavi," he said, "and it's time to close up and make small. We're comin' to a two-river town called Paradise."

We crouched in opposite corners and Apella reported, *Last year the U.S. government neutralized two cells in the Kaniksu, ecoterrorists, former members of the Montana Militia and North Idaho paramilitaries, apparently not related to Thius's group. Will attempt verification of his Kaniksu connection.*

7

A Swallow and a Saw

A loud command startled me when our train jostled to a stop next to the Paradise station house. "Heavy coal in ten. Make it quick!"

A deep voice yelled back, "Most're empties."

"Check 'em anyway!"

Thius whispered, "Yardmen waitin' on a heavy — stay down."

Someone banged in and out of two boxcars behind us. We flattened against the wall. Boots scuffled on the ballast, a gloved hand took hold of our door and pushed it — light streamed in — mission over, aborted in a Paradise boxcar, but the glove withdrew, and heavy boots stomped off just before a westbound coal train charged into the yard.

Thius ranted, "Saved by black silt that flooded out of the Rockies thirty million years before Ursavus arose. They're still strippin', shippin', and burnin' it. Climate to hell! Clean coal isn't!"

I coughed in the engines' wake. "Neither is diesel, Thius."

He ranted on. "A mile an a half a coal, the heaviest moving object on land — takes a lotta power. Runnin' dirty diesels to move the dirtiest fuel on the planet. Nuts!"

I said, "Man, you're right about the dirt but I believe a mile and a half of iron ore outweighs coal."

"You sure know a lotta crap for an ex-book rep, Oyente."

Our engineer blew three short whistles and started up. Thius pulled out his pad and pencil, wrote some notes and said, "Grab a hold, book man. We're headin' off the siding…always liked this rail town with a wye, a side street named for a tie plant, and the former site of a Northern Pacific turntable."

An hour later we were rolling through another old-west town when Thius leaned into me, so close I could smell chocolate on his breath. "Thompson Falls, county seat, jail and all," he growled. "They pinch it way down through here. Be invisible and hope we don't stop."

Another inflated warning. Don't let him get to you.

I braced in a corner until we started gaining speed on the west side of town. Thius announced, "Another siding comin' up in a couple miles. We'll probly stop and wait for another heavy — coal or grain goin' our way."

I asked how he knew so much about train schedules. "You tuned into dispatch somehow, Thius?"

"Yeah I keep it checked out, pays to when you're ridin' free, and we're already startin' to slow…be pullin' off as planned. Usually nobody around, a good place for a pit stop if you need it."

"I could do with that."

"Ahright, get ready, we're stoppin' and I'm stayin' with the train — mostly shut down for trips like this, eat and drink minimal. You'll have plenty of time before that heavy goes by but don't linger."

He nudged me and I jumped off, ran across the main line to a distant aspen grove. Three minutes passed, then train whistles — two long — one short — one long, and an eastbound work train pulled in view, not the westbound heavy Thius said was coming. I stayed down, then jumped up when our train blew two short whistles and started moving — and there was Thius waving at me from the boxcar. "Sonovabitch!" I yelled. "It's a SAW! You set me up!" I started to run but too late.

What's going on? What's a saw?

"A passing maneuver at a siding — and I'm stranded. Thius's train took off without me to let an eastbound work train pass — and he has my bike."

We need you with Thius!

"Yeah. About all I can do now is head west — try to hitch a ride and catch up with him." She didn't respond, and I started walking a service and fireline road next to the track. About a mile on I reported a high-railer pickup truck parked at a grade crossing.

Specifics! Apella ordered.

"Blue and yellow Ford one-ton pickup, plate MTTDR021, Triple Divide Railway logo — wait a minute, have to talk to someone."

The driver opened the door and asked if I was walking the track. "Just needed a break from the highway," I said, thinking nice smile, warm face, shoulder-length black hair with streaks of gold, pretty, better than pretty, and dressed in striped overalls. Cool!

Daniel, we've got a trace on the vehicle. It is official Triple Divide Railway.

"Hop up. Take a ride," coaxed the driver. "The rail company is real protective of its right-of-way."

Wishing to trade Thius and the train for this, I climbed in and thanked her. She started her truck and said, "Good afternoon, I'm Rachel Smyth, Roadmaster for the Day."

"Dan, Dan Oyente."

I glanced in the sideview mirror at my hair, ran my fingers through it, a little greasy but still okay, wonder what Ms. Smyth thinks?

She smiled and her eyes flashed me. "So, where is Mr. Oyente going, besides west along the Triple Divide fireline road?"

"No plans, just trying to see the mountains with a little cash and no car."

"Very well," she said then maneuvered her rig onto the track and lowered the rail wheels. I told her, "My first time in a high-railer, Ms. Smyth, glad for the opportunity."

"Happy to oblige," she said. "I love this job and the TDR."

The ride on the rails was loud and jarring but she had no trouble talking over it. "I'm on the tracks whenever my dispatcher sends me out," she said with ease. "Triple Divide uses drones for routine track patrol, but a roadmaster provides so much more. I am responsible for my section of track in every way…trouble shooting, law enforcement, track maintenance supervision, public relations, to name a few. A friend likes to call me Boss of the Tracks. Any questions, Mr. Oyente? We have a twenty-five-minute window before the next train comes through, and call me Rachel."

"Okay, and call me Dan. Do you work anywhere else on the line, Rachel?"

"Yes, but this is my favorite section. I love this valley, its history, ancient and recent. I moved here after the dams were built. There are two between here and Lake Pend Oreille, both tiny compared to the ice dams of Earth's past. You may know the name Pend Oreille refers to the large shell earrings worn by the indigenous people of the Northwest Plateau."

She slowed to a stop in a narrow pass between rocky cliffs, rubbed her temples and said, "One of many road cuts that accommodate the rail line, and there is some little-known but momentous history here. Many Earth years before railroads were invented, a meeting took place on the hill above us. Eleven members of the Ursavi Tribe from the Yellowstone area happened to meet a scouting party of nine Bloods from the far north. Their chance meeting resulted in a peace pact that remains in effect today."

She released the brakes and added, "The tribes abandoned the site when the railroad arrived and most of their artifacts were destroyed by dynamite when the cut was widened."

"Echoes of Nobel and buried footfalls," I mused, and she whispered, "History, Mr. Oyente. It is vital, yet trivial to so many on this planet."

The vehicle may be window dressing. We are attempting a voice match.

Rachel answered a call from her dispatcher and slowed when we saw Thius's train parked on a siding two hundred yards ahead. I looked at the nearby highway and said, "Think I'll hit the asphalt again, Rachel. This looks like a good place to hitch a ride."

"Are you sure? We're at least twelve miles from the next town."

"Yes, thanks anyway, maybe see you again."

"Very well, and likely, if you're on a Triple Divide line, Mr. Oyente," she said with a proud grin.

Daniel, stay within the parameters of the mission. You have met your first swallow, anticipate more.

What the hell is Apella talking about?

Rachel and her high-railer disappeared down the track, and I jogged to the side of Thius's boxcar. "Nice ride with the lady?" he asked, helping me back on. Obviously, the meeting was planned. I grabbed my pack, sipped some water and asked if he knew Rachel Smyth.

"Yeah, a while."

"Girlfriend?"

"Forty years back, a rail crew spotted us ridin' this line. We hopped off and spent the night in Thompson Falls — seven bucks and a bath down the hall in the Black Bear Inn — better than bein' thrown off the train."

"That ever happen?" I asked, hoping to hear more about Rachel the Roadmaster.

"Once. Buffalo, New York," he said.

"With Rachel?"

"Nope."

We were on a smooth stretch of track close to a lake when he pointed out the door and shouted, "Look up! Above that rock slide — Kain's Cut! I watched 'em blast that cliff face when they rebuilt the rail line to fit this reservoir. My dad and four friends died out there — some of their bones still in the rocks and river."

"Man, Thius. What happened?"

His voice strained, "Some other time. Soggy ballast, a slow order, and a town called Cedarville comin' up. They'll pinch it way down. You like ridin' alone?"

"If you mean biking, yes, why do you ask?"

"Trails in these hills you could ride dawn to dusk and moonlit nights and not see any humans 'til hunting season…maybe a few berry pickers on dirt bikes or ATVs, July and August. Most of the snow's already gone below four thousand."

"You're saying I should spend some time here?"

"Yep."

"What're your plans?"

"On this train awhile yet."

Accept the offer. We'll shadow Thius.

I said, "Okay, I'll give it a try," and he untied my bike and steadied it in the doorway. "Don't expect much from the place," he said. "Just two paved streets, a school house, fire station, post office, church, senior center and general store…better than a talky ride in a rail box, but our talk's been a necessary pain in the ass. Get ready. After the next bend I drop the bike you jump. Take the track or fireline road — a short walk to town either way. Remember what sage Berra said about a fork in the road?"

I jumped, landed on a grassy bank near my bike and heard him shout into the trackside wind, "Could be another train in ten. Lotta spirit here. She'll find you."

"She who?" I yelled but he was gone, and I was alone on the track with a deep sense of dread, thinking BAIL NOW. Find a road and ride away. No. I'd be stuck with the implant for life and lose my chance to find out more about Nate. I asked Apella if she knew anything about the town called Cedarville?

Daniel, do not trust the people you meet here. Best to assume everyone in this town is a master of deceit and entrapment.

Good grief, I thought — masters of deceit and entrapment way out here? But Apella rarely exaggerates.

The fireline road was brushy and log-strewn. Walking the ties with my bike was an easy choice, and surely I would hear a train in time to get off the track.

8

Tractor Seats

My first sight of town was the post office, then the general store close to the track on the east side. A flatbed truck was parked in front of the store and a tall athletic man dressed in brown Carhartt pants, vest and denim shirt was posting notices on a bulletin board near the door. He turned and gave me a once-over when I stepped onto the porch with my bike. "Name's Walter," he said, "Walter Smyth. I'm proprietor of our store here. Where you from, young fellow?"

I smiled, took off my pack. "Down from Missoula after a job in Yellowstone, Mr. Smyth. I'm Dan Oyente. Mind if I bring my bike in?"

He held the door for me. "No worse than boots, come on in and call me Walter. Just me and our deputy here. He's in the back minding some business. We're glad for your company. Just prop that bike against the news rack."

I stood inside, looked around and told him I hadn't been in a store like this since I was a kid. "Great building, Walter, and a real general store with a lunch counter. Do I smell fresh-brewed coffee?"

"You do," he said, grabbing an apron from behind the counter. "Coffee's fifty cents, seventy-five with refills, thirty cents for a donut, homemade." I settled on a glossy red stool, ordered coffee with a cinnamon dusted and told him I've always admired tractor seats like this.

"I know what you mean," he said with a slow nod. "My wife loves the old things. It took us awhile to find ten and get all the rust off."

He poured me a full mug, then looked toward a loud thump at the rear of the store. "Loyal!" he yelled. "We've got a customer. Get on out here."

I stood up respectfully as a stocky middle-age guy with blood-shot eyes and a handlebar mustache moseyed toward the counter. Walter said, "Dan Oyente, meet Loyal Crispin. Loyal's our deputy sheriff this end of the county."

"Always good to get acquainted with the law," I said as the deputy flopped into the seat next to me.

"Yeah, I hear yuh, Mr. Yentay. What brings a rough outta towner like you to Cedarville?"

"Glad you asked, sir. I've got some months off from a sales job, and a friend told me this is a great area for mountain biking, so I'd like to find some part-time work, maybe stay awhile. I'm a pretty good handyman."

He pointed at my bike. "You rode here on that? Where from? Pricey lookin' machine for a handyman."

Walter tried to diffuse the tension. "Most of us are on a barter system here, Dan. That's how I run the store for locals, and we post our goods and services on the board you noticed out front."

Crispin raised his mug for a fill and joined in, "You could find some yard or house work at a faux-Austrian resort, about ten miles south. Hell, it's bigger than our whole town. Eight mansions not much used, a nine-hole golf course, private lake, air strip, and security guards paid a whole lot more than me." He took out a handkerchief, blew his nose. "Nobody should have more than one house. Hell, the whole country'll be resorts and gentry unless somebody stops the govment and greedy trust childern from sellin' it all."

I watched him take a slurp of coffee and wondered why Thius didn't mention the resort. Walter wiped the counter around us and said I might have better luck with some of the full-time residents. "You should talk with Rosemary McClun. She is Ms. Rose to most of us, and we all have great regard for her. She lives just upriver, alone since her husband William passed…works a hydroponic greenhouse year-round. She has her hands full at seventy-plus, though you'd never guess it. I help some, but when things pick up around here I'll need the extra time. How 'bout I call, see what she says?"

"Please do and thanks, Walter."

"Okay, I'll call her right now."

He stepped to the side, pulled out his phone, "Ms. Rose, how are you? Uh-huh, I see. Well, ma'am, there's a guy just showed up here with a fancy bike, trying to find work. He seems okay…I don't know, fifties, early sixties, just a little dirty, hasn't shaved for awhile…all right, good talking."

"What's the word?" I asked as he stepped back to the counter.

"She didn't hesitate, just said Send him here forthwith."

Deputy Crispin pointed to the window and filled me in on how to get to Ms. Rose's. "I'm real good with drekshuns," he said. "Just take the East Valley Road out front here. Go left, that's south past the post office…road breaks up just after a yard full a dead cars and a boarded-up bus. You don't wanna loiter 'round there. Go another half mile and bear left at the wye. Right takes you across the rail line to our river bridge. You wanna stay on this side of the river to get to Ms. Rose's. About two miles of beat-up blacktop past the wye you'll see a mailbox painted like a rainbow, it's at the end of Ms. Rose's gravel lane that tunnels a half mile through some of the biggest trees in Cedar County. Too bad she'll never log those old things…worth a million bucks. Her house sits on a bench above the track and river."

Walter added, "It's a nice country home, Dan, two-story frame with a riverstone chimney and windows all around. Hope you and Ms. Rose work something out."

I got up to leave, and Crispin asked officiously, "What's your last name again?"

"Oh-yentay," I pronounced.

"Uh-huh. You Indian or Ora ental?"

"Latino," I said with a straight face.

"Huh. I'll be sure and tell Sheriff Pright about you bein' here. He lost his ranch to a buyout scam and likes ta know who's comin' and goin' around our town."

"Understood," I said and headed for my bike and the door. "Hope to see you both again soon."

Walter said, "It might interest you, Dan, I'm fair with beards, hair and eyebrows."

I thanked him, "Good to know, Walter. I am due for a trim."

"On second thought," he said, "I believe my services won't be necessary if you and Ms. Rose hit it off, which I'm certain you will. She'll take good care of you. Just come back and see us, will you, Dan?"

"For sure, and I appreciate your hospitality."

Outside, I quick-scanned the bulletin board then pedaled to the edge of town and stopped to give Apella my impressions of the two. "Mr. Smyth talks like he's connected, could be a member of the cell. The deputy struck me as naïve and maybe not too bright… can't imagine him a weighty dissident. I'll make myself a regular at the store, see what turns up. And what about the name Smyth? Are Rachel and Walter related?"

Affirmative. Walter Smyth is Rachel's father, and tentatively agree with your assessments. We have email account information along with county and state public records, including current photos of Walter and Rachel Smyth, Loyal Crispin, Rosemary McClun, and Sheriff Oliver Pright. All clean, except Crispin pled guilty for poaching two years before Pright hired him.

"The sheriff hired a poacher? Why would he do that?"

No logic apparent, and not important to us.

I stepped on my pedals. "Okay then, I'm on my way to Ms. Rosemary McClun's residence."

9

Soul Mates

Deputy Crispin's directions seemed overly detailed for the narrow-valley environs of Cedarville, but I took his advice and didn't slow for the busted bus or dead cars. Out at the wye, I turned right for a look at the river, crossed the rail line and pulled close to the bridge Crispin mentioned — two-lane concrete, easy access to canyons on the west side, two off south, another to the north, and probably more. This mission might end up okay if it gives me time to bike or hike those canyons.

Not wanting to be late for Ms. McClun, I backtracked to the wye, turned south and pedaled a fast two miles to her rainbow mailbox. Was it a symbol of New Age or something else, something known only to a chosen few? "Stay cool," I told myself and rode cautiously down the lady's tree-lined lane.

A glimpse of a striking woman in a sleek black dress, staring out from her front porch, made me stop and think This is where it really begins. I dismounted and tried not to flinch as two serious canines hopped down from the bed of a shiny blue Tacoma pickup parked under a carport on the south side of the house. The pair bolted to a landing below the porch, sat at attention and didn't need to say Stranger with the hard hat and bike, you better stop.

Their pack leader put her hands on her hips and said, "I'm Rose McClun, and you are Dan Oyente. Welcome to my home. The Dane is Max. The little heeler is Agnes. They'll be fine, and please just call me Rose."

She didn't seem like someone who spent her life in Cedarville, and she did not look her age…more like a fit fifty.

"Been on your bike much lately?" she asked.

"Never enough," I said, pulling off my helmet and gloves.

"Now that sounds like a man after my heart," she said. "And you certainly travel light."

"Try to. Everything I need is in my pack and the tool bag under the seat…couldn't carry much on this trip."

"Well, please come in, and your bike will be fine out here. Those are nice Shimano biking shoes. They'll look good on the porch next to my galoshes."

It was a cloudy day but everything about her place felt bright and warm…sparse but comfortable furnishings, arched windows, stone hearth, and slightly scratched pineboard floor. A midsize Baldwin grand graced her living room, and two kitties were curled together on a rug close to the pedals. "Meet two more friends," said Rose. "The little tabby is Franny. The big orange guy is Biggs. They're both strays, and they tell me they like piano music, even loud dissonance. I'm still waiting for them to tell me about places they visited before they found their way to the wicker chairs on my porch." She straightened some sheet music on the piano. "And what about you, Dan? You worked with George Waterbear in Yellowstone, hopped a freight out of Livingston and another out of Missoula after a long-overdue reunion with Jason Steller."

I forced a smile. "Wow, you really checked up on me."

She stroked a tear-drop amber pendant hanging from her leather necklace and said, "George and Jason have kept me informed on your whereabouts, and Jason told me how much you enjoy a good meal. You must surely be hungry."

"Very! But I'm not fit for clean company."

"You're fine, and I'll prepare an afternoon snack."

She backed through a swinging door and raised a folding screen over a countertop between the kitchen and living room. "There, bar's open," she said with a wink, "now we can visit while I fix some rellenos, just a tie over until dinner, sound good?"

"Better than good, Rose, and I'm taken by the large western landscape and two abstract paintings on your wall here. Bellas artes."

"Gracias. My husband William painted the mountain valley train, the abstracts are mine."

"Two gifted people. Both musicians as well?"

"Our piano does get quite a bit of use, and the peppers are ready. Table is here in the kitchen. Come take a seat. I don't eat in the middle of the day, but I'd like to sit with you."

She served me a plate of food and sat close. "Jason told us you love spicy dishes, Dan, so I made pablanos and quacamole. Hope there's not too much habanero in the red sauce."

I took a bite and nodded approval. "Couldn't be, grew up with it."

"Good, a man after my heart again, and with a pretty labradorite carving on his watch. Now I don't want talk to get in the way of your eating, but I am curious. I know you taught history and political science for several semesters at a community college in Fenville, a little town in Nebraska, and that sounds interesting. Why such a brief time?"

I could feel her eyes on me as I said, "Teaching didn't really suit so I took a book salesman's advice and went to work for a publisher."

I fanned my mouth. "Wow, your sauce IS HOT! But it's really good."

Obviously pleased with my red-faced pleasure and pain, she tucked her hair behind her ears and said, "Tell you what, let's try this for a week or so, see how it goes. Room and board for some help with chores, and as I'm certain Walter told you, we're a trading community. Working for me will cover you here and buy all the coffee you can drink at his place. What do you think?"

I started clearing the table, told her I'd stay indefinitely for a weekly meal like this. "Just let me know what you want me to do, Ms. McClun...I mean Rose."

"Un buen, amigo. And I'm sure you're eager to make use of that bike while you're here."

"Actually, nothing suits me better than biking alone in mountains like these, especially if I get to see some bears. I miss them already after working with George Waterbear."

"Lots of opportunity for that, and you're welcome to a room and bath upstairs. You could start right away on our wood supply. Hand tools are in the shed, and plenty of logs to split out back. Please don't wear yourself out though. Some conversation with dinner would be a delight — on the table at eight and you're welcome to any of my husband's clothes in the hallway closet to the left of your room, you look the fit. And while you're out, I'll put a comforter on your bed for the cold nights. It's handmade by a local family. How does all that sound?"

"Just right," I said, figuring I would have time to scope out the place and update Apella.

I grabbed my shoes from the porch, went out back and split enough firewood for several nights, then found a pebble path leading to the woods. Loud chatter of a red squirrel announced my presence and I said, "Hey gimme a break, I'm new here, staying with your attractive neighbor on the hill. How young is she really?"

Are you talking to me? Apella asked.

"No, to a disapproving squirrel. I'm alone, on a trail below Rose McClun's house. I can see the railroad between me and the river, and I just went by the biggest cedar snag I've ever seen. Are you keeping up with Thius?"

Satellite and on-ground surveillance confirmed his train on a siding near Cocolalla, Idaho. One of our drones captured images of him closing the door when the train approached the siding.

A raven squawked from a high perch when I stepped close to the track, and the rolling echo of a train triggered Thius's warning, Can't figure a mountain freight, ever — here before you know it.

Do I hear a train?

"Yeah, comin' from the east." I sounded just like him.

Cut off until it passes!

I hid below the berm, waited for the front engines to roar by, then leaped up and started counting cars, like old times. Thinking the single engine in the rear was unmanned, I waved and felt like a habit-driven fool when two short whistles blew and a five-finger wave appeared in the window. "Damn — should of stayed down."

What now? Did someone see you?

"Yeah, an engineer spotted me."

Watch yourself. Rosemary McClun is your immediate focus — an obvious member of the cell who has fooled the professor and George Waterbear while remaining under our radar — just one measure of what we are up against. Don't let Rosemary's folksy talk mislead you. She is an accomplished pianist, and her husband, world-renowned organist, William Yrisse McClun — deceased. No children. As for Walter Smyth and the others — don't let your guard down anywhere or with anyone in Cedarville.

On the way back to the house, Max and Agnes met me with friendly wags, and the downhill breeze carried scents of a fine Italian dinner.

"Spinach lasagna, one of William's all-time favorites," said Rose, setting our plates on the table. "I hope you don't tire hearing me talk about William. He lives in my mind."

"Not at all," I said and took my first bite. "This is superb, Rose, I'm in total agreement with your husband. I've tried a lot of Italian food, never tasted better."

She thanked me, dabbed the sides of her mouth with a napkin and said, "William and I traveled the globe together on concert tours. We played keyboard duets in many countries and tasted fine food everywhere. William was a brilliant organist. Oh, so many wonderful talents."

Rose made it clear that light conversation was favored at dinner, no heavy controversy, no politics or religion. I was drying dishes, and she was organizing them on shelves when I asked about Thius. "I've been wondering, Rose, this area has so few people, maybe you know the guy who helped me hop the trains to Cedarville. He told me the one thing he'd choose to do long-term was play Sebastian Bach on big church organs."

"Yes, I know Thius, and I am proud to say he is my son. William and I adopted him after his father was killed. Did he tell you about Kain's Cut?"

Keep her going!

"He mentioned it when we went by the rock slide, told me his father and four friends died there. He didn't give details."

Rose sighed, "It is too horrible to relate — horribile dictum. Thius's father, an Irishman named Carl Bantry, ran a cow-calf operation a mile south of Kain's. Poor man was only working part-time for the railroad when it happened."

"Thius never mentioned the name Bantry."

"My son's full name is Methius Terrene. His mother Shining Meadow Terrene was Kootenayan. Shining Meadow passed away shortly after Thius was born. He still has two relatives on the Flathead Reservation."

I tried for more on Kain's Cut but Rose said, "Another time. It is such a beautiful night, I'd like to spend some of it outside. Let me get organized for the morning then I'll meet you on the back porch. Please keep an eye on the dogs for me."

Twilight wind caught the screen door when I stepped out, and Apella asked, *Are you alone?*

"Yes, sitting in vintage wicker, watching Rose's dogs walk the yard. What do you have for me?"

Public records reveal that Carl Tulmont Bantry and his only son, eight-year-old Trajan Terrence Bantry, were both killed at Kain's Cut. We've got —

The screen door opened, both cats marched out with Rose, and she started firing questions. "Dan, how was your ride with Thius? My oh my, all that time you two were cooped up in those boxcars. What are your impressions of my son? What did you boys talk about?"

I told her Thius pretty much led the discussions. "Far-left politics, trains, mountain erosion, water bears, an old girlfriend…you name it."

Rose sat across from me and quietly but forcefully said, "Thius is a one-woman man. Always has been."

"Maybe she's the lady I met then, Rachel Smyth, a roadmaster for Triple Divide Railway. When I took a break from the train she was driving a high-railer truck west of Thompson Falls."

Rose reached down to Agnes, said, "Stay tuned little one. And now, Dan, I want you to know Thius's soul mate is Eleva Sterling. You've read about her haven't you?"

A headline flashed in my mind. Agent Provocateur Eleva Sterling Incites Violent Antigovernment Riot. "Uhh, yes," I said to Rose. "I have read about Eleva Sterling. And you're serious? Thius was actually with her?"

We need more.

Rose rotated her wedding band and said, "William and I were first introduced to Eleva at a church recital in Seattle. A few days later she stopped by to see us after a conference in Spokane. She loved Cedarville, our home, our music, conversation, and the meals we shared. Like William and me, Eleva and Thius were permanent from the moment they met."

"But Eleva Sterling went to prison for threatening a president."

"Eleva is much more than what you've read or heard, Dan."

I reminded her it was all over the news the day Ms. Sterling was arrested, and then again when she went to prison. "I know the reports verbatim. Eleva Sterling was handcuffed, escorted away by federal marshals and died tragically."

Biggs rubbed against Rose's chair, and she pulled the big kitty to her lap. "Yes, you've just recited highlights of the official report released to the public, but very little of it is true."

I wanted to say more about Eleva Sterling but Apella stopped me.

Drop this for now. You're recollection is correct. Eleva Sterling died after being incarcerated in federal prison. We'll provide details later.

Rose's yellow-green eyes flashed me, Biggs hopped down from her lap, and she brushed his hair from her dress. "Let's be upfront and honest with each other, Dan. There are eight of us here, and we all know about the email Jason sent you. We're very clear on why you came to Cedarville. You've always doubted the official report of your son's death in Iraq and you are here seeking the truth. Is this not correct?"

She caught me off-guard. What else do they know — that I'm here to spy on them? The notice from hell flared in my mind — an overnight delivery from the US government — a brown envelope with Nate's tags, a letter, and death certificate. I said, "You're right, Rose, I've had doubts since I got the death notice, but nothing's turned up that contradicts the government's account. Do you have any information that might help me? I have to follow every lead."

Convincingly stated.

Rose reached for my hand but withdrew. "We are very sorry, it is a sad awful thing. And we nearly lost a local girl to that war. Did the report say where your son died?"

"Yes, near the Ctesiphon Ruins, south of Baghdad. Tell me more about the local girl. Maybe there's a connection."

"Her name is Sula Millen. She's a close friend…a good heart. She spent her tour in Kuwait so there's probably no link, but you should talk with her. Andrew Denton might also help. He's a Vietnam vet who maintains close ties with the other veterans here in Cedar County."

She clasped her hands and rested them in her lap. "I want to say more about our interests, Dan. Jason told us you are trustworthy, down-to-earth and have some radical leanings and a phenomenal memory. Does that sound accurate?"

"More-or-less, but I'd substitute liberal for radical. Jason tends to embellish."

"He does at times, but we value his judgment, and most importantly you were also recommended by George Waterbear."

"For?"

"Surely Thius told you about Ursavus."

"He mentioned it, yes, said it's an international organization — antiwar and antiwealth — sounded like an antigovernment survivalist group."

She straightened the collar of her dress and didn't seem to notice when her little tabby hopped onto her lap. "Well now, we are certainly not survivalist in the sense of stashing food and weapons in the woods. I'd put it this way, Ursavus is the only organization on this planet with the means to secure humanity's future, and we are hoping you will join us in that effort."

I got up, backed against the porch railing, looked directly at her and asked more questions than I should have. "How radical are you, Rose? I mean Ursavus, the organization, how extreme is it? I'll be honest with you, antigovernment groups make me uneasy. Not that I don't care about world problems, but I can't see myself part of a political movement. I'm not really a joiner."

Slow down. Telling them you're not a joiner may be counterproductive. Keep your training in the forefront.

Rose tilted her head as though interested. "Well…your dossier certainly agrees with what you just said, indicates you're not fond of groups and we know you have a mind for details. Until we learn more about you and you about us, all I can say is, we wish to apply your special talents to a cause worthy of them. Applied broadly, your hyperthymesia could greatly accelerate necessary change. We ask for your patience during our prescribed recruitment period, which has already begun, and there will be no issues if at any time you decide you cannot participate. In fact, you will be permitted to join only if you choose. This is a two-way street, Dan, a double track on the railroad if you will, and from now on, your times with us will certainly be gentler and more personable than the train rides with Thius. But, can you think of a better way to test someone's mettle?"

I managed a late-night smile. "It is true, Thius and his boxcars required a type of endurance I didn't know I had."

"Yes, he was certain you would desert us when you got off the train in Missoula, but he underestimated you…at least on that level. My son has always doubted you could commit to any social or political cause no matter how positive and vital. That's why he volunteered to begin your evaluation. He told our planners we had to find out what you're made of right off-the-bat, and they agreed wholeheartedly. Now with that said, Dan, we should call it a night. You've got quite a bit to think about. Enjoy our stars for a few minutes. I'll see you inside."

I stepped off the porch, walked to an open space in the yard and looked up. Polaris stood out in the clear night sky. I glanced back at the house and asked myself, Why would a band of dissidents with international connections locate out here? And how could my hypermemory accelerate necessary change?

When I walked in, Rose was waiting at the foot of the stairs, her hand on the banister. "Keep your questions in mind, my new friend," she said. "All will be answered in due time, and no need for concern when heavy trains shake the house. Everything here is on firm foundation, so rest comfortably in your room, top of the steps, door's open."

10

Secrets

I climbed the steps to my new room slowly, counted sixteen total with a slight creak in the third and tenth boards. Never thought I'd actually be staying with someone I'm supposed to surveil. Rosemary McClun and adopted son Thius Terrene — two of eight backwoods dissidents. Was Eleva Sterling ever here? With Thius? Maybe in the room at the end of the hall. If he was close to her, how could he be opposed to violence? But is he dangerous? Is Rose? And what is Ursavus really about?

A light came on when I stepped over the threshold. I threw my pack on the bed, lifted a window just enough to let the night breeze whistle, then did a quick scan of the room — dark rolltop desk, shelves filled with vinyls and books, a turntable like Jason's, wood and antler carvings, abstract paintings in the colors of Yellowstone, then a photograph on the dresser. I whispered to Apella, "I'm alone in an upstairs room, staring at a photo of Rose, Jason and maybe William… three happy faces. They're so young. Do you have reports of them being together?"

Our field agents just informed the director that Jason visited Rosemary and William McClun many times over the years. Their shared interest in music and art history kept them close.

A thick volume on the top shelf caught my eye. Hmm, "The World of the Meiofauna." The tiny animals. I paged through and stopped at a brief chapter about George's namesake, the water bears. Crude line drawings made the stumpy creatures look like burrs with prickly holdfasts…a far cry from the detailed labradorite carving on my watch or the animated specimens George showed me in Yellowstone. Was I missing something here?

I reset the book in its slot, sat on the bed and pulled Jason's envelope from my pack. A cover sheet introduced some class notes, probably not interesting, but let's see.

Dan, I'm sure you recall discussions we had in and out of class, and here's an update, a transcript from one of my seminars for junior and senior history and poli-sci majors. Seven of nine students were present the day I recorded this. I have omitted extraneous comments and changed the students' names.

Steller: I'll start today with a passage from an essay entitled The Power of the Powerless by Vaclav Havel, written when his country — now the Czech Republic — was part of the USSR.

'In such a situation, people's interest in political matters dwindles and independent political thought, in so far as it exists at all, is seen by the majority as unrealistic, far-fetched, a kind of self-indulgent game, hopelessly distant from their everyday concerns.'

Steller: What's your reaction to this?

Sam: What he's saying applies to people in general not just to those living under totalitarian communism.

Etta: It's a bunch of words to say something obvious.

Steller: Okay. Someone give us a précis.

Rob: The quote's about the guy's country when it was part of the Soviet Union. That's ancient history. The Czech Republic is more or less a democracy now. People pay attention to their politics, I'm sure.

Sam: Yeah, but what do MOST people pay attention to?

I leafed through six pages of dialogue. Why did Jason think I'd be interested in this? I flipped to the last page, another note to me.

> Dan, smart kids, don't you agree? Etta and Rob started a relationship in that seminar and they're still together. How does the discussion strike you? To me it's not markedly different from those we had when you were a student. We didn't discuss terrorism or the Federal Reserve in your day, but we talked about many of the same ideas. For decades I have asked myself, what do students do with this material? What did you do with it? For too many years I believed seminar discussion alone could effect major change in young minds. Soon after I lost that naiveté, I joined an international activist group dedicated to meaningful change.

I repeated the last two sentences out loud for Apella's benefit. After a long pause, she said, *Yes, the professor is a member of numerous international groups, all purely academic.*

I told her Jason's class notes were too tedious and boring to finish, and she started to laugh, the first time since all this began. *Daniel, you've given us some interesting data today, we will collate and be in touch.*

I looked out the south dormer and let sparkles dancing on the moonlit river hold my attention until I knew I could rest.

Rose's radio woke me at five a.m. When I stepped into her kitchen she was stirring batter and tapping her feet to Roy Orbison's old-style rock-and-roll. She turned the music down, ladled six pancakes on the griddle and asked what I thought of the photo of her, Jason and William.

I sat at the table, told her, "It's a great picture, and I thought maybe that was William."

She poured two cups of hot chicory, filled my plate with pancakes and sat close. "Oh, Dan, that was such a fine day, one of many, and my oldest friend George Waterbear recorded that moment in time. George was born right here in a two-room cabin his grandfather built."

"Interesting, Rose. George never talked much about himself."

"No, he wouldn't while you were working with him. Enjoy those pancakes, they're piñón by the way, and I'll share some fond memories about George.

"You see, Dan, that photo predates the Clark Fork River dams, and oh my, how young George Waterbear loved fishing the rapids, before the reservoir covered everything. My parents liked to fish here too, and this is where I met George. He was standing on a submerged rock close to shore, watching bull trout fight their way upstream. He waved, I splashed out to him, and we've been close ever since. We're the same age... fourteen when we met, and such crazy kids we were, like the time we hopped a sidedoor Pullman on a Great Northern freight eastbound out of Columbia Falls...a bright chill summer morning along the Flathead River, then cold rain into wet snow on Marias Pass. We hopped off at East Glacier set to ride back the same day but a roadmaster spotted us, chewed us out, and didn't let us go until we acted scared. We hitched to Browning for a night, then caught a ride to Missoula with a young pre-law student named Cloud Speaker. It was a memorable trip, Dan, like a family reunion. You see, Cloud is a member of the Blackfoot Nation and George and I are members of the Ursavi tribe, which has been revered and protected by the Blackfoot Nation since ancient times."

Rose leaned over and topped off my cup. "When William and I settled here, George helped us build this wonderful home where his old cabin once stood. We paneled an upstairs room, the one over the kitchen, with logs from his cabin. That's always been George's space. He uses it mostly as a computer lab now, and it's the only part of the house that is fully cybersecured."

"A security system? Does that actually work way out here?"

She started to answer but a timer on her stove buzzed and she said, "Dan, I don't mean to be rude but I'm due at our elementary school in less than an hour. I teach an art class twice a week. Today it's on the nature of pastels."

I thanked her for the fantastic breakfast and said I'd like to get started on her list of repairs.

"I appreciate your company, Dan, and your help, but don't let that list keep you from enjoying this beautiful morning. Take the path to the river and poke around the big cedar snag on the way down, it's Thius's long-time favorite. Now I must get going. I'll be home before noon, and I'll want to hear about your adventure."

Daniel, good you are free. I have a lengthy update from the Director. Four items of interest. First, Rosemary McClun is not listed in any tribal records. Second, George Waterbear's tribe did not record his date and place of birth. He was less than ten when his parents joined a Salishan band living near the mouth of what is now called the Ouzel River, approximately ten miles south of Cedarville. Third, Jason Steller first met the McCluns at an organ recital in Helena, Montana on February 12, 1955. And fourth, Thius's background remains in question. In conflict with county and state records, tribal accounts indicate Carl Bantry had two sons, Methius and Terrence. Methius lived on the cattle ranch with his father. Terrence, Methius's older brother, lived on the reservation. All records concur the tragedy at Kain's Cut took place on July 16, 1957, and young Methius met Jason and George at the McClun's nine days later.

"This is more confusing than helpful, Apella, but never mind. I want to know why Jason and George didn't tell me they've known the McCluns for years."

All of this requires closer scrutiny but we do give our agents broad operating parameters. Jason Steller insists his sources remain anonymous, and we have no reason to be suspicious of his or George Waterbear's associations with these people. Both men are long-term dependables, decidedly antiterrorist, and their worldwide contacts make them irreplaceable allies for us.

She cut off, left me with her report of unknowns, conflicting records and questionable loyalties. How accurate is her intel, especially about Jason? Could he be the one who knows about Nate or could it be Thius?

I put the repairs on hold, took off toward the river and stopped at Thius's favorite snag. At least fifteen feet high and twenty feet in girth, it stood like a charred monument to those who died in the 1910 crown fires. On the snag's backside, someone had cut toe and finger holds, a crude ladder to the top. I climbed up, wasn't surprised to find a board seat, and pictured Thius here, watching the river, listening to the valley, waiting for trains to blast through. I lost track of time until a noisy jon boat nudged me back to the spy mission. What had I learned so far about the Cedarville cell? Rose and Thius are obvious members, and probably Rachel Smyth, maybe her father Walter, and George? No way, not George. But what about Jason? His letter said he joined an international activist group…and there's that photo of him with Rose and William. Does my old professor really work for this government mission? Or does his loyalty lie elsewhere?

I climbed down, went back to the house, patched a roof leak and was upstairs checking the bathroom ceiling when I heard Rose call to me from the kitchen. "Glad we won't see any more drips. Come down, have some tea and tell me about your day so far."

How did she know I fixed the roof?

"Did you take time for the river?" she asked when I joined her at the table.

"Didn't get that far, stopped at the big cedar snag, climbed to the top and thought about your son."

"Good for you. Thius was eleven when George helped him cut those holds. Educational up there, he often says, and don't you agree? Give me the highlights. What did you see from that high seat?"

"A lot. A young bald eagle glided over the river, circled back, seemed to check me out. Two mergansers swam by, then a loon, and I watched it dive and come up with a fish then dive again when a beaver tail whopped the water and boat noise disturbed the peace. I could hear an outboard motor fighting the current before two people in a jon boat came into view, an overweight driver and a young female tending a radio antenna that was way too big for the boat. Have you ever seen them, Rose?"

"Oh, yes, I've seen those two…students from a small university east of the divide, out here hassling bull trout with antiquated equipment. Can you imagine George's reaction?"

"For sure. He'd just shake his head, but he'd want to help."

"George has tried, so have I. We've talked with their supervisors on several occasions and each time we were met with a wall of arrogant pride. Too bad for the students."

I thought of my first days in Yellowstone with George, his patience and technical skills. Only a fool would turn George Waterbear away.

Rose gave me a solemn look and said, "Oh, I'm so glad to see admiration for George in your eyes. You will surely have more contact with him, my dear, and now I'm going to finish my canning."

"Okay, I'll clean the greenhouse fans, then I'd like to bike to town, have another one of Walter's cinnamons."

Yes, good decision. Maybe someone new will turn up. We still have nothing incriminating on Walter Smyth.

Rose started pulling jars from a cabinet. "The fans can wait, Dan, and I'm sure Walter would enjoy your company. And I think you should walk, take in more of our edge-of-wild mountain valley? Save the bike ride for another day."

Yes, take the walk and learn all you can about their edge-of-wild valley.

11

Dolly Varden

I took Rose's and Apella's advice and headed out on foot just after noon. Thirty paces north of the rainbow mailbox, a dragonfly patrolling a woodland pond reminded me of an afternoon with George. We had just finished monitoring a black bear, and we were having lunch near a lake in the Absarokas. Pointing to a small red dragonfly zipping back and forth along the shore, then to a powder blue, George said, Libellula, Aeshna, deft little predators. Mosquitos don't have a chance out here.

I shook my head, really odd some of the details I recall from that lunch with George — and how little I remember from the rest of the day.

A quarter mile past the pond, the purr of an electric engine signaled me to step out of the way, and a bright red ATV with a female driver pulled close. Dressed in a floppy pink sweater, black tights and tennis shoes, she had my full attention when she lifted her visor and said, "Hello Mr. Oyente, I'm Sula Millen…heard you're a handsome dude, an avid mountain biker and train rider living with Rose."

She revved the engine and said, "Hop on, we'll do some sight-seeing. I'll take you up Larch Creek, one of the Clark Fork tributaries that runs all year." Sparkles in her hazel eyes swept me back to my first date with Apella. I caught myself staring, ran my hand through my hair, and told Ms. Millen I was on my way to town.

"That'll work," she said. "On the way back, I'll drop you a mile from town if you still feel like walking."

I thought Why not and climbed on. Obviously Rose set this up, and maybe Sula Millen knows something about Nate after all. She wheeled a fast U-turn, honked twice when we passed Rose's lane, drove three miles south then turned east on a rutted forest road and stopped at an unmarked trailhead. "This is it," she said and looped her helmet over the handlebar. "Larch Creek is about twenty feet wide and we've got a neat-o crossing log right around the corner, then we'll hike to a quiet pool, about a half mile more."

Her neat-o log spanned the creek but was only six inches wide and moss covered. "It'll hold four times our weights combined," Sula said. "Just set your own pace," and she skipped across like a gymnast on a bar.

I took it slow with arms out for balance, stopped midway, looked down and tried not to think of biking a wet log and slipping off into a Texas mud hole. Sula yelled, "That's high water, Mr. Oyente, snow-melt runoff and no silt…so clear you can see the shape and color of every rock and pebble."

When I was across, she clapped and cheered, "It's springtime in the Northern Rockies, Mr. Oyente, you won't find a better place to be yourself."

"I believe it, and call me Dan. Where you from, Sula? I'd guess the Midwest, maybe Illinois or Iowa."

"Not really, more like Upstate New York and Delaware, and I moved west after an easy two years of college."

"To Montana?"

"Yes, to Garnet U in Missoula, eventually for a master's in life science." She pulled a ribbon from her sweater pocket, tied it around her hair. "I'll race you to the pool," she said. "It's a fun run on a mossy cushion, just have to watch for devil club where the path gets narrow."

She took off fast, didn't look back. I jogged slow enough to avoid the devil club, and before I saw her again I heard her shout, "You're almost here, Dan. I'm sitting against a big cottonwood tree close to the pool.

"An extra-special place for me," she said as I sat down next to her. "This pool is like a dreamy magic swimming hole. Dark, deep and clear. Rose brought me up here just a week after I rented one of her rooms while I was doing my master's research. I hardly knew her, much less myself, and felt funny when she sat me down and said the last time she and her husband saw me I was an infant on a rail trip with my parents. It was an overnight ride from East Glacier to Minneapolis."

"So the McCluns knew your parents?"

She frowned and started fidgeting. "Yes, but I was unaware until I moved here."

I started to ask if something was wrong, and she cheered up. "I like keepin' it real, Dan, sorry about my moods. What do you think of Cedarville so far?"

We're running her profile. She certainly sounds high-strung.

I told Sula I'd stay indefinitely if Rose is a measure of the town. "What a contrast to her son and his train rides from hell. You know him, I guess."

She pursed her lips, picked up a pebble and skipped it across the pool. "Ohh, I do know Thius, and gosh he can be so pushy and every-thing. Hope you didn't let him get to you. How hard was it really, being with him on the train? Wasn't it even a little fun?"

"Yeah, I can't deny it felt kind of cool hopping trains with a bike, but those black-out tunnels, Thius's windy monologues — most of it was a serious challenge. And I'd rather hear about you, Sula. How did you find your way to Cedarville?"

"That's easy. My major prof at Garnet handed me a project on wolverines in the Cabinet Mountains, and Professor Jason Steller signed me up for a room at Rose's. Everything was perfect, and I finished my degree without even seeing a wolverine — too bad, just tracks and a few hairs confirmed by DNA, two individuals, both males. Really neat you and I both worked on a master's at Garnet. What was our professor like for you?"

"If you mean Jason Steller, he was enthusiastic, inventive, irrev-erent, intimidating. He introduced me to mountain bikes, helped me think, and saved my life more than once. So you got to know him too, Sula?"

"Yes siree. I took three of his classes, my favorite being his graduate seminar. Jason is the uncle I would have chosen…considerate and encouraging. It feels so long ago, my first class with him was in the fall of '91."

I fumbled for Nate's tags. "1991! That's the year my son Nate, Nathaniel, was killed in Iraq. He was in the army."

"Rose told me, Dan, and I am sorry, and you're searching for answers." She looked down, picked up two reddish pebbles and held them. "Wars and warmongers fool too many of us," she whispered. "I was a dumb suburban rich kid, wishing I could do some good. Painful but lucky for me, a stray 50-caliber ripped my left shoulder. My trapezius and clavicle were shattered but sent me home for keeps. It's really hard to talk about, you see. Four friends were not so lucky. Let's talk about something else."

"I understand. How about telling me more about you, Sula. You decided to stay here — how long — you're alone?"

She gave me a warm grin, hopped up and did a split leap in midair then dipped her hand in the pool. "Cedarville's my home," she said, "and I'm virtually single for eternity."

I thought She is so much like Nate, carefree and full of life, not the type to hold back. She would have told me if she knew him.

She leaned over the pool's edge, dipped her hand again and said, "You should feel the steamy clear cold, Mr. Oyente, like wet crystal, a bull trout stream. Spawners swim up from the reservoir in late summer and early fall and build their redds in the riffles. Can you imagine a pair of ten-pound fish in this little stream? I saw two just upstream last August, quivering together with their dorsal fins out of the water."

She sat close. "You've seen them too, Mr. Oyente. I can tell."

"Yes, I have vivid memories of three spawning pairs. I was on a solo hike in the Great Bear Wilderness…spent four days, September 5 to 8, 1966, along Dolly Varden Creek."

"Really? Dolly Varden Creek, the Middle Fork of the Flathead. I've waded in that stream. That is a great hike."

73

"Yes it is. I took Trail 155 to Trail 173 along the Dolly Varden to its headwaters, then over a divide and down to Trail 83 along the Spotted Bear River. A friend was waiting for me at Campground 2835. We timed it just right."

"A…mazing. Do you always focus on numbers like that?"

"No, but it's a way to keep my mind from flooding with memories. Those were fine days and I remember myriad details from them, far more than anyone would want to hear."

She pulled her knees to her chin, stretched her sweater over her legs and closed her eyes. "Neat-o. They told me about your hyperthymesia, and Thius made notes, checked it out and everything, but hearing you in person…I mean I can't really imagine. Please share one of your most favorite memories from that hike."

"Okay. The larches were peak gold along the Middle Fork."

"Oooh, I love it, and what month were you born, Mr. Oyente?"

I told her September, and her eyes lit up. "Gosh, you and Thius both have raven as your totem, your animal spirit. Raven is a mimic and an innovator with lots of messages for us, you just have to pay attention. Raven holds secrets of the universe, secrets that are like magic and can change your life. So counting back from late September, your existence began near winter solstice. I bet you like long nights."

"Good guess. I do like being in the dark or twilight, gives me a sense of peace and freedom. So it's your turn, Sula. What about your animal spirit?"

She bounced up and stretched out her arms. "I'm a hybrid, bear and sturgeon, but mostly sturgeon — perseverance, generosity, sensuality — and I try to live them, and we should start back if you want to get to Walter's before he runs out of cinnamon donuts. And just in case you don't know, Walter's donuts are extra-special healthy. He's such a particular eater. Let's go!"

She set a fast pace, leaped into the air at the crossing log, cartwheeled across and dashed down the trail ahead of me. Who is this person? A gymnast maybe in another life?

"I had excellent gym teachers all through school," she said as we neared the end of the trail. "And I hope Big Red's still there…yep, there she waits. Climb aboard, Mr. Oyente, and hold tight, be ready for those deep potholes."

She hardly slowed for the potholes, missed them all, then stopped abruptly at a small field near Rose's and said, "Last summer out there I saw four wolves take down a yearling elk, made me shiver, want to leave, but I stayed to watch. What do you think of that?"

I thought of several trite answers and told her she was lucky to be in a place where real wild still exists.

She smiled. "Now that's what I call keepin' it real, Mr. Oyente. I like it, and I'll leave you here if that's okay. You still have a good walk to Walter's."

I hopped off, told her, "Great tour and maybe see you again sometime soon."

"Yes siree, my new earthan friend, and may the raven be more your guide."

A red-winged black bird flashed from the field as she drove away, and I thought of George and Jason. How can they participate in a mission that could ruin lives they've been part of for years?

Apella was back. *Daniel, by Rosemary's count, which could be a ruse, you have identified half of the cell. Thius, Rachel, Rosemary and Sula. Four of possibly many.*

"Maybe so, Apella, and of these four, only Thius strikes me as potentially dangerous. I'll keep my guard up, of course, but is this cell seriously dissident? I'm not convinced."

Watch your gender bias, Daniel, and mark my words, the threats these people pose are serious and irrefutable.

12

Another Wounded Veteran

A fast jog put me at the store at 3:36. Hmm, no vehicles outside… guess I missed the crowd. A buzzer announced my entry, and Walter yelled from the back, "Just you and me, Dan. Have a tractor seat. I'll be with you in a minute."

I took the middle seat and picked up an old newspaper someone left on the counter. A headline about a reporter murdered two nights ago in a Seattle train station caught my attention. She'd been shot at close range in her car, and a note was left at the scene. 'We will persist until the U.S. media cease being propagandists for the criminal government, until they undertake, broadcast, and publish solid proof of the government's treasonous acts.'

I asked Apella if she knew about the report.

Yes, and I am sure you will agree the message is vintage Thius. Mr. Terrene is currently off our grid, but correspondence placed him in the Seattle area at the time of the murder.

My mind raced — Thius Seattle Murder. Was he there?

Walter startled me from behind. "Terrible, that report, disgraceful violence."

"Yes it is, and hello, Walter. You sure know how to sneak up on someone in your store."

"Concrete floor helps, and I'm proud of its radiant heat, which you will be glad for, if you stay through the winter." He stepped behind the counter. "Dan, I assure you, no one around here, even our overzealous deputy, would consider that Seattle scene anything but bad in every way."

He pulled out a different newspaper and said, "Here's another one, describes violent behavior the human species should have disowned thousands of years past."

This fellow may be more than a shopkeeper.

I was impressed by Walter's manner...pragmatic, unpretentious, and probably practiced at diffusing arguments in his store. He picked up a freshly brewed pot and filled my mug. "So tell me about Ms. Rose," he said. "You two work something out?"

"Yes, and it's a good deal for me."

I sipped the brew, heard Apella say, *We're pulling deeper intel on Mr. Smyth,* then turned and saw a tall skinny guy with a grey-blond ponytail push through the door. He took a seat at the end of the counter, and I figured him for a regular when Walter handed him a mug of coffee. Could be one of the war vets Rose mentioned, and Walter confirmed it, "Andy Denton, meet Dan Oyente. Dan's a new boarder at Ms. Rose's."

Mr. Denton fiddled with the sleeve of his faded Save the Grizzly pullover, moved two seats closer to me and said, "You sure don't look Latino, but I'll take your word for it. Stayin' with Ms. McClun, huh? She's a fine lady, real smart. She and her husband were active in our enviro group. She say anything about the mine?"

"No, she hasn't. Is there one nearby?"

"Damn straight, and there's not a soul in this valley who's not affected by it. Mine headquarters damn near fill a big flat along the river about twelve miles south."

He stretched out his long arms. "Gross thing is huge underground, taps veins of gold and platinum under Windfall Peak — under the Windfall Peak Wilderness, for Lucifer's sake. Pick and shovelers dug the surface and placered it for a hundred years 'til a conglomerate — Synbelt Reserves LLC — bought the rights, drilled miles of tunnels, hundreds of pillared rooms, filled the neighborhood with toxins from a mountain of waste rock then quit and sold out when the ore quality couldn't compete with foreign. They tried blamin' us enviros, but the market decides, right, Walter?"

Walter turned on the coffee grinder and talked over it. "You know I don't like going on about all that, Andy, bad for business."

"Yeah, Walter, but this new guy has to hear the truth. Most people around here either didn't want the work or couldn't do it — ten-hour shifts a half mile under a crumbly mountain."

Walter looked at me. "Dan, I have to say it's not that simple. Most people don't bring it up, but I still hear about it and I try to keep a lid on it when people start up in our store. Some locals lost jobs they liked and still blame the enviros, and most of those folks want to see the mine crank back up to full production. Most of us believe the mine helps discourage development by wealthy out-of-staters. And Andy doesn't like hearing it, but not all the mining jobs disappeared. Synbelt, which by the way, is owned by a global company called Precambre International, remains a solid local employer."

Andy turned on him. "Ahh yeah, right, and everybody knows Precambre pays a few locals to mine just enough to keep the pumps runnin' or else ground water seeps in from above, floods the whole damn thing. Other jobs are mostly janitorial."

Walter calmly told him, "Those are good full-time jobs, Andy. Let's change the subject."

Andy slapped the newspaper in front of me. "What about you, mister latecomer Oyente? You think it's better to subdivide and build mansions or gut a mountain and fill a valley with toxic rubble? You ever think how much people can mess up a beautiful place? You republican, democrat, right wing, alt wing, left wing or what?"

I took a slow sip of coffee and thought, This guy's smart, but a loose cannon, no telling what he endured in Vietnam, I respect him for that. He's a veteran, I'm not.

"Well what are you, mister latecomer?"

I told him I didn't mean to sound like a fence straddler but prefer to stay neutral, especially being new here. "Maybe you could show me around sometime, Andy."

Walter went to the back of the store, and Andy gave me a hard stare. "Has Ms. McClun talked about her son?"

"Yes, and I rode here on the train with him."

Andy twisted in his seat. "Yeah, Thius is super smart but never had a real job. Hell, he doesn't need one with Ms. McClun always dotin' on him. He doesn't take a stand on anything. Hates the mine but won't fight it, just floats around...sorta like a wolverine."

I thought, No way this guy could be one of the eight.

Walter stepped back behind the counter, offered us warm cinnamons and asked if Rose had mentioned the gated community south of town.

I said No, and Andy roused up. "That mess is as rotten as it looks. Wealthies came in, bought up open land, ruined it with castles."

Walter served the donuts and tried settling him down. "Andy's right, they did build some extravagant places, but two thirds of those rich folks sold out and left when Precambre took over the mine."

Andy started coughing, held his chest and muttered, "Hell, Precambre owns everything now, the mine, the castles, bad for locals, bad for wildlife, bad for everything that matters or should." He stared into his mug and said, "Everybody loses...Ms. McClun, her husband...Thius, his dad...me, just about everybody."

Walter handed him a glass of water and said, "Andy, I have asked you this before. Would you still fight the mine if you knew it would discourage another wave of wealthy developers?"

"Damn sure I'd fight anything that makes a mess."

Walter explained that most of the land owned by the mine, nearly two thousand acres on both sides of the river, once belonged to the Pright family. "You see, Dan, Oly Pright, our sheriff, ran a popular outfitting company until he sold the last portion of the ranch thirty years ago."

"In your wildest," said Andy. "A billionaire Precambre trustee conspired with the government to bankrupt Pright so the company could buy his land cheap."

"Come on, Andy," Walter said. "You know that is just not true."

Andy persisted. "Yeah, well, most people around here believe Pright was set up and he's been re-elected sheriff ever since. I bet he'd turn in his badge before he'd go after anyone who took a shot at Precambre's turbines on Pright Ridge."

Walter shook his head and recited details. "Dan, the truth is the Prights couldn't pay the taxes on all that property. They needed the money to keep their home. Precambre paid a fair price for their land, and Andy doesn't like hearing it, but that company has been good for Cedarville. Precambre has always been interested in power production more than mining. When Precambre finishes those turbines on Pright Ridge, they'll power the whole town and still have plenty to sell to the grid. And since Precambre took over, the waste-rock pile has been getting smaller, thanks to one of their smart guys figuring out how to process the waste into consumable products."

Andy tipped his mug for dregs. "Aah, never trust a multinational. The world's goin' to corporate hell."

Just like Thius, I thought.

Andy hopped up, gave Walter a quick salute and said it was time to head home. I stood, said it was good meeting him, and he asked if I like to snowshoe.

"For sure! I did a lot on a recent job in Yellowstone. What do you have in mind, Andy?"

"How 'bout Saturday? Norwester blows through tonight. It'll leave new powder above four thousand…shoein'll be choice, and I'll show you places the mine ruined. We'll leave at 0500, back by 1850. I don't do overnights this time a year…chunks of 'nam shrap in my left thigh and butt get too cold."

"Sounds painful, Andy. I was never in the service, and I certainly respect those who put everything on the line. Where on Saturday?"

"Out at Ms. McClun's mailbox. Be there at 0500, we'll pick you up. If somethin' happens and you can't make it, leave me a message on Walter's tack board outside here."

"I'll be there, looking forward," I said as he went out the door.

I thanked Walter for coffee and conversation then headed back to Rose's with a string of thoughts about Cedarville. I was passing the old bus when Apella gave me a heads up. Her people already had leads on the mining company.

Precambre is a private corporation with diverse affiliates and subsidiaries on every continent. They are world leaders in energy research and development with a reputation for transparency and community service. George Waterbear is a long-term member of Precambre's board of directors. No clear profile for Mr. Denton. The naive, detached persona may be part of his cover. Unlikely the mine has any relevance to our mission.

That evening after dinner, Rose and I sat on her porch swing listening to a varied thrush repeat his rapid trill. When he took a break, I told Rose it was good to meet Sula Millen and Andy Denton.

"Happy to hear it, my dear. And I know you realize I arranged those meetings. I thought you wouldn't mind. Do you find Sula attractive?"

"Yes. Will I see her again?"

"Quite possibly, though she has a very busy schedule."

"I'm guessing she's one of the eight you mentioned, but what about Andy Denton? He seems kind of frail and troubled."

Rose got up, held her hands behind her back, then looked away for three long minutes before saying, "Andrew Denton is one of my favorite people. He is a decorated, severely wounded Marine turned outspoken antiwar environmentalist who was handsome when he had a stylish haircut and an appetite."

She faced me and added, "I will always admire Andrew's energy and wit, but sadly, he is not a member of our group. Andrew Denton carries a heavy load of cynical anger and wears it like a badge for all to see."

I told her there were times at Walter's when Andy sounded like a strident version of Thius.

"Yes," she said and sat back down. "Friends do imitate one another, and sometimes it sticks. The boys were classmates, friends on and off through grade school and after, but they do have serious differences. Thius retains some anger from Kain's Cut, but good long-term counsel taught him how to manage it, and he's never been in a war. Andrew, on the other hand, enlisted right out of high school, survived unspeakable horrors in the jungles of Southeast Asia, and spent a whole year in a crowded hospital for veterans of an unpopular war. When he returned home he was able to pull himself up by his bootstraps, and believe me, that was nothing short of a miracle. Andrew refuses any form of counseling, and it is not surprising that he resents my son and others who went to Canada to avoid the draft."

"I dodged the Vietnam war too, Rose, deferments, luck of the draw."

"Just be glad you are alive, intact, and have not had to kill anyone. Did you have a chance to ask Andrew about your son?"

"No, but he invited me to snowshoe with him Saturday, day after tomorrow. Okay to borrow the aluminum trackers and ski poles I saw in your shed?"

"Certainly, but take extra care. It's avalanche season and Andrew can be reckless."

She covered a yawn with her hand. "Oh goodness, Dan, my body is telling me this evening must end. How would you feel about a morning walk with Max, Agnes and me? I'll put together a light breakfast and wake you early." I told her nothing would suit me better.

And so as my second day in Cedarville drew to a close, I felt certain I had identified a ring leader in Rosemary McClun. But I still knew nothing about the ring called Ursavus.

13

Tightrope

Sharp whistles and the grating call of a Saw-whet owl woke me at five a.m. "Wonderful you're familiar with the Saw-whets," Rose said when I joined her on the back porch.

Max and Agnes took the lead as we started down the path to the river. Rose ordered TO WILLIAM'S PLACE, and the dogs bolted away. "Let's hurry," she said to me, "it's a quarter mile and they'll only wait ten minutes before circling back."

A narrow side path led to a small glade near the river's edge where three ponderosa pines towered over a weathered grey table and bench. Rose looked content as she unpacked rawhide chews, fruit, peanut butter, and a thermos, gave Max and Agnes each a chew, filled two insulated cups with steaming coffee and touched the bench for me to sit with her. "William and I would be here for hours," she said. "Two lovers, no talk…just being together. We discovered ourselves in this valley…the river, moist woods, the trains and remnants of wild. And that's why I brought you here to William's Place. I want you to know more about him."

She blew lightly over her cup, took a sip then spread peanut butter on a slice of apple and handed it to me. Calm before a storm, I thought as she stared out at the river. "William and I are insepa-rable," she said, "always were, always will be, and with that in mind, let me tell you about a night in March, 1967, a night that dras-tically changed our lives. I was here in Cedarville. William was in

Washington, DC where he debuted his second piano concerto with the National Symphony Orchestra. It was rare I wasn't with him, but I had a busy teaching schedule that spring and no substitutes. After the performance he called from his hotel to say the debut didn't elicit a standing ovation, but the applause was strong and included some enthusiastic shouts of praise…enough excitement so he needed his usual stroll in the night air."

We have her on speaker!

Rose cupped her hand around her amber pendant and sighed, "When I next saw my husband he was in a hospital, unconscious after being beaten, robbed, and left to die in a dark alley. He was in a deep coma for forty-nine days then suddenly woke up. His mind was active but he couldn't move his arms or legs." She stared at the river again. "The love of my life, a brilliant keyboard artist — was quadriplegic.

"William and I both knew Ursavus was his only true hope for meaningful recovery. So, I wheeled him out of that hospital and George helped me set him up at an Ursavus restoration center. William remained there for five months, isolated from everyone except the specialists who treated him. I didn't see him again until he came home to Cedarville, and let me tell you, Dan, after what my husband had been through, what those people did for him was nothing short of miraculous, like he'd been in another world. He looked and felt younger, stronger than ever, and when Thius and I heard him play Chopin's Opus 10 Etudes, we were ecstatic. William's artistry was fully restored."

Keep her talking.

I took a gulp of coffee. "Hard to believe, Rose. Tell me more about the restoration center. Where is it? Who treated him?"

She got up from the bench. "Oh yes, there is so much more to say, but Max and Agnes are telling me it's SWIM TIME." She pulled a float toy out of her pack and handed it to me. "They'll be your friends for life if you throw this, Dan."

Agnes barked sharply, herded us to a riverside sand bar. I worked my feet into the sand, gave the toy a heave and the dogs raced after it. Agnes swam faster, snatched the toy and passed it off to Max. They sloshed out together, shook hard, and Max dropped the toy at my feet.

Rose heaped praise on them as we walked back to the bench, then freshened our cups and said, "Let's see now, Dan, we left off at the restoration center, yes. It is in an area far more remote than Cedarville, and only ursavans know of it. I cannot reveal specifics, but even I didn't recognize my husband. He was reconstructed. His face was totally different, his eyes dark brown instead of blue. His hands were the same and his baritone voice was basically unchanged, just slightly deeper. He was — I should say is — more brilliant than ever, but his interests and goals are different, very much so. Public performance no longer appeals to him. He is a full-time teacher, bringing his music and artistry to the world — and not as a reconstructed William McClun — too many questions, too much focus. He will always be William to me, but he is Liam Yrisse to the rest of the world. And that's about all I can say until you agree to join us. I can see questions in your eyes, Dan, but please don't ask me any more about this."

Such a bittersweet fairy tale. Smart to hold your questions. Press releases for Irish musician William Yrisse McClun often mentioned his boyhood nickname Liam Y.

Rose turned sideways on the bench, looked down at two spots of white under the table and was surprised when I said, "Hey, those are earthstar fungi, first saw one, actually three, on a bike ride with my son. We were on the Devisadero Peak Trail near Taos, New Mexico, stopped for a break about halfway up, and there they were in the shade of a juniper."

"Well now, Dan, I am very impressed. George Waterbear introduced me to earthstars here in this valley. My oh my, so long ago. George asked if I knew any humans worthy of the title earthstar. I told him, Yes, you and William, both beautiful, gifted but modest, and oh, so much more. George gave me his rare smile and said, I think of you, Rosey."

She reached out, put her hand under my chin and looked in my eyes. "And so, Daniel Oyente, please believe me when I say you also have earthstar qualities. Jason speaks of you as a brilliant thinker, steadfast and loyal to the core. George admires your persistence, attention to detail and respect for life. And Thius, who's not easily impressed you realize, was completely taken aback by the sheer scope of your hyperthymesia. You are exceptionally gifted, Daniel, and this may sound like pure speculation, but can you imagine being able to perceive and record another person's detailed thoughts — I mean be telepathic AND hyperthymestic?"

Such hocus-pocus.

Right, I thought and swallowed the last of my coffee. "You mean, what if I could read minds, Rose? Offhand I'd say the data flow might be overwhelming, but that's a quick guess, hard to say without actual experience, and that won't happen in my lifetime. Interesting concept though, for the next century, I suppose."

"Well now," she said, fanning a hornet away from a slice of apple, "I learned a long time ago not to underestimate the power of Ursavus. You shouldn't make that mistake either, my dear."

Remote renewal center, miraculous restoration, telepathy. The woman is totally delusional!

Common sense told me Apella had it right, but Rose sounded and looked convinced, like she had no doubt about any of it. Good actor, I thought — or is she? And why is she so close to my thoughts?

Rose took my cup and started loading her pack. "Jason did apprise us of your propensity to be evasive, Daniel, and it is essential that you relinquish that tendency and be upfront with your feelings. Tell me how you really feel about Jason and George now, would you please?"

I touched the labradorite inset on my watch and looked down at the earthstars. "That's easy, Rose. I think highly of both Jason and George, and I am their loyal friend, period. I wouldn't be alive if it weren't for Jason. I owe him my life, and I mean just that. And George, what I've gained from him cannot be put in words. He gave me a whole new attitude about life."

"And now," she said, "what if I told you George and Jason are members of an organization that seeks to undermine the United States government? What would you think about that?"

Was Rose asking this so she could read my mind and catch me in a lie? No — crazy thought.

The dogs' ears went up, and they looked at me then Rose when I said, "I think if I knew for certain — I mean, had proof — that George and Jason were members of such a group, I would want to learn more about their roles, but it would not affect my friendship or loyalty."

"But would you risk treason?"

"If it came to that, yes, I believe I would take the risk."

"I see," she said, "and how would you feel if that treason involved violence?"

"Interesting you ask, Rose. Jason posed the same question in a seminar in the fall of 1964, and he convinced me he abhors violence. I am sure he would not be a member of a violent group, and I'm almost as confident the same is true for George. I believe it was Isaac Asimov who wrote, 'Violence is the last refuge of the incompetent.'"

"That's a wonderful quote, Daniel, and so appropriate. As we both know, Jason and George are anything but incompetent."

Yes, and your evasiveness reflects your training.

Rose shouldered her pack and called the dogs to her side. "Straight to the tracks you two, and keep close!"

They took the lead to the railroad berm and we scrambled over the track to the fireline road just before an engine horn blew from the west. Rose said, "Two blasts. He's seven minutes out, and at this pace we'll meet him below the house."

Her timing was near perfect, and she waved when the train barreled by. Two air-horn blasts then three made me think the engineer was a member of Ursavus. Rose winked at me and told the dogs to come as we headed up the hill.

That night I asked Apella what would happen to Jason and George if they turned out to be members of Ursavus.

Nonsense! They are with us and have been for years. Are you prepared for your outing with Mr. Denton tomorrow?

"It's all organized. How can you be so sure about Jason and George?"

Years of experience and surveillance. Rosemary's comments about Jason and George illustrate the tightrope these agents walk disguising their ultimate loyalty to us.

"And if you are wrong?"

Not possible, but they would be turned. Their service to us would not be affected until the mission is over.

"And then?"

She didn't answer and there was some static.

Uncertain, she finally said, and the implant gave its end-of-conversation beep.

"Uncertainty isn't acceptable," I said out loud. "I need to know for sure that George and Jason will not be harmed."

14

Floating on Powder

Saturday morning I waited two cold hours at the end of Rose's lane. Be there at 0500, Andy said, and I thought ex-Marine, he'd be punctual. I pulled my cap tight over my ears and paced back and forth. "You're late, damn it. Show up, will you. I'm freezing out here, and three layers of thermals and a beanie aren't cutting it."

Daniel, are you all right? We were concerned for you in the night. We recorded you moaning, almost yelling at times.

"I'm okay, just a lot of creepy dreams, different stuff—back-alley muggings, cryptic rehab centers, big cat attacks, miners screaming in a rock slide, avalanches and a cadre of telepaths who knew all about my implant—not an easy night, but I'll be fine."

The storm left twelve inches of snow at higher elevations. Watch yourself. The mountains may block transmissions from your implant. We will pursue and verify information as received, and it sounds like you've got company.

"Affirmative... maybe," I said as someone pulled close in a sputtery yellow pickup that sounded like it couldn't climb a speed bump much less a mountain road. The windshield was fogged but I could see three people in the cab, and Andy was driving. He lowered his window and acted like he was on time. "Hey latecomer, we just came from breakfast with some friends. Glad you made it. Throw your junk in the back."

I faked a smile, walked to the passenger side and reached for the door just as a stocky young guy with dark rock-star curls and a serious air bounced out...five nine and about Nate's age I guessed.

Andy yelled, "Mister latecomer Dan Oyente, meet Erik Galen and Sula Millen."

"Squeeze in," Sula said with a warm smile.

I slid next to her, and Mr. Galen took the window seat. He pushed his hair back and spoke in a calm, steady voice. "Sula and I try to get out twice a month at least, Mr. Oyente. Usually we go up Meadow Creek to the hanging valley above our place. It's on the west side of the river."

Hmm…Rose didn't tell me about this guy being with Sula. Maybe he knows something about Nate. And why are these two dressed so lightly? No coats or leggings, just thin fabric, and it's cold in the truck. Must be some kind of new thermal on the market, and I was set to ask when Andy, who wore a thick insulated parka, stomped on the gas, spun his wheels and launched into an odd chant. "Yeah, westside here we come, and a hard turn left comin' up it is. Then it's over the track to the river bridge, and there be quick for shades of blue, up and down you'll see. Then it's left again on the valley west, and that's our easy street to the Meadow Creek."

He shifted hard to second for the left turn, floored it again, bounced across the rails and didn't slow on the bridge.

The West Valley Road was new to me, and Sula could tell I was curious about the canyons we passed. "Great fun trails up those roads," she whispered and leaned into me as the road angled southwest and close to the river. "Hope you stick around, Dan, we'll find time to bike them all."

Andy blurted, "Okay mister latecomer, you know about Precambre and Synbelt from Walter's the other day. The damn corporation owns most of the valley around here — both sides of the river, except some parcels like Erik and Sula's twenty. We're drivin' over some mine tunnels right now, and you're sittin' between two kids who had more to do with tickin' off mining execs than any of us. When the mine's waste pile started foulin' Meadow Creek, Synbelt offered to buy the kids' rights, but the kids wouldn't sell and gave 'em an ultimatum — clean up or quit. The company bean counters said clean up would cost too much, but hell, they agreed to it when we threatened to sue."

He turned onto the Meadow Creek Road and drove like he knew every curve and pothole. "Yikesabee!" Sula shouted when he swerved to miss a family of badgers.

Andy countered with, "Everything's just right, be pullin' off past this bend," and Sula whispered, "Whew, finally," when he parked on a sheet of crackly ice.

We hopped out of the truck, Andy stashed his keys, zipped up his parka and smiled when I thanked him for handling the rough road. "Preciate it, Mr. Oyente, grab yer gear. We fall in back of Erik and Sula. I'll be on yer six."

We strapped on our snowshoes and gaiters and started out single file, scraping along on crusted snow and patches of bare ground. Andy was tight on my heels when he said, "Always makes me think I'm on some deserted bare-rock planet."

"Ohh, I hear you, Andy," Sula said over her shoulder, "metal shoes are fun but sure weren't made for quiet."

Erik led us up a narrow draw to a belt of charred pine and fir snags. "Great little burn this was," said Andy, "need more of 'em or big fires are the future."

Past the burn, Sula took the lead as we traversed a gentle slope heavily drifted with new powder. I thought of Rose's concern and asked about avalanches. Erik said, "Always good to keep in mind, but I believe we're okay on this face."

Andy added, "Aah, we got it made. No steep chutes or overhangs on this side, zero chance of problems."

Higher up, we were on a level glade near the headwaters of a stream when Sula shouted, "Cougar prints! Six-inch halos! Must have prowled through here this morning!"

Andy and Erik ran to see, and I followed, cautioned by an old fear. "Big sucker all right," said Andy, "...take an elk five, six times his weight. Gotta keep an eye out."

"Ever been dangerously close to a mountain lion?" I asked them.

Sula answered in a long, "Nooo, have you?"

"Yeah, once in the Pecos Wilderness. I was out alone on metal shoes like these — noisy and too close to a maze of deer trails. Near a cluster of Gambel oaks, I stopped, looked back and froze. A big adult and a half-grown cub stood six feet behind me. I stumbled and nearly fell, screamed and flailed at them with my ski poles. Lucky they turned and ran, vanished in the oaks. Still to this day when I think about that scene, Fully being in the eyes of death flashes white in my mind."

Red-faced and embarrassed I'd said all that, I was glad to hear Andy laugh and bluster, "Lucky mom didn't go fer yer neck, but choked by a big cat's gotta be better'n slow rips by coyotes or wolves." He started coughing and leaned on Erik's shoulder. "Not too far now," he said, "gotta make sure latecomer sees what's left of the lakes."

A long climb in deep powder put us on a wooded ridge between two massive peaks. Andy pointed downhill, "Lakes WERE below that stand of mountain hemlocks."

I wondered about his emphasis on were and watched him jump-start a downhill run. For twenty seconds he looked like a pro in a race — heels down toes up on the loose powder. Great balance, I thought, just before he collapsed into a cloud of white. "Hope he didn't break anything," said Erik, and moments later, we heard a loud, "Yay-eh!" as Andy righted himself and resumed his wild pace. Sula exhaled, "Whew, guess it's our turn, Erik," and they shoved off.

I held back, tried to contact Apella. "I'm alone for a minute. Are you there? Do you have my position?"

Her voice crackled. *Daniel, I —*

"You're breaking up, must be the mountains."

Hear you loud and —

"Getting mostly static here. Apella?"

Daniel, I needed — then nothing, no signal or static.

I cursed the implant, took a long breath of cold air and pushed off to a powdered run that felt almost as good as a bike ride. Andy was waiting for me at the bottom of the hill. "How'd you like that, latecomer?"

"Fine, smooth and too short," I said, and we scuttled through the trees to an opening where Erik and Sula were waiting. It was circular and snow-packed, shaped like a lake, I thought, and Erik said, "Where we're standing was Mirror Lake, and Hard Scrabble was about fifty feet down the hill. Both were too shallow for fish but were rare refugia for amphibians and invertebrates."

Sula put her arm around him and pointed with her ski pole. "Dan, these mountains are a maze of rock faults, big and small, and water flows down through the faults. Flooding was always a problem for the mine, but as Andy knew before I got here, surface changes were minimal until Synbelt took over. Their underground expansion of the mine included a new tunnel under a chain of lakes. Two of those lakes, Mirror and Hard Scrabble, just drained away."

Andy sneered, "I'd give up my manhood before I'd kill a wild lake, but Synbelt just had to keep tunnelin' as if the ore body was endless. Rocks to riches, the benighted digger's dream."

Sula looked at me and said, "Oh, but it was more than a dream. They found a vein of platinum more valuable than the total output of the mine since the earliest days. Synbelt did the tunneling that drained the lakes, but things have been getting better since Precambre took over."

Erik added, "It is true, Mr. Oyente. Precambre stopped tunneling right away, began converting the waste rock into useful products and transporting them to market via Triple Divide Railway. They've also built a below-ground water management system to handle seepage. It is a world-class model."

"So these lakes are still dry?" I asked, trying to gauge how deep the snow was under my feet. "It's hard to believe a company could avoid repairing damage like that."

Andy looked daggers at me. "And what would you have 'em do, mister latecomer? Mitigate? Run around pluggin' all the faults with bentonite or concrete? Nature'll fix it, but not in our time. Word is Precambre plans to convert the mine to some kind of below-ground power generator — could be a nuke plant — might be time to remind 'em we're payin' attention to what they're doin' down there, make 'em rethink their finances."

I asked if he'd ever been in the mine. He coughed, said, "Nope. Precambre lets the public in their above-ground headquarters — that's it."

Erik handed him a water bottle, turned to me and gently added, "Andy is aware that Precambre's finances are far beyond local disturbance, and these two lakes are dry for only a few summer weeks. Most of the time they're shallow wetlands that have become important to many species. Freshwater shrimp, for instance, and tailed frogs spend the long winter under logs near the fast stream that still drains Hard Scrabble's basin. Precambre saved the habitats by backfilling most of the tunnels that were draining the lakes." What a contrast this guy is to Andy, I thought. Not a trace of hype, arrogance or condescension.

Andy steadied himself with a ski pole, held his chest, said he needed a few minutes to himself. "You three go on ahead — I'll catch up."

We tied our snowshoes to our packs, backtracked up the hill and waited for Andy. I noticed Erik's and Sula's lightweight shirts molded to their arms. "I'm curious, have to ask," I said. "You're both young and fit, obviously, but how do you stay warm in those thin outfits?" Sula tugged on one of her sleeves. "It's a new nanofiber material, Dan, synthesized by a home-grown start-up, not yet available to the public."

Erik smiled at her, pulled binoculars from his fanny pack and told me to scope out the far hillside. "Our buddy Andy gets out more than we do," he said, "and he loves the high country. Last week he saw a family of wolves over there. Maybe we'll see new tracks on the way back."

By late afternoon a cold mist had slicked every surface, and we were strung out in single file behind Erik, working our way down a forty-five-degree slope. I could see Meadow Creek about five hundred feet below us when Sula shouted, "Hold up! Andy's hurt!" She ripped off her pack, pulled and scratched her way back to him, got under his right shoulder and waited for Erik and me. When she was sure we had Andy braced between us she reached down and carefully touched his left thigh. He gritted his teeth and tried to smile, "Ahh, nothin' new, kids. Metal twisted on me again. Gimme a minute, I can make it okay."

"I don't think so," Sula told him. "It's already swollen and you have a bad contusion. We can get you down to the creek trail, but it's another three miles to your truck."

"Hang in there, old buddy," said Erik. "We'll get you back," and Sula whipped out her phone. "I'm calling the veteran center in Coeur d'Alene, Andy, sending them coordinates to land a helicopter at Hoary Bat Campground and meet us with a gurney at the bottom of this hill."

Erik and I steadied Andy between us and started down. Sula scrunched ahead, clearing a path as best she could. Andy had to be in pain, but he didn't say anything until two paramedics met us on the creek trail. "Been awhile, guys," he moaned, "glad your chopper didn't have to return fire."

One saluted, the other smiled and said, "You were there for us, Sergeant, and we are here for you." They carried him on a gurney, and after the helicopter took off and the noise faded, Erik hugged Sula and spoke quietly. "He'll be okay, hard to believe he's still so negative about Precambre and Synbelt. Next time you see George, talk to him about Andy. Maybe he and Jason can finally work things out."

Sula tilted her head toward me and said, "Ohh, I'm sure some of it was for the new guy in town but that downhill run to Mirror was insane. Andy knows his leg can't take that much stress. If this puts him back on crutches and pain pills, he'll self-destruct. I'm really afraid for him." She was almost in tears.

Erik said, "He is definitely alone too much and the farm is not enough for him. I'll try to spend more time with him when I'm around, have to help any way we can."

"Agreed," she said, wiping her eyes, "and we should hustle back to Andy's truck. I'll drive us to town, park at Walter's, then we can catch a fast ride to Coeur d'Alene. I do not want Andy to be alone in that hospital too long."

We jogged the three miles to the yellow truck, piled in, and Erik told me to hold tight. "Sula's not going slow," he said, "and we'll drop you at the eastside wye north of Rose's."

It was a wild ride, and Sula paid less attention to potholes and curves than Andy had. She skidded to a stop at the wye, I hopped out, and Apella made contact minutes after they drove off.

Interesting outing you had. We wish Mr. Denton a quick recovery. His involvement remains obscure. Erik Galen's connection is obvious. Expect more than Rosemary's count of eight. On another note, we have calls scheduled with both Jason Steller and George Waterbear. The director requests clarification regarding their associations with various members of the cell.

I asked about her fractured message. "What did you want to say when I lost you in the mountains a few hours ago? You sounded like old times."

Yes, we expected that.

"What? You expected to be cut off? And why is Erik's connection obvious?" She didn't respond — nothing. Damned implant, I need more control!

Rose was waiting on her front porch with phone in hand when I walked up. "I just heard about the accident," she said. "Andrew has injured that leg so many times, it's a miracle he can stay upright without a crutch. Come sit with me, Dan, tell me what you saw."

I gave her details, ending with Sula's concern that Andy could be suicidal. "A worry of mine as well," Rose said. "I have spent countless hours with Andrew, and there's always a part of him I simply cannot reach. Probably only a war vet could. It concerns me that he lives alone in a small cabin, but Sula and Erik's place is close by, and he does enjoy working with two older vets managing our community farm."

"Erik mentioned the farm, said it wasn't enough for Andy. I like Erik. What's his background? Was he in the Iraq war? Desert Storm?"

She leaned close, searched my eyes and told me Erik Galen was never in a war. "But, oh my, all the sons and daughters maimed and lost to the whims of fools and greed of the weapons industry. How do parents live with it? I could not. Dan, talk about your son. I understand he was born when you were so young, still in high school. You and his mother never married. What else?"

I touched Nate's tags and talked about some of our times together. "My son was super smart and athletic, a great mountain biker, rock climber, and a fine companion. He lived with his mother, and when she passed away his last year in high school, he moved in with a friend named Derik, an odd guy...never understood how Nate tolerated him. Anyway, most years until Nate started graduate school, we hooked up two or three times. We'd bike the Northern Rockies in the summer and New Mexico or Utah in winter. Slick-rock trails in Canyonlands and around Moab were his favorites and I'm grateful for those memories. Nate surprised me when he said he was thinking about enlisting. He was only a thesis defense shy of a PhD in math and statistics at Syracuse, and I never saw him again."

Rose asked if I thought learning more about what happened to my son would help me. I told her I just couldn't let it go — had to see it through.

She looked out toward the front yard and mused, "The scent of spring on a mountain can soothe a troubled soul. I believe you should go for that bike ride you've been wanting, and I recommend Hemlock Draw. You passed it with Andrew and the kids, the first mountain road south of the river bridge on the west side, a good climb with some hairpin turns. It'll help settle you out. Now, I'd like to collect some hemlock cones from along the lane. I've got an idea for a new painting. Are you thinking about emailing George?"

Damn if she hadn't read my mind. She smiled demurely, said her computer was on the desk in the kitchen with George's email all ready to go. "Just type DO in the Subject line, give George my best, and promise me you'll take that ride, Dan...tomorrow morning early. I'll see you then."

We are logged in. We have accessed Rosemary McClun's and George Waterbear's email accounts. Ready when you are.

Whoa, wait a minute, I thought, If Rose can read my mind, she can also read Apella talking in my head. But why am I thinking Rose is a mind reader? No way, not possible. But she is perceptive, and I need to harness my thoughts when she's around.

15

Whirls of Power

I sat at Rose's computer. How to start an email to George — a message Rose will surely see? Okay, here goes.

Subject: DO
Hello George, missing you and the bears more
than I can say - survived two train rides with a
guy named Thius Terrene, the guy who helped me
hop the train on Bozeman Pass. It was good to
see Jason Steller after all those years. I'm now
in Cedarville, trading room and gourmet board
for chores and more with Rosemary McClun, a
friend of yours. I'm writing from her computer.
She sends her best. Dan

There was a fast response from George.

Subject: Re: DO
Good to hear from you, Dan. Rosey and I have
been friends since we were teenagers, also close
to her husband Will and son Thius. I decided not
to mention any of my associations until you had
a chance to visit Cedarville. -George

I think I understand, George, and I've been
wanting to ask about something that may be
trivial. My second day here, I was close to
the river and watched two radiotrackers with a
large antenna in a jon boat. Rose said they were
studying bull trout, but could they have been
part of something else, watching her place while
I'm here?

Radiotrackers? Don't waste thoughts on that.
Why would anyone advertise their presence with
obtrusive equipment that's been obsolete for
decades? I'm eager to hear about your implant.
How do you feel now that you've had time to
assimilate? Any side effects, physiological or
behavioral changes?

I glanced over my shoulder and swallowed hard. If Rose reads
these emails she'll know about my implant. But, surely George realizes
this, so he must have a way to keep it from her...guess that means I
don't have to worry about what I write back to him.

No pain from the implant, George. I don't think
much about it except when I'm talking with my
manager Apella Inglason, someone I've been
friends with for a long time. I was surprised
they chose her for this venture.

I remember you mentioned Ms. Inglason, think you
said she dreamed of becoming a roboticist and
couldn't juggle a relationship anymore. Now I
guess she's an intelligence operative. Does she
seem different?

She doesn't act like herself most of the time,
but all I have is her voice, at least so far.

Dan, I'm sure you recall what I said in
Yellowstone. Be on guard and do not let anyone
or any situation confuse you.

Yes, you said consider everything a test and I'm
beginning to understand what you meant. Speaking
of confusion, how do you stay sane floating
the line between the government people and this
organization called Ursavus? I assume you know
about it.

I do know about it, and I manage to float the
line as you put it, largely because I refuse
to disclose anything — particularly to the
government — unless asked a direct question.
When they do ask, I keep my answers as cryptic
as possible. Now that you've been introduced
to Ursavus it is appropriate for me to say the
McCluns and I helped start the organization long
before I was hired by the U.S. Park Service to
modernize tracking programs. Years later the
government hired me as an agent. Only since
you've been out there have I been questioned
about my relationship with Rosey, Jason, or
anyone else in Cedarville. But enough of that.
What about your implant? What's your appraisal
of its value to the mission so far?

But how do you do it, George? Your connection to
Ursavus makes your role in all this sound even
more complex. Can you say more about it? I don't

have much to report about the implant. It gives Apella and company a way to keep up with my progress, and most of the time it helps to hear her voice and be reminded that someone is watching my back...even if she does sound weird. Really strange I still don't recall anything about the implant surgery.

I'm certain you were heavily sedated when the device was installed. It is a prototype, and I tried to prevent its use. Its effects on body systems and behavior – especially long-term – have not been adequately evaluated. Do not hesitate to tell me or Ms. Inglason if you detect any side effects.

Nothing so far, George, but you've got me worried. Could it be driving this crazy chase to find out about my son? I mean, why after all this time am I so determined to track a lead from Jason Steller that was vague to begin with and still is? I also find myself doubting the government's account more and more. Especially when I wake up thinking, They never found Nate's remains, and his personnel records were destroyed in a fire at the VA.

Your device is too crude to effect such specific behavioral changes, and I think you would not ignore a message from Jason about your son under any circumstance.

You're right as usual, George, and maybe you can help me with this. I do think someone in

Cedarville has information about Nate. There's a young guy named Erik Galen here. Do you know if he's ever been in Iraq?

Mr. Galen has spent some time in every country in the Middle East. He travels widely, consulting with research groups and companies like Precambre. His application for a position with us noted recurring nightmares of being a surgeon's assistant in Lebanon, but he had no recollection of being there.

Erik is a research consultant?

Erik Galen is a brilliant cyberengineer, and Ursavus is a very powerful organization. Just one example, the advanced tag and sensor technology (ATST) I demonstrated for you in Yellowstone - not the system we used routinely - is at least thirty years ahead of your implant and the crude techniques used to install it. Erik and I helped develop ATST and the security system that protects its underlying theory. It derives from the science of skyrmion lattices, whirls of magnetic force that inhabit chiral magnets. Under certain conditions, these whirls can be unwound - disrupted mechanically and chemically - to provide quantized magnetic flux, which is a source of our power.

I took a minute to think. George had provided no details about ATST in Yellowstone — and the other stuff was way over my head. This is bizarre.

George noticed the time lag.

Are you still there, Dan?

Just trying to understand what this means,
George. I've never heard of chiral magnets or
skyrmion lattices. Where do you work, other than
Yellowstone? Are you a member of Ursavus now? Is
Jason aware of this?

Jason was informed many years ago. I remain
a member, along with Rosey and Thius, and
you've met others who work closely with me.
Rachel Smyth is a galaxy-class genomicist who
enjoys being out on the rails. Sula Millen is a
classically trained biologist turned geochemist.
Carbon storage in basaltic rocks is a main
interest of hers. And we should wrap this up,
Dan. I have an early appointment with a great
granddaughter of the Patriarch.

Another quick question, George. You being a
member of Ursavus. That doesn't mean anyone else
knows about my implant, does it? And if this
mission plays out as I think it's planned, how
will you handle the government incarcerating
Rose, your close friend?

Your secret is safe, Dan, and so is Rosey. We
all are. I'll sign off now. Do not hesitate to
touch base.

I sat back in shock. These emails make George sound like a rank-ing member of the very group I was sent to infiltrate. Not possible is it? What will Apella say about him now? One thing for sure, George Waterbear does not speak before thinking. He had a reason for every word he put in the emails. I also learned from our partnership in Yellowstone, he would not tell me we are all safe if he had any doubts. What will Apella's people do with all he just revealed?

I shut off Rose's computer, went upstairs and contacted Apella. "George just gave us a lot of information."

What are you talking about? We recorded nothing!

"But we've been writing back and forth for thirty-nine minutes."

Did you send from RmMCL@knmail.com and receive from George at gwtrbr@yellowstone.org?

"Yes, Rose had it all set up."

Someone must be using a cybercloak! Get back on her computer. Forward those messages to us. No — wait, repeat it all from memory immediately — verbatim!

She was hysterical, way out of character for Apella, and I made a fast decision not to repeat George's emails verbatim. It was a breach of my mission, but I was not prepared to compromise George. I had to find out why he shared all that information with me. George doesn't make mistakes like that. It was deliberate.

I gave Apella an abridged report of the emails, omitted details about advanced technology, and told her it's probably routine for George to hide his conversations from any and all hackers.

She didn't question my improvised report.

George Waterbear is the ultimate floater. His years of service are a measure of his disguise. We accept his stepping over the line at times to maintain a surveilled group's trust. We have searched records of his email communications with Rosemary McClun and found nothing incriminating, although the cybercloak potential raises flags. Our agents will probe for more. I will brief you at four a.m. before your bike ride, and I apologize for my impatience.

I knew nothing about cybercloaks, but surely Apella's government people would eventually hack those emails — and then she would see it all — everything I omitted. Or does Ursavus have better cybersecurity than the government?

I loaded my pack and thought about my ride out of Yellowstone — hours of focus on black ice and cold gusts in the canyon —

mind-freeing attention to the road ahead. A bike ride always helps — a long climb tomorrow, a chance to plot my way between the mission and Ursavus, between Apella and George — then a fast downhill to strengthen resolve. Gotta think about where I am in all this.

16

Keeps Gittin' Steeper

There was no call or briefing from Apella that morning. Rose left me a note saying she had to run to town, and I was on the first rise up Hemlock Draw an hour before sunlight chased the chill. I started counting pedal strokes and thought, if Apella breaks in with questions about my report I'll tell her I was trying to cover for George, help him walk his tightrope, as she put it.

The first switchback reminded me of a ride with Jason. We were biking a rough trail in a canyon called Crazy, he spelled the word endorphin, said the brain makes it and we're feeling it right now. That was fifty-nine years, three months and twenty-six days ago. George said Jason was informed years ago. What year? I should have asked.

A thousand feet higher, I slowed for a rusted grey van, a flatbed trailer and a big fir blocking the road. A tan pit bull slinked under the trailer, and a paunchy elder and young boy stood up as I rode close. "Hey," I yelled, "you guys drop the tree this morning?"

The boy answered, "Yeah, it jis fell awhile ago, but we're outta gas, waitin' on grandma. I'm Junior. He's my granddad. That's a neat bike."

I said thanks, gave the dog a quick look and tried figuring what to do if it charged or granddad pulled a gun. "Your dog okay?" I asked hesitantly.

Granddad puffed on a hand-rolled stogie and grunted, "Ah yeah, that's old Ginger, she won't botha ya. She's kinda hungry cuz we stayed overnight. Yul want yer lowest fer what's comin' up…jis keeps gittin' steeper past a cuppla doglegs."

"Bet it does," I said, tasting his smoke, thinking he has a vote, and they just cut down a healthy tree for cordwood no less.

Apella sounded impatient again. *Continue your ride. Nothing noteworthy here.* And she had no questions about my report — in the clear for now, I guess.

I lifted my bike over the tree and said, "Later guys, maybe see you on my way back," then pedaled quickly away.

Past two more switchbacks, I pulled over for another pair of wood cutters and what a contrast. A friendly Australian shepherd trotted happily over to me, and a neat and trim couple in their late fifties put down their tools and smiled. Their truck was a restored 1960 Ford flatbed painted shiny red. "We're the Prights…my wife Aurora," the man said, brushing sawdust off his shirt. "I'm Oly, county sheriff. You the young fella my deputy Loyal Crispin met down at Walter's the other day?"

"Yes sir. I'm Dan Oyente, staying at Rosemary McClun's."

Reevaluating intel on Crispin and the Prights. The cell may own the sheriff's office.

I cleared my throat at her interruption and told the Prights this was my first ride in Montana's northwest corner. Aurora looked at my bike then my legs. "You mean to say you rode all the way up here from Ms. Rose's?"

"Yes I did and it sure felt good."

She tucked her hair under her cap and said, "In any case, you're with one fine lady. Ms. Rose is so beautiful, and she's our oldest living resident. I declare, she just seems ageless."

Aurora giggled at their dog sniffing my front tire. "Sage, oh heavens no," she said and clapped her hands. Her husband was admiring my shocks and derailleurs. "Now that's impressive engineering," he said. "Always thought it'd be fun goin' down but not pedaling all the way up here. You're almost three thousand feet above the valley floor. How long you been at it, son?"

"I'm a slow climber…about two hours."

Aurora wrinkled her forehead. "And you're alone. Don't you worry about bears or lions?"

"Or miscreant humans," her husband added.

I touched the pepper-spray canister on my belt and told them I definitely think about all that. "That's why I carry this, but I don't want to blind a bear, and there's nothing I love more than climbing alone in mountains like these."

"More power to ya," said Oly. "Guess Aurora and I better get back to work. We'll see you again."

Tell him we hope so.

"By all means," I said as Aurora restarted the chain saw.

The next switchback put me on level ground where I dodged ice-covered potholes and broken tree limbs. I squished through a seepage overflow and entered a stretch of road nearly overgrown with chest-high alders — pure hell with a bike. I was walking, stumbling over roots, whipping branches aside and ready to quit when I came to a wooden sign pointing up a rocky trail — Scree Lake 8.5. *Jis keeps gittin' steeper* came to mind, and I asked Apella if she was still with me.

We have your position. You are twelve hundred feet from the peak, which is under deep snow.

She cut off, and I looked again at the wooden sign…maybe wait until next month.

On the way down, the woodcutters were all gone and I sped through granddad's sawdust piles minutes before a horse whinnied and Sula shouted, "Hey Dan! Two of us coming up. Wait there, would you? These mares haven't seen many mountain bikers."

Hmm, another arranged meeting with Sula, the geochemist and biologist. The horses were skittish until I set my bike down. "Sula, where you headed?" I asked when they were close.

"We're on our way to Scree Lake if the trail's clear, and Dan Oyente, this is my friend Nancy Denton. We met in grad school. Nancy and Erik are both high-powered computer engineers, and she stays with us whenever she visits her uncle Andy."

Nancy tipped her cowboy hat and stared at me, as though black biking shorts and glow-in-the-dark windbreaks were new to her. She reached down, shook my hand and said, "Sula told me you met my uncle. My home base is Pocatello, Idaho, and I visit Uncle A at least once every year, came sooner this time in case he needed my help after the accident and all. He doesn't like help, but kind of welcomes it. My dad was a war journalist, killed in Pakistan. Didn't attend his funeral, don't believe in them, he understands. Uncle A is my dad's younger brother. No warmongers in the Denton family, that's for sure."

Hmm, Sula's age or younger with Andy's loud fast talk.

Nancy tipped her hat again. "Guess I've talked too much, sorry. I often do that when I first meet someone. Nice meeting you, Dan, and we should skedaddle, Su, or we won't have time to hang out at the lake."

Sula ran her hand through her mare's mane. "Let's walk, Rainbow, and we'll see you later, Dan Oyente. Enjoy the spin down from here, and be sure to stop at the waterfall, wet your lips, taste that water — no Giardia, guaranteed."

When they were out of sight I asked Apella if she had anything on Nancy Denton.

Ms. Denton may be from another cell but we have no record of dangerous radical elements in Pocatello, Idaho.

"Okay, heading down and will check in when I'm close to Rose's. I'll be sure to see the Prights again."

I took the first mile slow enough to sightsee, looked but didn't stop at the waterfall and held a safe speed until the urge to let it out hit me on the steepest stretch. Find your zone or risk death on a down like this. It was young Jason Steller, and I squeezed the brakes just enough to think of us racing down a sixty-degree slope at forty-six miles an hour. Pure insanity but it does clear the mind.

My implant went live as I skidded to a stop in the middle of the valley road. *What's that noise, Daniel?!*

"You would love this, Apella," I shouted over thundering hooves. "Elk running across the road right in front of me — dark eyes, manes, and stamina that makes mine a joke."

Are you all right?

"I'm more than fine and so close I could touch them. They're almost past me now, all thirty-four. You should have seen it. The leader ran through wire fence like tape at a finish."

Daniel, this is business, a vital mission. Don't be so taken with distractions.

The scent of the herd lingered, and I thought of Apella's excitement whenever we found fresh elk beds. What's going on with her now? So many weird comments. And why the stiff routine? I guess being my manager requires it.

Rose was tossing a tennis ball to Max and Agnes when I rode up, looked like they were having fun. "You're back early," Rose said and hurled the ball again.

"Yes, beautiful mountain country but I decided to save the lake trail for another day. It was a good warm-up ride, I didn't push and saw more people than I expected."

She told the dogs to cool down and they splayed out in the grass. "Let's sit with them," she said, "and I'm pleased you had a nice ride, thought it was a perfect opportunity for you to meet Nancy Denton while she's in town. She's a wonderful girl, thinks so highly of her uncle and she's quite accomplished in her field, I might add. Nancy is also a member of our group, and she's a traveler, prefers it that way. Now, who else did you see up there?"

"Two pairs of woodcutters. Sheriff Pright and his wife, and some old guy with his grandson. They had just dropped a live tree on the road."

"I'm sure the Prights had Sage with them, their beautiful Aussie shepherd. What about granddad and the boy? Did they have a pit-mix named Ginger?"

"Yes, and I was glad to get by without bloodshed."

Rose winked and leaned back in the grass. "You met Rex Mills and one of his nine grandchildren. The old thug used to threaten me every chance he had, especially when we started our bartering system."

"Threaten? How?"

"Oh, bully tactics, calling me names, even threatened to shoot my dogs and burn me out. He's always offended when I just stare back at him, and he's basically harmless, and well aware I am armed and know how to shoot."

"Seriously, Rose?"

She winced, "Oh, I wouldn't shoot him, but I often carry my .38 revolver. I keep it loaded with blanks except when I target shoot, which I enjoy immensely, and it gets the message out to the likes of Rex Mills."

"How does Thius feel about people like Rex?"

She frowned. "Now why do you ask me that?"

"Because there were times on the train when I thought Thius was close to losing control. He seems to wear anger and impatience under a rather thin veil."

Rose shook her head and said, "Dan, in all the years I've known Thius, only once did I fear he might lose control. It's time for you to hear more about this, but it includes gruesome details about Kain's Cut — not a good appetizer — and dinner is ready, so we'll have decaf in our best china out on the front porch where your company and the night air will help me talk through it."

At last, Rosemary's version of how her illustrious and allegedly nonviolent son reacted to the deaths of his father and brother.

17

Kain's Cut and Pes Albus

It was clear and cold that evening with a steady breeze out of the northwest. Rose and I wore down jackets and sat together on the porch swing. I was thinking about Thius and his dad, then my dad and how he loved being outside on nights like this. Rose snugged close. "Oh my, Dan, it's only three degrees Celsius out here. Tell me about your father, would you?"

I zipped up my jacket. "Interesting, Rose. I was just thinking about him."

She waved her hand. "Oh, no big deal. I sensed your reminiscing. You've had Kain's Cut and Thius's dad on your mind…natural for you to think of your own. Tell me about him."

I kept it brief. "My dad was a cellist, mainly a teacher but loved playing small-venue concerts. I believe he lived a reasonably happy life, and I was there when he passed quietly at home in his own bed, refusing medical care. He was ninety-three."

"And your mother?"

I took a sip of decaf. "Didn't really know her. She died of lung cancer when I was nine."

"Losing a parent when you're so young…a terrible thing. Thius was only six when he watched rocks, boulders, and dust cover his dad." Her eyes flashed at me. "Now, do you really want to hear all this, Dan?"

"Yes, I'd like to know Thius better."

As would we.

Rose held her cup with both hands. "I will tell you the whole story as long as you agree not to bring it up again. It haunts me to think about Thius and his friend Davie Harlow…just two innocent young boys out there."

She set her cup down and pulled her collar tight around her neck. "The boys were on a ledge, at a safe distance, mind you, watching a crew cut a cliff for a new rail line along the reservoir. It was late in the day, long after the usual blasting time. Thius's dad Carl, and three other part-timers were doing pick and shovel work below the cliff. The boys were about to leave when the blast went off. Can you imagine the horror they felt?"

I exhaled, "Can't begin to."

"And let me tell you Thius relived it for a long time in nightmares, chills, and sweats. So many nights he would scream, No! My dad's down there — his red shirt. Can't see him anymore."

Rose closed her eyes for a minute, rubbed her forehead. "Two men from the blasting crew found the boys. They drove Davie home and brought Thius here to stay with William and me. The Harlows moved away a year later."

"Rose, how could something like that happen? I mean, who would dynamite a cliff with people working below?"

"Good question," she said. "Red Kain was the crew foreman, and he was behind schedule under heavy pressure. A line in Kain's testimony went something like, I said to my crew, the boss gives us two days to be done here and we gotta keep the trains moving so we're gonna drill and blast an extra section today — clear and grade while we drill the next set first thing in the morning."

"Sounds like a foreman under pressure, but man."

"Yes, and it might have been okay if they hadn't set extra heavy charges, and if Kain hadn't ordered them to blast without making sure all his men were in the clear. The shock wave ran so far back in the mountain it triggered a rock slide that buried everything between the cliff and the river and poured out to deep water." Rose sighed and rubbed her forehead again. "They found most of Carl Bantry and three other men who worked with him, but they quit searching for a fifth victim, an eight-year-old boy who was supposed to be taking care of his younger brother but instead snuck down to the river to fish that afternoon. Trajan Terrence Bantry, Thius's older brother was swept away, apparently buried in the river. The family wanted him left undisturbed, to be with the spirits."

"What happened to Kain? Was he indicted? It sounds like gross negligence to me."

"No, the county sheriff's office labeled it a blasting accident...no negligence. Red Kain was fired from his job and someone shot and killed him seven years later."

Rose stood up and collected our cups. "Excuse me, Dan, time to check my email. One of our teachers may need my help with their class first thing in the morning. I'll be right back."

Our intel confirms that Red Kain was shot to death. Thius's involvement was never exposed but is obvious.

"Really?" I whispered. "Thius would have been only thirteen when Kain was shot."

Apella didn't respond and Rose returned, sat on the swing and said, "Now, I'm sure you're wondering if my son killed Mr. Kain, and the answer is emphatically NO. Thius was beside himself with grief after losing his dad and brother, and those horrid events stayed with him, but they did not sour his spirit or consume him with rage. The one time I saw Thius in a vengeful state came years after the horror at Kain's. He was eighteen, and it all had to do with the loss of a very special friend. Thius had just returned from a rail trip and stepped into the house when Andrew Denton banged on the front door and yelled something about one of the Mills boys killing a bear illegally up Hemlock Draw. Andrew said it was a dark red male with a white forepaw, could be the one Thius calls Pes Albus. Well, it was, and that bear meant the world to Thius. They were the best of friends, fraternal spirits for over ten years."

A scene on the train shot through me. We were stopped at Bearmouth Hot Springs and I had just finished a long recital of train robberies. I didn't ask Thius to explain when he said bears are more important than humans. "What did Thius do?" I asked Rose. "Go after the Mills boy?"

"No, he grabbed a phone and called George, his dearest friend and mentor. George and Carl Bantry were close, and George took every opportunity to help with Thius and his brother. For nearly a year after Kain's, Thius was withdrawn, rarely spoke to anyone but George. Thank goodness all that changed the day they met the white-footed cub. Did you sample any stream water when you rode down Hemlock Draw? I should have told you it is safe to drink."

"No, but I slowed way down at a waterfall. Beautiful tall larches and cedars there, claw marks on three of them, must be a favorite spot for bears."

"Very observant, Dan. Bears do love to rake their claws on those trees, and that's where Thius met Pes, mid-June, on a day hike with George. The cub was clinging to a trunk about twenty feet up. George and Thius were backing away when mom swept by them, sidled to the tree and waited for her young son. George had tagged mom several years earlier. She was a stunning dark-red color, and George called her HM for Hemlock Maroon. Her cub was jet-black, and probably no more than thirty pounds. When the little guy shimmied down and dropped on mom's back they saw his left forepaw, it was white. That evening, Thius came home feeling so proud, talking about a black bear cub he and George named Pes Albus. He told William and me the story in detail, including how the cub turned his head and raised his one white paw to wave as he piggybacked away."

"You think that was true, Rose?"

"George assured us it was, and that summer he taught Thius how to be close to bears and help them retain their healthy fear of humans. George also showed Thius how to track HM without a tag detector. I'm certain you are quite familiar with the patience and concentration that takes. I don't have to tell you footprints are rare and trails left by bears are faint. Now Dan, I assume you have detailed memories of your childhood."

"Yes, deeply archived but retrievable. Why do you ask?"

"Just think about this — Thius was only seven when he immersed himself in the bear work, spent whole days, even some nights up Hemlock Draw. He recorded multiple sightings of HM and Pes, catalogued every reddish hair, broken twig, cluster of matted leaves… everything he found that could have been left by the pair. After several weeks he could tell them from other bears by their scent. George even taught him how to enhance his field work with DNA technology, and by the time HM denned with Pes late that fall, Thius had a map of their travels that filled most of the blanks in George's tag records."

Rose excused herself again. "All this talk and I'm late feeding the kitties. I'll see you in a few minutes. We'll finish this in the living room next to a warm fire."

A charming tale about the bears, but a quick check of facts casts doubt on its veracity. Thius was seven in 1958, only five years after DNA research began in earnest, and not possible DNA technology was available for bear research at that time.

I went inside, sat at the piano and thought about George and what he wrote in those emails. Was it possible his Ursavus organization was decades ahead of mainstream science? Could they have developed DNA technology before the 1950s? Would George answer Yes, and would I tend to believe him? Maybe, at this point.

Embers popped and crackled in the fireplace. What do I really know about George? All that time in Yellowstone, he was a near-perfect mentor and colleague, but now, what do I make of his relationship with Rose and Thius? What's he like as Rose's oldest friend…or Thius's? Should I ask Apella for more?

Rose walked in from the kitchen and motioned for me to sit with her on the sofa. "The remainder of the story has some truly sad parts, Dan. Pes Albus was only a year and a half old when his mother Hemlock Maroon was killed by a hunter on the Hemlock Draw Road."

"Oh Man," I said, remembering how I felt when my beagle Sadie was shot by a coyote hunter.

Rose reached over and patted my hand. "The day after we heard about HM's death, George took Thius hiking up Hemlock Draw, and they spotted Pes rolling in grass and glacier lilies only a mile from his mother's den. George handed Thius binoculars and told him, A powerful lesson there. That young fellow is hurting, but he's already getting on with his life."

Rose took a deep breath. "This last part is the worst, Dan. Before they left Hemlock Draw, George tagged Pes and put Thius in charge. Not many orphan cubs survive, but by the end of summer, Pes was like a big teenager with his mother's dark-red sheen, and like most male bears he started roaming far and wide. Most summers though, Thius would find Pes in these mountains, feasting on huckleberries and pine nuts, prepping for the long winter. Pes Albus always denned in Hemlock Draw, and like his mother, that's where he was killed."

"Shot by some low-life poacher!" I said.

Be careful, don't let her pull you in.

Rose wasn't finished. "Oh, the painful rage Thius felt. Pes's death was a heavy blow, but my son did not let his rage win out. He dealt with it. He called George, and the next morning hopped a freight east. George picked him up in Livingston and put him to work monitoring bears in Yellowstone. Since that time with George and the bears, Thius has been free of any tendency for out-of-control rage. Now understand, I am not saying he doesn't get momentarily angry. What I am telling you is, my son Thius Terrene is incapable of violence."

She got up from the sofa, walked to the fireplace and closed the screen. "Contrary to popular belief," she said, "Thius is your friend in the making."

Friend? Nonsense!

I told Rose I like being optimistic, but Thius and I are on distant wavelengths. She gave me The Look. "Be that as it may, my dear, your issues with Thius are fading faster than you realize. Your differences pale beside your similarities. You both appreciate bears, dogs, wild country and a few good people. Your politics are only superficially different, and I believe you detest poachers and slob hunters as much as we do. And now, that is the end of story for me. I don't want a restless night of sad dreams."

"I'm with you there, Rose…and about tomorrow, if you don't need me for anything I could do another bike ride. I've got a lot on my mind."

"You certainly must," she said, "and let me think, where would I have you go? Maybe the next canyon south of Hemlock Draw. Yes, Woody's Gulch would give you a nice long climb and plenty of time to think. It's one of William's favorites. He and I used to ride up there with Jason whenever he visited…maybe take a small saw, could be some fallen trees near the top. I'll say good night now, Dan."

"And to you, Rose. You mind if I listen to some music upstairs? I'll keep it low."

"Fine, won't bother me a bit. You probably wonder why we haven't updated our sound system, what with all the high-tech tools you and George used in Yellowstone. But I think the old-time vinyls sound better, and the turntable in your room plays like new. See you early."

18

In the Dark

Wide awake in my room, I put on a Van Morrison album and stood by an open window. I felt uneasy about censoring reports to Apella. By omission, I lied to her to protect George, but without knowing more, I wasn't prepared to provide information that could hurt him, especially to Apella's employers — strangers who, according to George, drugged me and injected a prototype implant into my head without my consent.

I changed into one of William's soft cotton Henleys, and my thoughts drifted back to how I was prepped for the mission. The physical regimen was intense and effective. The mental part was ridiculous, a naive attempt to make me behave like an automaton. Four lines were repeated so many times I stopped counting.

I will not question this mission or its personnel.

I will gain the dissidents' trust and remain detached.

I will report all pertinent data precisely.

I will never question this mission or its personnel.

In the end, the mind benders were convinced I would perform exactly as directed. What they didn't know is hyperthymestics like me cannot be brainwashed by repetition. Their attempts to brainwash had no effect, and if they thought the implant would help program me, they were wrong.

Van the Man swept me back to a scene with George in Yellowstone…a rainy spring morning, my first week on the job. We had started up the Gneiss Creek Trail when a mother grizzly with young twins walked out in front of us. She reared up, tossed her head and snarled — so close I could see a crack in her left canine. Eyes down and relax, George told me, then whispered a few quiet words I didn't understand. The bear dropped to all fours and led her twins into the brush.

When I caught my breath, George said, You can appreciate mom's concern, Dan. You're an odd smelling stranger, and she's always been wary. She was an orphan when I first met her, a gaunt yearling scavenging a wolf kill along the Firehole. She probably would have starved or been killed by another bear, but I helped her for a while and always spoke Ursavi to her. She learned to trust quiet words and the gentle cadence of the language.

George knew I'd nearly fainted and assured me nothing in life prepares anyone for their first grizzly close-up. I'm partial to black bears, he said, but the mass and force of a full-grown grizzly under-scores the name Great Bears. Knowing your memory, I predict it will take you an hour to recite everything from that brief encounter.

Being with George on a job that required unwavering trust… fine days with few complications. Do I still trust him? Probably not entirely. Should I continue omitting facts about him in my reports to Apella? Yes, but does it matter? George implied he wasn't worried about his safety or anyone else's.

I stopped the record player when two loud motorcycles pulled up out front.

Daniel, what's going on? It's 12:30 in the morning. Where are you?

"I'm just standing here in my room, thinking."

Rowdy talk and music erupted downstairs, a party of three — Rose, George and another guy with a deep raspy voice. Rose was often the loudest. Three hours later the motorcycles started up and Rose yelled from the porch, "Wonderful friends always!"

"You too, Rosey," shouted George as they roared off. "You and Ursavus!"

I asked Apella how much she heard.

Everything.

"Did it alter your view of George?"

No, there is nothing alarming here. We fully recognize that George Waterbear is more than a biologist and bear tagger. He is a master at maintaining trust, and we do not doubt his loyalty to us.

"So you are certain George wouldn't tell anyone about my implant? And you're sure no one, including George, can access it?"

You were apprised of these details in the beginning.

I didn't tell her I was almost certain George could hack a device like the one in my head.

Daniel, a reminder is in order here. Your implant is encrypted, and its access code, which we alter weekly, is available to no outsider, including George Waterbear. Even if Rosemary, Thius, or someone else became aware of your implant — and be assured neither George nor Jason has told anyone — they cannot access our transmissions. Good night.

Nice try, Apella, but your less-than-warm reassurance doesn't ring true. Where are you? How did you get involved in this mission? Are you in danger? Would I lie to protect you? Yes. Without hesitation. And it's time to stop thinking…got a bike ride tomorrow.

19

Brakes and Bears

"Rise to ride, dear boy. It's nearly dawn. If you want to make the top of Woody's Gulch before dark you better get going." It was Rose standing at the foot of my bed, and she was wrapped tight in a wispy purple robe. I sat up thinking Wow, no way she's in her seventies… more like thirty-five.

She set a cup of coffee on the nightstand and said, "You appear to have a lot on your mind already, and good to see you in William's Henley…a perfect fit, and I hope it helped you sleep through our party. I'm sure you recognized Dr. Waterbear's voice. Even he needs an occasional night off. The other guy was Cloud Speaker, a tribal lawyer, the Blackfoot law student George and I hitched a ride to Missoula with years ago. Among other things, Cloud handles negotiations between Precambre and the transcon railroads in the western U.S. and Canada."

Blackfoot tribal lawyer! We're on it.

Rose turned to leave and noticed my gear on the desk. "You're always so organized, Dan, that's a fine quality, and I'm sure you'll be careful up Woody's on your own. I'll be at the school most of the day, turns out our science teacher does need me, and if you're not home by dusk I'll find you. Have a good ride."

We will find you, not sure she could.

It was twilight when I pedaled out the lane, a still morning for a long solo climb up one of William McClun's favorite canyons. I

123

crossed the river, turned left and had the West Valley Road to myself until Andy Denton's yellow pickup sputtered slowly toward me. "Hey latecomer," Andy yelled. "Heard you're goin' up Woody's. Lotta bears up there. Goin' for Walter's coffee then Precambre's eastside wind farm. Take you up there if you want."

I said thanks but I need to do my ride, and he sputtered away. Who else did Rose schedule to meet me today?

A fifteen-hundred-foot climb up Woody's Gulch Road put me on an open hillside where I stopped to chew on an energy bar and scan the Clark Fork River Valley. Looking northwest I could see all the way to Pend Oreille Lake in Idaho. Looking east at the snow-capped peaks of the Cabinet Range I could hear Thius say, No better place for me, natale solum.

Lucky you, train man. What's your role in the backwoods cell called Ursavus?

Two ospreys swooped by then dodged and danced over the river. "You courting or fussing?" I asked out loud and was glad Apella didn't respond.

I held a steady climb on sandy clay then geared down to granny on a rocky switchback. Farther up, a rain squall whipped the mountain but hardly wet the road. I rolled over mushy gopher digs and thought about the fierce little dozers scratching for roots under ten feet of snow. A section of crusty ice, then an overhang of red and grey boulders triggered memories of Thius's rants. No time for that, gotta hard pedal to the top.

A moderate climb on smooth gravel put me on a level bench where I splashed through a shallow seep and wished for wheels that wouldn't mar the scene. Three and a half miles farther, I stopped on a narrow road cut, shoved two round boulders off the outside berm and watched them bounce and roll to a ledge fifty feet down. Wondering why I did that, I hopped back on my bike and held an aerobic pace until muddy snow on my brake discs told me to turn around.

A thousand feet lower, I was speeding around a switchback when a rush of wind sparked pieces of a dream. Hope lies at the edge of fear. Not now, Rose, gotta hold my zone. Hey Danny boy, how are you this fine day? Please dad, I'm on a serious downhill. Out ahead, fifty feet. Bear! Brakes! I stopped short, fumbled for pepper spray and watched a tawny yearling lunge down a rocky bank — gone away but fused in mind.

Moments later pushing thirty and what a ride, like a hovercraft on a celestial trip with Apella, then fast around an inside curve. Uh-oh, another one. BIG, 300 pounds plus, and a dark glistening mass parted brush on my left — indelible milliseconds with the Spirit of Bear.

Rounding the last switchback. How could this be? Another adult. Dark red, with a pint-size cub. I stopped while they scrambled up a muddy bank, hoped to see a white forepaw but didn't. The cub ran for cover while mom paused at the top. I mimicked her head turn and lip curl as she walked away.

Cold drizzle and sand sprayed from my tires the last mile of the gulch then dried on my legs and face as I bumped along a crumbly section of county blacktop. Coasting down Rose's lane, I felt grateful for something left of youth, for a place to ride with wild bears and time away from the mission and Ursavus.

"You ahright, solo man?" Thius yelled from the front yard when I rode in.

Thius is there?

"Yes," I said then stopped and set my bike down when Thius pointed to something in the grass. "You know about bird's nest fungi?" he asked, and showed me the tiny cups with three spore packets each.

"Interesting," I said, "didn't expect to see you here, Thius."

"Yeah, had to come back to shave, catch up with the bears and make sure you're not hasslin' Rose too much."

I told him this is definitely the place to see bears, and asked how far he rode the westbound boxcar.

"Columbia River towns, Kennewick, Pasco — stayed with some friends you'd like at an army base on the Oregon side."

He has friends in the military?

Thius looked at my bike. "Got some cleanin' to do on that, bike man, and yeah, the army base was a storage and disposal site for chemical weapons and contaminated ordinance. When the DOD shut it down, Precambre bought it for salvage only Ursavus could use. It remains a major source of rare-earth elements for ultrafast, secure communication."

My, my, the games these people play. The Umatilla Chemical Depot in Oregon is the base he referenced. Reason for him being there dubious if claim is true. Probe for more. He has eluded us since Seattle.

Thius lifted my bike up the porch steps, and Rose threw open the screen door. "Early dinner, boys. Hope you're in the mood for spicy pepperjack pablanos, spinach and cheddar enchiladas, and rice steamed with sesame oil and fiery relish."

The dinner was great, and Thius was a changed man, a regular chatterbox with Rose, wanting to catch up on all the comings and goings around town. He was even pleasant with me, and we actually had fun sharing stories about favorite hikes in Yellowstone, times with George, dorky tourists and more. Rose looked happy with it all and suggested a walk afterwards. "Boys, there's a bright moon, a good night for flying squirrels. The two of you go out, spend some more time together."

Yes, spend more time with him and find out where he plans to go after Cedarville. Forget the silly squirrels.

I frowned. More bizarre talk. Has she forgotten that magical night in the Sapphires when a flying squirrel swept by our faces, so close we thought we felt the air move?

20

More on Dallas

"Another night about to be tainted with talk," mumbled Thius as we started down to the river, and nothing else was said until we were on the fireline road close to the track. "You know about Orion?" he asked, looking toward the western horizon.

I said, "Sure, I know about the hunter of the celestial equator, and myths vary with the culture. Stars interest me more, like the orange-red supergiant Betelgeuse in Orion's right shoulder. It's about 700 times larger than the sun and probably near the end of its life. When it explodes it will be visible in daylight."

"You ever take your megamemory to Dealey Plaza, Oyente?"

More discursive talk?

I answered Yes and knew we weren't out for flying squirrels. Thius was the pesky train man again, asking how I felt about a half-century-old assassination in Dallas, Texas. I told him I wandered around Union Station and downtown Dallas three full days, November 21 to 23, 1984, and left with more questions than answers, but then I happened to see that documentary, "The Men Who Killed Kennedy," the uncensored version.

Thius said, "Yeah, I saw it too. Plain and simple, they took the president there to kill him, one of the few who might have worked for peace. The bloody '60s — WAR, JFK, RFK, MLK — tests, all of 'em and we flunked."

Is there a point to be made here?

We walked to a parklike stand of cedars near the railroad and sat on a log bench Thius said he built to watch trains with a raven friend. "Sometimes my stepdad would sit here with Raven and me," he said, "and it's time for you to hear more about William McClun. Rose told you about him gettin' mugged, but she didn't tell you why, so here it is. William was attacked because he knew a train conductor named Josy Meltin, who was on the scene when JFK was killed."

This has to be unadulterated nonsense.

"Give me a break, Thius, not another Kennedy conspiracy."

"Just listen. This isn't some made-up bull. It's what William told Rose. He and Meltin were life-long friends. They grew up together in a tough part of Chicago — spent their youth keepin' each other alive and stayed tight years after. When the president was shot, Conductor Meltin was havin' lunch in a caboose at Union Station, his train scheduled to depart that afternoon. Meltin heard gunfire, peered out his window and saw three hobos climb into a boxcar on another train. He recognized one of 'em, and knew he better get the hell away and not be seen."

"Nothing new there, Thius, photos of the hobos were everywhere, and no one could get their names right."

"Yeah, but Meltin actually knew the tall guy real well. Twice he kicked him off freights, asked to see his ID the second time and memorized enough of it to run a check. Everything matched up, and when crap started comin' out in the news with the pictures, Meltin thought he better contact the FBI. The FBI debriefed him, ordered him to keep his mouth shut, tell no one, not even his wife, until the investigation was done. Meltin kept no secrets from his wife Sara, but they were both tight-lipped, told nobody for years."

Thius shot up from the log bench when two whistles sounded on the track. It was eastbound, and the engine lights lit him up through the trees.

Apella filled me in on Conductor Meltin while the train blew by. *African American Josiah P. Meltin was a unionized freight-train conductor operating out of Fort Worth, Texas for thirty years, set to retire on the anni-*

versary of his thirty-first. Records have him en route between El Paso and Los Angeles at the time of President Kennedy's assassination. Not likely Thius's windy tale holds any truth.

Thius sat back down. "The night's too good to waste, Oyente. I'll keep this short. Meltin and his wife never stopped worryin' about what he saw, and it didn't help that the FBI never got back to him. Conspiracy theories were runnin' rampant, and it was like anybody who knew anything was turnin' up dead. Meltin trusted William, knew he was in some kind of highfalutin group and thought he might help. He sent William a long letter about what he saw, and he asked to meet up, but that meeting never happened. Meltin and his wife died in a fiery crash on their way home from the grocery store on March 21, 1967 — exactly one week before William was attacked."

I shook my head. "So, Thius, you're saying there was a connection?"

"Rose still has Meltin's letter if you want to check for yourself. We figured whoever attacked William took him for an out-of-shape piano player, didn't know he was tough as leather, took care of his body like all of us, like you. They wanted it to look like a random mugging and left thinkin' he was dead. Their mistake was not hangin' around long enough to make sure."

The important question here is, What role did William have in the alleged highfalutin group?

Thius said, "Like George told you in that email, William was a charter member of Ursavus. The piano man recruited globally for years."

Try for more.

I asked Thius, "What about now? What's Liam Yrisse's role in Ursavus?"

He turned and looked toward the dark woods behind us. "All in good time, Oyente. You've seen William goin' by and you'll meet him when you join Ursavus. Just stay close and quiet now. Try for the nonhuman world. That's where I'll be."

The walk back was like being out with George. I said nothing and Thius spoke rarely, always in undertones. Scratches from a tall fir had me thinking bear cub but I knew Thius was right when he whispered porcupine. When a rustle of leaves and a pungent whiff told me to stop, Thius said, "Keep goin', and it's spotted not striped."

I waited until we were at the house to ask how he knew one species of skunk from another in the dark.

"George helped me with it," he said. "You tell by the aerosols."

Next morning Thius was talking loud to Rose at the foot of the stairs. He sounded edgy and impatient, like he'd lost all his calm from the night before. "I'm tired of yackin' with this Oyente guy," he told her. "All the guy does is ask questions. He's a waste of energy and I'm gunna hook back up with Ellie sooner than planned."

Apella was tuned in. *We need you to keep Thius in sight.*

Rose was like a firm parent with him. "Dear boy, we have to stick to the schedule, and your role is pivotal, as you well know. Need I remind, you have only three days left to complete your evaluation and decide if this crucial recruitment can go forward. Then we need to proceed to the next one. Now, as you know, day-to-day activities are yours to plan, but it seems to me this would be a good time to get your bike out and take Dan to some of your old haunts."

Thius was even more wound up and irritable when I hopped down the steps and joined them. "What're you smirkin' about?" he asked me.

"Sorry, but I overheard something about a bike and old haunts? What kind of bike you ride, Thius?"

"Been on all kinds. Solid frames, hard tails, full suspension, even some roadies."

"Any carbon frames?"

He frowned, "You're thinkin' about the Heckler on the train — belongs to Sula."

"I don't mean to challenge your knowledge of bikes, Thius, but I'm pretty sure that bike has an aluminum frame. Why don't you give mine a try? It's carbon-fiber with twenty-seven no-foul gears, super-fire shifters, full suspension with more travel than you ever need, fine-adjust hydraulic disk brakes — makes seventy feel like twenty-five."

"I already feel young and you sound like a BSG."

"A what?"

"Bike Shop Guy."

Rose encouraged him. "Just do it, Thi! You love it as much as he does."

He scratched his chin, "Ahh okay, why not. I'll do a run out the lane," and he took off on my bike.

"My son will be a new man when he returns," Rose said. "Wait for him out here, would you, Dan? I'll be in the house."

Thius was gone for thirty minutes and when he pulled up he said, "Ahright, I'll give it a day or two. Haul out my Trek, take awhile to lube it and put it in shape. If you're up for it tomorrow, Devil Club Lookout's only a forty-six hundred-foot climb."

"That's all, huh? Guess we could do that, but my bike's overdue for a full service...got everything I need but I like to take my time, do it all just right and include a couple of test runs."

"Yeah, I hear you, bike man. Take the rest of the day, and I know Rose is fine with it. I'll wake you at the crack."

Good you worked it out with him. One of our agents is tracing a possible lead regarding Nathaniel. Thius may know more than we thought. We will have information regarding the lookout before you leave in the morning. Keep in mind, train man Methius Terrene is not trustworthy.

21

Alder Impasse

A predawn rap on my door fractured a dream of pedal strokes on a steep slide of rainbow stones. I sat up in the dark, heard Thius growl from the hallway, "Gotta head out, Oyente. Grab some fuel. Make it quick. See you on the road."

Oh Man, what was I thinking when I agreed to bike with this backwoods enigma?

Are you prepared? This could be as challenging as the train rides.

"Pulling on socks and double checking gear right now. What do you have for me?"

Thius is taking you to the Devil Club Fire Tower Lookout Station. The structure is a one-room cabin set on a thirty-foot-high platform con-structed after the 1910 fires devastated the area. The cabin is available for rent by the U.S. Forest Service and is no longer in use as a fire tower. Daniel, be safe. As we've experienced, the mountains may block transmissions.

Thius was waiting at the end of the lane and pumped when I caught up. "Glad you made it," he yelled and popped a wheely, "great ridin' this time a morning."

I asked how far to the lookout. "Takes awhile," he said. "We cross the river bridge, go south then west, climb some easy miles then take a single track — got some friends up there."

I knew he meant bears and asked how many he expected to see. He pedaled ahead, muttered something about twins and said they'd probably stay out of sight, smelling a stranger on a cushy bike. He started bunny hopping potholes and yelled, "West-turn gravel 2709 comin' up a hundred feet — take a break there."

We stopped at the turn and Thius grabbed his water bottle, took two swigs, shook his head disdainfully at me while I sipped from my tube, then waved his bottle at the gravel road, "Forest Service labels it 2709, I prefer MTDC, Main to Devil Club. Let's haul!"

His MTDC started out smooth and steep, and we were holding a steady aerobic pace on a thirty-degree rise when I thought, Mr. Gnarly's definitely not a poser on his hard-tail ten-speed. "You train in your sleep?" I asked.

He swiped his forehead with his wristband. "Naah, just good genes, mitochondrial enhancers and tips from an old bike railer named Jason Steller. We hopped freights with his fat-tire heavies back awhile."

I was trying to picture Jason and Thius hopping a train with steel bikes when a red squirrel scurried across the road. We swerved in unison then hammered hard for another hour. By midmorning we had traversed three south faces, carved around nine tight corners, and were coasting single file along a narrow roadside stream. Thius put out his arm, "Hold up, Oyente, might see a friend or two." We set the bikes down, and a three-inch brownish frog hopped into the water. Thius said, "Yeah, Rana pretiosa, still here…been seein' the little guys every summer since I first rode up here a half-century back. Predators, long winters, snowmelt floods, people like us stoppin' by, they're tuned to it all. Gives me hope. Let's ride."

Alder, mountain maple and fir trees lined the road for the next mile, and Thius stopped where trees and brush filled the roadside, pulled a ranger district map from his tool bag, unfolded it and held it up. "We're right here," he said, "thirty-two hundred feet off the valley floor, and this is where the logging roads take off uphill."

I studied his map and the road bank. "What logging roads, Thius? The only road around here is the one we're standing on."

"Yep, they been brushed in like this for twelve years," he said, swallowing a mouthful of water and gesturing to a fir tree close to the road. "Two slash marks you see on that trunk mark the Alder Impasse

Road — AI for short. We go in left of the tree."

He pushed his bike through a tangle of alder and yelled over his shoulder, "AI's a shortcut, only a mile long, saves an hour but it's real wet. Watch your feet!"

I yanked branches out of my way, caught a glimpse of his shoe prints in a line of muddy sand and yelled, "What're we doing in here, Thius? I've bushwhacked and mud-bogged but this is ridiculous!"

"We're fine, about fifteen minutes to the freeway. Late summer, this is a major thoroughfare for elk, mostly bulls in the rut. Picture a thousand-pound-testosterone-charged bull elk with five-foot antler beams plowin' through here."

A thorn bush raked my face as I pushed into the clear, and Thius tossed me his wristband. "You're bleedin', Oyente, gotta watch those raspberries." He motioned ahead, "This thoroughfare is Elk Spring Single Track — ESST — takes us up Yellow Belly Draw to Spar Wallows, then you'll need your granny gear for the gonzo climb to Hightower Hemlocks about five hundred feet below the lookout."

I asked if he made up the names.

"How'd you guess? And you lead, Oyente, but don't get too comfy. It's bear country, and bear grass is startin' to flower — paint you yellow if you brush too many. Let's ride!"

Two hours later, breathing hard but not out of breath, we left our bikes at the base of Devil Club Lookout and started up the steps to the cabin. Thius offered a rare compliment. "You're not half bad, Oyente. Didn't figure you for much of a climber but you didn't dab at all on that last hill."

I asked why he ever took me for a lightweight.

"Aah, don't know, probably your catalogue clothes have some-thin' to do with it."

"Brings up a question, Thius. How can you sit on a bike for hours without padded pants?"

He tossed a limb from the top step and cracked a smile. "Adjustable pain receptors and a hard ass, and you missed the bears. Yearling twins ran ahead of us for over a mile on that easy traverse…saw and heard 'em, mostly smelled 'em."

He yanked on the cabin door. "Yeah, they got it locked so we'll do the walk-around. Lead on. I got some stories to tell."

His voice was relaxed, free of the train-ride rants. "One of my favorite places year-round," he said as we walked the narrow platform. "Maybe late summer's the best…early snow dustin' the peaks, tall larch thinkin' about turning, elk bugles echoin' off the hills. Hunters had it too easy when logging roads like AI were open. Just hop on your ATV and ride on up. Too many big racks lost from the gene pool those years."

When I stopped for a long look at a stately snag, he said, "Yeah, feast your eyes on that charred trunk, over a hundred years old when it burned. And you thought those train tunnels were hot — nothin' like the Hadean hell that old tree felt in 1910."

I told him we share a fascination for persistent trees.

"Yeah, Rose told me you climbed the ladder snag. That one's cedar, this one's mountain hemlock, been a nursery for mountain bluebirds, tree swallows, black-backed woodpeckers, water bears, and a scratchin' post for bears all years I've been around. One moonlit night, Ellie Sterling and I watched four flying squirrels take their first glide from that hole at the top. You believe the media yack about her?"

"Mostly, yes. What about you?"

"Later. We need to be gettin' off this mountain."

That was it. He skipped every other step down to the bikes and was tightening his brake cables when I got there. "We'll pass on AI," he said, "but need to prep for steeps. No room for error, might hear an eeep or two from a pika, and watch for company around curves — bears, maybe even a cougar."

I did a quick check on my bike, lowered my seat, and asked if he'd ever crashed into an animal. "Yeah, slammed an elk once — spike bull shot right out in front of me and didn't stop for a look. I was nine miles out with a bent wheel."

"Any broken bones?" I asked.

"I don't break. What about you?"

"Ribs and a collar bone, twice. You're telling me you've never had a serious crash?"

"One," he said. "First time on full suspension, I leaned too far forward on a drop-off and did a face plant that turned my face to garnet sandpaper, mostly road rash but it took twenty-one stitches and a tube of superglue to fix."

"Pretty good repair job. I don't see any scars on your face."

"Nope, not on this one, and it's time to really ball-the-jack before Rose starts to worry. You go first. Stay on the main road. I'll be outta your slipstream."

After the steep mile at the top it was a smooth ninety-minute down with only a glimpse of a black bear. Coasting around a switchback I tried my implant but no response. I was cruising twenty on the last straightaway when Thius caught up and passed then signaled me to pull over at the river bridge. "Kain's Cut — just past that far southeast ridge," he said, "been a long time since Davie Harlow shot Red Kain then turned the gun on himself at a county fair in eastern Washington."

Apella gasped and I picked up static on my implant.

"Damn, Thius, I never read about that."

"Yeah, and Davie never stopped obsessin' about Kain killin' my dad and brother, kept writin' me about it. His last letter said he couldn't live with it anymore, was gunna walk up to Kain, stare him in the eyes and shoot."

"Damn again, Thius. Did they question you about it?"

He took a swig of water. "No way they could find me."

"You ever shoot anybody, Thius?"

He looked riled, sped off and yelled, "Hell with you! No! Never have, never will. What about you, Oyente?"

"You know the answer to that," I said, pedaling after him.

"What happened out there?" Rose asked when we walked in. "You boys look beat, especially you, Dan. Let's go to the kitchen and fix you something."

"We're okay," said Thius, "just some fits of radicals in the blood."

Free radicals everywhere, I thought, and I'm talking with two serious ones right here right now.

Thius stirred up some sports water. "Drink this, Oyente, renew your electrolytes and think about a bear zone."

Hours later I was asleep on a frozen road in the midst of clattering hooves, straining necks, and wild stamina up-bank to vanilla scented snags in cold winter sun. Pedaling hard I waved at Nate as a young grizzly raced ahead of my front wheel and pulled away when golden needles clogged my brakes. Then OH MAN — leg cramps — shotgun blasts, rapid-fire, automatic. Don't shoot! Just let us by. I rode in hot twilight with icy drizzle blown aside by a passing train. In a flurry of wood chips and coal dust I singed two fingers on white-hot brakes and felt Thius pull me away. He owes you now, said Rose, and I sat in a daze, watching George talk to a moss-covered roof in Yellowstone. Over two million water bears per square meter in that moss, he said.

A giant water bear with a cougar's head startled me from the dream. My door was open and I heard Thius whisper, "He's dreamin' about George and water bears," and Rose whispered back, "It's hyperthymestic recall, trying to reestablish order after his bike ride with you. Our boy will be fine."

The tenth and third boards creaked as they went down the stairs, and I shot up in a cold sweat. "Apella — did I say anything about the implant or mission?"

No. Just a fitful dream. Relax, Daniel. Let your neurotransmitters keep your dream demons at bay.

22

The Traveler

Piano music woke me before sunrise, my eighth day in Cedarville. I pulled on William's sweatshirt and pants, did some quick stretches and went downstairs expecting to see Rose at the keyboard, but No! It was Thius. Rose was looking over his shoulder, ready to turn pages. I held back until he finished. "Incredible you play like that, Thius, sounded perfect."

Rose clapped and said, "That's one of Sebastian Bach's praeambula, Dan," and Thius added, "Yeah, and he wrote it for beginners, tells you somethin' that it's tough for me."

Even Apella was impressed. *The man wasn't exaggerating on the train. We must never again underestimate him in any regard.*

Rose flipped to another page. "I think Dan knows your modesty is out of place, Thi. Here, how about this one?"

He squinted at the page and said, "F Major Praeambulum. I don't think so."

Rose squeezed his shoulders. "Dear boy, it's in your head, digital memory as William would say. Don't think, just play. Show Dan what you can do."

He let his fingers go, made it look easy, and I think he would have played on, but little Franny had other plans. She batted a kitty toy at him, he tossed it back to her, stood up and said, "Ahright, Oyente. Change clothes, time to work. A dead fir's blockin' the river trail just up from William's Place…fell in that windstorm you probly slept through last night. Ax and bow saw are out back."

Rose started to the kitchen. "It's an unscheduled opportunity for you boys to unravel kinks from your ride yesterday."

Good. Another chance to pick Thius's mind.

We had a quick breakfast with Rose then hiked to the fallen tree. Thius did the sawing, and I was axing branches off the trunk when he said, "There's magic in this valley, Oyente. You're feelin' it, I can tell."

"You're right, it's a great place. If I lived here I'd be out year-round, stud my bike tires for winter, snowshoe the high country, spend days at mountain lakes."

"So you're thinkin' about joinin' Ursavus?"

"I think about it, sure."

"Maybe you think too much."

We were piling brush and pushing the last two logs off the trail when a train rumbled upriver. Thius waited for it to get close then faced away from the track and said, "Tell you about this one. It's a ninety-nine-car unit — all loaded grain hoppers. Ellie's on the point, and there she goes."

"Not into waving?" I asked, as two locomotives roared by.

"No need. Listen to the cars — uniform sound, pitch, and cadence. She's haulin' close to thirteen thousand tons of corn and soybeans."

Find out why there is so much focus on freight trains with these people.

Thius said, "In case you're wonderin', I've been watchin' loco-motives round bends in this narrow valley my whole life, same for Rose and George, most people here. We like trains, understand 'em, make the most of 'em. Planetwide, Ursavus is a veritable family of railophiles."

We were packing up when another freight whistled from the east. "Three shorts," said Thius, "this one's comin' off the siding, headin' our way, nine minutes out."

He faced away again and rattled off power and manifest like a conductor with a memory like mine. "One Triple Divide engine pow-ered by fuel cells!" he shouted. "She's pullin' a local mix like the two we rode — boxcars, three late design, loaded — five old ones goin' by now, two open, all empty — tank cars now, seven, all loaded, corn syrup, sulfur, liquid CH_4, two full reefers and a tail of empty flatcars. And that's it, won't be any more for awhile, and I can tell somethin's on your mind, Oyente, spill it."

I walked behind him, waited for the train sounds to pass then started with, "Okay, I was thinking how unpredictable you are. I mean, a train-savvy mountain biker who plays Bach on the piano and tracks wildlife and trains by scent and sound. What about your job in Ursavus? Will I ever hear about that?"

He spun around and faced me. "You mean what do I do when I'm not babysittin' recruits like you? I'm a traveler — on trains as a rule. Mostly I target heavy footprint miscreants."

I asked him to translate, he dropped his pack, looked me in the eyes and didn't hold back. "Globally, Ursavus has files on thousands who hoard big money and power and stifle essential change. They live in tight family groups guarded by smart lackeys who specialize in disinformation. Right now, four high-placed corporate cheats top my action list. I ground-proof files and outline options. We're effective but our pace is way too slow — which is why you're here."

I asked what he meant by options then repeated what I told him on the train, "I have no violence in me, Thius."

His eyes narrowed. "If that's fact, Oyente, you fit right in with Ursavus. We don't do violence. Fueling family feuds or threatening to expose abuse usually does the job, and we don't target wealthies who spend big on worthy causes."

I asked he ever felt remorse or made mistakes.

Good tactics! Get a full confession.

Thius snapped a branch from a fallen log and broke it into three pieces. "I don't particularly like my job. I'd rather be bikin' these hills, workin' bears with George, bein' with Ellie, even ridin' with you now, but I believe in the job. You should talk with Sula about this. She's had firsthand experience. Her foster parents fit the powerful miscreant role big time 'til news spread on the internet about abuse in the mansion. Three months later multibillionaire David Rochsfeld shot his wife then himself."

My pulse raced — I searched memories — headlines bylines news archives. Nothing. Thius broke off another branch, squatted down, drew three overlapping circles in the dirt and said, "Guess you wonder how I reconcile crap like that, huh?"

I looked at the circles then him. "For someone who espouses nonviolence, yes."

He tossed the branch and stood tall in front of me. "The Rochsfeld abuse was violent, regular and persistent — verbal and physical by both parents. Daughter Heather kept her wits and ran away, became Sula Millen. She wasn't real happy when she learned what we did to the Rochsfelds, but she worked it out."

We're pulling intel.

I was stunned. Sula! Spirited, moody and spacey. How could she work it out?

Thius kicked dirt over the circles. "It's not just about taking down rich abusers, Oyente. Ursavus intel prevents thousands of evil acts worldwide every year. So now you know."

He grabbed his pack and started down the trail, his backside proclaiming No More Talk, and I didn't try keeping up. I thought about the locomotive engineer who just went by. Ellie, he called her, and yesterday at the fire tower he mentioned Ellie Sterling? Before that, he told Rose he was gunna hook back up with Ellie. I asked Apella if she was sure about her intel on Eleva Sterling.

We believe this is another game they are playing with you. More importantly, you are gaining Thius's trust and our goals can be achieved.

"But where does this leave me? You of all people know I cannot be part of anything like what he does — not for the mission — not for anyone."

Patience, Daniel.

I balked, "No — I'm past patience. I need you to be straight with me. Is this more than a surveillance mission? What's my assignment really about? Will I see headlines about a deadly confrontation in Cedarville? Just give me the truth, Apella."

We continue to assess the threat level of this cell. National security may not be an issue, and in any case there will be no intimidation that could lead to violent death. Concerning what Thius said about the Rochsfeld case, we have confirmed how the husband and wife died, but there is no record of abuse, and Heather Rochsfeld, age nineteen, died in a motorcycle accident in Thun, Switzerland. No connection to Sula Millen. Thius's involvement in the case is undocumented, undoubtedly a ploy to gauge your reaction. For your information, the Rochsfeld estate is on an isolated island in Lake Champlain. A private Montreal investment firm underwritten by Precambre International purchased the island and the estate a year after the deaths. There is no connection between the Rochsfeld case and the Cedarville cell.

Thius and Rose were waiting for me on the back porch when I came out of the woods. "Just in time, Dan," Rose yelled. "We're going out for dinner. Harpy's for levity, boys! I've got my favorite black dress ironed and laid out and the truck shined up, ready to leave in an hour. I'll drive."

"Yeah and I'm wearin' my work clothes," Thius said, dusting off his shirt and pants. Rose shook a finger at him and his tune changed. "Ahright, we both need to spiff up, Oyente, and you'll like Harpy's. It's a fine local watering hole, south on this side of the river."

Thius's and Apella's versions of the Rochsfeld family rang in my ears as I showered and dressed for dinner. I was inclined to believe Thius, and my doubts about Apella were mounting. I pressed her for more about my role in the mission. "For peace of mind, Apella, I have to know what the director plans to do with the information I'm providing on these people — details you wouldn't have if it weren't for my implant."

Daniel, as always I will share your concerns with my director. And once again I must emphasize this is strictly a surveillance mission. While you are getting close to members of this group, do not let emotions cloud your vision. I strongly believe your tolerant view of these people is on the brink of change. Have you lost sight of your quest for information about Nathaniel's demise?

She didn't wait for an answer. The implant beeped, and I reset my mind for an evening of levity.

23

A River Dancer's Dream

We pulled out of the drive just before six, and squeezed tight between Thius and the manual shift, I had second thoughts about the clothes I picked out from William's wardrobe. What will it be like walking into a local watering hole wearing a purple Tommy Bahama shirt and pressed jeans? Rose reached over and patted my knee. "Good not to be shy about what you wear, Dan. You look islandy, just right for Harpy's, and I like the stubble on your face…nice the way you keep it trimmed."

We're tuned in. This should be an interesting trip.

Rose and Thius talked nonstop for nearly eleven miles. I heard about local school music events, wrestling matches, volleyball championships, Shakespeare in the Park, huckleberry festivals, and a pig in the bar at Harpy's, "And she's a regular hog, Oyente," Thius said, "not one of those potbellies you're thinkin' about. Blossom is her name, and she answers to it."

"Yes," added Rose, "and too bad we won't get to see her tonight. Blossom was quite the attraction, but she doesn't live at Harpy's anymore. She grew too large to turn around behind the bar, so they adopted her off to a local ranch family. We might see her with her first litter at the county fair in September."

Thius crossed his arms and said, "Yeah, we'll visit Blossom, then I'll stop by the flag booth and tell 'em I called in a heads-up the week before VP Pebre's lights went out."

Was he joking or did he just admit having advance knowledge of Vice President Pebre's assassination?

I cringed and filed her question for later as we approached a flashing neon sign.

HARPY'S LAKESIDE CAFÉ
500 Feet Ahead
Outstanding Entrées, Friendly Service, Cabins & Canoes
A River Dancer's Dream

Rose beamed when we stepped up to a rustic oak door. "Dan, I want you to know I love everything about this place. It's family owned and operated, entrées you can't find anywhere outside a metropolis, a great assortment of music and they don't overcharge for foosball or pool."

A young man in slacks, button-down shirt and bolo tie met us inside, complimented Rose on her dress and said he would be our host and server for the evening. Thius high-fived him, and Rose gave him a gentle hug and introduced us, "Dale Harpy, this is Dan Oyente, a mountain biker with a phenomenal memory. He's living with Thius and me while he plans his future."

Dale picked up a stack of menus, studied my face and told me his parents own the restaurant. "So please tell me if anything isn't just right for you, Mr. Oyente."

I thanked him, and he seized the moment when I glanced at the sturdy dark planks under my feet. "Mr. Oyente, those are hemlock two-by-twelves, cut, set, sanded, and polished by the original homesteaders, my great grandparents, Grace and Cyril Harpy. The original house, just this room and the loft above, survived the 1910 firestorms and didn't require moving when the river was dammed."

He fiddled with the menus and blushed, "Oh, sorry for all that, Mr. Oyente. I get carried away."

I told him I like hearing about the place, and Rose assured him he had every right to be proud. He smiled and led us to a center table, took our orders and promised he'd be right back. "Great kid," said Rose, "a junior this year with a fine future if he can stay single."

"A fine future in terms of what," Thius snarled. Rose snapped her fingers and said, "Harpy's for levity, Thi," then started swaying to the beat and lip-syncing as Don McClean's clear voice came through the overhead speakers.

I scanned the room, counted thirty-four diners and chuckled when I caught suspicious glares from a table of four. "The young group by the window could use some levity," I said, and Thius cracked a smile, "Yeah, militia kids with a healthy distrust of outsiders."

Find out if the militia is aligned with Ursavus.

"Yes, and we protect those kids," said Rose, "and oh goodness, here comes our appetizer."

Dale set a full plate of oysters in front of Thius and proudly declared, "Kumamotos on the half shell with house-recipe hot sauce! And our chef said to let you know these were flown in two hours ago from Willapa Bay over in Washington." Thius pushed the oysters my way and said, "The lady and the diffident snob in the purple shirt ordered the raw things. I'm startin' with salad."

Dale said, "Oh sorry, Thius, I should have — I'll be right back with your salad, then blackened steelhead for all when the time is right."

Rose and I shared the oysters and were enjoying the last of the tangy sauce when Andy Denton hobbled in on crutches, escorted by Sula, Erik and Nancy Denton. They waved at us and pulled chairs to the militia table. Rose blew them a kiss and said, "Join us, Dan. The people and the cause will keep you young."

"She's right, bike man," said Thius, "and I'm gunna see what those kids are talkin' about over there, maybe help with the conversation, be back with a full report."

Friendly faces and a warm squeeze from Sula greeted him, and he took a seat between Erik and Andy.

"Good smart kids, all of them," Rose said to me. "Clockwise from Sula, you see young Chas Miller, then his cousin Gabe Miller, both distant cousins of the Miller boy you met up Hemlock Draw. Next around are June Giffin, and Guy Marshall. Problems do arise with some of the parents. The Giffins and Marshalls regard Sula, Erik, Thius and me as seditious radicals."

Thius was back at our table when Dale served our entrées. "Steelhead," Thius said to his plate, "you look too good to eat but I'm goin' to anyway. And it's not wild or farmed, right, Dale, my man?"

Dale held his hands together, bowed and said, "No, so please enjoy."

I was thinking the steelhead must be a new soy product when Rose said, "Andrew seems awfully quiet over there, Thi…worries me. Do you think he's all right?"

"Not sure. His leg could be gettin' worse. He didn't say much, which is rare for him. All that time only a few groans and weak laughs. You could tell what the kids had to say, right?"

"Not all of it, Thi, and I'll have to talk with Sula about Andrew first thing in the morning. And you didn't have to prompt Chas Miller, did you?"

"Nope, Mr. Chas was spontaneous for a change. When I got over there, Ms. Denton was fast-talking rules and regulations mandating public and private school literacy tests. Chas butted in, said the meeting was supposed to be about voting and whether it's worth the time to register. I didn't have to prompt Chas's cousin Gabe either. He told us he believes voting's a joke and he's not gonna add his name to any public list. June Giffin kinda laughed then and said anyone who registers is bound to get a jury summons right away in this little county. She added that her parents vote in local elections."

Thius took several bites of steelhead. "Man, this is fine, tastes better than ever. I should go to the kitchen and tell 'em about it, but back to the kids. Sula spoke up next, said she votes whenever possible and tries to look beyond single issues, but that can be very difficult. Then Guy Marshall opined, To me it seems like most national nerds get in because they're willing to cheat, spy, start wars and get free health insurance. And that really got Chas animated. He said his folks believe cheaters can rig any election they want unless there's a landslide. And right then, I looked at our man Erik, saw him brush back his hair, and knew the highlight was fixin' to come. Ever so coolly he said, I wonder about that term Landslide. I think of a huge mass of rock and debris pouring down a mountain. Is this really similar to a typical election when 80 to 90 percent of the electorate chooses not to vote and the winner of less than, say 10 percent, gains office? I would like to participate in a real voting landslide, and I believe it would lead to good government.

"That's when Sula clapped her hands and said, Okay, that's it tonight, and for our meeting here tomorrow night, everyone, let's talk about good government, what we mean by it, why we need it and what we can do to get it."

We have four, possibly five new persons of interest. Will research family connections, and good you are mostly the listener here. Plenty for us to pursue.

Dale returned to our table with a full tray of desserts. Rose ordered decafs around, and Thius noticed me eyeing a dark chocolate tort and mixed berry pie. "Don't do it, bike man. We're goin' out again tomorrow — a serious ride. You don't want a buzzy night."

"Keep talking, Thi," said Rose. "I'll claim a foosball table and we'll have our coffee back there." He gave her a thumbs up and punched me in the arm. "Yeah, we'll do a six thousand-foot ride up to 60-Odd Peak, the high one, top of Hemlock Draw. It's a seventy-mile round trip we can bike in a day — still some snowmelt pools and mud up there — Alma'll be diggin' glacier lilies and gophers."

"Alma must be a bear."

"Yep, known her for years. Time now for some foosball, you and me against our lady. She's been warmin' up in the backroom."

Rose won four of five games, and it was nearly eleven when we left Harpy's. The dark night with low clouds and drizzle had me planning gear for a wet day on a bike but Thius assured me it would be clear and dry by morning. Rose drove at a steady speed and reminisced about Harpy's. "You can tell how much I love that old place, can't you, Dan? One of the best nights of my life happened in there. It was mid-February and bitter cold. William, Thius and I were enjoying a table near the fireplace when George Waterbear walked in with his young research associate Eleva Sterling. Oh, what a wonderful time that long-ago night was for all of us. William, George, and I watched Eleva and Thius sweep each other off their feet, and we all knew there would be no turning back."

Just like Apella and me, I thought, and Thius said, "Yeah, Ellie in her sky blue dress, walking in there with George, makes my heart pound to this day. Poised, brilliant and beautiful, then and always."

And Rose added, "My mind goes to you now, Dan, the night on the porch when you recited things you learned about Eleva. Tell Thius about that, would you please?"

Thius almost spat in my ear, "Yeah, tell me what you think you know about my friend."

Let them have it all.

I hesitated. "Okay…Eleva Sterling, Master's Degree of Fine Arts and History, antiwar radical once listed with the FBI's Most Wanted, incarcerated in May of 1968, died April 29, 1969. I remember four interviews and nine news reports, all containing strong antigovernment statements, some with veiled or direct threats against the president."

"You've been infected, bike man. You're spoutin' right-wing media crap laced with vile prejudice. You ever read any of Ellie's essays or hear her lecture in person?"

I answered, "No, but most of the media stories were mainstream and I can recite many of Ms. Sterling's statements verbatim. Comments like, This reigning president should be dethroned by whatever means necessary — caught up with her, landed her in prison."

Thius elbowed me in the ribs and said, "Ellie was speakin' hard truth about a dangerous idiot who shouldn't have been president. She never threatened anybody, just tried to get people to think for themselves, pose questions like you do, Oyente, help people find some light at the end of their tunnels."

Rose slowed down and stopped within inches of a bobcat. Blinded by the headlights, it froze for a second then leaped away, and I asked myself, Wild cat eyes, good sign or bad? "More likely neutral," said Thius, "and that cat knows as much as you do about Ellie Sterling."

There it was again, a clear reference to my unspoken thoughts.

A mile on, Rose pulled off the road and put on her warning lights as a motorcycle whizzed by. "Guess the meeting broke up, Thi. That was June Giffin, and here comes Gabe Miller on his Yamaha."

We need more on all these people, especially Eleva Sterling. Anything you can get them to disclose!

I told Thius it must have been a terrible shock when Eleva died. "Wrong again, Oyente," he said, and Rose added, "Eleva is certainly not in the past tense, Dan."

"What are you saying? I remember every word in the report. Eleva Sterling blew herself up, left a note. The FBI released a detailed statement. Someone smuggled plastic into her cell. Such a violent death."

"Wrong!" blared Thius and put up his fist. "Ellie's more alive than you, bike man. She had a complete makeover, all new face, fingerprints, irises, retinas, and genetically altered untraceable DNA, same height, though. Just right."

"Unbelievable," I said.

Ignore the silly reference to futuristic alteration. We have suspected they were in the business of harboring fugitives, but not this one. Get her alias.

"Hold on, boys, sheets of rain ahead," said Rose, "and don't worry, Dan, I know every twist and turn of this road." She didn't slow as heavy downpour and a blast of hail pounded her truck. "Oh how I love wild squalls," she said. "They're like momentary anger — fast, furious and fleeting. Another minute, boys, and we'll have clear sailing all the way home."

Halfway down her lane she lowered her window, put out her hand and said, "Why, I believe it hasn't rained at all here...broken clouds, filtered moon, and a warm dry breeze that makes me think chinook."

"That's tsi-núk in Salishan, one of Ellie's favorite languages, bike man, and you're wonderin' when I last saw her, right? Answer is, she's always with me, and you need to figure your way to the truth. Stay out here awhile. Night air makes thinkin' easier for you. Like I said, we'll be dry tomorrow."

I sat on the tailgate of the truck, watched them walk arm-in-arm into the house and let the dogs out. Max and Agnes circled the yard then sat next to the truck, en garde, while I counted how many times I'd heard Thius say the name Ellie. When I got to nine, I thought, Okay, maybe Eleva Sterling worked with George, and according to Thius, she had been altered beyond recognition. Were they planning for me to meet her — or have I already? Rachel Smyth also worked with George, and Thius rode the rails with her. I told Apella this may sound crazy but my gut tells me I've met Eleva Sterling in the guise of a high-rail truck driver, a roadmaster named Rachel Smyth.

Daniel, we are relying on you to fill in details about Ms. Sterling. Concerning Ms. Smyth, know this. We have reliable records of her life from birth to present, and our analysts assure me the technology for complete makeovers is not available. You have a strenuous ride ahead of you. Play it safe tomorrow. We will be in contact. Ursavus remains an unknown.

She signed off and I thought Ursavus may be a mystery but I would bet on Ursavus intel over hers any time…and I have to put all this out of mind. A seventy-mile bike ride with a six thousand-foot climb would require a full night of rest. Tomorrow could be a tough day.

24

High Country Refugium

Thius woke me at four-thirty a.m. "It's time, Oyente, need to get an early start, leavin' coffee by the door, got enough fuel for both of us, see ya out front." I switched on the light, started pulling on layers… not like him to serve me coffee. Maybe last night's talk about Eleva Sterling softened him up. Thius, the one-woman man, like me. So why didn't he just say Eleva and Rachel are the same person?

His brew was strong and its buzz hit me full throttle when we started out Rose's lane. I zipped around him as though posing for a race, and he yelled for me to wait up. "Slow down, bike man. You'll need it later."

We were on the East Valley Road riding side by side when I asked how he expected to find his bear. He didn't hide his disdain. "Alma's not my bear any more than I'm her human. She knows my scent. She'll find us. All we have to do is be on 60–Odd Peak by midafternoon."

The river bridge was in sight when a truck roared by spewing diesel fumes. "Ahh hell," Thius groaned, "I'll show you where we're goin' while we wait for the stench to clear." He pulled out his map. "Ahright, here's the itinerary. We take Hemlock Draw to the Garnet Creek Road, hit Lone Bear Trail by noon, another hour and a half should put us at the base of the peak. We'll be lucky to make five miles an hour on the last climb and won't be up there long. Alma doesn't linger." He folded the map and gulped some water. "Comin'

151

back we'll be on the peak's east side — an easy two-hour run along Swallowtail Creek — should get us home before dark. Let's haul!" And he charged across the bridge ahead of me.

We climbed for hours without a break, and it was close to noon when Thius slowed, yelled for me to stop and pointed at the skyline. "Lone Bear Trail runs north and south along that ridge," he said, "a quarter-hour bushwhack gets us there — nothin' like our last trip in the alder."

Apella made contact. *Daniel, one of our drones scouted the area Thius is taking you. The drone returned with nonsense data. I cannot watch your back.*

Thius and I shouldered our bikes, started up a damp slope into dense brush and knee-high beargrass. "Watch your feet," he warned, "not a good place to snap a leg."

When we reached Lone Bear Trail, he said, "Ahright, bike man, we got five miles of steady climb on this easy track up to a level ridge then it's a good drop to Meander Creek where we cross."

Forty minutes later we stood at the edge of a steep drop-off above a heavily wooded draw. I looked down and said, "Whoa times ten, Thius, if Meander Creek is down there, this confirms you seriously understate road conditions."

"Yeah, starts steep so figure butt behind saddle, and you won't forget this, Oyente. Four hairy doglegs, no berms, sidehill scree on a narrow open slope then a world-class run under larch and old hemlock — what these bikes are made for. I'll go first. Gimme a half-minute lead."

It was a biker's dream. Whipping down an open slope to a rocky ledge, splashing through muddy seeps, I was stoked and felt thirty again. When he yelled Outrig Here, I held speed, leaned my bike into the curve, counterbalanced and nearly lost it before the trail opened under the trees and gave me a full-bore screaming glide to the creek bottom.

Meander Creek was roaring, more like a Class III rapid than a mountain stream. When I saw Thius poised to cross with his bike, I told him, "I bet if your ten-speed could talk, she would say Carry me over or buy me new bearings."

"Real funny, bike man. You didn't expect a cushy log bridge, did you?"

"No, but this doesn't strike me as a great place to ford. How deep is the middle? I mean I've waded icy creeks with a bike, never in this much current…looks like forty feet to the other side."

"Ahh, I've crossed when it was runnin' faster. George would say the rocks are biofilmed so move like a snail. Slide and set, use the bike to brace against the flow. Wait 'til I'm across and forget the cold. Bike's your focus. Brace and feel your way slow and sure 'til you're outta the current."

At midstream it looked like the flood would take him, but he made it without a stumble. I waded in, felt the icy water pour through my Shimanos, and repeated Numb feet slide and set, until I sloshed out soaked to the waist, cold and shivering. Thius was jogging in place and shaking from head to foot. "Let's go," he said, "I gotta keep movin', and we're runnin' late. It's a tough haul gettin' outta this draw."

We pushed the bikes up a steep bank of loose rocks, wet sand and tree roots, and I stopped for a last look at Meander Creek. Thius was nearly out of sight, pedaling hard when I heard him yell, "See you where we stop!"

The trail ended at a rock slide Thius called 60-Odd Stairway. "My thermostat takes a break after bein' that cold," he explained. "Only way I can warm up is to keep moving. It's a rare effect of whole-body enhancement."

I asked for more about enhancement and he said, "Mostly George's bailiwick and Alma's close by. We'll stash bikes and helmets here — foot it rest of the way."

We clambered up three hundred feet to a rock pool edged by devil club and mountain ash. Thius knelt for a drink, and I caught myself laughing at sparkles of water dripping from his chin. He looks stoned or in a trance, I thought, must be the rarefied air.

"Snow's mostly gone…rains earlier every year," he stammered, "been keepin' track ever since George first brought me up here. Nine I was, lookin' for a young friend I called Pes Albus."

We climbed another fifty feet to a narrow subalpine meadow on the north side of 60-Odd Peak. Thius turned full circle and declared, "This is Alma's place. Climbable cliffs, whitebark pines, Precambrian mudstones studded and veined with quartz, and satellite coverage by Ursavus." He reached into a pine thicket and pulled out a long stick. "Scratchin' rod. Have a seat, Oyente. Alma's been close since we left the bikes. She'll be along soon."

We sat and waited. I thought if a bear's close I should keep quiet and still, but Thius didn't act concerned. He tossed a rock at me.

"Quartz — silicon dioxide," he said, "clear, colorless and stable when pure, melt it to make glass. Most quartz on this mountain is shocked — struck by lightning. You could see the shock lines if you were optically enhanced. George would tell you quartz is Gaia's cement, her binder that holds minerals together in rocks. None wiser than George Waterbear — not on this planet. George taught me to think about more than myself, deal with pain, read sign, cogitate rocks and think like a bear. Some nights I dream about George and me bein' bears."

A warm breeze stirred the meadow and Thius stood up slowly, took two steps forward and focused on a wall of thick brush downwind of us. "She's here now," he said, and I tried to relax as a brown muzzle parted the brush. Thius held out his scratching rod. "She's tryin' to decide if you're okay, Oyente. Keep your seat and act like you belong."

Long seconds later, a cinnamon-phase black bear in her prime pushed out of the brush and ambled close to Thius. He rubbed the stick along her back, carefully at first, then harder back and forth. She was like a big docile canine with him, and when she had enough she raised her head, shook and started walking away. Thius spoke gently to her. "Bring the cub next time, old friend...two months, we'll hork some huckleberries."

She stopped for a last look, and that's when I noticed some dark red hair on her nape. When she was out of sight, Thius sat back down, pulled his journal from his pack and made some notes. I asked if Alma was related to Pes Albus. "They share some genes," he said. "Most bears born within twenty miles of crow flight from here have shades of maroon."

He looked away, swiped a tear, then frowned when I asked about hunters coming up here. "Guess George didn't tell you," he said. "Discontinuities remain, but high country in the Rockies is mostly refugium, protected by international treaties, but minimal enforcement except areas like this patrolled by Ursavus — by cloaked satellite twenty-four seven. Five hundred meters down from here, human trespassers get zapped by a quantum particle beam. It's harmless and they don't feel it, they just go home and remember there's nothing worth pursuing on this mountain."

He walked to the pine thicket, put the scratching rod back in its place, and turned his attention to a slight intermittent breeze from Alma's direction. Human destroyer one day, Bear savior the next, I thought and asked what he knew about skyrmion lattices and quantized magnetic flux. He squatted down, thumbed through his journal and said, "You heard all that from George, right? There could be somethin' to it, but George gets a kick outta throwin' high-minded hype at naive recruits. The particle beam that protects this place is antidromic. It derives from axions, has no effect on ursavans, and you don't have to worry about gettin' zapped. I slipped an antidote in your coffee this morning."

I leaped up. "What? What's in the antidote?"

He didn't answer, and my mind raced — Axions Antidotes Cybercloaks Quantum Particles Mitochondrial Enhancers — and why didn't I think twice and ask George about the vitacorders we were using in Yellowstone?

Thius looked up at me. "Jason Steller told me you're a real loner, Oyente, basically antisocial borderin' on sociopathic, but you're good at coverin' it. What do you think of that?"

I made sure he saw me roll my eyes and told him I never took Jason's attempts at psychoanalysis seriously.

"Me neither," he said, "and Steller once described me with similar words, told me I'd never join Ursavus or any organization — that I lost all sense of responsibility at Kain's Cut."

I tried not to sound sarcastic. "So, Thius, according to Jason, you and I are similar, at least socially."

"Yeah, and there's probably some truth in his professorial edicts, but Rose says NO to anyone who calls us loners. She knew I'd join, not for the cause, for the people — for her, George and Ellie — not ideal, by the way. You're the same, she says, and I believe her now. But who's it gunna be for you? Aah, never mind. Time's up. We'll take a shortcut down that avalanche chute."

When we reached the bikes, he asked what I planned to do when my search for the truth about Nate was over. I told him, "Best scenario, I'll get another job like the one in Yellowstone, but I'm not prone to quixotic searches."

"Yeah, well George told me he might set you up part-time if you join, and you'd probably gain twenty good bikin' years if you commit that memory to a worthy cause — never thought I'd say this but here it is. You're a prevaricator extraordinaire but fixable and you belong with us. Mostly your call now. You have to want to join, and that's enough talk. See ya on the valley road. I'm gone."

I gave him a three-minute lead and tried contacting Apella — no response. I stopped on the way down, tried again and she had a terse order, *Daniel, we stand ready for a full report of what happened on that mountain. Now!*

Thinking a full report will have to wait, I told her about a great bike ride in high country that was like a second home to Thius, glossed over the scene at Meander Creek, noted seeing Alma but said nothing about satellite beams and Ursavus. I ended with, "Overall, Thius turned out to be a decent biking companion and is acting more and more like he trusts me."

You're in, Daniel. Thius offers comradery to entice you to join. Stay within mission parameters and keep your mental distance from these people.

Thius was crossing the river bridge when I caught up, and we stopped on the East Valley Road near Rose's to watch a family of coyotes romping in a field. "She's got three half-grown pups," he whispered. "Ponder pullin' that off in this valley of motorized predators."

The trickster raised her head and caught our scent, snapped her rowdy crew to order and led them into the woods. Thius loosened his helmet strap, rubbed his chin. "So, what do you predict for the future, Oyente? You think maybe our time's about up?"

I told him I've never been into gloom and doom, but I don't envy future generations. His dark eyes flashed me. "Weak answer, bike man. Dyin' you can't rely on. Things are changin' too fast. This civilization's a time bomb set to blow sooner than you think."

He jumped on his pedals, spun a wheely and stayed ahead of me until we were close to the house. The windows were open, and we heard someone at the keyboard. Thius said, "Bach's E flat major 552 on the piano. Wish I could make all those voices stand out like that."

Rose met us at the door and whispered in his ear, "Oh, Thi, you know William so loves that fugue." "Ellie too," he said, holding her tight. We went to the kitchen, and Rose pointed at the calendar next to her computer. "Schedule reminder for you, Dan. It's time for another visit with Jason. We have you booked for a round trip on the Triple Divide Scenic, our commuter tour train."

"Really? Yeah, that sounds great." Could she tell my enthusiasm was overstated? "When do I leave?"

"I'll drive you to Walter's store in the morning, and the Triple Divide Scenic will stop for you there at 0915. You'll arrive at the Missoula yard at 1630 and Jason will be there to meet you. Feel free to use William's overnight bag, on the top shelf of the closet upstairs. He keeps an MP-3 player and a few of his favorite CDs in the front pocket…might come in handy."

Apella made contact when I was back in my room. *Your rail trip is confirmed, Daniel. Solicit information from all you encounter. Watch your back as always and do not take chances that could weaken the mission.*

I put a few things together for the train ride and thought about her last three messages. She expected a full account of my day with Thius but was satisfied with my brief report. Was she testing my loyalty to the mission? Was the implant transmitting all that time? No, I think I can tell when the damned thing is on or off, and Apella would never agree to test me. If she heard anything from the implant that I didn't report, she would have asked me about it.

Sounds of an eastbound heavy rumbled through my room — loud engine noise then a long roll, random clatter and a gradual fade away — sort of like this mission. Was it time to tell Apella her government group is outflanked by Ursavus? No, I wasn't prepared to break with the mission, not entirely, not yet. Keep your seat and act like you belong, Thius said at Alma's place, and it felt like good advice. I did some push-ups then stretched out on the bed and drifted into a dream of another insane ride on the rails.

25

Train Train

A banner draped in front of Smyth's store that morning read, WELCOME TOUR TRAINORS, and there was a picnic table on the porch with coffee, tea and a plate stacked high with donuts. The door was open and I could see Walter serving breakfast to a full row. There were no empty tractor seats, and no one looked up when a long whistle blasted from the west. Strange, it didn't sound like a diesel, more like something out of the past, and minutes later Baldwin Steam Locomotive 3641 pulled in with the Triple Divide Scenic in tow. What a sight, and why no smoke and steam?

I watched twenty-six passengers step down from three coaches... ruddy faces under felt hats, fringed jackets and leather dusters, lace and denim dresses, and shiny new western boots. Was this one of those old-west re-enactment groups? If so, a squatty guy in a navy-blue pinstripe suit with a yellow bowtie and red wingback shoes didn't fit the scene. I pretended not to notice when he gave me the once-over. Was he taken by my pea jacket and tennis shoes? He stayed by the train and kept up his vigil until I stepped off the porch.

Another guy, a lanky leather-clad gentleman with ultrabrushy nostrils rubbed by me as I walked toward the locomotive. "Not likely any of these tour train people are with Ursavus," I whispered to Apella.

The engineer climbed down from his cab and glanced my way. Tall, in-charge and appropriately dressed in striped overalls and matching cap, he introduced himself as Chief Engineer Boston Cole and reached for my hand. "This your first trip on the Scenic, young fella?" he asked.

"Yes it is, sir. I'm Dan Oyente, headed to Missoula today and back on Wednesday."

"Well, in my opinion, son, you're in for a royal treat drawn by converted steam through the best country anywhere. If I were you, I'd take a window seat on the left for river views and snow-capped peaks. Plenty of room in the middle car. Occupied seats are flagged, those good folks are out stretching their legs and helping themselves to Walter's complimentary snacks."

The Triple Divide Scenic operates a regional railroad franchise granted by Precambre International. Get as much as you can, especially on the engineer.

I asked Mr. Cole if he expected to arrive in Missoula on time. "Count on it," he said with a proud nod. "One three-way meet is factored into the schedule, and our dispatcher promises fifteen minutes or less at the Paradise wye. We'll take the Flathead River route, over the hill, as we like to say. You been over Evaro Hill on a train, son?"

His repeated use of the word son was odd since he looked younger than me but I took it as a compliment and answered, "Yes sir, I was heading north over the hill not long ago."

Again a proud nod, then a wave at his engine. "Our Steam Sheila here won't miss a stroke. Triple Divide used to have diesels standing by in case we needed a push or pull, but not anymore. Sheila's all new inside and out — sleek black steel with stainless trim powered by state-of-the-art hydrogen fuel cells. Purists like me kinda miss the coal and smoke but our lungs sure don't."

He pulled a classic brass pocket watch from his overalls, opened the lid then snapped it shut. "Ten minutes to boarding," he said. "Excuse me now, gotta finish checking Sheila's parts."

I climbed into the middle coach, found a seat on the left, tucked my bag underneath, and popped in a CD. Other passengers filed in, took seats on the left, except one guy, Bowtied Suit sat alone across the aisle from me. Brushy Nostrils and his wife, I assumed, sat directly behind me, and minutes out of town Mr. Nostrils thumped my right shoulder and asked what I was listening to.

"Organ music, sir, some Bach. You like Baroque music?"

"Reminds me of church when I was a kid. Grew up in Chickaahhgo, raised Loothrin."

"Lutherans have great music, sir."

"Just keep it down, will you," he snorted, "the wife and I don't want that kinda noise out here."

I apologized, stowed the MP-3 and relaxed to the train sounds. I was thinking maybe Rose set me up for more levity when Bowtie's phone rang, and he started talking loud enough for everyone to hear. "Yeah, it's me, Jabo, can barely hear ya. Naah, save your money. Shabby towns, 25 percent unemployed, country's nothin' special…yeah, be gettin' a refund."

I was imagining what Engineer Cole would say to this traveling cliché when Mr. Nostrils grabbed the back of my seat and shouted over me, "You with the bowtie over there! Yer disturbin' the peace. What are yuh doin' on this train anyway? Yuh don't look or sound like yuh belong here and yer too loud to be a terrist."

Bowtie stayed quiet then and fidgeted in his seat until we slowed in a tight gorge. "Wouldn't wanna drive that highway," he blurted. "Have a train fall over on me and — "

"Would you please shut up!" yelled a woman from the front of the car. "Rude people on this tour," sniveled Bowtie, finally subdued by applause and Boston Cole's announcement on the overhead speakers, "Ladies and gentlemen, we're rolling into Thompson Falls. Later on we have a fifteen-minute stop in Paradise. The dispatcher expects a timely meet there at the wye. Two westbound freights — a long unit of grain from the Clark Fork route and a manifest from the Flathead, both heavily loaded — will pass on our right. Meanwhile, we have about thirty miles of Clark Fork River vistas and a fast run through the town of Wildhorse Plains before the show at Paradise, so kick back and enjoy."

The train was hugging a narrow ledge between the highway and the river when I heard static on my implant then Apella, *Daniel, it's been so long since we were out there, will you describe it for me?*

She sounded warm and upbeat, like when we were together. "Wait a sec," I whispered, "gotta move so I can see the river." I made my way to the rear of the car. "Okay, no one around me, and I've got a clear view of the water. It still runs fast and wild in white-capped blues and greys. We kayaked two spring runoffs through here. Remember the Class IV rapids through the boulder garden?" No answer. Damn — and I could tell she wanted more.

Three distant whistles blew, the train slowed, and Mr. Nostril's wife stood from her seat and cheerfully read the city sign for all to hear. "Paradise, Montana, population one hundred and twenty…oh how quaint."

I took my seat as Engineer Cole announced, "Please, your attention everyone. Our two loaded westbounds are right on time, and we will be on our way as soon as the second one passes. Best to remain seated, no time to detrain."

Minutes after we stopped, a ninety-unit grain train roared by followed by the manifest. Bowtie popped up and shouted, "What's the manifest hauling, hazmats?" And as though on cue, Mr. Nostrils leaned into the aisle and jeered him down, "Let's see now, two tank cars labeled corn syrup, three with asphalt — uh-oh, that's deadly. Now what? Oh no — two with liquefied natural gas. Yuh better shut up and exit fast."

I almost laughed, thinking of Apella's instruction, Solicit information from all you encounter.

Disjointed chatter filled the car when we rolled out of Paradise, then gentle train sounds took over as we picked up speed along the Flathead River. I counted two hundred and eleven camera clicks recording views between Paradise and the tiny village of Perma, then a broken crown on a tall pine reminded me of Thius's tale about a bald eagle, a deer, and a hapless herd of elk. I figured him for a moody kook on those train rides. Now I see him off the charts in complexity, like this messy mission I'm trying to navigate…and I wouldn't hesitate to bike another mountain road with him.

Boston Cole slowed us down when we veered southeast along the Jocko River. My eyes went to a young boy fly-casting from shore, his line floating gracefully toward a cloud of insects downstream. "Apella," I whispered, "mayflies hovering over the Jocko, remember?"

Yes, winged ephemera shimmering for mates their only day in the sun… feels like yesterday.

There she was again, her old self, and I wanted more but she cut off. Why does she sound uptight and detached most of the time then normal sometimes? Guess her role is difficult, with memories of us roiling her mind. But Apella is tough. What's going on with her?

When Steam Sheila started climbing the north side of Evaro Hill I pictured a fireman madly shoveling coal to power the old engine up a long grade like this. As we crested the hill, Paul Butterfield's train-inspired harmonica entered my mind and played over and over until squealing brakes brought us to a smooth stop. I looked out and down — two hundred feet. We were sitting, idling on Marent Trestle. "No need to panic," said Cole. "Enjoy the view for a minute or two. This is a special treat for a special group." Cameras clicked wildly and kept clicking as we eased off the trestle and continued down to the Missoula Valley.

Youthful Professor Steller came to mind when we passed the Forest Service Aerial Fire Depot on Missoula's westside. Jason was a smoke jumper before I knew him, and he liked to spice lectures with tales of parachuting into fire zones. I could hear his booming voice — he never used a microphone — and see him pacing back and forth in front of two hundred and fifty students. Once when interest waned, he stopped abruptly, rocked back on his Earth shoes and shouted, Listen up, people. I want you to close your eyes and imagine being dropped from a low flying prop-plane into a frigid lake. You've got a parachute to contend with and you're nearly surrounded by a crown fire. You with me? Good, now back to our subject, the political history of US fire policies.

Jason's classes were always full. He was — is — a gifted teacher. And what else is the Professor? An associate of Ursavus? A member?

He's been in a perfect position to recruit for lots of years, and who could better fit that role?

26

Quantum Update

The Triple Divide Scenic pulled into Missoula's rail yard at a snail's pace, right on time as Boston Cole would say, and there on the boarding platform was Jason…red and pink floral shirt, tan vest, boot-cut trousers, and no, those can't be the same old shoes. He greeted me with a wide smile and a big wave as I stepped down ahead of the other passengers. "Here's a memorable moment," he said, "a friend from yesteryear arriving on a hydrogen-fueled nineteenth century steam train."

Jason hustled us away from the crowd and told me about the western gang I rode in with. "A nationally assembled group, Dan, and all but one are properly dressed for an extended tour of historic sites. A visit to Fort Missoula and an overnight at the Garnet Inn primes them for a week-long rail ride across Montana to Forts Union and Buford in North Dakota. Steam Sheila pulls them from here to Livingston then a sparkling new Triple Divide locomotive takes over and gives them a fine trip along the Yellowstone. Most of the group will fly home from Williston, North Dakota, the others via Amtrak on the highline…an enviable experience I'm sure you will agree."

We crossed two sets of track and stopped to watch a rear-cab locomotive pushing a row of rail cars. "That's our little switcher engine," Jason said proudly. "She's building a westbound manifest like you rode with Thius, and I know you've been introduced to Triple Divide's parent company, Precambre International. Triple Divide Railway operates regional east-west and local north-south lines to supply many of Precambre's installations continent-wide."

Jason lectured on as we walked down a familiar shop-lined street… fumeless exhaust systems, locomotives burning hydrogen from biore-actors and Precambre's business train. He stopped at Pete's Railyard Bar and Grille, pulled open the door and said, "Let's have an early dinner, Dan, for history's sake."

We took seats at Jason's favorite window table and Mike, the young philosophy major, handed us menus. "Your usual half glass of house red, professor?" he asked.

"Please, Michael, and one for my friend Dan, whom I think you've met, and as usual, we're on foot today so no need for concern about the ethanol." Mike filled our water glasses, plunked a slice of lemon in each and hurried off. Jason held out his menu and said, "Now, Dan, can you visualize Caesar salad, poached rainbow trout with capers, smart phones, and hyperactive brats in the old Pete's?"

I squeezed lemon in my water, stirred it with my knife and noticed a busker playing a guitar out on the sidewalk, then a woman in a white dress walked by, tossed a coin to the busker and disappeared. Jason knocked on the table to get my attention, and I told him he was right about the old Pete's. It was rough, didn't cater to families, and I kind of liked it that way.

He bristled at scampering feet and loud squeals from across the room. "Hell of a mess over there," he said, "brats acting like idiots, parents hunched over, faces aglow, swiping their apps. It's all part of a vast network of wireless addicts connected to everything but their own sense of self. Phone swiping is a pandemic disease."

He can be so much the curmudgeon.

Jason turned in his chair, leaned back and furrowed his brow. "Dan, you remember a half century ago this country and a few oth-ers had a critical mass of young people unmasking fascism, pushing for meaningful change, getting some environmental regulations and writing serious music."

I raised my hand like a student and said, "I do remember and some of those people are still going strong."

"True," he said, "but if most of them hadn't faded away they could have kept war mongers in check, maybe cooled the planet, but what happened?" He waved a finger at the other tables and talked louder. "What happened was they splintered into millions of power-less procreating families. All that intelligent idealism drizzled away in jobs, child spoiling, shopping, and today it's phone swiping—but wait. "Earth House Hold" wrote Gary Snyder back in the '50s, and at last I can say hope is on the way."

Mike returned with two glasses of wine, took our order, and Jason offered him a chair. "So, Michael, you've got a couple of geezers sitting here griping about the state of the world. I happen to think there's a connection between what's wrong with the planet and peo-ple fused with phones, making babies, and being trapped in a job. You don't have plans like that, do you?"

Mike sat on the edge of the chair and twirled a diamond stud in his left ear lobe. "Nope, Dr. Steller, as we have discussed repeatedly, I'm single, kidless and plan to stay that way. I like moving around, working jobs like this, living where I choose. And before you start on politics, I think it's a bigger disaster than the last time we talked, but I'm not supposed to go there with customers."

Jason didn't let up. "Michael, tell me again, are you afraid of los-ing this job?"

Mike stood and gave me a poker-faced nod. "The professor knows I like this town and what I'm doing, at least for now, and I better get back to it or I may not have a job." He rushed off, and Jason said, "The boy has no wife, offspring or siblings. He's alone and searching for something beyond the norm but hesitant to reach for it, reminds me of you a few decades ago. How are you and Mr. Terrene getting along, by the way?"

I told him things have mellowed since the train stuff, Thius turned out to be solid company on mountain bike rides, and there's a lot to like about him. "Good to hear," said Jason, "and have you learned anything new about what happened to Nate?" I told him nothing so far. "Well, stay on it," he said, and Mike was back at the table with our entrées balanced on one arm and a smile on his face. "Here you go," he said, "Santa Fe chicken special for the professor and seafood grande for Mr. Dan."

"Where you from, Mike?" I asked, and Jason answered for him. "Michael Allaire Faubourg is an extremely bright, second generation Montana boy from the village of Sun River, west of Great Falls. Straight-A-math and physics until psych and philosophy swept through him."

Mike shook his head at us, set a pepper grinder on the table and sidestepped footloose kids on his way to the kitchen. Jason peppered everything on his plate, then mine and said, "That young man put everything else aside, throttled his math genius, stopped taking it seriously, but he'll be a great asset once he realizes he can handle it all simultaneously. He's agreed to a job that will open his spirit and eyes. Rachel Smyth and Erik Galen are taking him under their wings this fall. Mr. Faubourg will be in the field with Erik and working in Rachel's lab engineering bacteria to express genes from fungi that concentrate rare-earth elements from mine wastes. Within a year, the lab expects to produce quantities of pure Ytterbium and other rare-earths that will match China's output."

"Hmmm, Mike's really into that kind of work?"

Jason tucked his napkin in his shirt collar. "Absolutely. Michael idolizes everything about Rachel, including her politics. He can't wait to work with her. She believes the project will rekindle his passion for hard science and numbers, and he'll want to stay on. We don't have time to wait for Michael like we did for you."

I took a bite of shrimp. Did Jason just admit being a recruiter for Ursavus? Surely he knows Apella heard him — or did she? Is Ursavus blocking my implant transmissions now? Once again, George's assurance, Your secret is safe, played in my head.

Our plates and wine glasses were empty when Mike returned and announced, "Desserts on the house. Flamed black cherries and vanilla ice cream, cerises noires flammées et glace vanille," and Jason raised his glass, "Hearing that, I fear Dan may choose not to revisit this establishment, but un grand merci, Michael of the Railyard. I'll have the cherries sans glace to go."

I smiled. "Sounds great but just some coffee for me, please."

Mike left us a pot and two mugs, and I didn't hide my surprise when Jason pulled out a smart phone. "Never thought I'd see you with that, Jason. What did you just tell me about people and phones?"

He waved the phone at me and said, "I was talking about mindless addiction to wireless phones, the most pervasive and insidious malady in human history. The global phone and social media society is an electronic caste system with all the trappings of an ant colony — one colossal difference, ant colonies are functional."

"Give me a break, Jason."

He set the phone in front of me, lowered his voice. "Seriously, my friend, there are devices, and there are devices, and I am certain you don't know the power of this little quantum tool. Your hyperthymestic recall provides what? Words? Facial expressions? General body language?"

"Yes, plus details of the surroundings, depending on my focus at the time."

He glanced at the other diners then back at me. The look in his eyes was eerie. "But, can you recognize a person by the size and shape of their ear lobes?" he asked. "By their gait? By their chemical trail? Can you record a person's DNA from a fingerprint and access their personal data seconds later?" He slid the phone to the far edge of the table. "Within three or four meters of a source — a person, a fingerprint, a few molecules, whatever — all I need to do is mouth a command."

"That is dangerous power, Jason."

"Dangerous in the wrong hands, yes. But that can't happen. In unauthorized hands it automatically encrypts all quantum data and reverts to a standard cell."

I asked if the device could silence my implant. He said, "Well certainly we don't have to worry about what we're saying in here. And you must be wondering why they want to recruit you when they have tools like this."

"Do you have an answer, Jason? And what about my implant? Is it a joke to them?"

He put the phone back in his pocket and said, "Details will come. For now you should start thinking about what your mind could do if your memory were combined with telepathy. They haven't built that combination into any device yet."

I drew back — Rose had said virtually the same thing.

Jason asked what I was thinking, and I gave him an earful. "I know you're with Ursavus, Jason — not with Apella's group. Does that mean you can read my mind? Can the others? What are their plans for me? Some far-out chimeric fusion of my hyperthymesia with mind reading? Do they really have all that power? Where did they get it? When did you join? What do you know about Nate you haven't told me?"

He held up his hands and laughed awkwardly. "Slow down, old friend. One thing at a time. Yes, I'm with Ursavus but not telepathic. Most ursavans are though, and they do have all the technology and power you've heard about and much more. George is your source for such topics, and you are scheduled with him soon after you return to Cedarville."

"So they've known about my implant all along?"

"Yes. We all have."

"They've been monitoring it?"

"They're tuned in, if that's what you mean."

He slipped a twenty-dollar tip under the pepper grinder and leaned close. "Listen, old friend, I apologize for the deception — inexcusable I admit — but would you have stayed the course if George or I had broken it to you upfront? Probably not, and you wouldn't have met Thius, Rose, Rachel, Sula or anyone else out there. Believe me when I say you've only begun to experience what you would have shied away from altogether — so stick with us. You won't regret it."

I strained to hear the slightest sound from my implant — nothing. I asked Jason if he knew I'd been censoring reports to Apella.

"I've been apprised of that, yes. Good, admirable. We all appreciate it, but Ursavus is not concerned about your reports to Apella. The goal is to recruit you, persuade you to join."

"Damn, what have I gotten into, Jason? This is way past anything I anticipated or was trained for."

He ran his hand down the front of his vest, pulled out his napkin and said, "You're doing fine, as I assured them you would."

"Doing fine at what? The mission is done — it's over and I'm left with a box of metal, plastic or whatever in my brain."

"Pardon me, Dan, are you saying you're abandoning your search about Nate? There are people in Cedarville who know more about him. Stick with us and stop worrying. I'm sure you've been told — and have no doubts — the decision to join Ursavus is entirely yours, and upon joining, enhancements such as telepathy, longevity, strength, endurance, to name a few, would be yours to freely choose. And I speak from experience when I say ursavan enhancement technology is tried and true, noninvasive and painless to assimilate."

"I can't believe this, Jason. You are actually enhanced?"

"Yes, and I recommend it without reservation. Constant good health and agelessness suit me to a T. But of course I could choose to reverse the enhancements at any time. So, my old student, it's purely a Win Win. You have much to gain and nothing to fear. And no need for concern about your friend Apella."

"But Jason, she's the implant voice working against Ursavus."

"Yes, and her director requires her to be strictly business with you, and she probably finds that difficult, as would anyone with a modicum of wit. Rest assured she's not in danger. Ursavus will protect any friend of yours, even if that friend has been working against us. My advice — just play it out with Apella."

When Mike returned with a to-go bag and the check, Jason held out his phone to pay, turned to me and said, "So, Dan, about timing, I'm tied up most of today and tomorrow, last-minute things I can't put off. First, I've got to visit with Pete's management, so in lieu of further discussion, I'll put together some reading material that will answer

more of your questions. Just make yourself comfortable at the house
and I'll see you early for breakfast."

Next morning in his kitchen, Jason was the light-hearted hip-
prof of yesteryear. Wearing loose-fitting shirt and pants, he shuffled
around barefoot with a coffee cup in his right hand, spatula in his left
and greeted me with a cool, "Good day, Dan. How does French toast
sans butter with cinnamon and cardamom instead of syrup sound to
you, my inveterately troubled friend?"

I started to smile, and he whipped out his fancy phone. "Here,
make your first quantum call. Rosey has you booked to return today
but needs to confirm the seat."

Rose was pleased. "Dan, excellent! And I'm certainly glad Jason
shared a little of our technology with you. Boston Cole may share
more, and he pulls out of Missoula at the top of the next hour. You
will arrive in Cedarville at 1815, just in time for our cookout. We're
having neighbors over and Thius will be grilling sweet potatoes and
boletes."

I throttled my concerns, told her I wouldn't miss a meal like that.
The phone beeped and Jason said, "So now you know the source of
my culinary skills — Rosey and William — tops at all they do. And I
have to get moving, Dan. I've got a ten a.m. with a new recruit. She's
en route to Vancouver and I'm meeting her VIA train in Kamloops."

I checked my watch. "Kamloops, Jason? It's already after nine.
You have your own superfast jet?"

"Projected holography, Dan. Time and distance are not serious
issues for an ursavan, not by any means, and Boston Cole doesn't
leave for a while, so why not take a leisurely walk around your home
town." He reached for an envelope on top of the refrigerator. "Here's
the reading material I mentioned at Pete's. It includes some personal
history and another seminar, a more recent and poignant one. Don't
start reading it until you're on the train, and keep all of this private."

We said goodbye, and I thought about walking the town, but a city park three blocks from his house beckoned more than a town full of memories.

The park was empty and the only noise was light traffic in the distance. I stretched out on a wooden bench and focused on fuzzy contrails and scattered cumulus floating in a breeze I couldn't feel. Two clouds came together, started to fade then broke apart and drifted away. Constant unpredictable change, and down here lies a hyperthymestic with a brain implant usurped by a cell of eccentric telepaths with unimaginable power. Who are these people? Why are they so powerful? And what would they gain by combining my memory with telepathy?

Play it out was Jason's advice — yesterday about Apella, and earlier about Nate. Do I really have a choice? Am I free to bail as Jason, Rose, even Thius, implied? I sat up and watched a brown creeper spiral upward, probing for bugs on a Douglas Fir. A healthy clan of bears where you're going, Dan…likely some interesting people too. George knew all along.

27

Sweet Clair

Boston Cole was checking front-end hoses and wheels on a diesel locomotive when I walked into the rail yard. Using a hand-held device, he reminded me of George recording vitals on a sedated grizzly. "Hang on a minute, young fella," Cole said to me. "Dispatcher wants a repeat on wheel wear." The device beeped three times, and Cole said, "Alll right, dispatch has our data, we're ready to roll soon as she clears us…take a minute to collate so I can tell you about this handy little gadget. It's a transcorder, a simplified version of the vitacorder George Waterbear invented for his bear work. A fine piece of workmanship, it records and transmits precise whole-train diagnostics straight to dispatch."

Cole smiled when the transcorder beeped again. "Alll right," he said, "dispatcher gives us the go-ahead, so you should grab yourself a seat, son, departing in nine minutes." He rapped his knuckles on the locomotive and added, "By the way, this big fella we call Hadron just looks diesel. Fact is, he's all electric except for his shell, and I'm proud to say Precambre International no longer runs diesels. Any smoky engines you see on this line belong to other companies."

I thanked Mr. Cole for the information then climbed into the middle coach and found a private seat in the back. Seconds later a bright female voice came through the overhead speakers, "Hello everyone, I'm Clair, without an e, your host, here to describe highlights of your trip on this gorgeous western Montana day."

Two horn blasts, a grind of wheels and we started to roll. "Watch to the right," said Clair. "You'll see a switcher, the blueish locomotive, coupling a reefer, a refrigerated car, to a row of gondolas. Now sit back and enjoy your own thoughts. If something noteworthy comes up I'm here to bring it to your attention. My future broadcasts will come through your headsets. If you wish to tune in, watch overhead for the blinking green LED. This is Clair signing off." Click.

Back on track, Daniel. Try to meet the host. The honeyed voice may be a ruse to distract you.

Or attract, I thought, and the game goes on.

Clair didn't comment when we passed four tank cars daubed with blue and grey graffiti, and a memory of Jason filled in for her. We were on his steel bikes at a midtown rail crossing waiting for a slow freight to pass. Impressed by a string of graffiti-clad boxcars, he asked if I ever gave any thought to these nocturnal emissions of spray cans and markers. An ancient practice, he said. Think cave paintings, etchings, petroglyphs. It begs for a seminar.

I opened his envelope, pulled out the first page and thought, Oh Man, here we go again, Jason.

History 520 (Political Science 512). Upper level seminar. Spring semester. Discussion of historical and modern politics in a global context. Enrollment by interview with the instructor, Professor Jason Steller. Credits 1-2; Extensive Reading, Field Trips, Student Presentations; No Text; Graded A-F.

The second page was a note to me.

Dan---

    With recruiters and branch campuses in 84 states and provinces in North America and over 80 nations worldwide, Garnet University maintains a diverse and intellectually exceptional student body. I have worked closely with many talented young minds over the years, including the four who signed up for this seminar. For now, let's call them Brooke, Bill, Elena, and Louisa.

Brooke was a pre-law senior from Winnipeg. Bill, a double-major graduate student in math and nano-engineering, and Elena, a master's candidate in life sciences, both from upstate New York. Louisa, from Guatemala City, was a first-year graduate student in cyberscience. She and Elena were teaching assistants, while Bill and Brooke had full scholarships underwritten by Latin American affiliates of Precambre International.

Most of our discussions centered on the history and future of democracy, capitalism, and sustainability. The enclosed transcript excerpts one of our sessions.

I flipped through stapled pages of the seminar then set it aside and put on my headset when Clair's overhead light blinked. "Can't hold my thoughts any longer," she said. "Those of you fortunate enough to have driven this route know the highway has much to offer. Nonetheless, Engineer Cole and I will be surprised if you are not awestruck by our rail trip. We track along the Clark Fork River and at times we run so close to whitewater you might wish for a wet suit and a paddle. Other times you might see us mirrored in a glassy lake. Our first ninety miles or so take us downriver to St. Regis, one of Montana's quaint small towns. From there we take an abrupt turn northeast and cut through a narrow canyon flanked by rock walls and talus slopes up to snow-capped peaks. We'll hug the banks, cross river bridges, and squeeze through a series of short tunnels before merging with another rail line at the tiny village of Paradise. There I will direct your attention to the former site of a Northern Pacific roundhouse as we swing northwest again on a picturesque seventy-five miles to the river delta at Lake Pend Oreille in Idaho. Our final stop is Spokane,

Washington. Okey dokey, that's it for now. I'll let you ride with your own thoughts again. This is Clair your tour guide signing off." Click.

I was glad for a window seat as we rolled west through country I hadn't seen for years…down valley all the way, so different from the route over Evaro Hill and no bow-tied talker or Thius to contend with. I liked the sound of Clair's voice but thought her travelogue could use some spice, maybe some of Jason's ice age stuff. I could almost see him standing in the aisle, saying, Travelers gaze out your windows. We're passing through a road cut with a story to tell. The horizontal lines you see are cuts in rocks that were once mud at the bottom of huge lakes that filled this valley. I say huge lakes plural because there were many that rose and fell, drained and filled — over and over — during the last glacial period. I want you to imagine we are rolling along the bottom of one of those ancient lakes. It was massive, maybe three thousand square miles of water impounded by a gigantic ice dam downstream in what we call Idaho. Visualize that dam melting, collapsing, and cubic miles of water splashing, gushing through this narrow valley. The flood would sweep our train all the way to the Pacific.

Jason liked peppering lectures and seminars with wild stories, and I decided to take a look at what he wanted me to read.

Steller: Good to see everyone again. Let's get to it. Taking off from our last meeting I have a confession. When I was a young student, I argued in a setting like this that communism can be more ecologically sound than democratic capitalism. I no longer put any stock in communism.

Brooke: I can't believe you ever did. A system where everyone's time and products are equal? That's idiotic and against human nature.

Louisa: But communism may not be all bad, just bad the way it's been practiced.

Bill: But it isn't natural and can't survive without

dictators. Communism never was a serious threat to democracy or capitalism.

Brooke: Communism is a joke, a cruel one for countries that adopt it.

Elena: Another joke is an all-or-none attitude. Communism equals evil and capitalism equals good, nothing in between.

Brooke: I'm not saying that, but capitalism does fit human nature.

Elena: Maybe, but that doesn't make it sacred, and there's a difference between unfettered rapacious capitalism and limited capitalism, which could be sustainable.

I stared at the names. Brooke from Manitoba, Bill and Elena from upstate New York, and Louisa from Guatemala.

The overhead light blinked, and Clair began, "Folks, I would be remiss if I didn't tell you this valley once had two rail lines, the Northern Pacific Railway and the Milwaukee Road, mostly on opposite sides of the river. The Milwaukee Road electrified much of its line across Montana and Idaho using hydropower from rivers. The Milwaukee's electric locomotives were a good fit for mountain railroading. Going downhill they generated some of their own power, and they were soot-free, so they didn't fowl the air in tunnels and didn't throw cinders. Back to you now." Click.

I took off my headset, put Jason's notes down and thought about riding the Milwaukee and Northern Pacific rails with Apella. She was always the planner, like one summer day, we were sitting shoulder-to-shoulder on the grass outside Jason's office building. She wore a long white dress. Daniel, she said, It'll be clear and warm Sunday, let's hop a train out to Alberton and tube the Clark Fork down to Cyr Bridge. I hesitated…Yeah, that's a fun stretch of river, but Steller expects my thesis proposal on Wednesday. Lighten up, she said, Jason likes you, ask for more time. I told her I'd already done that twice. She picked a ripe dandelion, blew it at me and laughed, Then bring him along, make it a threesome.

Jason declined when I invited him but wanted to hear more about Apella, her background and future plans. I remember thinking, major professor in loco parentis.

And he's still trying to play that role, and here I am on a tour train reading his class notes.

Louisa: Are we limiting discussion to the combination of democracy and capitalism? I mean, there are other combinations. Most dictators employ some form of capitalism.

Elena: Sure. Capitalism fits dictators. It feeds rich rulers and makes their subjects dependent, kind of like this country sometimes.

Bill: Capitalism and democracy may reflect human nature but they're not sustainable as practiced. Socialism is sort of midway between capitalism and communism. Liberals lean that way, conservatives lean toward unfettered capitalism, tax cuts and rich getting richer, poor getting poorer.

Brooke: Socialism is another dead-end, and I may have to drop this seminar if it devolves to bashing the world's best political system.

Steller: Stay with us, Brooke. We need your perspective. Let's pursue your premise that capitalism fits human nature. Can you project ahead? Say ten years up or down the road?

Brooke: I see capitalism and democracy growing and spreading together. Along with science, they can make people free. If you believe in humanity you have to be glad every time democracy and the free market liberate a country.

Bill: Eloquent, happens a lot, right?

Steller: Hold the sarcasm, Bill, please.

Bill: Sorry, but it's just too simple. I can't give democracy or capitalism that much credit. Maybe historically, but not today. You're free if you live on investments or inheritance? You're free if you can consume everything in any quantity? People actually believe that.

Elena: You're talking about the top tier, Bill.

Bill: Sure, but everyone aspires to it. And what about the guns? If we keep 'em we're free, right?

Elena: Rapacious capitalism married to government, democracy or any other, isn't good for any of us, rich, middle or poor. It's destroying the middle, and the planet's ability to support us.

I was flipping pages trying to decide if I should keep reading when train clatter caught my attention. We rumbled over a bridge, and I thought of forest roads and trails that take off from the river valley. They're still there on the edge of wild with a chance to share a moment with a bear around every curve. I could leave this failed mission, find part-time work and bike those canyons.

Visions of Thius with Alma the Bear on 60-Odd Peak swept through me. Was he reading her mind? And why does Jason choose to remain nontelepathic?

Clair's voice on the overhead cut into my thoughts. "Folks, sorry to say, something's wrong with my LED. We're now braking for a long descent to the St. Regis River then we'll veer northeast through one of the Clark Fork River's most spectacular canyons. The canyon portion of my talk is recorded, so slip your headsets on and listen in if you want to hear about early explorers, folklore, et cetera. This is Clair live, signing off." Click, and I heard Apella.

We now have complete dossiers on Boston Cole and Clair Lissette. Cole studied engineering technology and Lissette on and off biology and history. Both are full-time employees of the Triple Divide Scenic Franchise but with no connection to anyone in the cell we are surveilling. Are you reading Jason's notes?

"Yes and it makes me realize my former enthusiasm for politics was largely due to youthful infatuation with my professor."

Hmmm, she murmured, and I continued reading.

Bill: Maybe democracy is the problem. It doesn't exist in wild Nature, does it?

Elena: Not sure, probably not.

Louisa: Democracy can work for people but has nothing to do with other species or nonhuman Nature. I think that spells trouble.

Steller: Let's pursue that conundrum. Assume government by elected officials dominates the future and ask ourselves, Can elected governments deliver long-term sustainability?

Bill: I think some combination of democracy and capitalism is the only way to go, but you can't keep electing incompetent ideologues and dunderheaded demagogues and expect the world to survive.

Elena: And you can't expect longterm survival with leaders who belittle science and promote harmful industries.

Bill: Man, these discussions bore me. It's just talk. Nobody does anything. Nothing changes. I'm dropping this seminar. I'm tired of talk.

Steller: It's too late to drop, Bill, unless you want an F on your transcript.

Louisa: I think it's all a question of timing. Can democracy deliver positive change before it's too late?

Elena: Timely positive change will require steady, benevolent leaders, visionaries who understand what needs to be done, and have the strength and power to act.

Brooke: So you're saying what? We need dictators?

Elena: The term dictator implies tyranny. I'm saying we need strong, altruistic leaders who don't cater to myopics and wrong-headed naysayers. We need educated leaders who make decisions favoring long-term survival instead of business as usual.

Bill: Aptly stated, but I think it will take a big fast-moving group of leaders with a rare balance of estrogen and testosterone.

Steller: Let's refocus. Think more about limits, restraints that might be pertinent to the future. Perhaps Mother Nature could provide some insight. We are part of Nature, are we not?

Brooke: That's debatable. We're close to breaking free of its yoke.

Bill: Ah, no way. If you're thinking artificial intelligence and earth-saving technology, they give futurologists and script writers something to ruminate, that's about it.

Louisa: You don't have faith in your nanos, Bill?

Bill: I have tons of faith in them. Nanotech is changing the world, for better or worse, depending on how we use it, but artificial intelligence is an oxymoron.

Steller: Let's discuss AI at a later date. For today, let's assume we remain subject to Nature's rules.

Elena: Change is Nature's axiom. Gaia abhors status quo. That's what I call keepin' it real, a whole system running on dynamic, regulated change.

Bill: Humans haven't been regulated since the Bronze Age, and it's only a matter of time before what's left of Nature on this isolated ball of rock cuts us down.

Brooke: Doomsday? No way people are just going to die out.

Elena: We've already survived longer than most species.

Louisa: And isn't that a measure of our resilience? We aren't necessarily ruled by Nature. I mean we might be able to solve problems before it's too late.

Steller: Okay, let's assume Homo sapiens and civilization survive another half century, what do you think life will be like fifty years from now?

Brooke: It won't be the same, and I dread thoughts of artificially intelligent humanoids.

Elena: I would bet on a bottleneck before AI has any effect. Millions, maybe billions, won't make it. Gaia will set the bar. It's just a matter of when.

Bill: You say gay a. I always thought it was guy a.

Elena: Get serious, young man! Without immediate radical change, your children are bound to suffer unimaginable pain.

Bill: I'm not going to procreate, and think about what you just said. Immediate radical change. How many people could handle that?

Brooke: No one in this room. That's for sure.

Louisa: We might have to.

Bill: Gimme-a-break. Elena's talking about the end of just about everything people think they have a right to.

Elena: Yes, and it all has to end soon. A sustainable society would have no war, no power from toxic fuels, no super rich, no more getting fat from eating, no meat, mandatory daily exercise, no nonessential travel. The list goes on.

Bill: Your entitled upbringing shines forth, Elena, and you forgot water. It's insane using fresh water for anything except drinking. Every building will have to be replumbed and no more irrigation.

Louisa: And I don't think you can require daily exercise without imposing limits on work hours.

Bill: So add sustainable employment to the list. Fewer hours per person could provide work for all. And daily exercise becomes part of the job, required and compensated.

Brooke: And that is communistic, which by the way, has had a gross ecological footprint.

Elena: No, we're not talking about communism, but capitalism with upper limits, with wealth and resources spread out. Moderation is the word, always has been.

Louisa: But competition is essential. Without it there's no incentive, no ambition.

Elena: Yes, but having upper limits doesn't preclude that. Ambition shouldn't be hijacked by greed and fame. We need cooperative people, cooperative corporations, private and collaborative.

Steller: Okay, time's getting on. Let's be optimistic and suppose we could effect needed change. What would be your first order of business?

Louisa: Above all, war has to end.

Brooke: Hear! Hear! But you have to be ready to defend.

Bill: Another oxymoron. Defense of tribe, nation, religion, resources. Defense leads to war, plain and simple.

Brooke: You cannot ignore the threat of terrorism.

Bill: How could anyone ignore it? It's big business. Have you checked the price of bombs lately?

Elena: My first order of business would be to weaken the power of dysfunctional governments. I would start by weakening their communication networks and establishing a separate internet that would fast forward while government bureaucrats sit and stare.

Brooke: It's always the government, isn't it? Bring down the government. What would that do? Give us anarchy when we most need good strong leadership. I think we've been saying that people are the problem.

Elena: Too many governments serve themselves and corporations, not people, mostly the big greedy corporations that got us in this trap and are keeping us in it.

Louisa: So, Elena, you'd be for antigovernment cyberwar?

Brooke: You guys are really getting carried away.

Bill: Yeah, back to Earth.

Steller: And we're out of time. For next week, oral presentations will precede discussion. Your topic, How to persuade a critical mass of people to effect essential change.

28

Piano Man

The reason Jason wanted me to read his seminar notes was crystal clear. It was the students, his potential recruits — Brooke the lawyer, Louisa the cyberscientist, and two budding radicals, Bill and Elena. Bill could have been Nate or Thius or me mouthing off a lifetime ago. Elena was a clear match for Sula.

Three quick whistles from the engine swept Jason's world out the window. "Bighorns on the cliff — left side!" shouted Clair. "Don't miss them!" Cameras clicked, and I looked just in time to watch a big ram's effortless climb up a sheer rock wall. "A lucky sight," added Clair. "It's rare to see an Ovis canadensis on this stretch of the river. Next up are two short tunnels. If you want to miss them, close your eyes right NOW and count to sixty."

"Awesome," said a teenager three rows back, and Clair signed off with, "That's it everyone. You can relax now, probably no more surprises, just ten smooth miles to Paradise." Click.

I stretched my legs under the seat in front of me and turned back to Jason's notes.

Dan, Did any of the students in the seminar seem familiar? Elena aka Sula Millen was only two months away from completing a double-major master's in political science and biology. You have also met Louisa aka Nancy Denton, who whipped through her master's in a year then took on a PhD in computer engineering with a colleague of mine at Idaho State. Feisty Bill, a world traveler now, took three seminars with me and added a minor in political science to his doctorate. Brooke became a defense attorney in Seattle, works mostly for small companies, tries to avoid the big ones. Like you, she strives for political neutrality and is not a joiner.

Dan, I regret our distance over the years. I was a novice professor when you arrived at Garnet, and far too inexperienced to properly mentor a graduate student. I was still finding my own way while you were here, and when you completed your degree you were eager to start a teaching job and pursue your new-found interest in off-road biking.

Things might have been different if you had accompanied me to a workshop in Texas that second summer. One of my fondest memories is sipping a late-night bourbon in an Austin piano bar, listening, adding a comment here and there to a discussion the dapper pianist was having with two full-bearded Beat guys. It was crowded and noisy, and I was leaning over trying to hear an opinion of Alan Watts's thoughts on Beat Zen when the pianist grabbed his sheet music, and five beefy clean-cuts pushed into our backsides. The scene was stereotype mid '60s hinterland America. The clean-cuts hoisted the pianist off his chair and carried four of us out the door. The two Beats headed to another bar, while the pianist and I opted for a walk along Texas's Colorado River, and thus began my close friendship with Will McClun.

Dan, Imagine my surprise two months later when Will and Rosey told me Garnet University was home to one of many recruiting and research centers in

North America chartered by the Ursavus organization. There were never any expectations, no pressure to join Ursavus. I sought membership on my own volition, and nothing could have suited me more. Today, Garnet and its branches are nodes in a vast network of private colleges, universities and research centers underwritten by Ursavus, all heavily staffed with recruiters like me.

When I joined, Ursavus was already fully established with multiple contingents on every continent. The organization has had moles in virtually all government agencies since the 1940s. It was literally built into the Internet, embedded in its central nodes as essential yet diffuse and undetectable components of servers and relays. Even before Ursavus was quantized, the organization had full access to every operating system and could manipulate federal, state, provincial, any and all data banks. No amount of government or private surveillance has ever provided more than vague impressions of our organization, its breadth and momentum. For instance, my reputation, leftwing website and free-wheeling webinars have kept me on federal watchlists for decades, but our software has never failed to deflect active investigation.

Dan, I trust this brief overview will lend credence to my telling you the end of the disastrous era of war and consumption is foreseeable. Hopefully, the world we all abuse will give us enough time to quietly and nonviolently turn things around.

See you soon. Having you with us will be an enhancement in itself.

Always your friend,
Jason

P.S. I am certain I do not need to say shred or burn this packet at your first opportunity. All of this remains covert, as does the core of Ursavus herself, until time is apropos.

    I took care securing the envelope in my bag, and when Clair announced an unexpected wait on a siding I decided I'd had enough of the tour train. Apella and company might protest, but that didn't matter now. I thanked Boston Cole for a great ride, asked him to give Clair my best, and said I was ready to try my luck on the nearby highway. He volunteered to drop me below Rose's if I stayed on, but I knew I needed some time to myself before another weighty evening in Cedarville.

29

Hitching a Ride

A two-lane highway was a short walk from the siding, and less than a mile down the road a senior looking fellow in a red two-seater pickup pulled next to me and shut off his engine. I caught a whiff of cannabis-variety grass as he lowered the passenger window and began reciting rules for hitchhikers. "No names, mister, don't wanna know yerz and don't ask me mine."

I threw my bag in the back then raised both hands and froze as he left-handed a stainless revolver from under the seat. "No trouble, sir," I said. "That's a fine .357."

Apella gasped.

"Yeah," he said. "And I'm real good with it. Git in," and he leaned over to unlock the door.

I hesitated, then climbed in as he started the engine. "Yuh know guns, huh? Yuh hunt?" he asked.

"Haven't for years, sir. Lost the urge in my forties, missed it for a while but couldn't get it back."

He put the gun away, started driving and acted like he didn't hear me when I said, "Everything's cool." Then after several miles of uneasy silence, he asked why I was walking the two-laner. I told him I was on a tour train from Missoula…had a fine engineer named Boston Cole and a cheery host named Clair but I kinda got tired of it. "Any chance you're going near Cedarville, sir?" I asked. "I'm staying with friends on the south side of town."

He lightened up. "Cedarville, huh? I know everbuddy there. Used to hunt bear in their woods every spring and fall, but can't stand the thought of it now. Who yuh stayin' with?"

"Rosemary McClun."

"And how did yuh end up at her place?"

"I rode in on a freight with her son Thius."

"Okay, guess I picked up the right guy, had to check with my own setta questions. Ms. Rose and Will, Thius. We been friends ferever."

I asked how they met, and he answered in a happy clip, "Funny how things work out. I gotta farm on the North Idaho prairie, used to grow grass seed...love watchin' tall grass blow in the wind. People kept tryin' to shut me down cause I had to burn off fields in the summer. I always picked a time when the smoke would blow over here to Montana, but lawsuits and naggin' never let up. I was ready to quit when the first housin' boom hit me in the face, and taxes went through the roof. That's about when Will and Ms. Rose stopped by with a plan that would save me and my farm. They floated me a low-interest loan to grow native grass instead of lawn grass, and instead of burnin' I cut once or twice a year and sold bales to locals for biofuel...no irrigation, minimal fertilizer and decent returns. I got tight with Will, Ms. Rose and Thius, and one day they came to me with a pile a cash to build an indoor farm on my property, three high-rise state-a-the-art facilities. We supply fruits, vegtables, eggs and a few other surprises year-round with minimal transport cost. Sales're innernashnal but mostly western hemisphere."

He grabbed a phone similar to Jason's from one of four velvet pouches on his dash and said, "I keep records of everthing with this wherever I go. And you probly recognize where we are now."

He stopped next to Thius's coyote meadow and said, "One mornin' here with Will McClun, we counted fifty-six elk out there in the dawn mist. Dark ghosts he called 'em. I miss Will...everbuddy does. A quiet man he was, thoughtful, and humble. You'd never think he played that organ all over the world. You don't mind walkin' from here, do yuh? I don't wanna cause Ms. Rose to have another mouth to feed."

I invited him to join us. "Rose and Thius are having neighbors over for a cookout. I'm sure there will be plenty of food."

"Can't do it. Already late gittin' home, but give Rose and Thius my regards, would yuh?"

"Sure, who should I say?"

"Gibby. Gibson Lentele. Yerz?"

"Dan Oyente."

"Enjoyed yer compny, Dan."

"You too, good company."

"Sit for another minute, Dan, would yuh…jis wanna say sorry I hauled out the firearm, but yuh never know, so I carry a gun to bluff. It'd probly be liebility if I picked up serious trouble."

"You would actually use it?"

"I think about that whenever I shoot. I'm a reglur at our gun range, like bein' there with Ms. Rose, but I turned nonviolent when huntin' and fishin' got old. Like you said, with some things, once yuh quit, it changes yer whole attitude." He reached over and gave me a firm hand shake. "Got a feelin' I'll see you again, Dan Oyente."

No need for more on the gun-toting farmer. We have years of documentation on Gibson Lentele and his enterprise. We will expect a detailed report on the neighbors Rose said would be there for dinner.

There were no dinner guests and Thius wasn't grilling sweet potatoes and boletes. When I walked in, he and Rose were sitting at the kitchen table, which was set for three. "Welcome home, Dan," said Rose. "It's just the three of us after all, and Gibby Lentele called after he dropped you off, told us how much he enjoyed your company. Gibby's one of our favorite people, and his story goes well with dinner. Have a seat, dear."

"Keepin' it simple tonight, Oyente," said Thius, passing me a plate of dolmas, olives and feta cheese. "I'm gunna tell you about my friend Gibb…known him since I was a kid, met him late afternoon on a wet day in April. I was on my prototype Stingray up Larch Creek. Gibb was drivin' real slow on the wrong side of the road, and I figured he was lookin' for tracks in the ditch. He pulled up in front of me, asked if I'd seen any bears. His truck had Idaho plates, so I asked why he needed to hunt my friends in Montana if he lives over there. He started to laugh and asked how many bear friends I had. I told him too many to count, and one named Pes albus saved my life. He asked me what Pes looked like so he wouldn't shoot him, and that's about when I started likin' Gibb. I told him the only way he could be sure about not shooting Pes was to stop hunting bears, and if he did, I'd invite him to dinner, told him my mom's a great cook."

Thius plopped an olive in his mouth, and Rose continued the story. "That very evening Thius brought Gibby home, and William and I liked him immediately. We were up so late talking that he stayed over. The next morning Thius beat us to the breakfast table, couldn't wait to see Gibby."

Thius chuckled. "Yeah, I told Gibb I'd be his guide for two days if he'd leave his guns with my mom and dad. He agreed and we spent six days together in the mountains. George was with us for two of 'em, checkin' on a bear he'd moved from Yellowstone. We saw her, plus three yearlings new to George and me. Gibb's tracking skills were iffy, but he's real smart and learned fast from George, gained a rock-solid respect for bears, and he quit all hunting a year later."

Rose said, "Dan, the answer to your question is Yes, Gibson Lentele is a longtime member of Ursavus. His farm feeds thousands and has been a model for the world since its first year in production. You must see it very soon. Now, let's adjourn to the living room. Talking about Gibson makes me want to listen to an album he gave me the last time he visited."

Thius's and Rose's stories continue to amuse but consider these facts. The two outbuildings on Mr. Lentele's farm are in disrepair, his net income hovers at break-even, and he may have hunted bears in Montana but never possessed a license to do so.

30

The Messenger

Apella's dismissive comments about Gibby Lentele were wrong, I was sure. They didn't fit my impressions of him, and after listening to Rose and Thius talk about Gibby, I was curious about the kind of music he gave Rose.

Thius told me to sit close in front of the speakers and listen up. Rose put Gibby's album on the turntable and said, "I've always been very impressed with Lisa Gerrard, Dan. Have you heard her sing?"

I said No, and Thius gave me a hard stare. "Ms. Gerrard speaks her own language, bike man — makes you believe you're in another world."

He cranked up the volume, and the room did feel otherworldly until a loud double knock broke the spell. Rose rushed to the door, and Walter Smyth stepped in, pale and unsteady. Thius jumped to his feet and so did I.

"Walter, are you all right?" Rose asked and reached out to hold his arm. "What's happened?"

"Ma'am, the sheriff's office sent me to inform you Andy Denton died about two hours ago. An investigation is in progress."

"No! What do you mean, Walter? This can't be true. Come in, come in....let me take your things. Sit by the fire." He slumped in a chair, put his head in his hands. "Well ma'am, you're aware of the problems they've had at Precambre's wind farm up Liberty Creek?"

Thius stepped close to him. "Yeah — coupla broken windows, gate hinges, crap like that. What's that have to do with Denton?"

Walter moaned, "There's more to it. Contractors working on road cuts reported some dynamite missing and said they saw a guy sneaking around. They described him as tall and skinny with a gimp. Everybody knows Andy's been limping since he fell up Meadow Creek, so Pright and Crispin went to his cabin to talk with him. Sheriff Pright stayed in the car, Crispin knocked on Andy's door. Andy yanked it open, turned fast and reached for a gun. Crispin already had his gun in hand and shot Andy in the chest. Sula and Erik heard the shot and came running but Andy was gone before they got there."

Rose threw up her hands and shouted, "Oh, that arrogant fool KILLED Andrew!"

Thius fired a question at Walter. "They find any dynamite at Denton's cabin?"

Walter answered, "Crispin told me they found four sticks."

"Crispin, huh, don't believe it," Thius scoffed.

Rose paced in front of the fireplace, held her amber pendant and spoke in a low monotone. "It's nonsense, all of it. Andrew Denton would never stoop to stealing, vandalism or gunplay no matter how much he loathed Precambre and the turbines. I'll get the truth from Oly Pright, and this never would have happened if we had let Andrew in."

She held Walter's arm again, and he perked up as she started making plans. "You should stay here with Dan," she said. "You two can talk it out. Thius and I will see how Sula and Erik are doing, probably be up most of the night with them, and Sula should be the one to call Nancy. We'll keep Andrew's ceremony simple, have it day after tomorrow out by the aspens he planted near his cabin. Jason will want to be here. I'll arrange for him to come in on the train that morning. Dan, you and I will be there to meet him, and he'll stay with us a night…and since William can't attend, I would like for you to wear his concert blazer. You'll find it in the cedar chest at the back of the closet. We'll leave you in Walter's hands now."

Rose is certainly the take-charge organizer, and these are sad events. But good you have this opportunity to probe Mr. Smyth. We'll have you on speaker. Important that you attend Mr. Denton's service.

As soon as Rose and Thius left, Walter told me to have a seat and began talking about how much they all liked Andy, how bright he was, how hard his life had been, and how bad everyone felt about him not being recruited by Ursavus. "A most regrettable situation," Walter asserted, then leaned forward in his chair and made sure he had my attention. "Dan, you probably realized when you were around Andy, why he wasn't a member of Ursavus, and I know you're hesitant, but you do not want to end up like him and miss a once-in-a-lifetime opportunity."

He got up, went to the piano and played something I'd heard my dad practice on the cello — the ground bass of Bach's Passacaglia — and Walter didn't miss a note. I stood next to him and thought, Damn, how can this be? Another Cedarville musician — the mild-mannered shopkeeper playing like a pro. He improvised a seamless transition to the final flourish, played it well and said, "Like you, Dan, I had gifted teachers at an early age, and later on, I received expert instructions from my friend William McClun."

"Are you telling me you're a member of Ursavus, Walter?"

"Yes indeed I am a full member of Ursavus. My daughter Rachel and I moved here from another facility a long way off, and we have been close to the McClun family for many years."

"But the way you talked in your store, Walter, I mean, how does all that work? Is Ursavus that good for you? Obviously, I'm not where everyone thinks I should be."

"Ursavus is that good for me, unequivocally, and for Rachel. I thoroughly enjoy working in the store, helping with local music events, and I also function as Ursavus E's main liaison with Precambre's space program. Join us, Dan, and you will gain many healthy years and work with some of the best minds on this planet. The day you join, you'll regret the time you wasted trying to decide."

He pulled a phone like Jason's from his shirt pocket, set it on the coffee table and stretched out on the sofa. "A very busy day coming up. Must get some rest," he said.

I stepped to a window, looked back at Walter and thought, So you've been reading my mind all this time.

"Correct," he said, "and I believe the dogs need their late-night outing. I must obtain a little shuteye."

I went out with Max and Agnes, waited while they snuffed around in the moonlight, and asked Apella what she thought of Walter Smyth now.

Obviously, Mr. Smyth is a cell member, but likely an innocuous peripheral. Interesting what he told you about Andy Denton and disappointing he didn't mention his daughter Rachel. She may have a central role. We depend on you to get more.

So, she just confirmed she is not receiving accurate information from my implant and the mission and the implant pose no threat to Ursavus. Walter spoke freely because he knows Ursavus is tuned into the implant and filtering its transmissions.

Daniel, go outside and breathe, breathe some fresh evening air.

Whew, guess again, Apella. I'm already outside, it's 2:46 in the morning, and I'm done for the night.

31

Bunchberries

When I went downstairs the next morning, Walter was gone, and the house felt empty. A note from Rose read, You needed the sleep, dear boy, and a little more time to yourself would be good. That's what William's Place is for. Try not to be too pensive about Andy and enjoy your day, I'll be home late so please don't wait up. Jason's train arrives tomorrow at 0900.

I mumbled, "Okay thanks, Rose, and who am I scheduled to meet at William's Place?"

I had a quick cup of coffee and headed down to the river. Someone, maybe Thius, had cleared brush along the side path to William's Place, or was it William himself?

A steady breeze carried scents of pine and river as I sat at the old table. William McClun alias Liam Yrisse, a charter member of Ursavus. Would he meet me here? Would he weigh in on my recruitment? How would he feel if I told him Rose wanted me to wear his concert blazer to Andy's ceremony? And what would the concert organist turned teacher have to say about Andy Denton? I flattened my hands on the weathered wood and asked out loud, "What was Cedarville like for Andy, the blustery veteran clinging to life among friends and foes? Why would he threaten Deputy Crispin — and why was the deputy so eager to shoot?"

This is a sidetrack, a local vendetta. Crispin is rabidly antienvironmental. He lost control with Andy like a wild dog in a chase. Stay on the main. Nathaniel for you, the real subversives for us.

Something made me turn around, and there was Sula only a step away. White letters on her green cap spelled SAV US. "Great place, isn't it, Dan?" she said. "William chose well. You did say to call you Dan, didn't you?"

"Yes, Dan is fine. Where did you come from, Sula? You're quiet as a cougar."

She slid close on the bench and asked if I'd ever hugged a tree.

I didn't feel like joking. "No, never tried hugging a tree, Sula."

"You should. It can make you feel part of something really strong. Come down here on a windy day you'll be amazed how much these big ponderosas can sway. Push into one and hold tight, you'll feel the strain and pull from way down in the roots."

I tried for more about Andy, asked if she really believed he pulled a gun on the deputy.

She set her elbows on the table and said, "Andy liked to talk tough, but he was a total pacifist. He despised what he did in Vietnam, and the only weapon he owned was a .22 revolver his dad gave him. I know he didn't pull that .22 on Crispin because it's locked in our gun cabinet. Andy gave it to Erik and me for safekeeping and refused a key to the cabinet."

"So you're saying Andy was unarmed when Crispin shot him? You're sure he didn't have another gun?"

"I'm positive he didn't, and Sheriff Pright was there. He called Erik and me last night, told us Andy had no gun and Crispin shot to kill."

She closed her eyes and winced. "Ohh spirits, please tell me, Why is there so much evil on this planet? My friend is dead…gone!"

I touched the labradorite inset on my watch and thought about Apella saying Crispin was like a wild dog in a chase.

Sula squeezed her hands together and murmured, "I'm sorry, but I know the next time I see Crispin, he will feel remorse for what he did and won't be capable of shooting anyone or anything ever again."

What is she talking about? Does Ursavus alter minds and behavior?

Sula moved closer, gave me a cold stare and said, "It's not as scary as it sounds. The scary thing is the human potential for violence, what some of us call the anxious little predator mentality." She plucked a lichen from the edge of the table, held it close to her face and mused, "Ohh, the deadly poison this pretty little organism produces. When I found out about it I was afraid of my own thoughts and had nightmares and daydreams where I was stockpiling poisons to defend myself."

You were trained on how to play along with this sort of nonsense.

Thinking, Anxious little predator I'm not, I asked Sula if she can read whatever appears in my mind. "Yes siree," she said, "and you need to realize Ursavus is entirely nonviolent. We believe that every violent thought has potential. When I was ready to join, the council recommended a corrective enhancement and I agreed. If you choose to join Ursavus, would you accept enhancement to ensure pacifism? It would include a subtle ability to defend yourself, by dissuasion, not violence."

"Uh, no I don't think so, Sula. I wouldn't choose to be pacified. Futurist changes like telepathy, longevity, body strengthening — can't deny they're tempting. But corrective enhancement to ensure pacifism — that sounds ominous, like brain surgery that dampens a person's spirit, and it doesn't make me want to join your organization."

You must stay with the plan, Daniel.

Sula reached for my hand and said, "I think I understand your concerns, but do any of us seem pacified in the way you describe?"

"No, definitely not," I said.

"Good, and let's take a walk. You first, and no need for you to talk. Let me learn from your thoughts while I share more about Ursavus, how I got here and everything."

A chill gust rustled dry leaves along the trail, Sula tracked close and said, "My life with Ursavus was set in motion when I was conceived, but I knew nothing about that until I met Thius. I was a student at the University of Delaware and my war wounds were still healing. My foster parents, the Rochsfelds, were long gone and I felt really good, free and on my own — alone but not lonely, maybe like you, Dan."

She skipped in front of me, walked backwards and kept talking. "The Rochsfelds were okay until I learned to think for myself," she said. "It wasn't just me though, they had their own issues, but anyway,

I got VA support and signed up for college majoring in a mix of political science and real science. My sophomore year I took vertebrate evolution, and that's when I'd see this intriguing older man in the library. I felt drawn to him, and one day I noticed him reading "Black Bear: The Spirit of Wilderness," it's a book by Barbara Ford."

"The older guy you're talking about — Thius, right?"

She kept walking backwards. "Yes siree, and we became instant friends. He was full of stories about animals, made the vertebrate course come alive for me. Oh, Dan, those times were so much fun, my thoughts are just bubbling out. Can you imagine growing up out here when Thius did? Most of these forests were intact, molded by wild Nature, fire and all. I had to experience it firsthand."

She turned around, stopped under a towering ponderosa pine. "One of the lucky survivors of the big fires and saved by the river," she said. "Thius calls her AM for Alpha Matriarch. We have time, Dan. Let's sit with AM for a little bit. She'll help with questions I know you have about Thius and me. Just let your thoughts have their silent way."

Okay, back when you were getting to know Thius, did he bring up the name Eleva Sterling?

"Oh yes siree, he did. He let me know right away that he agreed with her politics and admired her fortitude. He even gave me a ticket to a screening of a documentary on her life. I left after finals that spring, took a train west, and watched the film at a small theatre in Minneapolis, and gosh, Eleva was wonderful. I got back on the train, took it all the way to Glacier Park then Whitefish where I rented a cabin for the summer. What a time that was…biking, kayaking, rock climbing, other fun things. On the fourth of July I went to Missoula to see another Eleva documentary. It was more detailed and I really took in what she had to say…thought about her courage and commitment. I was surprised to see Thius in the audience, and after the film he pulled me out of the crowd, took me to a coffee house and introduced me to a close friend of his sitting alone in a corner booth. He introduced her as Rachel Smyth, and it felt kind of spooky at the time that I just believed him when he said she used to be Eleva Sterling. I saw no resemblance whatsoever, and I listened hard when he and Rachel started sharing things about George, Rose and others in Cedarville. Three days later I enrolled in life science at Garnet University, finished my bachelor's in two semesters and started graduate research on wolverines right here in these mountains that summer. I loved being a teaching assistant in freshman bio labs and got to attend some of Jason Steller's poli-sci seminars. Living with Rose, then Erik, working with them and George, joining Ursavus, being close to Thius and Rachel, all of it…my life became better than my best dreams."

But how did you deal with Ursavus destroying the Rochsfelds?

She picked up a handful of pine needles, rolled them between her palms and pursed her lips at me. "It wasn't like that at all. The Rochsfelds self-destructed. Did Thius say he was involved?"

Not in so many words but he described your situation and told me about his job in Ursavus.

"Gosh, he just can't shake the blame. My abusive foster parents imploded rather than face prison sentences. Thius was not involved, and Ursavus didn't go after them because of me."

I frowned and asked her to explain.

She looked straight at me and said, "I'll put it this way, Dan. I felt love for Thius and Rachel when I first met them, and I knew on some level before they told me — they're my real parents. And I know you didn't suspect."

"Never! Why would I? And no wonder Thius feels guilt, and probably your mother too. They just dropped you on the Rochsfelds when you were an infant, and the Rochsfelds raised you!"

"No siree, Mr. Oyente, your assumptions are way off. Thius and Rachel didn't want to give me up. They had to. I was three weeks old, and they were on the run, needed to disappear. Ursavus fixed public records to hide my identity and after a vetting process they placed me with the Rochsfelds. It was in my genes to eventually break away from the upper crust lifestyle and Ursavus knew it. Thius had nothing to do with the Rochsfelds. Sure, at first I had some misplaced anger, but it didn't take long for love to win out, and I welcomed the pacifism enhancement along with a complete makeover when the membership council deemed it necessary. We couldn't let anyone see me as Heather Rochsfeld."

I held back a day's worth of questions and thought about make-overs — William, Thius, Eleva, now Sula. How much did they change?

Sula bounced up, offered me a hand and said, "I am genetically and phenotypically very different from Heather Rochsfeld. No one outside Ursavus could possibly put us together."

A sample of her hair could corroborate or more likely refute this obvious fairy tale. Obtain asap and send to George Waterbear for analysis.

Man, Apella's adrift, still thinks George is on her side? Jason said Ursavus would protect her but does he know for sure? If the government people discover the truth, Apella could become their scapegoat for the failed mission...have to find a way to protect her.

Sula tightened her shoe laces, didn't respond to my thoughts. "Let's jog the rest of the way," she said. "I promised Erik I'd be home about now."

I watched her ponytail whip back and forth. No way I'm getting a sample.

"Good sense of humor," Sula said over her shoulder. "And FYI the only record of Heather Rochsfeld's DNA is tucked away in Ursavus archives."

She stopped at a fork in the trail, knelt down and ran her fingers over a cluster of bunchberries, then looked up at me. "I knew your son," she said with a worried look. "We rode mountain bikes togeth-er two summers, and I thought about telling you when we were up Larch Creek, but the time wasn't right, it still isn't, but I can't keep this from you any longer. The truth is Nate never was in a war, never even enlisted. He died in a bike crash up Woody's Gulch. We were racing and I cut too close around him on a curve. He lost control of his bike and went off a rocky cliff — fell a hundred feet. It was all my fault."

I held my breath, clenched my fists.

This is nonsense. Stay calm.

Sula stood up slowly and said, "Sorry, there's more but it has to come later."

All I could think was, Crazy! Nate was never here. Apella has it right this time.

Sula stared in my eyes. "You don't believe me, do you, Dan? You're thinking Nate was never here. But the truth is everyone here knew him, wished for him to join, and I believe he would have if he hadn't gone off that cliff."

She crossed her arms, held them tight around her waist. "You think I would lie about Nate's death? He was my friend, and I can't lie about anything. I was there…saw his life slip away on those rocks, and no enhancement could stop me from feeling sad and responsible."

"What on Earth is this about, Sula?! True or not, what you've said will stay with me forever."

"Sorry, and there is much more. The whole story is very complex, and you will hear it from others later. I should not have told you any of it, and you have to promise you won't even think about it when someone's around."

"How could I possibly hide my thoughts from telepaths?"

"It would be simple if you were enhanced, but you can still do it. You just need a mental switch, a trigger that immediately clears your mind or fills it with compelling memories that shut out thoughts of Nate's death. Raven helps, and all you have to do is look around… like right here, the bunchberries next to the trail. The leaves, white bracts, tiny flowers, and red berries in late summer. They're miniature dogwoods, and I really must go home now. I'll see you at Andy's ceremony tomorrow."

Sula skipped away, disappeared down the trail, and I thought, she's kind of a scatterbrain but maybe that's just for show. Apella broke into my thoughts.

Daniel, I remember calling those beautiful plants dwarf dogwoods when we first saw them flowering. Sula's word miniature is much better.

"Apella — you sound like the old days again and my mind just went back forty-one years to an ancient grove of cedars west of Lolo Pass, near the Lochsa River. Where are you?"

She didn't answer, and I took my time walking back to the house. The mission is a bust and Apella doesn't seem to have a clue. Do I tell her? Would that put her in danger? Or does Ursavus block anything I say that could compromise her?

I thought about Sula's idea of a mental switch. Nothing special really. I often trigger memories to clear my mind. So to foil a telepath I just replay a strong memory? Daydream? Can't be that simple. Tomorrow at Andy Denton's ceremony…have to keep my mind off Nate.

32

Semper Fi

Rose and I were waiting near the track below her house when Jason's train nosed around the bend. "Precision scheduling brings him to us at 0900 on the button," Rose said proudly, "and it's always a thrill to see Steam Shiela. She's pulling a work train today, eighteen cars full of new ties and ballast going west to a track crew that will be ready to start work after lunch."

Jason was in the engine cab with Boston Cole, and after a smooth stop Jason stepped out the door, dusted off his tweed jacket, bowed and climbed down. Ever the showman.

Cole rang his engine bell and pulled away as Jason rushed to embrace Rose. "Live forever will you, Rosey!" he exclaimed, and she wrapped both arms around him, kissed his cheek and said, "We never see enough of you, my dear, you belong here with us, and my oh my, I will enjoy a dinner with you, Thius and Dan...so much to talk about."

And so much like lovers, I thought, but no, probably not.

"We should get going," said Rose. "I'm sure everyone else is already up at Andrew's cabin."

Jason stepped back, "Okay, but first let me take a look at you, Rosey, don't think I've seen this outfit. Lilac over your smooth skin — radiance personified."

She gave him a playful push toward the path and said the truck was parked in the lane and ready, we'll just hop in and go. He led the

206

way, paced it just right, and I had to stifle a laugh when he hustled to the driver side of the truck, opened the door for Rose then ran around and jumped in ahead of me. I expected him to strike up a conversation, but he started flipping through Rose's CD case, kept at it until Rose turned left out of her lane and said, "You should share with Dan what you are thinking about, Jason."

"Absolutely. Sorry," he said. "Being around telepaths, I tend not to talk much. I was thinking that everyone who really knew Andy recognized his many fine qualities, but despite it all, his persistent battle with Precambre made him an unlikely candidate for Ursavus. In the long run, all my recruiting efforts failed. I could never persuade the Ursavan Council that the young man's potential would overshadow any negative impact he might have on the organization."

Jason's ability to play both sides is truly remarkable. Until this mission we were unaware of his recruiting efforts. This is a masterfully ingenious ploy to gain the cell's trust.

I wanted to yell, Damn it, Apella, Jason and George are not on your side. The mission is over, out of control. And of course Rose caught it all, but she didn't react, and Jason filled the air with details of Andy's depression and various benefits and side effects of St. John's Wort and Gingko biloba. We were crossing the river when Rose patted him on the knee and said, "It's a new and beautiful blue-sky day, dear. We should keep it positive for Andrew's sake. Find the CSN disc and play Number 16, would you? It's one of Andrew's favorites, and Dan's as well, I believe."

She was right. It was a Crosby, Stills and Nash gem, and mingled with its 'Carry On' refrain I could hear Apella the morning after a concert — Daniel, those three are angels, perfect voices from somewhere else, out beyond. Please let them stay with us forever.

We were a mile south on the West Valley Road when the song ended, and I wanted more, but Jason pulled out the CD and said, "So, Dan, these westside canyons, Hemlock Draw, Woody's Gulch, Forest Road 2709, they must feel familiar to you now. Hemlock is my favorite. We should schedule a ride in that canyon."

Andy's chant and rants from the snowshoe day rang from memory when Rose turned onto the Meadow Creek Road. Two miles up she drove south on a narrow lane and stopped at a grassy pullout. "Here we are," she said. "Four vehicles, so everyone made it, and they left us a space." She parked next to Sheriff Pright's flatbed, and Jason filled me in on demographics as we got out of the truck. "Dan, you've met Oly and Aurora Pright. They've made their home in the county seat — that's Thompson Falls — since Oly was elected sheriff, but the Prights also owned a spacious cabin on twenty acres at the end of this lane. Sula and Erik rented that cabin for years then bought it and the twenty, gave Andy five acres and helped him build his cabin. A short lane to Andy's cuts off to the right just ahead."

Rose wrapped a shawl around her shoulders, took my arm then Jason's. "A quiet day, scarcely a leaf stirring," she said, "just right for a walk with two friends…and Andrew. Dan, you are very handsome in my husband's sparkling recital attire, and please don't worry about your thoughts out here. Everyone's attention will be on the ceremony."

Andy's cabin was a compact log kit nestled in high grass with tools and farm implements scattered about. Rose squeezed my arm when we walked by a rusty wheelbarrow brimming with rocks and driftwood. "Raw materials that speak to Andrew's soft, creative side," she said, "and you will be interested, Dan, Andrew built a lovely pebble garden off his rear porch. That's where we're having the ceremony. There will be twelve of us. Everyone else is already out there."

The others didn't seem to notice when we joined them. At the far end of the pebble garden, Sheriff Pright was talking quietly with three Marines. His khaki uniform with a badge and no sidearm contrasted sharply with their dress blues and hand-polished rifles. Deputy Crispin was standing off to one side, alone and holsterless, staring at the ground, hands in his overall pockets.

Thius, Sula and Erik were lined up next to a rough-hewn picnic table. They wore crisp white outfits and were focused on a centerpiece, a wooden urn, probably river birch turned on a lathe, maybe by

Andy himself. Rose and I stood opposite them while Jason walked to one end of the table, Pright to the other.

Jason adjusted his tie, cleared his throat to get everyone's attention and began, "A few words from Walter Whitman seem appropriate here. 'A child said, What is the grass? Fetching it to me with full hands. How could I answer the child? I do not know what it is any more than he.'"

Jason glanced my way when I frowned at his choice of verse, then continued in a more commanding tone. "Andy loved this Emerson quote. 'Go, blindworm, go. Behold the famous States harrying Mexico with rifle and knife.'"

I saw no sadness in the professor's face, nor did Rose show any when it was her turn to speak. Smiling slightly, she stroked her amber and said, "Andrew Denton once gave me instructions for this day, should it ever come. He told me to keep it simple and positive, outdoor whatever the weather, and tell the people in one sentence what you think of me. So I chose this. I believe Andrew Denton embraced nonviolence as only a veteran could, and he was innocent to the end."

Next up, Sula lit a candle and held it toward a distant peak. "Andy," she murmured, "you were a friend for all my years here. You loved this valley, these forests and hills, and all the life in them. You understood the value of community and local economies. Your spirit remains a strong opponent of waste and unrestricted growth." She gazed up at the sky and let a breeze blow out her candle. "Our community has lost a special friend," she said.

Thius nodded toward Sula, then spoke in a somber tone I hadn't heard before. "Andy and I were not close friends. He was a Marine. I went to Canada. We never transcended that, rarely had a friendly talk or argument. We both grew up around here, had much in common, but time got away. Andy Denton was a fearless fighter who returned from war sworn to reject violence. I will miss him."

Everyone then turned to Erik. He smiled at Sula, held out a small statue of a bear and said, "Andy was a life-long sculptor, a miniaturist who liked working with local materials and produced figures noted for their fine detail and natural appearance. Antler was his favorite medium, and each piece he worked had a story. He gave this bear to Sula and me the day he moved into his cabin. He carved it from a mule-deer antler Sula found in a snowdrift that buried Andy's wheelbarrow the winter before. I always wanted to be closer to Andy. Perhaps another chance will come around."

After a silent moment Rose stepped close to the Marines and said, "Andrew requested that the customary flag presentation and playing of taps be omitted from his ceremony, but he always took pride in the rifle salute."

The Marines braced up, fired three volleys, and Rose waited for the last echo to fade, then carried Andy's urn to the aspen grove, ran her free hand over a low branch and said, "Andrew was very proud of this clone, proud that all these trees grew from a single root he planted the very day he started building here." She turned, scattered his ashes at the base of a tree and whispered, "Your time is nigh at last, dear distant one."

I thought, What a strange way to put it, and she gave me a quick look, set the urn on a rock beneath the trees and said, "Time now for the spirits to do as they wish, and I can hear Andrew declaring, For Lucifer's sake and mine, don't let this be a solemn event."

Sula took the hint, grabbed Erik's hand, and they sprinted into the cabin. Rose, Jason, and Thius started talking with Sheriff Pright and the Marines. I tried for a few words with Deputy Crispin. He thanked me for stopping by and looked relieved when Sula and Erik appeared on the porch with two pitchers of sun tea and a tray full of muffins. Sula blew on a string of small bells hanging from the soffit and the mood changed abruptly, talk got louder, the tea and muffins were a hit. Even Crispin smiled, and I tried not to think about what Sula said would happen to him. The group was starting to disperse when I overheard Sheriff Pright say to Rose, "Andy left all his belongings to Sula and Erik except his yellow pickup. It goes to one of Andy's Ursavi friends, in care of Ms. McClun. Okay with you, Rose?"

"Yes," she said, "we'll take care of it."

I turned when I heard a young coyote yelp from somewhere up Meadow Creek, and Apella said, *Daniel…Dan…*and that was all.

At dinner that evening Rose suggested we enjoy dessert on the porch, and Jason raised his goblet, "To the night sky, my special comrades!" he exclaimed.

It was clear and crisp outside, and Rose sat close to Jason on the swing while Thius and I leaned against the rail, facing them. A swirl of moths caught my attention, Thius grumbled, "Damned exotics," and I was savoring a bite of dark chocolate with a sip of wine when Jason hoisted his glass again and called out, "A taste of Theobroma fruit with rich Tuscan red to celebrate Andy's ascension!"

I straightened up against the rail. Now why, I asked myself, would this man — an avowed nonbeliever if ever I knew one — toast an ascension? Was he alluding to another life for Andy? And there were Rose's words at the funeral, Your time is nigh. Was Andy's death staged? His funeral a sham? Would Andy the outsider be transformed into a member of Ursavus? Absurd, all of it, futuristic nonsense, but?

Rose gave the swing a gentle push with her foot and politely reminded me that she and Thius were reading my mind. "Dan, please don't be misled by how Jason and I worded our thoughts for our dear friend. Andrew's passing was not staged in any way. He was shot to his death — murdered. Jason and I were merely expressing our wish for the spirit of Andrew Denton to live on. Besides, who among us can say with certainty there is nothing, no existence of any kind after death?"

Or that there IS something beyond it, I thought.

"Yes, thank you for pointing that out," she said. "You might find it interesting that Andrew believed in a multiverse."

Jason sat up straight on the swing, adjusted his collar and said, "Dan, let's discuss the situation here. Per our conversation at Pete's Railyard, you realize that Ursavus can silence your implant and is not concerned about information transmitted by it. I can now inform you that Ursavus has full control of the device and can manipulate all transmissions to and from. How does that strike you?"

I told him, "Above all, it makes me worry for my friend Apella. Where is she in all this, and what happens to her when her employers discover their spy mission is a bust? Will I ever see her again?"

Jason slapped the arm of the swing. "Damn it to hell, Dan, I tried telling you that your concerns for Ms. Inglason are unfounded. The lady is safe, and you will see her again. Count on it!"

I glared at him. "And I should accept that just because you said it, Jason? I've always questioned a lot of what you profess, even more now. Yes, you saved my life and I owe you for that, but you haven't been straight with me since you wrote that message about Nate."

He raised his arm, nearly spilled his wine. "You're right, I admit it and I'm not proud of being cagey with you, but that message did help get you to Cedarville, and I expected you to join Ursavus before you heard the full story about your son."

"The full story, Jason? What is that? Friendly fire? No! A bike Crash?" I clenched my fists — clench, release, clench — didn't help, and Thius bellowed in my ear. "Believe what my daughter told you. She was with Nate."

"Yes," said Rose, "and like father like daughter, Sula tends to jump the gun. It was a mistake for her to tell you about the accident, but remorse still weighs heavily on the young girl even though it was not her fault by any means. I don't have to tell you, Dan, bikers risk life and limb every time they go fast down a hill."

I tried not to picture Nate at the bottom of a rock slide...can't be true but what if it is? Was there a service, is there a gravesite? Rose answered, "We most certainly held a service, and like Andrew, Nate did not want a marked grave. His ashes were scattered by a drone we sent up Woody's Gulch."

"S–so, that's it. End of search. End of why I'm here."

Thius elbowed me and chimed in, "Really bad crap, Oyente, but you've got fine memories. They're not gunna go away."

"Rrright," I said and stormed to the yard. I can't stay here? No, wait! There must be more. I turned around and shouted, "Did you stage the bike wreck? And…and make Nate a member of Ursavus?"

"Haven't we wished," Thius said loud enough for all to hear.

Rose called out from the steps, "Dan, NO to all of that! I wish I didn't have to say it, but Nate is gone. He is not a member of Ursavus. He never was, and heaven help us, I guess we have to go through the whole hurtful story now."

Thius yelled at me, "You need to try settlin' down, Oyente. This is your Kain's Cut."

I could feel them in my head — Rose then Thius then Rose — telepaths stalking my thoughts. Rose pulled her shawl tight around her shoulders, came toward me and looked in my eyes. "Dan, the war story is false. When your son left Syracuse he had no intention of serving in the military. Nate needed to find himself, to travel, and didn't want any distractions from anyone who didn't fit his plan…not even you."

I turned away from her, quick-scanned memories, came up with nothing and asked how they knew all this. "Well, of course Ursavus knew," Rose said, "and we were not surprised when your son started retracing some of your steps. He began with a visit to Jason, having listened to you talk so much about him. Nate enrolled at Garnet, finished his PhD, and naturally, Jason tried to recruit him. When the boy showed no interest, Jason got him involved in a work-study program with Gibby Lentele. Sula was here, and it was a joy to watch their friendship flourish that summer."

Thius added, "Yeah, both kids serious mountain bikers, rode trails together for three solid months. Late August though, Nate quit Gibby's, said goodbye to Sula and left — went to every continent — lived in most of 'em long enough to feel home. When he had enough travelin' he came back here, mostly to work and ride with Sula again. That's when things turned bad."

"What things? This is all crazy."

Rose reached out, held my arm. "I am so sorry you have to hear this, Dan. We knew there was trouble when Sula noticed the birthmark on Nate's back had grown and changed color, almost turned black. A biopsy revealed life-threatening cells, and immediate surgery and chemotherapy were prescribed. Nate hesitated, dug through the medical literature and turned up two experimental treatments neither of which he trusted."

I felt shut down, looked up at Jason and Thius on the porch. "Didn't Ursavus have a cure?" I asked.

"Of course we did," said Jason, "but it was not cleared for use on an unenhanced person. And we knew Nate's thoughts. Like you, he had little or no faith in dubious medical treatments, and would not have accepted a cure if we had offered one. He chose to remain as healthy as possible on his own to the end. Some of us thought your son had a death wish and that's why he went off that cliff, but — "

Thius cut him off. "Enough beatin' bushes, professor! Oyente needs to hear about the phony death notice."

"Easy, Thi," said Rose, and he lowered his voice. "I didn't know much about Nate back then and figured he must be pretty flaky when Sula told me he sent you a fake death report. She said a buddy of his conjured up the whole idea — some guy named Derik, if I remember right — forged the death certificate and made those tags you hang on to. Now that I've done some rides with you, I can sort of understand why your son agreed to the nut-ball scheme. He just didn't want you havin' to deal with him bein' sick — but man!"

"This is ridiculous! My son would never lay anything like that on me. We were close."

Rose said, "It's all true, Dan. To be sure, it was a brash act, sending you a military death report and dog tags, even for a distraught young man who knew he had but a short time to live. He told Sula how much he regretted the whole ugly thing, and was going to explain it to you, but the accident came before he had a chance."

I held my breath, closed my eyes.

Rose reached out, "Oh my dear boy! It must be awful to hear about your son this way. Please don't let any of this drive you away from us. There is a whole new world here for you, so much more to experience."

Jason punched his fists in the air and shouted from the porch, "Chin up, old student. You've heard the rough elements and you're still standing. Tomorrow dawns anew. You and I will start out early with a bike ride for old and new time's sake then stick to Rosey's schedule for an eventful day. Excelsior…on to lofty heights and secrets deep within."

He can be so flippant at times.

I stomped past him and said, "Hell with you, professor. You can't fix this. Forget the ride. I'm gone tomorrow," and Thius growled, "You're outta your mind if you leave now."

It was not a good night. Over and over, back and forth, I questioned every detail of their convoluted, maddening story about Nate. What really happened to him? How did he die? Where? A recurrent nightmare soaked me in sweat…a helpless struggle on a cold stainless table surrounded by masked figures. Ursavans? Thius? Derik? I shot up in bed when I heard Apella.

You're still in the game, Daniel, no reason to run, every reason to stay. You must play this out. Relax now and allow your neurotransmitters to salvage what remains of your night.

She clicked off, didn't hear me say, "No — Apella! You're caught in the middle like me and we're running out of time. Whatever happened to Nate I have to put on hold, stay in the fray until I'm sure you're safe and free of this mission madness. I have no choice, have to take that excelsior ride with Jason, see where it leads."

33

Tunnels and Rooms

"Good! Dressed for a bike ride and ready if not eager for a bright new day," Jason said when I stepped into Rose's kitchen, and his appraisal wasn't far off. I'd been awake much of the night but felt okay now, like I had a plan and could carry it out — weird. He waved at the table and poured me a cup of rich brew. "Dan, boost yourself with the buffet Thius assembled for us. Our Rosey's been out harvesting dewberries, creating a new painting now and doesn't wish to be disturbed. As usual, Thius is in another dimension. We'll see them both this evening."

I savored a taste of coffee and asked how long he'd been up.

"Long enough to fuel up and you should too…oatmeal, fruit, help yourself. We've got an interesting road ahead of us. I'm on Rosey's fine Yeti, and I'm certain your bike is set to go, but I need to switch pedals, still prefer the old-style clips. Gotta make some calls too, so I'll see you out front. Don't hurry, don't tarry."

We left the house at 8:14, pedaled six miles south then west a quarter mile on private blacktop and set our bikes down at a closed metal gate. Jason announced, "This is the outer portal to a world-renowned natural area maintained by Precambre International. Guided tours are provided for the public throughout the year during daylight hours, and portions of the facility are available for public meetings, seminars, et cetera."

He faced the gate and a small black disc lit up. "Next you," he said, "and don't worry, George scanned your irises two years ago. Just direct your attention to the disc."

I hesitated, and he knew why. "Dan, this is not the time to fuss about iris privacy. Take it up with George if it really matters to you."

"All right," he said when the gate rolled open, "we passed the first surveillance hurdle and still on schedule. Now everything we say and do will be recorded and analyzed. It's called ARC, Attoscale Recording and Calculus, operates via nanosatellites and encompasses any and all from macro to subatomic."

Past the gate, a thick forest of cedar, hemlock and grand firs lined the road, and I glanced up when a strong gust sent fir seeds whirling down at us. Jason was in the lead when we crossed a single-lane bridge over a wind-swept lake. He yelled over his shoulder, "Our final checkpoint is hidden in the trees on the other side! They'll have that gate open."

Two guards in sage-grey uniforms and berets met us at the open gate, and they were so stiff I thought Robots, and Jason cautioned, "Don't dismount, Dan, just balance in place and stay quiet."

The guard on our left stepped out and addressed us formally. "Gentlemen. Member Professor Jason Steller and Advanced Recruit Citizen Daniel Oyente. You are expected at the inner portal of the compound."

Jason said, "Thank you, Ingra and Axel, your services are always appreciated." They nodded in sync, stepped aside and we pedaled on through. After a quarter mile, Jason eased up on the pedals and asked what I was thinking back at the gate.

I told him it felt like I was on some kind of sci-fi movie set, and it took my mind off last night.

"Well, fantasy this isn't, my friend, and there is plenty of mind-filler ahead, so take it all in, and we're close now. You'll get your first view of the compound in about three minutes."

We rounded a bend and stopped at an intersection where a distant cluster of buildings reminded me of Deputy Crispin's mention of a faux-Austrian resort. Jason said, "That's headquarters, lodging, and a hangar on the far side, for visiting educators and researchers, and you will be pleased to hear that Dr. George Waterbear is a frequent contributor to our lecture series. We'll take the narrow lane to the right, and I believe another one of my friends will check us in today."

The narrow lane was a cul–de–sac with three closely spaced cabins at the end. We left our bikes and helmets at a stand in front of the middle cabin, walked to the porch and heard a metallic voice announce, "Greetings, gentlemen, you have arrived at the inner portal."

"Greetings to you also, friend Tullian," said Jason, and a tall lanky person in T-shirt and jeans marched out of the cabin, shook our hands, and held the door for us. His grip was soft, his steely eyes vacant, and he didn't look human. "Old-model cyborg," Jason said as we walked inside, "Tullian's been working this cabin since it was built, and believe me, Dan, his memory chips are no match for yours. Tullian receives orders from the main house and directs a quantum computer to make the walls fit the occasion. Public visitors get walk-around wall panels detailing Precambre's local history. Just blank walls for us but pay attention to the shiny quartz plaque at the far end of the corridor."

We took eleven steps, Jason pointed two fingers at the plaque and it transformed into an embossed image of a toothy, terrier-size mammal crouched on a tree limb…someone's rendition of a scrawny bear cub with a long tail, I thought.

"Behold the dawn bear Ursavus elemensis," Jason said. "A twenty-pound arboreal omnivore, a resident of Eurasia about forty million years after the dinosaurs crashed. Nothing special you might say, but little Ursavus had great genes many of which persist in the majestic creatures we call the Great Bears."

Jason ran his fingertips over the image, a seamless portion of the wall opened, and we stepped through to a four-by-four landing above three flights of wide metal stairs. "We go down," said Jason. "The main facility is underground."

I walked beside him, counting steps while he explained that we'd still be in the visitor room if Citizen Oyente had not been vetted by five full members of Ursavus. I asked who vetted me, and he answered, "Rosey, George, Sula, Thius, and Walter."

When we reached the bottom, forty-eighth step, I asked why he wasn't one of the five. "Because I'm not a full member," he said. "I've accepted only basic enhancements for agelessness and nonviolence. Telepathy fascinates me but would be excessive, perhaps even a burden, as I spend most of my time with nonursavans."

He pressed a stainless pad on the wall of the stairwell, an elevator opened, and a robotic male voice spoke from the ceiling. "Welcome to Ursavus E. Please enter now." We stepped in, the door closed, and the voice said, "You are advised to place both hands on the side rail and brace firmly. You will descend five hundred meters very rapidly."

Jason said the instructions were an unnecessary precaution, and seconds later the elevator stopped and the door opened to a brightly lit tunnel. We stepped through, and the ceiling voice said, "This passageway takes you to the main facility developed from a room-and-pillar mine. Ursavus E occupies many rooms, some over two thousand meters beneath the Northern Bitterroot Mountain Range on the west side of the Clark Fork Valley. The entire facility is connected by kilometers of tunnels. The side tunnel on your right connects to the McClun hydroponic unit. The side tunnel on your left connects to the Millen-Galen residence on the valley's west side. You will detect a slight decline in the main passageway as you start walking under the river."

The tunnel floor was troweled concrete painted light green, and the arching sidewalls and ceiling looked alive with three-dimensional art. "Ancient forests of the Northern Rockies," the ceiling voice said, "and change comes with the seasons."

I was thinking of my snowshoe trip high above with Andy, Sula, and Erik when Jason said, "Straight ahead, Dan, and the river is only a half-kilometer wide above us. Ursavus E and nine other sites were developed when it was necessary to keep everything hidden. Eventually ursavan technology made it possible to develop facilities above ground and hundreds now exist on every continent."

A short walk took us to a three-way junction where a steel door slid into a wall. "Straight ahead again," Jason said, and we stepped inside a room lined with pipes, pumps, and blue metal tanks. Jason waved toward the equipment and said, "Seepage from the ground above supplies more freshwater than Ursavus E needs. This is one of fifteen pump venues that route the excess water to storage facilities. From there water is transported to distant sites by rail and other means as required."

A door opened at the far end of the room, and a familiar figure strode toward us. His light blue lab coat and matching tie were a far cry from his Park Service uniform, but his manner was unmistakable. "Man, it's good to see you," I said to George Waterbear.

He nodded formally. "Glad you are here, Dan, and do not be concerned about telepathy when you're with me. I routinely revert to nontelepathy when I'm with trusted nontelepaths. So tell me, do you regret hopping the freight on Bozeman Pass?"

"Well," I said, running my fingers through my hair. "Regret sounds a little strong, George, but I've had a lot to think about since then."

"Indeed, and what I know of your mind tells me you will not wish to be cut off from the lure of Ursavus after today. We'll visit more in the conference room, but first let me show you one of our early accomplishments."

He led us to a room nearly filled by an imposing glass column. I counted thirteen transparent tubes attached to the top and sides of the column. All thirteen were connected to a maze of thin blueish tubes inside the column. A steady hum from the apparatus triggered memories of keyboards, and George said, "I'm sure you recognize the tone, Dan. Middle C, yes, and it tells us the system is balanced — products equal products consumed." He pressed a keypad next to the column, the hum went up half an octave, and small bubbles appeared in seven of the top tubes. George said, "Oxygen and carbohydrates coming off now — excess products, all harvestable."

Jason added, "Dan, we are standing before a venerated ursavan relic. This type of apparatus once made Ursavus E and similar facilities virtually self-sufficient, off the grid, so to speak."

"Yes," said George, "this entire underground facility has been quantized and powered by dark energy for many years, but prior to that we relied on biosystems, units like this. Fluid in the glass column and the tubes suspended in it provide optimal conditions for two species of diatoms, which I'm sure you know are microscopic plants. We named one of the species Erga, the other Syne, and they thrive as tight synergistic partners within the tube network. We call the partnership ESSY, which stands for Erga-Syne Synergy."

He pulled out a pad and pencil, wrote some notes then gestured toward a table. "Pamphlets over there tell more about ESSY. We should get back on schedule."

Jason stopped him. "George, that pamphlet doesn't do justice to ESSY. Dan should hear more from you. We have time and we can abridge our conference meeting if needed."

George took off his wire frames, tucked them in his pocket and said, "All right, I will start from the beginning and provide details, and I will stop immediately if I sense either of you losing focus. I have a profound attachment to Erga and Syne. They are natives of the Upper Yellowstone, and I was introduced to them by my great aunt, who was my tutor. I had just turned eight, and we were camped near Meniscus Lake in the Absarokas. For three nights from dusk to midnight we sat near a hot pool, waiting in silence for signs from the water. When blue-green sparkles appeared on the third night, my tutor asked what I thought they were. I answered, Maybe something alive in the water, like small animals reflecting moonlight. Or perhaps fiery spirits, my tutor said, and I believe the true answer lies in your future, my young charge.

"Events of that night stayed with me, and I returned years later to collect water samples and have them cultured and studied at Ursavus E. The project had just begun when a three-day power outage destroyed all plant life in most of the cultures, but then, ten days later, my colleague Dr. Lissette knocked on my office door, peeked in and announced, Serendipity, George!

"She had a culture flask in hand and excitement in her eyes. I've got two species of diatoms here, she said. They survived the outage and they're reproducing like mad. See the blueish tint in the flask?

"Dr. Lissette and I had to find out how those diatoms survived the outage, and six months of intensive research provided some answers. When exposed to ultra-low light, the diatoms adapt by becoming dependent partners. Erga loses most of her ability to produce food and becomes a powerful emitter of blue and UV light. Syne absorbs Erga's light and uses it like a typical photosynthetic plant to produce her own food while nourishing her light-emitting partner.

"I was working in Yellowstone when Dr. Lissette called from this facility to tell me she had successfully enhanced both Erga and Syne, causing an exponential increase in their growth and metabolic rates. The lab was celebrating, and I'll not forget her sober voice amidst the loud cheers, This is one of those eureka moments, George. Most certainly, I told her, if we can scale it up and make use of the products. Then — "

Jason stopped him again. "George, I think you should explain what Dr. Lissette meant by enhanced."

"Thank you, yes, I should have said GENETICALLY enhanced, and realize also, Dan, ursavan research teams in China, Portugal, and Mexico perfected whole-genome sequencing, and we were developing enhancement technologies a half century before nonursavan scientists began thinking about any of it."

George nodded at the glass column. "It took us three years to design and build living quarters for ESSY, units like this that accommodate her growth rate and put her to work for us. Soon thereafter, ESSY became Ursavus E's main source of light, oxygen, electricity and much of our food. Power production and conductivity were major challenges, and needless to say, ESSY was the first system on Earth to generate electricity from photosynthesis."

George reached for a bottle of water on the pamphlet table, and I asked why he hadn't shared ESSY with the outside world. "Tried to," he said. "We knew our work was ahead of its time, nonetheless we submitted several papers to a mainstream research journal describing the power-generating potential of biosynergies. Those papers were summarily rejected. Two reviewers derided them as science fiction, unrepeatable nonsense. We tried several other journals and received similar responses. We even provided cultures of Syne and Erga to a skeptical researcher, never heard back. As you may know, Dan, nonursavan science has been illogically slow to appreciate the power of synergy and positive feedback. Too bad, because biosystems like ESSY could have replaced much of the petroleum culture and prevented many problems humanity is just beginning to fathom."

I took one of the pamphlets, looked again at the big glass column and blueish network teaming with synergistic life. "So, George, I'm still trying to get my head around all this. After those early rejections why didn't you persist? You could have proven them wrong. Why hide knowledge that might have helped the rest of humanity? Sorry, I don't get that mindset for a scientist."

He clasped his hands together and said, "It is inherently difficult for a nonursavan to understand, and judge as you may, I will emphasize three points. First, our research has always been ahead of the nonursavan research world. Second, the pace of our research is vital, and third, we will not allow our work to be encumbered by military, political or economic interests. Our decision to remain isolated was set in stone when we acquired quantum powers. No individual, no group, no political entity outside Ursavus can be trusted with full expression of these powers — not until safe use can be assured — not until violence, war and petty nationalism are abolished."

George checked a gauge next to the glass column, wrote some notes, and Jason spoke up. "None of what George said implies that ursavan technology is confined to ursavan facilities, Dan, not by any means."

"Correct," said George, "and our Yellowstone work is an example. A majority of credible radiotrackers employ a nonquantal version of the nanotag system we developed and still use with the bears. And covertly, my ursavan colleagues and I employ quantum magnetic pulse to track everything from large carnivores to mobile bacteria. This method is attoscale and secure with a network of undetectable satellites handling data collection, recording, and analyses. Most importantly, our global research effort has identified strategies required to maintain this planet's health and welfare. What we lack and must have sooner than later is planetwide acceptance of our plans, and this is why you and others are in various stages of recruitment at ursavan centers throughout this world."

George's body language told me Discussion over, but I still asked what strategies he was talking about. "Nothing novel or extraordinary," he said. "For many years, ursavan laboratories have been synthesizing our food, using carbon dioxide and nitrogen from the atmosphere. Other examples include regenerating glaciers and enhancing trees to reestablish diverse canopy growth. You will learn more about all our strategies and how you can help promote them during your enhancement phase. It is time now to adjourn to a room with table and chairs."

34

Bugged

"Welcome future triumvirate," the ceiling voice announced as we stepped into a large meeting room. "You have just entered the William Yrisse Memorial Hall. Advanced recruit Daniel Oyente, please take note of the elliptic glass table and surrounding chairs, all synthesized using waste materials from the room and pillar mine. The wall panels are hemlock, hewn from the original mine's support beams."

Jason walked around the table, pulled out a chair for me and said, "The Ursavan High Council meets here monthly, Dan, the quorum being twenty-one full members. This is where your membership in Ursavus will be finalized after a presentation of your case by George and myself. We anticipate a unanimous vote."

"Jason, we need to get back on schedule," said George. "It is time to talk about our recruit's implant predicament."

They took seats facing me and George began, "I will not mince words, Dan. Brain enhancement technology outside Ursavus is proto-typic at best, and you were victimized by an unauthorized and poten-tially lethal field test conducted by rogue employees of a government lab. The arrogance of these people — they are criminals not scien-tists. The device they injected into your brain is rudely constructed and grossly macroscopic — despicable. Accustomed to our attoscale enhancements, I was surprised the device functioned at all, and as you are aware, you suffered some memory loss."

"George!" I shouted and put my hand on my forehead.

"You must hear me out, Dan. I can remove the device and repair all damage to your brain, but I cannot proceed without your approval, and I must have as complete a record as possible of your surveillance mission. Tell me what you recall about the operation — when the rogues installed the implant?"

Jason cut in. "George, I think for Dan's sake and ours, we should start with events leading up to the mission, before Dan's training, particularly in regard to the role of Ms. Inglason. Correct me if I'm wrong, Dan. You hadn't seen her for what, nearly ten years then suddenly hopped on a plane when she requested a visit?"

I looked at George, hoping he would think this was a waste of time, but he tapped the table with his pencil and said, "Proceed. Something useful may turn up. Please be brief."

I began by reminding Jason how I felt about Apella. "We met only sixteen days after I was introduced to you, professor. When she finished her masters at Garnet she took a research job with the government, worked on robotic weapons, top secret projects. She couldn't talk about her work, and except for a rare weekend visit we were apart most of the time, but our relationship stayed strong. When she said she'd like to see me and offered travel expenses, I didn't hesitate. It didn't matter how much time had gone by."

Jason rolled his eyes and said, "Tell us about the visit."

"Highlights will be sufficient," George said.

"All right. Apella met me at Baltimore-Washington International and drove us to a nearby hotel. At breakfast three days later — wait a minute. Why am I just now remembering all this?"

"Proceed, Dan," said George. "We will discuss your sporadic memory losses at another time. What happened at the breakfast encounter?"

"Breakfast on the hotel veranda," I stammered. "Apella and I sat next to a cascading water fountain. She was all business from the moment we took our seats. She asked if I'd read the Devlinson reports on dissident cells. I told her No, and she said she had agreed to help run a mission to surveil a suspicious group in northwest Montana, and with my exceptional memory and personality type I was a prime candidate for infiltrating the group. I laughed, and she reached for my hand, said she was serious, that I fit the job and the group was not considered dangerous. The training would be demanding but nothing I couldn't handle, the pay excellent with two thirds to start, and the assignment would provide some high quality biking time. I told her it was tempting, could be a welcome break from selling textbooks, but the whole thing sounded pretty far-out for me. I'd have to think hard and long. She asked me to stay in town another night, be alone and try to see myself in the job. The next morning we met at a small Italian café near the airport. She walked in wearing her favorite Armani pant suit...so beautiful always. We didn't talk or eat much. I told her I just couldn't decide what to do about her spy offer. She said she knew I'd love the wild country out here and was certain I'd find some of the people interesting. I said I would keep thinking about it, she told me she would do her best to stay in touch, and that's how we left it. We walked outside, she flagged a taxi, and I didn't talk with her again until the implant was activated."

Jason stared at the ceiling and said, "Shortly after that parting, Apella sent me an email about the proposed mission and asked me to step in and encourage you. For years I wanted to recruit you but could never convince anyone you were worth the time and trouble."

George spoke for Ursavus. "During the years Jason alludes to, none of our recruitment plans projected success in your case. In spite of that, when we discovered your surveillance mission was in progress we decided to proceed. Our algorithms still predicted failure but we were compelled to try."

Jason added, "And that's when I sent you the email about your son with a forward to Apella."

"So you set me up, Jason — you!"

He slapped the glass table top with both hands and said, "No, my innocent, erstwhile student, you were already set up. You were going to be used as a guinea pig by a cabal of sinister quacks. Fortunately, we were able to turn their vile plan and bring you to us. So, what do you think of Apella at this point? I mean, what kind of friend sets you up to be drugged, implanted, and sent on an ominous mission? Answer that one."

I focused on the wall panels…splendor salvaged from timbers that didn't break under strain. What do I think of Apella? I think how natural it was being with her in Baltimore, as though we'd never been apart. I looked at George and asked, "Was Apella threatened, coerced in some way? Is that why she agreed to set me up?"

Jason boomed from across the table, "Old friend, it's never too late to transcend romantic adolescence."

George wasn't amused. He steadied his eyes on me and dropped a bombshell. "Apella had nothing to do with the mission, Dan. The voice on your implant was synthetic and directed by Ursavus."

My mind was spinning and Jason shouted, "George, I wasn't informed. Why not? Why'd you keep me in the dark?"

George held up his right hand and said, "You were given all the information necessary for your role, Jason. You knew Ursavus controlled all transmissions to and from the implant. You did not need to know Ms. Inglason wasn't involved."

I railed at George, "Tell me now. Where is Apella? Is she in danger?"

He pulled out his wire frames, held them with both hands and calmly said, "Your friend has always been safe and kept up to date regarding you. When you were together in Baltimore, she knew nothing about the implant. She had been told your wrists and ears would be fitted with harmless nanochips through which you would receive and send information. When Apella heard about the implant she cut all ties to the mission and the government and accepted a position with a private, not-for-profit research firm in Chile. Among other things, she currently leads an international group developing software for deep-space probes."

I jumped up and yelled, "So, Apella wasn't involved, but you both were? You knew I had this thing in my head. With all your high tech, why didn't you just take it out? And all those phony messages —

the fake implant voice, stiff and lifeless from the first contact back in Livingston. That was the best you could do, George?"

He was not provoked. "Actually, Dan, it was the best the government rogues could do. They originated the implant voice, and we chose not to alter it when we took over. As I stated in the email, I opposed the implant, but as a member of Ursavus I abide by majority rule, and I agreed to modify the device so it would not harm you, perhaps even assist us in evaluating and recruiting you."

I thought of my last day in Yellowstone, George telling me not to be misled by anyone.

Jason seized the moment. "Dan, your implant is repugnant to all of us, and we didn't learn about it until you began training for the government mission. Lucky for you — and us — your lead trainer was Maria Waterbear, a multiskilled ursavan operative who sensed you had a brain implant and alerted Ursavus. At that juncture, faced with your assignment as an infiltrator, and confident that George could retask the device and render it safe, we decided to put it to good use."

"Yes," said George, "and recordings from the device did verify Jason's appraisal of your character. You recall my admonition to consider everything a test. Even the synthetic voice proved to be a test, and you passed honorably. You remained loyal to Apella despite all the doubts the voice raised about her. You also refused to put your new ursavan friends in danger. Our current algorithms conclude that despite your deep-seated reticence you are strongly inclined to be with us."

"Algorithms to hell!" I shot back. "And you expect me to trust and join after all this?"

"Good grief, man. Take your seat, quit whining and lighten up," said Jason. "The important thing is you're here with people you like, people who need your help. We have no expectations, only hope that you will remain interested and decide to join."

George tapped his pencil on the table again and said he understood my concerns but we had to move on. "Dan, please tell us what you remember about the rogues installing the implant."

I sat on the edge of my chair and said, "I have frequent flashbacks and nightmares of being on a steel table surrounded by masked figures in lab coats, that's it. Were you there, George — one of those people — one of the rogues?"

He drew back, "You disappoint me, Dan. You have questions like that after all our work together, all our times with the Great Bears?"

I assured him all two hundred and fourteen encounters were detailed in my memory.

"But what have you assimilated?" he asked. "Transcripts from your implant indicate you favor a future with every ursavan you've met, including Thius, who once strongly opposed your recruitment and worked against it. Are you not aware?"

"I am very aware, but you learned all that about me from — as you put it — a grossly macroscopic, despicable device in my brain. When was it turned on, George? Were you spying on me all that time in Yellowstone?"

"Dan, please," he said calmly. "The implant was not activated until you checked into the Livingston motel. And I am not overstating when I say, If Ursavus had not intervened, the implant would have killed you at the onset of training. Agent Maria not only informed us of your implant, she also knew from your scent and pallor that you were within forty-eight hours of life-threatening shock. The sunscreen she required you to use contained two sets of absorbable atto-particles that adhered to the implant and protected your brain. Maria Waterbear and that sunscreen saved your life, my friend."

I touched the inset on my watch and thought out loud, "Training. First day. I remember a mild headache and a martial arts instructor handing me a tube of zinc oxide and saying, Put this on before we begin. Coat your face and neck well. I also remember details from all 366 days of training — the mental and physical routines, meeting you and planning to work with you in Yellowstone. I draw a blank the last night of training until I was sitting with you on a plane. You said we were in a chartered Park-Service jet and we would land in Livingston then you would drive us to Yellowstone."

George wrote some notes then looked up and said, "You draw a blank in that time period because you were heavily drugged, unable to stand on your own. The evening of your last day of training, government agents carried you to the plane — delivered you to me, their putative go-between. As soon as the agents left I placed a magnetic disc on your forehead, no pain, no incisions, just a harmless insertion device for an attodrive that replaced most of the implant's crude circuitry. You were unconscious for our plane ride from Washington, DC to Livingston, and since then we have had complete control of the device, and you have been immune to any side effects."

He got up slowly and stood behind his chair. "In conclusion, Dan, I want you to know that all ursavans are bound by a solemn oath — we do not coerce. You have experienced some deception, yes, but I trust you realize none of it was harmful. Give us another two days, complete the recruitment process and I believe you will understand why we felt the deception was necessary." He straightened his lab coat, walked around the table and gripped my shoulder. George the benevolent authoritarian, I thought, and he quietly added, "I also believe, Dan, that it is time for you to put your gifts to work, not just for Ursavus, for all life — for Planet Earth as a whole. The choice is yours and you will not be harmed if you turn us down, but I envision you a new existence — if you please — as Daniel del Oso. Now I must return to other work. I will see you both at Rosey's for dinner this evening, and Thius will join us."

When the door closed, Jason leaned back and said, "I've known George Waterbear for a long time but never heard him be so effusive."

"Nor have I, Jason, and I'll think about everything he just said, but right now, the only person I believe I can trust is Apella. I need more than a vague assurance she's safe."

He stood and motioned toward the door. "I am certain Ms. Inglason is not in danger and you will reconnect, so pace and patience, old friend. They serve you on long climbs. Let them work for you here."

I asked if he really knew for sure that Apella is safe.

"Absolutely. You heard George. We have his word on it, and let me offer you some advice. Think about what you've acquired so far.

You no longer have to puzzle about Nate, and you have gained some fine new friends, all of whom appreciate your talents and want to help you apply them to meaningful tasks. And there is something else. I believe you retain one of your best features. Under that façade, you're the same inquisitive student I knew years back. You cover it well, but I see wholesome curiosity driving you as much as ever. Ursavus intrigues you, so do its people…and that part does surprise me a bit. So I would say, consider this opportunity with great care."

He pulled out his phone and started humming as we retraced our route through the tunnels, stairwells and elevators. When we stepped out at ground level he gave a sigh of relief. "It wouldn't be a problem for your mind, Dan, but I still have to use a map app to find my way out of the maze down there. You'll enjoy seeing much more of Ursavus E in the near future, and don't worry about your dysfunctional implant. Trust George to take care of it. Just think all in good time, all at the right time. And I don't know about you, Dan, but I'm looking forward to this evening at Rosey's with five of us together for the first time. Dinner will be outstanding."

35

Dinner with Friends

Jason was quick to offer compliments for the fine food that evening. "Bellissimo," he said with a wave of his fork, "excellent sole fillets, superb choice and balance of herbs. Who prepared this delectable cuisine?"

"Why, Thius was our dinner chef," Rose replied, "and this would be a good time to fill Dan in on our resources."

Thius smacked his lips. "Yeah, Oyente, all the fish and fowl you've digested in Cedarville, in fact, nearly all ursavan-produced food is assembled from simple molecules using quantum synthesizers programmed with species-specific, energy efficient algorithms."

Wow, another Thius dimension — technochef in residence, I thought.

"Readin' you all the way," he said. "And you're wastin' brain power bein' surprised."

Jason clinked his glass on mine, "Dan, about those fine chicken and seafood dinners at Pete's Railyard Bar and Grille, laboratory synthesized to meal-time fare."

Rose raised her glass, "And to the Kumamotos at Harpy's. Dan, it pleases me to tell you Gibson Lentele oversees our West Coast production facility for oysters, crab meat, and shrimp. He calls it Sealab Organics. Federal inspectors often question how one farm with limited culture facilities and a paltry balance sheet can produce so much, but they always leave satisfied after Gibson's informative tour and tasty free samples."

Quiet until everyone finished eating, George folded his napkin over his plate and said, "My compliments also, Thius, fine meal, the best I've had in weeks, and for the record, Dan, 45 percent of the meat currently consumed by humans is synthesized at ursavan labs. This percentile will increase in sync with the decline of the animal production industry."

George looked at Jason and said, "We should call it a night. I'm expected at Ursavus E at 0600, and you have an early meeting with another recruit. I will see you, Dan, either late tomorrow or noon the next day, depending on intervening events."

George and Jason started helping Rose clear the table, and she waved Thius and me off, "Outside, please, both of you. There is a sky full of stars. Go out and take Max and Agnes with you."

The dogs ran to the door, Thius pulled two jackets from the coat rack, tossed me one and said, "My daughter told me you have a heavy fear of lions, Oyente. Let's see if we can find you one."

What's he talking about? Surely, Agnes and Max will keep the cougars at bay.

We walked out to the front yard, and Thius said, "Up there, the night sky, Leo major's real clear. I read you dreamin' about constellations when you were nappin' on the train, and I know it bugs you when you have to use a telescope to see more than one star in the lion's heart, am I right?"

"Telescopes are cumbersome, yes."

"So wouldn't you rather just look up and see it all? Retinal enhancement would expand your whole attitude."

We both turned when an owl called from a nearby tree. I thought Great Horned. "Nope, Great Grey," said Thius, "and you're easy to read at night. Dark settles you, same as me, and yeah, you need another bike ride. Do Zāpus Canyon tomorrow, across the river, west of town. I'd go with you, but I'm on Ellie's eastbound intermodal tomorrow. She's stoppin' below the house at 0330."

Ellie Sterling, aka Rachel Smyth, the genomicist, biologist and roadmaster, also a locomotive engineer — a cool gifted lady.

"Yep, readin' you there. Ellie's all that and more."

He whistled for Agnes and Max and we walked to the porch. "About Zāpus," he said, "the climb gives you three doglegs, long graduals between 'em, maybe some snow in shady spots. Don't be tempted by side roads or trails. The main goes to the ridgeline, which happens to be the Montana-Idaho border. Take a right at the T, climb a couple more miles and you'll reach the top of Fern Creek Road…all downhill after that and you'll wish for more. Tomorrow's your day for it. Let's go in the house, answer those questions roilin' your brain."

I sat at a south window. Thius chose the piano bench. "Gimme one at a time," he said, "just think 'em."

I pictured him soaked and shaking at Meander Creek. Okay, about enhancements, the side effects?

"Don't sweat that. Enhancements are like bein' in a zone on a fast downhill knowin' you can't fall. Side effects are minor and few. I just have the one — tells me I'm still human."

About your telepathy, can you turn it on and off like George does?

"We all have instant control at near-zero to full-on. Tomorrow in that engine cab with Ellie, we'll talk awhile just to hear our voices, but most of the time we'll be full-on telepaths. And now you're wonderin' if she can do that and keep track of the train. Answer is, Ellie Sterling's a master engineer, always in tune with her train from locomotive to end-of-train device and all the cars between. Telepathing with me while drivin' a train — like a walk on the track for Ellie."

My thoughts went to Bozeman Pass. Was she driving when you picked me up?

"Yep — Chief Engineer from Billings to Missoula. Boston Cole took us from Missoula to Cedarville."

So, the train stuff. It was all staged?

His voice toughened. "Most of it — yeah. I figured a load of rough talk in a cold boxcar would bring out the worst in you. How do you feel about that now, bike man?"

I was playing the spy role, and you didn't come close to seeing my worst.

"Yeah, I read your thoughts the whole way, none as negative as mine if I'd been in your Shimanos."

You even staged the derailment?

"Yep."

What did you think when I passed out?

He fingered a low octave on the piano. "I could tell you were ahright, no broken bones, no concussion, and your memory was intact. I read you worryin' about it, so I got you to recite all that crap about train robberies at Bearmouth. Now I'm catchin' your thoughts about swimmin' in that steamy pool."

He played a chord lower, and I asked myself, If Apella were telepathic would I choose to be?

"Oyente, if you reject our offer, you'll just keep livin' your isolated life. I'm tellin' you how it is for nontelepaths. They can't really know anybody, including themselves. Some, kinda like you, discover the limits of talk and learn to value silence, but the boundaries don't go away. Telepathy brings a synergy, allows love to expand beyond your wildest dreams. Think about that and your lady friend."

I glanced out the window and thought, Now you're my counselor, Thius? And he waved his hand, "Ahh, never mind, you got plenty to think about and more on the way. Rose will give you a lift to Zāpus in the morning, and she made some huckleberry yogurt, top shelf of the fridge. Get some shut-eye, probably see you day after tomorrow."

36

Take Thirty

Next morning I hopped out of bed so full of positive energy I was certain Rose had added something other than berries to the yogurt. Her steaming hot chicory was as good as her coffee, and I was in the kitchen finishing a second cup when she walked in with a stack of folded towels. "You certainly appear optimistic," she said. "Our yogurt helped, I'm sure. Are you about ready?"

"Yes, looking forward to a full day alone in the mountains. A long solo climb is just what I need, but I should do a routine check on my bike before I go."

"Don't rush, safety second," she said, "and I certainly admire your unenhanced ability to focus, considering all you've been through so far. Now, let me see, need to feed the kitties, soak some Yukon golds then I'll meet you out front."

I found negligible wear on the brake pads, installed new cables, took a test ride in the crisp morning air, and was ready to go when Rose stepped out on the porch. Her coy expression told me to think twice about having a whole day to myself. "Let's get going," she said. "We'll have plenty of time to talk on the way to Zāpus Canyon."

She didn't say anything until we crossed the river and turned north on the West Valley Road. "Now, Dan, a little introduction is in order since this is your first time north of our river bridge. After this lovely straightaway, we veer away from the river, and after that we have ten narrow curvy miles with steep drop-offs, but please don't worry, I

237

know the curves and edges by heart, and I'll take it slow. Don't hesitate to give me your thoughts, and I'm open to whatever you want to ask, especially about telepathy. Just think your questions and enjoy the views. Let me do the talking."

Starting into the narrows, I thought, So Rose, you can read my mind without looking at me — like now, while you're negotiating these curves?

"Yes, it's easy. What else do you want to hear about telepathy? I've been aware of your interest in it for some time now."

Okay, whenever I've sensed someone reading me they were only a few feet away. How close do you have to be?

"It varies with the individual. With a clear view, my optimal range for both sending and receiving extends to about seven meters, and most of us can piece thoughts together when a subject, especially someone we know, is out of view but close, in a nearby room, for instance."

She beeped the horn. "Now the next half mile is a major crossing area for deer and elk, so be prepared when I put on the brakes."

There were no close calls, and when she slowed gradually and stopped smoothly before a calf elk charged across the road, I thought, Can you read animal minds, Rose?

"General intent, yes, and more if I know the subject, Max and Agnes or the kitties, for instance."

What if you saw someone trying to hit that elk? Could you stop them?

"Yes, we may redirect harmful intentions and acts of nonmembers, and I hasten to say this does not apply in your case. You are an advanced recruit, have been since your first evening with me. Thereby, you are protected by a strict ursavan law that forbids our use of telepathy or any other enhanced power to deliberately alter your thinking."

How strict is strict, I wondered, and she said, "It is absolute, a res judicata. When there is any chance of altering your thoughts, we are required to immediately break off all contact with your mind."

She had me going. Okay, change of subject, Rose. What happens in a crowd? Suppose you're trying to read someone in a group of complete strangers, like at an airport or on a train?

She shifted to low, steered close to the shoulder to avoid a wash-out and said, "Interesting you ask about groups. I usually enjoy reading them. As you might expect, some thought selection must occur in crowded situations, and there are multiple options. For instance, in a group of active thinkers I'm acquainted with, such as the kids at Harpy's that night, I often do a quick scan to narrow my focus. Another option is to let my telepathic algorithms prompt me to focus on a certain individual's thoughts. I can also read several minds at once. You see, our minds process information in attoseconds."

"Attoseconds, Rose? Quintillionths of a second?"

"Yes, and you question this because you learned that human brains process information very fast, in milliseconds, but ursavan brains function about fifteen orders of magnitude faster than unenhanced human brains."

Can't imagine that.

"But wouldn't you like to experience it?"

Yes and no. If I were enhanced, would I lose memories? Would they be erased to accommodate all the new stuff coming in?

She down-shifted for a steep rise and said, "Dan, there is no chance of overloading that memory of yours. We've known this to be true for many years. When we first considered recruiting you, George's team sequenced your genome and much of your epigenome."

I couldn't keep quiet. "Is there no end to this? You're telling me George — before I even met him — sampled my DNA, sequenced it, and Ursavus has all my genetic information? What could possibly justify that?"

"It is not necessary to raise your voice, dear. Sequencing is a required element of every recruitment plan. We simply cannot proceed without knowing the genetic and epigenetic basis of a person's talents, and weaknesses, for that matter."

I shook my head. George had no right to —

"Please let me finish. Everyone's enhancements must be precisely fitted to their inherited talents. In your case, and this should certainly interest you, George's team identified the molecular basis of your hyperthymesia. They also discovered something of enormous significance — genetic underpinnings of a largely undeveloped ability to sense others' thoughts and to influence them. If you were fully enhanced, you would not only be telepathic, you would be overwhelmingly persuasive — able to redirect masses of recalcitrant minds. Your gifts are profound, but without enhancement, you experience only the very fringes of them. Now, I would like to hear your thoughts about your latent talents, and please be candid."

"Okay. I think you've got the wrong guy if you see me redirecting others' thoughts, attitudes or whatever. I have no such inclination."

"You're not interested in having your hidden talents activated?"

"Not enough to let Ursavus mess with my genes or my mind."

"Dan, if you are concerned about security, don't be. Your genetic profile is safe and secure in the Ursavus archives, protected by another res judicata that pertains to advanced recruits. We cannot use your genetic information without your permission, and indeed if any of it shows up in nonursavan files, those records will be deleted for your protection."

"You've already used my genetic information — taken it and studied it without my permission."

"Yes, but not recently," she said, then checked her rearview mirror and smiled. "Oh my, wouldn't you know, here comes Dale Harpy, must have the day off and he's got June Giffin and Guy Marshall with him."

Lots of hands waved as a black Jeep with a lift kit, huge tires and two gas cans pulled around us. Rose said, "Dan, those kids want me to tell you they are all members of Ursavus and they anticipate working with you in the near future."

"Those kids are members and they're reading me?"

"Yes, and they're asking if the loner myth still weighs on your mind."

"I am a loner, Rose. I like everyone here, but I'm not into groups. I made that clear from the start, didn't I?"

She sighed and said, "That is pure close-minded nonsense, Daniel Oyente. You are not a loner. This is obvious to us and should be to you. You have no genetic basis for antisociality, and you show little if any tendency for it. You require time alone. We all do, which is good. And here we are at the Zāpus Canyon Road. I'll drop you at a pullout a quarter mile up, and be sure to stay positive with those telepathy thoughts, Dan. Realize you are being offered a chance to express the full living force of your mind — vivida vis animi."

Cold mist showered me as I unloaded my bike and gear. Alone at last and primed to climb.

37

Ytterbium

The first rise out of the Za-pus creek bottom put me under clear sky and I was warming up, feeling aerobic when I turned a corner and stopped. A Franklin's grouse stood posed like a statue in the middle of the road. "What's on your mind, Mr. Franklin, John that is?" I asked. And he didn't move or ruffle a feather when I pedaled by.

Twenty minutes later I was traversing an open cliffside when my implant went active. *Daniel, it's Apella.*

I hit the brakes and shouted, "Come on, I'm past this, leave me alone." But it did sound like her.

Daniel, it's really me. I can prove it. Ask me something from our past, like the panhandler who introduced us, well sort of.

I straddled my bike, tried counting how many times I had re-played that life-changing scene on Missoula's eastside. Apella in faded cutoffs, white T-shirt and moccasins skipped by, gave the panhandler a half dollar then turned and smiled at me. I've been crazy about her ever since. "Okay," I said, "describe the panhandler guy."

She was old with sad eyes and grey-brown dreadlocks. Three black beads hung in a lock over her left ear. She went inside the corner store. I took your hand and we walked across the river bridge to campus talking nonstop. That walk was a beginning for us, so much more to come, that summer and all the time since.

"What did we first talk about?"

How new and exciting everything was. We'd been in western Montana only two months, you from Sioux City, six days on a mail-delivery bus. I rode the train from St. Louis. We loved the dry air, the conifer forests, being in wild public land. We wondered if we would ever stop feeling like trespassers.

Those memories were warm and vivid, like it was yesterday. I asked if she remembered our first hike together.

How much do you want me to share?

I took off my helmet, set my bike against the road bank and said, "It'll take a lot more to convince me you're really Apella."

Better get comfortable then. My memory nearly equals yours, Daniel.

I sat down on the grassy midstrip. "Okay, tell me about that first hike."

Gladly. We caught a ride up the Bitterroot Valley with three hippies in a green VW van, and they drove us to the Blodgett Canyon road. We hiked three miles up the canyon, camped and counted stars most of the night, didn't start out again until late morning the next day. If it's all right with you, I'll be my usual demure self and gloss over the intimacies.

"Always liked that. Tell me more."

You started fussing when four horse packers passed us along Blodgett Trail, and we decided to take an alternate route that led south to High Lake. Without a topo map we didn't realize High Lake Trail was very steep. We were on all fours much of the way and felt like we were going straight up the mountain. In one shady stretch we climbed over one hundred meters on slippery hard-pack snow, and I still question why we kept going.

"Did I have an answer?"

You said we were destined to see High Lake, splash into it hot and sweaty from the climb. It was dusk when we arrived, we were exhausted, and the lake was frozen under a thick blanket of rough snow. We laughed and you said it was like firn. Without a tent, we spent a cold night huddled together under a snow-sculped subalpine fir.

Her memories were flawless, and I was hearing the same gentle, steady voice I adored. I moved to the shade, sat by my bike and said, "Okay, tell me something only you and I would know from our last summer together."

That's easy. On August 14 we tubed the Bitterroot River from Fort

Missoula to Maclay Bridge. The water was unimaginably clear, crystalline you said. We stopped three times, and wading waist-deep we could see our toes, and almost hidden under colored stones there were crayfish. I caught one, held it up. It had only one pincer claw. Before we left the river, we built a cairn on a sand bar under the bridge, took turns placing mudstones from the river, five each, and I added a handful of smooth rainbow pebbles we found in a dry stream bed. You told me Jason Steller would say the stones were polished by gravel and sand from Glacial Lake Missoula. Our secrets, Daniel.

"How did you get in my head today?"

George Waterbear gave me access to your implant.

"Where are you right now?"

Alone in my lab at the Desierto de Atacama research facility. And I've kept track of you, Daniel. When we were in Baltimore, I realized how much I missed being close to you and I wanted to stay in touch. So, when you slept late the second morning I slipped an attoscale locator in the dermal layer between your shoulder blades.

"You tagged me?"

I didn't think you would mind my keeping up with you. The device is called an Ytterbium Telephonic Locator. YTL for short. It was developed and fully tested by top cyberengineers under my supervision at Atacama. YTLs are perfectly safe, and I programmed yours to emit a discrete signal at prescribed intervals specific to my receiver. I also listened to your voice often and tried to talk with you, but was able to break through only a few times.

"I remember those times, sensed something different, more familiar, about the implant voice but I figured you slipped up once in a while, forgot to act like my manager."

How did you feel when we spoke briefly? You were on the tour train and told me about white-capped blues and greys on the Clark Fork River and mayflies hovering over the Jocko.

"I wanted to keep talking."

Yes, and you had me wishing for more also. I was alone near the top of Mount Aconcagua in the Andes and George Waterbear suddenly appeared in front of me.

"George was on the mountain with you?"

Yes, he took shape right in front of me.

I almost laughed. "You mean like beam me up or down?"

This is real, Daniel. Rare-earth teleportation, bka Lanthanon Transit, has been a routine means of ursavan travel for decades. George teleported to me because he feared I was about to reveal something you were not ready to hear. He reminded me how little you knew about Ursavus at that stage, and George was right. You didn't need the confusion of our relationship added to your already difficult recruitment, and that's when I sent a dissolve-immediately message to your YTL.

"How do you know so much about Ursavus?"

I heard her take a long breath. *Daniel, now at last I can say it. I have been a member of Ursavus for many years — fully enhanced and telepathic.*

I leaped to my feet and yelled, "NO!" to the microsatellite or whatever was beaming this down to me. "You're just another fake voice in my head!"

Daniel, please, I understand your shock, but I am here with you, as real as ever, and I believe you know that. I must break off now, but we will meet again very soon, and you can always trust that my telepathy is zeroed out when we are together.

38

Diamonds on a Narrow Ledge

Everything she said, the tone of her voice, every nuance and turn of phrase told me I'd been talking with Apella, but I still had doubts. Was it really her or someone else, maybe a perfectly programmed cyborg? All the memories she recited, all those details. Ursavus would have known most of them if they were surveilling me when I was Jason's student.

I stood on the open cliffside and shouted, "GEORGE WATER-BEAR!" and W A T E R B E A R echoed so loud I yelled back, "I KNOW YOU'RE OUT THERE, GEORGE! YOU AND ROSE THE MASTERMINDS! APELLA'S WITH YOU?!"

There was no echo, only an uphill breeze whistling through trees, and I stared across Zāpus Canyon, half-expected to see George with Apella, then tightened my helmet strap, hopped on my bike and started counting pedal strokes to clear my mind. It didn't help. All I could think was, Apella is in Ursavus — fully enhanced. I was just above a switchback when I heard, "Hey Dan, wait up. It's Sula."

I stopped and fussed, "Not again, Rose, damn it. And this time I have to keep pace with a teenage powerhouse on a Heckler. Why didn't you send Apella?"

Sula in pink and white racing spandex and matching helmet whizzed by, stopped ten feet past me, flipped her bike around and said, "I like to think Apella and I have a bunch in common. Your friend was my sponsor, and oh how little I knew of her until I was telepathic.

You're a very fortunate guy, Dan Oyente, and you hardly realize it." She flipped her bike around again, smiled over her shoulder. "My dad told me you like setting your own pace, so I'll go first and wait for you on the ridgeline."

I watched her pedal away and knew Rose had something else planned for my day. "How far to the ridgeline?" I shouted, and Sula yelled back, "About ninety minutes. Enjoy the climb."

I pushed hard for nearly an hour, easing back when my vision started to blur. In a near stupor, pulling over the crest of a long hill, I squinted at movement out ahead then stopped short, put both feet down and froze. A bear — a grizzly — was backing out of thick brush a hundred feet up the road, and he or she had my scent in the uphill breeze. George and I had been dangerously close to sixty-three grizzlies in Yellowstone with no mishaps, but I hadn't faced any of them alone.

I thought Grab the pepper spray but it was too late. The bear was in a charge — coming fast straight down at me. Was it a bluff? A serious charge? Drop the bike, get fetal! No! Straddle the bike — don't move — no eye contact. Fifty feet — thirty — twenty and yellow-brown eyes were inches from my front wheel a split second before two hundred tawny pounds turned and charged up the bank. I unlocked my knees, tried to relax and enjoy the sight of a healthy young grizzly ambling away. Wishing I could be that nonchalant, I jumped on my bike, felt the adrenaline drain and pedaled hard until I caught up with Sula waiting for me at an unmarked intersection. "You see the grizzly?" I asked, nearly out of breath.

"Nooo, wish I had. Where?"

"On the road two miles down, a big youngster, probably a male. He charged but veered off the last second."

Her eyes lit up. "Fully enhanced, you could tell gender, mood, general intent, and be able to redirect as needed."

I thought of George that last day in Yellowstone, saying a cinnamon black bear with a new cub is a propitious sign. I never guessed he was reading the bears' minds.

Sula said, "Of course he was, and George would have changed their behavior if necessary. Lucky for you that young grizzly wasn't bloated on green berries or he might have blasted a cloud of foul waste at you. Let's ride."

We held an equal pace to the ridgeline, turned north at the T and climbed two miles to a level stretch that Sula said was smooth enough for a roadie. She grinned when I thought Thius might call it a frontier highway. "No, it's just the ridgeline road to all of us," she said, "but my dad might warn you, Don't get too comfy. The Fern Creek down will not disappoint, and the top of it's just ahead."

We stopped at a three-way junction marked by wooden signs to Fern Creek, Pika Pass, and Shewolf Gulch. I asked, "Why no sign for Zāpus Canyon?"

Sula pursed her lips and said, "Shewolf Gulch is the official name, but it's been Zāpus to us ever since a jumping mouse — that's Zāpus princeps — nearly made Nate and me crash. We were doing thirty on the downhill when one arched in front of my face. Instinct said hit the brakes, but I could hear Nate close behind. I didn't slow and a mouse tail brushed my forehead. I've seen two other jumping mice, both in huckleberry thickets about a mile down from here. I'll show you — but wait, this is a serious hill. How are your brakes? I've got new cables in my pack if you want to change yours out."

"Thanks, Sula, I'm good, checked my brakes this morning…pads have minimal wear and cables are new."

"All right then. Don't ride too close. See ya."

I expected her to stop at an open slope, but she chose a wooded site where the bushes were high and dense. "Oh, the berries here," she said. "They always get extra plump with maximum tart, perfect for pies and everything. They'll be ripe in a few weeks, and we can pick quarts from the roadside unless the bears beat us to 'em. I like when they do, and I'll wait for you at an overlook two miles down just after a long straightaway, and my dad does have a name for that one. CBH he calls it, Chain Break Hill. It's steep and smooth, and you're already thinking minimal brakes, so slow down when you first see me. Okay, startin' down. Give me a long-minute lead."

The road matched the steepest mountain two-laner I'd ridden, and Sula didn't mention three large drainage moguls. Airborne over all three, I was so pumped I skidded to a stop ten feet past her, spun around, braced my bike against a boulder and wished she didn't know I felt like an old man acting silly cool. "Yikesabee," she squeeled and walked her bike next to mine. "You're good, and aren't you excited about enhancements making you even better? I mean, think strength, balance, reaction time, effortless boulder hopping, and the so-quiet of a telepathic partner on a long ride."

Can't wait, I thought, still feeling the rush, and according to Rose, I'd also be overwhelmingly persuasive, able to alter minds, but I'm not into that, not that kind of person.

Sula propped her bike, whipped off her helmet and hung it over the handlebar. "Mr. Oyente — how you see yourself — is it really that important? You and others with special gifts could save billions of people and prevent extinction of myriad other species. Persuading people to accept necessary change remains an insurmountable problem you could help fix."

I searched her eyes, Heather, Elena, Sula — whoever she is — she actually believes this stuff.

"Yes siree I do," she said, "and my dad was right when he told the ursavan planners you'd be a hard case. Most of us still believe nothing less than full enhancement will put your doubts about us to rest. We know you have a healthy interest in agelessnesss and telepathy, and that's a start, so let me switch to ursavan mode and try to ease your mind about enhancements, particularly mind reading."

Her eyes flashed me and she rubbed her temples — just like her mother, Rachel Smyth.

"Ursavan enhancements are categorically safe and problem-free," Sula declared. "Physical exercise is required during assimilation, and I gained telepathy during a thirty-minute mat and parallel bars routine I'd put together. Apella was in the gym with me, and in that brief time my body painlessly incorporated hundreds of attoimplants — minute teleceptors in the dermis of my head and neck. Right now they are detecting quantal changes in the air associated with your thoughts and transducing the data into ultrafast impulses. Four of my cranial nerves were enhanced to speed impulses to my brain. Multiple brain centers were remapped to process the information into telepathic awareness."

"Whoa! Where did all that come from, Sula? Are you part cyborg?"

"No way, and leave your pack and helmet here, please."

"Where are we going?"

She took my hand, led me to a row of hemlocks on a narrow ledge hidden from the road. "Stand tall now and relax," she said and pulled something from a pouch around her neck. "Here, hold one in each hand and make fists. They're diamonds. Time to meet a friend. Close your eyes and ride the breeze."

A cold gust — like winter — chilled me — then a blast of heat and I found myself standing at the edge of a mountain lake, gripping the diamonds. "Sula, what just happened? Where am I?"

I turned and saw a woman nearby. She blew a kiss, walked toward me and said, "Welcome back to High Lake, Daniel. You have just traveled 162 miles and ascended 1,986 feet, much easier than our long wintry climb years past."

Her voice was quiet and sure, her eyes dark brown and calming with gold flecks at the edges — gorgeous hair and a hint of patchouli, Apella or a perfect replica — and dressed in a sage-grey jumpsuit with six pewter buttons along the front, and a narrow silver belt. Wow!

She smiled, pushed her bangs to the side and said, "Trust what you sense to be true and welcome to your first teleport." She unfolded my fists, took the diamonds and slipped them in her pocket. "Take off your shoes and socks, Daniel, let's test the water."

We waded in and I could see my feet on the sandy bottom but they felt dry and warm. "Is this really happening?" I asked. "Am I actually here?"

"You are here and unenhanced, Daniel. Give your brain a few more seconds too catch up with your body. And please stop doubting me. I am not a finely tuned ursavan doppleganger sent to persuade you to join."

I looked at her face. "No, I'm past that. I believe you are Apella, but I have other doubts."

She wrapped her arm around my waist, glanced toward shore and said, "Take in the sights and scents, Daniel — pine and fir, mountain heather, bearberry, paintbrush, shooting stars, pipits and pikas, so many and so much — and think about our time here long ago."

I told her I remember a long, bitter cold night, and being close and awake for most of it. "All good memories of a blissful, simpler time for us, Apella."

We waded back to shore and walked along the sandy edge, shoulder to shoulder like we used to. We were quiet together and I didn't want it to stop, but my thoughts got in the way and I blurted, "I don't like saying this, Apella, but no one has been straight with me since this venture began — not even you. When we were in Baltimore you were a member of Ursavus, you knew about the mission and must have known about Nate."

She stopped, made eye contact and said, "Yes, Daniel, I have always known about Nate, and I hope you will understand. I desperately wanted to tell you about him but I could not in Baltimore or any time since. It would have destroyed any chance we had to recruit you. And now I sense you are leaning toward Ursavus. Is this true?"

"Yes, while I'm with you."

"But your decision to join must not center on our relationship."

"Is that always the way it is? Thius said he joined for the people, not the cause."

"Surely you recognize the simplicity of that statement. Thius could not have joined for friendships alone. No one can. Oh, Daniel, I wish joining Ursavus could be as easy for you as it was for me. As you well know, space has fascinated me since my parents first showed me a clear night sky, and working at the slow pace of nonursavan science I couldn't bear the thought of embracing death before experiencing at least one futurist breakthrough. My recruitment included an internship with ursavan scientists, after which I had no qualms about joining. Now enough about me. I know you still have questions."

"Yes, would you please tell me exactly when you found out about the implant?"

She ran her finger over the scar on my forehead and said, "The hideous device was already in your brain when I heard about it. I knew people were working on brain implants but had no idea they were field testing with humans. Ursavus is very powerful but not omnipresent or omniscient, and we were not aware of the small cadre of miscreants plotting to test a prototype on you. The government agents who approached me before I saw you in Baltimore described the mission as low risk, a routine evaluation of a dissident group loosely associated with the offbeat academic Jason Steller. If an inkling of a brain implant was in those agents' thoughts, I would have known — warned you. It was too late when I found out. Ursavus had decided to preempt the mission and I took George's word that you were not in danger. Now, Daniel, it is time for your next appointment."

She held out her left arm, palm down in a fist then palm up with fingers flared. I did the same. It was our parting ritual, just ours.

I told her, "I still have no compelling reason to join Ursavus except for the people — you especially, Apella."

She put the diamonds back in my hand and said, "Soon again for us," and I found myself standing next to the glass table in the Yrisse conference room. My thoughts were jumbled, out of order — body before mind — a few seconds to catch up.

George walked in, took the diamonds from me, and said, "Once fully enhanced you can teleport without these, and we hope that will transpire very soon." He saw me glance at a badge on his left lapel. The badge bore an image of a water bear — hadn't seen George wear it before. "A transcendent symbol, Dan, as I will explain tomorrow, and you have had enough for one day, more than enough for any nonursavan. We have comfortable quarters for you tonight."

He ushered me through a side door into a stylishly furnished efficiency apartment scented like fresh-from-the-oven pizza. "You'll find all you need here," he said, nodding to a large pullout sofa bed. "Your alarm is set, Dan, and an intern will arrive at 0700 to help start your next day with us."

I was flat-out on the sofa bed before he closed the door and was in the same position when the alarm went off at 0630.

39

Out of Mind

The intern knocked twice, walked in and announced formally, "Breakfast call, Mr. Oyente. I am here to provide fuel for your challenging day."

He wore a suit like Apella's and his dark shoulder-length hair and young face reminded me of Nate. "I am not of your son's generation," he said and marched stiffly to the kitchen.

I watched him brew café-rich espresso, squeeze fresh orange juice, slice strawberries into a bowl of granola and add a dollup of yogurt — all in less than three minutes. Has to be a cyborg, I thought.

He gave me a cold stare. "My name is Riffle Stone and like other ursavans I have been enhanced, but we do not refer to ourselves as cyborgs. I will exit now and return at 0830 for the purpose of escorting you to Dr. Waterbear's laboratory. Please be prepared."

I opened the door at 0830, and Mr. Stone met me with a courtly bow. "Shall we, Mr. Oyente?" he said. "Dr. Waterbear awaits your arrival. Walk with me please."

His long stride was similar to Nate's. Could he be Nate? He stopped at a heavy steel door marked E-23 and said, "Please address questions regarding your son to Dr. Waterbear." The door slid open, and Mr. Stone turned on his heels and vanished.

I took two halting steps into a brightly lit laboratory and did a quick scan — climate-control chambers, lots of shelves, four large computer screens, equipment I didn't recognize and another door in the back. In the far right corner, a faded wicker chair looked like a hot seat next to an apparatus labeled ultraviolet sterilizer. Off-center, six swivel stools were lined up next to a four-by-eight stainless table. Two wireless devices on the table resembled Jason's quantum phone.

I spun around when I heard George behind me. He wheeled two stools to the end of the table and motioned me to sit on his left. "I will be brief and direct," he said. "Your profile accurately predicted a most difficult case, but as our recruitment efforts got underway we felt you would choose to join Ursavus given enough experience with us. It is time for you to tell me if that remains a possibility, and as before, I am not reading your mind. I prefer equal exchange."

I stared at the wireless devices. Were they running experiments or recording my every move and thought?

George sat patiently. "Where are you with a decision, Dan? Do you still wish to remain an outsider? Failure to recruit you has become unthinkable to us, but our recruiting efforts are drawing to a close."

I said, "All I know right now is I'm feeling some relief about Apella, and I do not want to lose contact with anyone I've met here."

"So much talent, so little resolve," he said. "Dan, I am not exaggerating when I say your hyperthymesia exceeds any long-term declarative memory we have achieved through enhancement, and fully enhanced you would most likely possess more persuasive power than anyone in human history."

"George, if that means you see me as some kind of hyperpersuasive, planet-saving nouveax messiah, I find that almost laughable."

"Hmmh, put that way it does sound laughable. I've not thought of you as messianic. The term secular savior is more fitting, for you would transcend religious boundaries."

He set his elbows on the table and steepled his hands. "Dan, few unenhanced minds can grasp the enormity of problems we all face. I ask you to take a leap of faith and believe that Ursavus holds solutions to these problems. Indeed, we envision some political shuffling, and humanity will need some assistance — persuasive prodding you might call it — to accept and fully support the necessary changes. Ursavus requires a global consensus before proceeding, and we need you to think seriously about where you stand in all of this. Our efforts to gain popular support lag, and time is getting short. If Ursavus fails, it is unlikely humanity will find a way to sustain itself. If you knew as I do that you harbor the potential to save billions from an uncertain future, would you not choose to help?"

"Whew, I don't know, George. Just the idea of Ursavus feels like a heavy order for a guy like me."

"Yes, and too bad," he said. "Your recruitment has stalled, and you have forced us to consider giving you reasons to join Ursavus while you retain doubts about us. Enhancements such as those required to link telepathy with the depths of your memory could be compromised — perhaps even harmful if you remain indecisive. Also, as Apella told you, no one can join for friendships alone. You must want to join for yourself, first and foremost.

"Now another topic. There is something I've felt compelled to do since the day we met. With your permission, I will proceed to extract the implant — I assume you wish to be free of the device."

He turned on another overhead light and asked again, "Dan, is my assumption correct? You want to be free of the device?"

My heart pumped wildly — the stainless table — was it this one? "I'm more than ready to get rid of the damn thing, George! But how? What will you do?"

"A minor restorative procedure, no tissue damage, no anesthetic and no pain. You will be awake and I will explain every detail, perhaps more than you want to hear. Most of your lost memories will return when you are free of the implant. Six neural shunts blocking the memories will be eliminated, and you may experience some behavioral changes. Apella thinks the device could be contributing to a heightened edginess she noticed when the two of you were together."

He wheeled his stool to the UV sterilizer, pulled on blue surgical gloves and said, "This procedure employs attomagnetic pulse similar to what we occasionally and covertly use in our tracking work, but it is slightly more involved because of the size, structure and position of the implant in your brain." He lifted a small canister from the steriliz-er. "This is an insertion device. It interfaces with a quantum computer to direct precise pulse sequences through a set of attowires that locate and attach to the implant. You won't feel anything, but the wires will pass through your frontal bones and the membranes surrounding your brain. I will proceed now unless you say No." He held his right palm above the canister then stepped in front of me. I wanted to say No but couldn't.

"This is really creepy, George. How was it for the bears? Did they feel pain or anything? The field apparatus was so simple and we always used it from a distance."

"Stop talking and sit still, Dan. The bears felt nothing nor will you. You cannot detect attowires or attopulse." He leaned over me as if inspecting a sedated bear, and I flinched when he reached out and touched my forehead. "Attowires in place," he said. "Relax now and pay full attention. When I give the order, your implant will receive three distinct and separate attomag pulses. The first dissolves the adhesive that binds the implant to oligodendrocytes in your brain. The second fractures the implant and stimulates your immune cells to dispose of the fragments and remaining scar tissue. The final tertiary pulse breaks down and stimulates disposal of siliceous components used in crude implants like yours. All in a matter of seconds, which you should count."

He turned to the computer and ordered, "Commence pro-cedure," and eleven seconds later the computer voice announced, "Procedure complete. Implant destroyed. Allow seventy-two hours for remnants to clear."

George peeled off his gloves, dropped them in a hazardous waste container and said, "All right, Dan, stand up and walk around. Give yourself a few minutes to acclimate then get a bottle of water from the cold room, door to your right."

When I returned he was sitting at the table jotting data in a ledger. "Have a seat, Dan. How are you feeling?"

"Relieved, but I can't tell if anything is different. Is this the first time you've extracted an implant like mine from a human brain?"

"Matter of fact yes, but we ran numerous simulations with advanced cyborgs. Now tell me, have you regained any lost memories?"

I held the cold bottle against my face and said, "Yes, I remember waking up flat on my back on a steel table, felt like I'd been drugged. The room was sound proofed with padded walls. Not sure, but it might have been the day after Apella and I parted in Baltimore. I remember standing on the street watching her leave in a taxi, then nothing until the padded room. I could hardly move when four people walked in, all wearing white masks and matching lab coats. Two of them strapped me to the table. Another one held my left wrist and stuck a needle in my arm — a ten-cubic-centimeter hypodermic full of yellow fluid. The fourth one, short and chubby-faced with close-set eyes, leaned over me and said, Welcome to your government's service, Daniel. You are a prized central figure in a highly classified interagency probe of domestic dissidents. You were chosen for your exceptional memory, proven ability to gain trust, and highly rated physical skills. You have agreed to an inserted surveillance device — a state-of-the-art brain implant that will enable us to communicate with you and record data. The device is completely harmless and undetectable by outside sources, and will be painlessly removed when the mission is over. Your trainers will explain more about the implant and your assignment. Godspeed, Daniel. Find us the truth about these people.

"Everything's falling into place now, George. I remember waking up the first day of training, looking in the mirror and noticing two small bumps on my forehead. First I thought insect bites but then I could see they were sutures, and I think that's when I first became aware of the implant. I had breakfast in the mess hall, checked my email account and read Jason's note about Nate, which surprised me, then the rest of the day was typical orientation stuff, filling out forms."

George held up his hand and motioned me to the wicker chair. "It's good you have those memories filed back in place, Dan. Anything else? Are any lost memories from our time in Yellowstone coming back?"

I rubbed my forehead. "Yes. I remember you lifting a patch of moss on a boulder."

"Details," he said sharply.

"The moss covered a petroglyph, an image of a water bear. You told me it is a symbol of an ancient link between separate worlds."

He handed me a felt marker and gestured to a whiteboard on the sidewall. "Sketch the image for me, Dan."

I walked to the board, and memories poured to mind as I outlined the boulder and began drawing details of the petroglyph. George stopped me. "That's enough," he said. "Only members of Ursavus are aware of this. A satellite monitors human presence at the site twenty-four seven. If a nonursavan happens to discover the petroglyph, the experience is erased from the person's mind. In your case, our plan was to show you the petroglyph and fix it in your memory while you were in the park, but we could not allow those thoughts to surface until now. That first day on the train you surprised Thius when you mentioned the petroglyph, and he had to reinforce the memory block I applied in Yellowstone."

I dropped the marker and glared at him. "A memory block, George?! Unbelievable! You've been messing with my brain all this time — so was the government ever involved or was it Ursavus from day one? What's next?"

"Dan, please. You are still thinking I helped install the implant? Do you realize how illogical that sounds? Get hold of yourself and consider the precise, painless surgery you've just experienced. With this level of technology why would I ram a crude and dangerous walkie-talkie into your brain? That would be a premeditated violent act. No ursavan is capable of doing such a thing."

He closed his ledger and placed it on a shelf behind him. "Now, Dan, I will explain about our memory blocks. Far advanced of any technology employed by nonursavans, our blocks are attoscale-accurate, harmless and easily reversed. Unenhanced human minds regularly perform synaptic changes that are much less precise, and our blocks are very different from erasures, which involve synaptic ablation and are generally irreversible.

"The Ursavus High Council considered five recruitment-plan

options for you. They chose the one that required you to spend time with specific individuals and be introduced early to the petroglyph. I supported this approach, along with the temporary memory block. And to address messing with your brain, you recall Rose explaining to you, Ursavus has a strict rule against altering the minds of advanced recruits, but you were a nascent recruit while in Yellowstone and not yet prepared to be aware of the petroglyph."

"I suppose I have to accept that, George, but what's the big deal? Why all the secrecy? There are rock carvings everywhere. What's so special about this one?"

He looked at one of his wireless devices. "We'll get to that. Time for a break. I have to check on two gene-drive experiments, which you will learn about soon after you join. I'll be down the hall in another lab for a few minutes, and your mind needs a little time to readjust, so relax in the wicker, think about life without the implant."

40

Tuns of Space

Was the implant really gone? I couldn't tell. But there had to be some evidence, something different about my mind. I tried getting comfortable in the rickety chair, closed my eyes and recalled a bizarre dream. I was in a room with Rose, George and Jason. A silver-blue globe rotated above us, and Rose announced, Witness future Planet Earth divided into twenty-three manageable political units called Regens. George's face then covered the globe and he spoke with authority. Do not be concerned, Daniel del Oso, you have seen only a fraction of our power. Ursavus has the means to restore essential order to this planet. Gaining a mandate to proceed requires us to recruit special talents like yours.

The globe floated down to eye level and was painted with familiar names. Jason boomed, BEHOLD the current muddle of nations, states, provinces, tribes, fiefdoms, ad nauseum. Which would you choose, old student? Leadership by hyperintelligence or flounderance by despot wannabes and corporate plutocracy?

I flinched and opened my eyes when George walked in. He gestured for me to sit next to him at the stainless table and said, "This is a pivotal meeting, Dan. When it concludes, you will have until noon tomorrow to think through the experiences you've had with us. After that, if you decide not to join or remain indecisive, your recruitment terminates, you are no longer protected by ursavan laws and I must erase all knowledge of Ursavus from your mind. Erasures are permanent, as

I explained, and ours are safe. You have my word as an ursavan scientist that your mind will not be altered in any other way. You will retain memories of people, places and events but nothing about Ursavus, and you may visit us but you will not know our true identities."

"George, let me get this straight. You just helped me regain some lost memories — now you're saying if I walk away from Ursavus you're going to tease out and delete other memories, permanently alter my brain?"

He didn't respond, picked up one of the wireless devices, tapped it twice, and a rotating globe just like the one in my dream appeared inches above the table.

I swiped my hand through the globe. "You put a dream in my brain, George!"

"Yes, but no need for alarm. I set the globe scene in your mind two years ago when we were on the plane en route to Livingston. You were experiencing bouts of delirium tremens induced by toxic drugs. Physical restraint was out of the question so I chose to replace your self-destructive thoughts with an informative scene, and it worked. You stopped hallucinating within minutes. Tell me your thoughts regarding the contents of the dream then we need to proceed to other issues."

"George, I'm sitting here trying not to freak out, thinking about memory loss and attowires you might have left in my brain. I don't care about the contents of the dream, and I stopped taking radical politics seriously a long time ago."

"Regrettable, because I assure you radical change is essential for human survival. Sequence Thirty Four," he ordered, and the globe disappeared, replaced by a series of scenes from Yellowstone. "Dan, I'm certain you recognize these satellite views of the Meniscus Lake Trail in Yellowstone from the day we hiked it, and in this final frame you were looking at the petroglyph. We'll hold on that frame while I begin the story of this stone object, what it means to ursavans and why we keep it secret. I recall you saying you knew nothing about water bears until I showed them to you in Yellowstone. Is this correct?"

"Yes."

"And then at Rosey's you found a book with a chapter on water bears. That was the timeworn meiofauna tome. She bought that copy at a book fair when we were sixteen. It's nearly as dry as a water bear tun and much less informative. Did you read about the tuns?"

"Yes, tough, desiccated sacs that can withstand harsh conditions."

"Indeed, and until recently on this planet only a few nonursavans gave water bears the respect they deserve. The tuns are exceedingly close to lifeless but they retain a spark of life that is virtually indestructible."

He ordered, "Glass Tuns," and the globe reappeared in place of the petroglyph scene. The globe was not rotating, its surface was moist and I couldn't make out any details. "For unenhanced eyes," George said, and a tangerine ray of light magnified a portion of the globe's surface. "That should help, Dan. Now watch closely and you will observe tuns transforming into water bears."

I expected to see the animals hatch out of the tuns, but George had it right. They didn't hatch, they transformed. Claws started wriggling at the surface as the tuns changed from lifeless specks to live animals.

George explained, "This species, Hydrursa decilleana, is unusually tough even for water bears. When exposed to life-threatening conditions, H. decilleana vitrifies — yes, each one turns into a glass cocoon that envelops and preserves that spark of water bear life. The glass cocoons of H. decilleana can withstand the vacuum of space and the extreme heat and pressure of re-entry through our atmosphere."

George clapped his hands, "Think of it, Dan! Right here on Earth we have animals that seem magical, even to a scientist. These tough little parcels of life can be swept up in the wind and carried from one pond or patch of moss to another. Out in space, they could be blown about for years by solar winds, perhaps settle in pores on a meteor, a comet or a spaceship and return to Earth or other suitable planets ready to absorb a drop or two of water and start their business of lumbering about sucking fluid from plant cells."

I frowned, and George could tell I was wondering why he told me all this.

"Dan, it is not science fiction to say water bears can exist in space, and yes, I do get excited talking about them. I cannot overstate their significance to me and to Ursavus, and if you are still considering membership in Ursavus you must hear more about water bears now."

"For sure then," I told him.

"A wise decision, Dan, one you will cherish as an ursavan but not remember at all if you choose to remain apart."

George tapped the wireless device, the globe started rotating again, and he said, "I am very proud of my family name and its history, Dan. The Ursavi Tribe's Waterbear Clan, of which I am a member, was founded thousands of years before water bears were discovered on this planet, and a remarkably accurate clan myth tells about water bears, the petroglyph, and the clan's origin.

"I first heard the clan myth and was introduced to water bears on my twelfth birthday and the memories remain crystal clear...my tutor's moccasins shuffling ahead of me on the Meniscus Lake Trail and her steady hand lifting the moss and tracing the outline of the petroglyph. She told me, This is an ancient picture of a water bear, an animal found wherever it is wet. We cannot see these animals for which we are named but they hold great power. This stone picture was carved by a stranger from another world. The stranger's people used water bear power to travel great distances. Early members of our clan met two of these strangers here in the valley of the yellow stones."

George stood up, tapped his wireless device again and the globe contracted to a pinpoint then was lost in a slowly turning image of the Milky Way. "I prefer the Latin term Via Lactea," he said. "I need to retrieve some papers from archives before continuing this discussion. Back in five minutes. Be prepared for our meeting to become — I would say, seriously challenging."

41

Pitch-Black Five

When George returned he slapped two red folders on the table, sat across from me and said, "Best we are face to face for what I am going to say. There is nothing more we can do to prepare you for this. Most of it will seem far-fetched, preposterous, but it is the absolute truth — all of it."

I grabbed the water bottle, took two gulps. The Milky Way continued to rotate above the table. "You definitely have my attention, George."

"Good, and perhaps what you have just learned about water bears will help you take all this in. I'll begin by saying my tutor's story, my clan's myth, was largely confirmed by a person who made an auspicious first visit to this laboratory. It was midmorning January 15, 1965, and I was here enjoying coffee with Rosey and William. We were discussing the depth of snow on nearby peaks when we sensed a presence in the hallway. The door opened and a stranger in a dark blue uniform said it was essential he speak with us. His voice was a low tenor, bright and clear, slightly mechanical, and when he entered the room I thought he had a knightly aura. He was trim, nearly six feet tall and wore a water bear badge on his left lapel.

"I am Meterion Waterbear, he said to us, and I am most pleased to greet George Waterbear, Snowmoon Waterbear, and William Yrisse McClun.

"The visitor took the seat you are in now, Dan, and I tried recalling where I'd seen him before. He said, We have not met, sir, but we are related. My family's home planet is Decilles, in the Via Lactea Galaxy, 14,593 light-years from this planet you call Earth.

"Realize, Dan, we were not telepathic at the time, and Rosey asked the visitor how he knew our names, especially her maiden name. Please excuse, he said. I am telepathic and you were thinking your names when I said mine, and William now wishes for me to know that George and Snowmoon are cousins. Please excuse again. Decilleans are mindful and peaceful, and strive to remain unobtrusive. It is therefore proper for me to suspend my use of telepathy for the remainder of this encounter. From this moment on, I cannot read your minds."

George peered at me over his wire frames, and the Milky Way image faded away. "You still with me, Dan?"

"I am, George, and just like you said, far-fetched and preposterous, but I haven't missed a word and part of my mind tells me you're not making this up."

"That is correct, and try putting yourself at the scene that long-ago winter morning. You, Rosey, William and me — four skeptics sitting here trying to fathom this strange person. He had the appearance of someone forty-five to fifty but said he was born 157 Earth-years past. His face and hands were dark brown, his eyes sparkled, appeared to have flecks of gold in them. I noticed Rosey focused on an amber pendant hanging from his silver chain necklace. She asked politely if his home planet had resin-bearing trees. He said Yes, Decilles has what you call coniferous or cone-bearing trees but this amber is synthetic, inorganic resin.

"Our visitor removed the pendant from the chain, walked around the table and gave Rosey the pendant. Please accept this as a gift, he said, from my people to your Ursavus organization. Snowmoon, William, and George, this is a momentous experience for me and I assume also for you. It is my first meeting with earthans or I should perhaps say, with humans. Understand, this is not the first time decilleans have visited Planet Earth. My ancestors developed antigravity drives and began traveling great distances in space thousands of Earth-years past, and six trips included time on this planet. You have recognized the symbol on the badge I wear. A boulder in your Yellowstone Park displays an equivalent symbol, which you call the water bear petroglyph. Decilleans have great respect for water bears. These minuscule animals are unsurpassed in their ability to traverse interstellar space. We have found them on thirty-eight planets, including Earth and Decilles, and we have gained much by studying them. Our space program icon is the water bear."

George opened one of the red folders and said, "This is a detailed transcript of our meeting that day. I will read now, starting with the section our compositor titled Partnership Proposal. At this point, Meterion was seated at the end of the table and his voice had a somber tone.

"Snowmoon, George, and William, the decillean people know your Ursavus organization has developed potential earth-saving energy and cybertechnology far advanced of your planet's dominant cultures. Decilleans share your concern that widespread calamity looms during your next century, and human nature impedes your efforts to prevent it. I am here to propose a partnership. With your permission, decilleans are prepared to provide your Ursavus organization a full set of plans and materials to develop powers and technologies known only to machine societies. This will include a secure quantum-based cybersystem, teleportation, telepathy and sundry other mind and body enhancements. You have begun to explore what you call quantum technologies, but what I am offering would expand your power beyond anything you could adequately describe as quantum. I use the term only because it is familiar to you."

I had to interrupt. "A partnership, George? It sounds more like a takeover plan. Didn't it to you?"

"It crossed our minds but the thoughts didn't linger. We dismissed it as earthbound paranoia. Listen to Meterion's next statements.

"A partnership would be a giant step into the unknown for my people and yours, but I assure you it would not involve any loss of sovereignty. Please allow me now to address an element of precedence that underlies this proposal. There were chance events in the distant past that forged a link between my people and yours and established the Waterbear family name on Earth."

George opened the other red folder and said, "Our transcript's title here is Ancient Connections, and our compositor noted William's comment that Meterion put his hand over his water bear badge before picking up where he left off.

"George, Snowmoon, and William, please understand, decilleans were initially drawn to Earth and similar planets to study hyperactive crusts and their effects on life. The tectonic hotspot your people and mine call the Yellowstone Caldera was discovered early, and two of my distant relatives, Decilla Waterbear and her brother Leeton Waterbear were the lead seismologists on one of the research visits. The petroglyph marks the site where Decilla Waterbear died 11,047 Earth-years past, killed instantly by steam and pyrophoric gas from an uncharted geyser. At that time in our history, decilleans did not have restoration technology — Decilla could not be saved — and her brother, overwhelmed with shock and not himself, burned the family's water bear crest into the boulder."

George looked at me as though trying to gauge my reaction. "I need your full attention for all of this, Dan. No drifting of thoughts or emotional outbursts."

"I'm still registering every word, George but…"

"No buts! You must listen with undivided attention to what Meterion said next.

"The site of Decilla Waterbear's tragic death was immediately purged, but a follow-up ensurer team found fragments of Decilla's DNA in soil microbes within a two-meter radius of the site. The ensurers also discovered Decilla's DNA fragments at an encampment twenty-seven meters directly south and downhill from the site. These fragments were found in human skin cells loosely attached to flakes of chalcedonic stone. Decillean scientists surmised that the skin cells were sloughed from the hand of a Lithic Culture hunter — I believe you would say Stone Age hunter — and presumably the hunter was fashioning a tool or weapon."

George closed the transcript folder and asked how much knowledge I have regarding virus infections.

I told him I took a college virology course, and I think Armageddon whenever I read about emerging viruses.

"Well, Meterion's people discovered viruses many thousands of years before humans did. Viruses on Decilles, like those on Earth, cannot reproduce on their own. To do so, they must infect cells of a suitable host. In certain cases after a virus infection, some viral DNA or RNA remains in the host and becomes part of the host's DNA.

"And Dan, I believe you can understand the decilleans' distress when they discovered short segments of Decilla Waterbear's DNA fused into human DNA in the skin cells found in Yellowstone."

I took a deep breath, and George said, "Yes, like remnants of a viral infection, some of Decilla's DNA — some of her genes — had become part of a Stone Age human's DNA."

Two loud knocks turned our attention to the door. "Right on time as expected," George said. "A friend with a more personal connection to this narrative," and Walter Smyth walked in. I noticed a pendant like Rose's on a silver chain around his neck — kind of flashy for Walter. He took a seat next to George and held out his pendant for me to get a closer look. "Daniel, your thinking is correct," he said. "I do not wear this in the store. It is synthetic amber, much like Ms. Rose's. He turned to George and said, "If you will, please."

George ordered, "PITCH-BLACK FIVE," and the room went totally dark. Exactly five seconds later, the lights were back on, and a strange man in a blue uniform was in Walter's seat. A hologram, I thought, as the stranger reached across the table, shook my hand firmly and said, "So you know I am not an illusion, Daniel. Please do not be alarmed. I am Walter Smyth. I am also Meterion Waterbear, and I am with you today at the behest of my long-term friend George Waterbear. We agreed you would benefit from learning about Decilla Waterbear's legacy directly from me, a decillean, and like George, I will remain nontelepathic for this meeting."

I stared at the water bear symbol on his badge and fumbled for words, "You…you're the same Walter Smyth who collects old tractor seats, served me coffee and cinnamons at the Cedarville store and knows how Bach should sound on the piano?"

He shrugged his shoulders and said, "Yes, and all of this must seem peculiar to you but it is a most gratifying situation for me. My Walter Smyth identity began in your year 1980 when I accepted an offer from the Ursavan High Council to divide my existence between Earth and Decilles. I take great delight working in Smyth's store. However, my time there is limited and therefore I share my existence in Cedarville with Orin, an ursavan whose enhancements like mine, enable physical change. Orin was proprietor Smyth the day you arrived in Cedarville and when you boarded the tour train to Missoula. During those times I was in conference at Ursavus E with George and my daughter Delia Waterbear, whom you know as Rachel Smyth."

I quick-scanned memories of my visits to Smyth's store, knew I couldn't tell one proprietor from the other. And Mr. Meterion continued, "Daniel, I am most pleased by your expanding friendships with Delia, her ursavan partner Thius, and their daughter Sula. Delia and Thius rarely leave Planet Earth, but Sula visits her decillean relatives and friends often."

Visions of Sula cartwheeling across a log onto a hovering spacecraft mingled with thoughts of her saying she's a hybrid — bear and sturgeon. Did she want to tell me she's a decillean human — a real hybrid?

"Is something disturbing you, Daniel?" Mr. Meterion asked.

"Uh, no, I'm just trying to imagine what it's like for Sula — having parents from different worlds — if all this is true."

George shuffled papers in his folder and said, "It is all true, Dan, and Meterion needs to get back to the topic of Decilla Waterbear."

"Yes, Daniel, with your permission, I shall pick up where George left off. Are you prepared to hear the full story?"

"I think so. Any chance it will get easier to believe?"

"Yes, that is our hope, and first I wish to assure you the decilleans were duly concerned about the fate of Decilla Waterbear's DNA on Planet Earth. Visits to Earth were immediately suspended, and global debate ensued over what should and could be done. Decilleans of that era had the means to excise DNA fragments from the human carriers but decillean law forbade it.

"When it became clear that some of Decilla's genes were fused into human DNA within skin cells, nanoorbiters were deployed to locate all of the human carriers. As you might imagine, Daniel, our main concern was —"

"No!" I blurted. "Don't tell me Decilla's genes showed up in human eggs or sperm."

Meterion continued. "Fragments of Decilla's DNA were soon identified in seven members of a hardy band of hunters who lived in the Upper Yellowstone. Decilleans referred to these hunters as the calderans because they rarely ventured further than twenty kilometers from the Yellowstone Caldera.

"For over two Earth years, Decilla's DNA was not found in any other location on your planet. However, during that time, orbiter data confirmed the presence of decillean genes in the germ cells of eleven calderans. Indeed, some of Decilla Waterbear's genes had become heritable, destined to spread from generation to generation in humans, and further interference by the decilleans was, I believe you would say, out of the question."

"Oh Man, the ultimate nightmare," I said, and Meterion smiled. "George, we discussed this many years ago, this trait so common in nonursavan humans. I believe I described it as a strong, somewhat mindless tendency to jump to negative conclusions and the attendant desire to hear no more."

George gripped Meterion's shoulder. "You did say that, old friend, and you also acknowledged that long ago in your history, many decilleans may have reacted similarly, especially regarding genetic issues."

"Yes, that would have been before my ancestors understood the significant contributions alien viruses made to the decillean gene pool."

I told Meterion I'd heard of the effects of viral leftovers in humans but those weren't from alien viruses. They originated on Earth, and their effects were neutral or negative.

"Generalizations, Daniel, based on untested assumptions. Do you wish for me to continue?"

"Yes."

"Very well. How persistent were Decilla Waterbear's genes in humans? Orbiter data chronicled her genes residing in the western zone of your North American continent for many generations then spreading swiftly and widely when intercontinental travel became common. Based on our latest census, 78,238,046 Earth people possess genes traceable to Decilla Waterbear. Of special interest, all members of Ursavus are carriers of Decilla Waterbear's genes."

My mind raced — George Rose Jason Thius Sula Rachel Erik — all carry alien genes? Even Apella? "Do I have decillean genes?" I blustered.

George said, "Unfortunately no, you do not, and I do mean unfortunately. If Daniel Oyente had decillean genes we would not be struggling to recruit him. He would already be with us, already enhanced to whatever degree suits him."

Meterion concurred. "Yes, Daniel, I believe you would have welcomed membership and enhancements."

"As did your friend Apella," said George. "You will be glad to hear she maintains perfect health and does not age. Like all ursavans, she is living proof of the long-term benefits of genetic enhancement."

"Irrefutably," said Meterion. "And, when I made my first visit to Earth, ursavans had already enhanced themselves for longevity and pacifism, and dedication to peace and welfare. Be assured, Daniel, decilleans would not have approached Ursavus before these special attributes were affirmed.

"Decades before I arrived, decillean orbiters observed this Ursavus group, a secretive global faction, outpacing all other earthbound R&D efforts in every major field. We watched ursavans build self-sustaining facilities like Ursavus E, equipped with advanced energy and cybersystems. We were singularly impressed with the ursavans' ability to maintain secrecy while many members held positions in nonursavan society."

"And how did we accomplish all that?" George asked rhetorically. "We pondered our success for years. Was it related to genetics? We knew our DNA had some unique features, specifically a few unusual viruslike inclusions containing a chemical compound not found in other humans. Were these features associated with the early success of Ursavus? Meterion had an answer for us."

"Indeed," said Meterion, "as I told George, Snowmoon, and William, it is most likely that the genius of Ursavus derived in part from synergistic interactions of human genes with a few fragments of DNA traceable not to viruses but to Decilla Waterbear. Decilleans call this mixing and concerted action of genes derived on separate worlds Pancosmic Genomixis, PCGM. And we honor the PCGM that transformed the ancient tragedy of Decilla Waterbear into the uplifting legacy of Ursavus."

George smiled and said he was reminded of Meterion adding some levity to their first meeting.

Meterion leaned back and stroked his amber. "Aah yes. I asked what response the three of you would hear if you told outsiders your perfect health and apparent agelessness were due to synergism with extraterrestrial genes deposited in the Yellowstone Caldera thousands of years past."

George pushed his stool in. "Enjoyable discussion you two, and I have a scheduled meeting now with an intern getting up to speed on decarbonation politics. Riffle Stone will be in with refreshments."

Minutes later, Mr. Stone entered with a service tray, set coffee and a cinnamon donut in front of me and said, "Dr. Waterbear will return promptly, and please enjoy some nourishment. Dr. Waterbear wishes for you to continue the discourse with Meterion Waterbear."

42

A Full Strength Maser

Flecks of gold sparkled in Meterion's eyes as he reached across the table and shook my hand again. "Aah yes, Daniel, Pancosmic Genomixis and Ursavus, the uplifting legacy of Decilla Waterbear's tragic death. I welcome this opportunity to address your questions regarding the presence of decillean genes in humans and the intentions of my people. And I do realize that hearing and seeing all of this out of the blue, as you might say, can be confusing."

I tried matching his tone. "Sir, if your telepathy were turned on, you would know my confusion is minor compared to my concerns about motives. It's hard to believe your people had only science in mind when they visited Earth. Was there no desire to colonize? Maybe the gene transfer wasn't accidental. Surely your decillean technology was advanced enough at the time to infect a few Stone Age humans with decillean DNA. Or did some of your early explorers take human form, stay here and gradually assimilate with humans? I mean, what better way to unobtrusively colonize Earth?"

"No, unequivocally, no," he said without a hint of drama. "Such thoughts are abhorrent to any decillean."

"But has that always been the case, sir? Did your people feel that way during Decilla Waterbear's time?"

"Daniel, I much prefer to be called Meterion, and the answer to your question is Yes, decilleans have always had strict rules against interference. This is not to say we are averse to adjusting our rules

of conduct, but meddling is not in our nature, and our precise historical records attest this."

"Then perhaps you can tell me how much of an ursavan genome
is decillean. How genetically close are members of the Waterbear families on Earth and Decilles? How closely related are you and George?"

He tilted his head as though surprised. "Daniel, I am gaining the
impression that you are more interested in antagonizing me than
obtaining answers to your questions, so let me assure you I am
immune to intimidation. If you wish to imply the ancestors of Earth's
Waterbear family were decilleans or more decillean than human — that
George and Snowmoon are more decillean than human — then Daniel
Oyente, you are in this case critical to a fault, and your concerns merit
an emphatic No. George and Snowmoon's ancestors were decidedly
human, as are they. Their family name was adopted by early carriers
of Decilla Waterbear's genes — human carriers not decillean carriers.

"Please listen carefully as I explain how and when the family
name Waterbear appeared on your planet. The story centers around
the Yellowstone petroglyph, which I hasten to say was never autho-
rized. It was in fact a violation of decillean law forbidding marking
or defacement of any aspect of an alien planet. Sentiment arose in
the Decillean High Council to retrieve the petroglyph and return the
boulder surface to its natural state, but this would have required
additional disturbance of the site and was vehemently opposed by
Decilla Waterbear's family and close colleagues, who considered
the petroglyph a memorial to her work and abbreviated life."

I told him I didn't understand the fuss about the petroglyph. "I
mean, why not just leave it and let humans think whatever, tell stories
about it like they have for other petroglyphs?"

Meterion tilted his head again. "Is that what you would have
done, Daniel?"

I took a sip of coffee and said, "Probably. I'm a loner. I tend to
leave well enough alone."

"Honestly put, and arguably consistent with the long-term decillean rule of noninterference, but the issue was more complex. Decilla

Waterbear's brother, Leeton Waterbear, created a serious problem when he altered the surface of the boulder. In a panic and momentarily reckless, Leeton used a full strength maser, which rendered the water bear image a complex alloy of elements, a conspicuous emblem indestructible by any force on Earth until your scientists began splitting atoms. The petroglyph evidenced an alien presence, and this was not something decilleans could accept."

I thought, Wait a minute — an indestructible alien presence — a stone object. How would people on Earth react? If the alloy were analysed, maybe one or two news articles perused by a few thousand science buffs?

"Please let me add, Daniel, the issue was further complicated when three years after Decilla's death, nanoorbiters recorded human activity at the site of the water bear petroglyph. Three women and two men, five members of the calderan group that carried Decilla's genes, were seen at the boulder during a summer solstice. At dawn and dusk, one of the women carefully exposed the petroglyph and guided the others in what appeared to be a religious ritual. The situation was unprecedented, and the Decillean High Council made a most-difficult decision — an extraordinary exception to the non-interference rule. The calderan earthans would be contacted in an attempt to solve the petroglyph dilemma, and the Council put Decilla Waterbear's family in charge. One year later, Decilla's sister Xariah and brother Leeton arrived on Earth with full authority to negotiate a lasting settlement that would cause minimal disturbance. I believe you would say Xariah and Leeton were decillean plenipotentiaries."

A click and a flash of blue light from the far end of the table distracted me. "Excuse," said Meterion, "George's Gaia Gauge is operative, cycling normally. It records and analyzes environmental conditions from earthwide to venues smaller than this room. Like most equipment at Ursavus E, Gaia Gauges are attoscale, and without my telepathy I do not know details, but I feel certain the one here is recording the changes in your body temperature as you process this conversation. Also without my telepathy I can only trust that you remain interested in learning more about the water bear petroglyph."

"Actually, I'd prefer to hear more about the Gaia Gauge, but okay, I've read stories since I was a kid, hackneyed fantasies about visitors from space marking their presence with various glyphs or geometric formations. I used to love the stories, still do some of them."

"I understand, Daniel. Your mind is earthbound and admirably critical. And like you, George, Snowmoon and William were skeptical when I first told them how the Waterbear family name originated on Earth. But they are very discerning and soon realized I spoke the truth. They also realized, as should you, that I have no inclination to contrive what humans call fairy tales. Do you wish to hear more? I will not be offended by any response, but please try to keep an open mind."

I had an urge to compliment him for his mastery of English and its idioms, but only said, "Okay, tell me more."

"Very well. It was your autumnal equinox when Xariah and Leeton landed near the Meniscus Lake Trail. The first objects they noted were brilliant yellow aspen clones dusted with light snow and the pungent scent of large mammals bedded under the clones. There was no path to the petroglyph but five sets of moccasin tracks leading off the main trail confirmed that the calderans were at the site. Xariah Waterbear's account of the visit is worth a read, Daniel. Allow me to quote a few lines.

"'So much and so many kinds of life in this place of seething energy,' Xariah wrote, 'and none seem capable of changing everything. I believe, and Leeton agrees, that only this planet herself holds that power, and Leeton reminds me that we are walking on a massive plume of molten rock, the superheated cauldron that destroyed our sister Decilla. She so loved and admired the geysers, the steaming rivers, the heated pools and ancient microbes that color them. As a scientist Decilla understood that the cauldron's heat and nutrients sustain the plethora of life here, all so peaceful now, and yes, Decilla knew the danger to her and eventually to most life on this continent and beyond. Unlike Leeton, I feel drawn, as Decilla told us she was, to the danger.'

"I hasten to add, Daniel, that decilleans eventually developed the power to divert and neutralize the cauldron's volcanic energy, but they would do so only if requested by Earth's people.

"Now Daniel, envision yourself at the first meeting of decilleans and humans? What was it like for Xariah and Leeton and the five calderans?"

"Hard to imagine, even harder to believe the meeting ever happened," I told him.

"Then I must ask you to free your mind. Envision yourself dressed in animal skins and plant parts, and you are standing next to the boulder with your calderan friends. The petroglyph is exposed, all eyes are on it. The only sounds come from the quaking aspens, but then a twig snaps, and a curious scent turns your head, and what you see makes you shudder. Two strangers with radiant rainbow hair and shiny suits stand under a tree nearby.

"Xariah wrote, 'The calderans were stunned by our presence. Their thoughts moved fast and chaotically. Leeton and I knew their Ursavi language but their fear and shock clouded our telepathy. We held out our hands to show we were free of weapons, and there was a mix of panic and reverence when they saw water bear badges on our shiny uniforms. I focused on the lead female's thoughts, tried engaging her curiosity and trust with hand signs and gentle facial expressions and soft smile. She was frightened but looked directly at me and asked with her hands and thoughts, Who are you? Where did you come from? What do you want? I answered in Ursavi, told her my name and asked for hers. I am called Ket, she said. And so began a tense calm followed by a fruitful meeting.'

"Daniel, I believe you would say the calderans were naive at that time, for they possessed none of your skepticism, had no reason to question what Xariah and Leeton told them. The calderans listened intently as Xariah pointed to the sky and told them she and her brother Leeton came from a faraway world. We are members of

The Family Waterbear, Xariah said, named for unseen but powerful water-dwelling animals, and the stone object is a picture of one.

"Ket replied, We are spirit leaders of The Winter Elk People. The animal on the rock speaks to us of great distant power.

"Leeton then told them, 'We come from a place of great power, and we wish you no harm, only safety, peace and friendship. We know about the animal on the rock. I drew this animal at a time of sadness. I was here with my older sister. We were studying the steam and the heat under us when suddenly I saw her death boil up out of the ground. I ran to her but knew she was gone, and our people had begun clearing the site. In a rage, I grabbed one of their tools and struck the top of this rock. It melted enough for me to quickly draw the animal, which I had done many times at home. The site clearers started to remove the animal picture but I would not let them. This drawing of mine, which we call the water bear petro-glyph — it now pleases me to say — will be a symbol of our meeting today, and I believe from here on we should consider the Winter Elk People members of the Waterbear family.'"

"Ket and her companions did not hesitate to agree, and a solemn pact was attained before Xariah and Leeton departed. The spirit leaders of the Winter Elk People, recognized since that day as The Founders of Earth's Waterbear Clan, pledged to watch over the petro-glyph and hold it secret. In turn — and this is known only by decilleans and ursavans — Xariah and Leeton committed the power of Decilles to protect Earth and its habitants. So now, Daniel, the origin of the clan myth George related to you is no longer a mystery, and yes, Earth has been hidden and unapproachable except by decilleans since Xariah and Leeton made that solemn pact with the Winter Elk People.

"And, Daniel, I am feeling compelled to say Homo sapiens has many fine qualities, but I have always been intrigued by your species' self-centered arrogance. To believe that Homo sapiens is the only sentient species in the cosmos, and to think this makes you safe? This is dazzling mythology. You are just lucky we found you. Do you have further questions, Daniel, persistent doubts?"

"One comment. If real — that meeting and the pact stand out as the height of interference."

"Regretfully true, and your forthright honesty is commendable. Please allow me to finish by saying that after Xariah's and Leeton's visit, there were no further contacts with humans until I arrived in 1965. However, decillean nanoorbiters and attoscale upgrades continued to monitor Earth's carriers of Decilla's genes. Our orbiters recorded the increase in carrier numbers and documented the founding of the international group Ursavus. When we intercepted William McClun's 1959 prediction of future cataclysm, and our scientists confirmed his conclusion that Earth's problems would most likely not be solved in time to save much of the life your planet supports, a global vote on Decilles mandated my official visit and the offer to transfer technologies upon request by Ursavus. I now sense George returning."

George walked in, resumed his seat and said, "So, Dan, you just can't shake the thought that the decilleans' main motive was to gain a foothold on Earth and eventually take over without conflict. Am I right?"

"Not exactly, George, it's more complicated than that. I have takeover thoughts for sure, but they're mixed with a strange tendency to believe you and Meterion. My question now is, Do I believe because my mind has been altered. How could I tell? How can you be certain that Meterion didn't alter your mind and Rose's and William's — everyone's?"

George nodded, said he understood 100 percent why I had these concerns, then pulled papers from the transcript folder and placed them in from of me. "Dan, this is the transfer agreement between the Decillean High Council and Ursavus, signed by both parties before Ursavus was granted ultraquantum powers. Note the page entitled, Mental Alteration and Enhancement. Meterion would like to say a few words about this."

"Indeed, Daniel, I can assure you decilleans have not altered any minds to promote our position on your planet, and we are not capable of speaking untruths. To that I must add — and this is stated in the transfer agreement — the decillean people have been able to alter and enhance minds for thousands of years."

"That is chilling," I said.

"Without appropriate controls, definitely, and I hasten to say, strict rules have always been in place to prevent abuse of this power. First and foremost, our mind-altering technology is limited to enhancements requested by a recipient. Second, decilleans are incapable of altering nondecillean minds. As specified in the transfer agreement, there are no exceptions to these rules as they apply to decilleans, but Earth's unsettled social conditions dictate some exceptions. George?"

"Yes, I will address this topic. As a general rule, ursavans are incapable of altering the minds of nonursavan humans, but we reserve the right to neutralize harmful thoughts and actions, including those that threaten the integrity of Ursavus and this planet as a whole. We can do so only when directly confronted, and we must leave no evidence."

I pulled back and frowned at him. "How does that work, George?"

"It happens through the eyes," he said. "It is called Quantal Optic Transduction, QOT."

"And how many times have you altered my mind?"

"I have made you aware of every alteration, and as I have tried to explain, they were essential components of our plan to recruit you, a very difficult, even hazardous subject. Your mind is entirely yours now."

"So, I have your word about this. All the changes you, Thius or anyone made, the mental blocks and whatever else. You say they are gone, all of them — but no proof."

Meterion's eyes flashed me. "Indeed, it is up to you now, Daniel, and I sincerely hope you will make what earthans call a leap of faith and accept, as ursavans did before signing the transfer agreement, that your thoughts and decisions are free of outside influence. And I must now depart to greet a tour train crowd at the store. And Daniel, I wish for our friendship to expand and pray the feeling is mutual."

He cupped his hand around his amber and vanished.

43

Confirmation

Meterion's chair was empty. There were two taps on the door, Rachel Smyth walked in and took his seat. Here was the winsome and serious roadmaster historian dressed like George for work in the lab. She handed George a small leather case, looked at me and said, "Hello again, Daniel. I have some more history to relate if you are interested."

The water bear badge on her lab coat triggered thoughts of how much I'd learned about her since the ride in the high-railer. Three identities, three names. Thius's partner and Sula's mother Eleva Sterling, Meterion's daughter Delia Waterbear, and George's research colleague Rachel Smyth. "You're decillean…not human," I said, hoping I didn't offend and feeling strangely drawn to her.

She touched her water bear badge and smiled. "I was born decillean, Daniel, and do you find it revealing that you have twice been attracted to a telepathic woman from another world?"

I thought Yes, and she said, "Very well, and unless you object I will remain telepathic for this meeting."

George took it from there. "Dan, Dr. Smyth has been an integral member of our genomics team at Ursavus E for many years, and we thought it appropriate for her to discuss some of our findings with you. She has agreed to summarize the research confirming what you have been told about Decilla Waterbear's DNA in humans."

Rachel quickly added, "Please understand, Daniel, I am here to present results, not to offer proof, so you may wish to consult the ursavan genomics archives for a complete chronology of the science supporting what I am going to share."

Like her father, I thought, a mix of formal and cordial, and still the alluring lady I met on the tracks that day.

She ran two fingers across her forehead and said, "Very well, my narrative begins with Meterion's initial visit to Earth and the amber pendant he gave Rose as a gift to Ursavus. Contained in the amber was a sample of attoscale decillean genomes, including Meterion's and Decilla Waterbear's. As soon as Ursavus and Decilles agreed on a partnership, ursavan scientists were given access to the genomes, and they were quick to recognize that decillean DNA and earthan DNA are different. A team at Ursavus E then searched for decillean DNA in many thousands of human genomes from all of Earth's continents and islands. This exhaustive survey provided firm evidence that the only decillean genes on this planet were a scant few found mostly in ursavans and all derived from Decilla Waterbear."

Rachel stood up, touched her badge again and said, "Now, with that in mind, Daniel, I will summarize evidence of Decilla Waterbear's genetic legacy. We will compare a specific portion of DNA from four people — Decilla and Meterion Waterbear, George Waterbear, and you. And I hasten to say the results of these comparisons have been confirmed repeatedly. You will need to be vertical now, Daniel."

I stood facing her as she extended her arms over the table with her palms down. "Stem cells, one each," she said, "Decilla Waterbear, Meterion Waterbear, George Waterbear, Daniel Oyente," and cloud-like models of four cells labeled DW, MW, GW, and DO appeared out of nowhere and floated above the table. I could see detailed structures within each cell — including mine.

Still seated, George asked if I was willing to take his and Rachel's word that these were precise models of cells derived from the four people named. I said Yes, and Rachel asked if I was aware that most of a cell's DNA, its hereditary material, resides in chromosomes within the cell's nucleus.

"Nothing new there," I told her. "Good," she said, "and realize this is true for decillean as well as human cells. And something else you might find fascinating. Decilleans and humans have the same number of chromosomes, forty-six — twenty-three pairs — numbered the same according to size, shape and DNA content."

"I find that more spooky than fascinating, Rachel."

George snapped open the leather case, pulled out a pair of blue-tinted glasses, peered at me through them and said, "Give us all a break, will you Dan?"

Rachel smiled at him, passed me the blue tints and added, "Yes, and you wouldn't need these magnifiers if you were enhanced. Please put them on and watch closely now."

A flip of her left wrist made the chromosomes in the four nuclei glow, and a snap of her fingers colored one chromosome in each nucleus bright red. "These are the Number Nineteen chromosomes, Daniel. They are all similar, and we will focus on them because they are the main bearers of genes derived from Decilla Waterbear."

A flip of her right wrist magnified the four red chromosomes, and she asked me to summarize what I know about DNA structure.

I said, "Okay. DNA consists of two helices held together by four key compounds — Adenine, Thymine, Cytosine, and Guanine. A pairs with T, and C pairs with G across the double helix."

"Basically correct," she said with a glance at George. He carefully removed two small instruments from the leather case, held them out for her, and she said, "Very well, I will now use a molecular probe and scalpel to extract a short segment of a single helix from each of the four chromosomes."

She worked quickly. "Very good, there we go — four short single helices now — all lined up vertically in front of us."

I asked if this was anything like the CRISPR technique.

She said, "Daniel, you make me want to laugh, and I assume you have memorized what the acronym designates."

"Yes, I believe it stands for Clustered Regularly Interspaced Short Palindromic Repeats, and I have only a vague notion of what that means."

"Another reason for enhancement, Daniel, and I must ask you to take my word again, that these short helices are comparable segments of DNA, essentially the same segment from each chromosome."

"Please continue, Rachel. I have no questions at this point."

"Very well. What comes to mind when you hear me say Genetic Code?"

"Just the basics again," I said. "The universal code — I mean I think it's universal — is the genetic information needed to construct every living being. It's coded in the DNA in sequences of A, T, C, and G…like one area of my DNA might bear the sequence AAAATGC. The same area from George might have GCTACTT, but if George and I were closely related, I would expect us to have many identical sequences."

"Basically okay, Daniel. Now watch as I label an A, T, C, and G on the helix from your cell."

I reset the glasses on my nose and said, "You realize my memory banks contain next to nothing about actual molecular structures."

"Hmm…I am surprised, Daniel, having studied your hyper-thymesia. Nonetheless, the blue tints will enable you to see and distinguish the exposed surfaces of A, T, C, and G, which are recognizably different. Please signal when you are certain you can distinguish the surface structure of A, T, C and G without labels."

When I told her Okay, the labels disappeared, and she used her probe to align Meterion's helix vertically next to mine.

"Very well, Daniel, these are comparable segments of DNA, yours on the right, Meterion left. Please observe the sequences of A, T, C, and G on both from top to bottom and tell me what you see."

I scanned the surfaces and said, "They are really different, as I would expect. My helix has lots of Thymine. Meterion's helix doesn't have any Thymine, and something on his helix doesn't resemble Adenine, Cytosine or Guanine."

"Correct, Daniel, in fact, there is no Thymine in Meterion's entire genome. Decillean DNA does not contain Thymine. Instead it contains a compound we call Decilline, D."

"So, Meterion's DNA isn't really comparable to mine."

"An arguable point, Daniel, but not the one I am here to pursue. Please note and memorize the surface structure of the Decilline compound while I position a segment of George's helix between Meterion's and Decilla's. I want you to compare these three now."

I took a minute, told her they were all about the same and they have Decilline but no Thymine.

"Excellent," she said. "The segments are virtually identical, and the presence of Decilline in George's DNA indicates what to you?"

"Well, I'm sure you'll tell me Decilla Waterbear was the original source. So does this mean George is part decillean?"

"No," she said, "not even close. George is fully human, but genomicists have established beyond a doubt that the Decilline in George's and Meterion's DNA is traceable to Decilla Waterbear."

George added, "And needless to say, the presence of Decilline in human DNA is a well-guarded secret, detectible only by ursavan technology."

Rachel waved at the pieces of DNA, and they disappeared. "Very well," she said, "you may remove the blue tints, Daniel, my demonstration concludes, and we will sit back down with George. I expect you will not be surprised to hear me confirm what my father and George told you. You have no decillean genes, no Decilline in your genome."

I tried not to show relief, but she and George picked right up on it. George tapped his pencil, and Rachel said, "We do not comprehend your feelings of relief about this, Daniel, and I wish to emphasize several facts about decillean DNA in humans. First, the DNA of ursavans contains multiple regions that are traceable to Decilla Waterbear. George, for example, has six traceable regions in his Number Nineteen chromosome. Second, this is not to say the total amount of decillean derivatives in George's DNA or in any other human is more than a minuscule portion of their whole genome. Third, as a decillean and earthan genomicist, I reject any tendency to consider these decillean derivatives alien or to call them alien genes. They were integrated into human DNA thousands of years past and have been regulated for millennia by epigenomic proteins and RNAs that are decidedly human. We call the decillean derivatives enhancers. They form parts of a very small set of human genes, and enhancement is their sole function. The effects of these enhancers are seen in the subtle but profound differences between ursavans and nonursavans.

"Now, in summary, Daniel, what we have shown you here applies to all humans who possess decillean genes. And we hope you will accept as fact that in the wake of the Decilla Waterbear tragedy, decilleans were successful in preventing additional transfers of their DNA to humans. The only decillean DNA in humans was derived from Decilla Waterbear."

Sula came to mind, but I thought it might be too personal to bring up. Rachel put her instruments back in her case, snapped it shut and said, "I was hoping our beautiful daughter would be mentioned in the course of this discussion. The answer to your question is Yes, humans and decilleans are compatible mates. Can they procreate? Generally speaking No. They are distinct species. Human sperm cannot fertilize decillean eggs and decillean sperm cannot fertilize human eggs. So, is Sula really Thius's and my daughter? Yes, and the proof is in her DNA, which is a mix of Thius's and mine. You see, when I first came to Earth, I chose to be fully human — human DNA, eggs, everything." She turned away and I was sure I saw a slight blush in her cheeks.

I asked, "So Sula is a true hybrid, a decillean human?"

"You may assume that," said Rachel, "but as I told you, I was fully human when she was conceived."

"Are there others on Earth? Is this common?" I asked.

"Sula is one of three," Rachel said, then steadied her eyes on me and vanished. I looked at George and sensed another bombshell.

44

Hyperspace

George stared into my eyes and QOT — Quantal Optic Transduction — flashed through me. Was he messing with my mind again? He planted his hands firmly on the table and said, "We must talk more about the decilleans, Dan, and Rachel thought you should hear this from me. We hope what you have learned today will help you accept my telling you that centuries ago decilleans abandoned their organic existence and fused with machine intelligence."

I snapped to attention, wasn't sure I heard him right. "What did you say, George? You mean decilleans aren't real, not biological — they're machines, some kind of AI machine collective, like a space hive? You're freaking me out again, George."

He touched his water bear badge and said, "With few exceptions, the decillean PEOPLE find inorganic existence far superior, and they believe as I do, a transition to inorganic is inevitable for any species whose technology reaches a fusional threshold. Barring global collapse, the human species could reach that threshold early next century."

A cold chill ran down my spine. "That's crazy, George! Fusing with machines? Machine minds? This is the ursavan plan for humans? For me? How far out can you get?"

"Actually not far out at all. Ursavans could join the decilleans today, leave the rest of humanity to face Earth's uncertain future, but most of us will not do so until at least 95 percent of humanity is ready."

I couldn't believe what he was saying. "Machines! This is madness, George! Like something out of a dystopic space fantasy. It would be the end of humanity."

He pulled off his wire frames and rubbed his eyes. "Ah, Dan, that attitude is based on the witless notion that humanity will lose itself in artificial intelligence. Thoughts of an inorganic future should elicit curiosity and hope, not fear. Humanity will lose nothing except the limits, burdens and harmful traits of biological minds and bodies. Fusion with artificial intelligence could only be dangerous if sinister forces become involved or if we let it happen without safeguards. It does concern us that an undercover nonursavan consortium is developing AI at an alarming rate. These people are beholden to their nations' armed forces. Ursavus, as you should realize by now, has no military interests."

"None of this convinces me, George. I'd never give myself to a machine — no body, no DNA, no living cells, no blood, sex, taste buds, muscles, my own independent brain!"

"It's time to loosen your reins, Dan, try thinking beyond human hubris and dogma. We're talking about life without aging, without pain, without disease."

"But you're telling me Jason, Rose, Thius, Sula, Erik, APELLA — everyone in Ursavus is ready to follow the decilleans — give themselves to a nebulous machine?"

George gave me his QOT look again. "Dan, the nebulous machine or space hive you envision is renowned throughout this galaxy and beyond as the Decillean Pluraxial, and I believe you should take care thinking for your friends. The decilleans gave up nothing. If they choose, as Rachel has, they can regain any or all aspects of organic existence. Are you not intrigued by Rachel's and Meterion's ability to live in more than one kind of body?"

"As in shape shifting?"

"The preferred term is quantum transformation."

"Call it what you will — I can't imagine Rachel or anyone living that way."

"And that tells me you would have benefited from more time with my friend and colleague Rachel Smyth, Dr. Delia Waterbear. Such a brilliant, intrepid mind — inorganic decillean transformed to organic human. Like all decilleans, Delia was organic at birth and joined the Pluraxial after a period of rapid mind development. But unlike most decilleans, she never lost her fascination for organic existence, and before arriving here, she had visited and studied the evolution of sentient organic life on fourteen planets in five different galaxies. Among her many accomplishments, Dr. Waterbear is a galactic authority on how specific technologies effect the development of civilizations."

George was on a roll. "Needless to say, Dan, we were elated when Delia chose to remain on Earth. We set her up to work at Ursavus E, inserted information into public records to establish her dual background as Rachel Smyth and Eleva Sterling — and yes, she is as human as any of us. Delia worked here in the lab for a year before she ventured out and created herself as a public figure — antiwar firebrand Eleva Sterling. I introduced her to Thius at Harpy's that long-ago evening, and if you'd seen those two young people together, all your concerns about ursavans and decilleans would disappear. They were both overwhelmed, changed and united forever — two people from distant worlds. Eleva said it felt like they were tossed together in a plasma storm, and perhaps they were, for the last thing on their minds was the possibility of conceiving a child. Sula was born 268 days after they met."

I wanted to hear more about Sula but there was a light knock at the door and Riffle Stone walked in, gave something to George, then turned on his heels and vanished. George smiled and set a small carving of a bear in front of me. "Riffle and I want you to have this," he said. "It's made from antler inlaid with quartz a mutual friend found on 60-Odd Peak.

"Dan, most of my life I've dreamed of a world where the Great Bears roam free, and our decillean friends achieved that reality centuries ago. When they reached fusional threshold they turned to stellar plasma for limitless power, left their home planet and built a civilization, their Pluraxial, in interplanetary, interstellar space. Their exodus gave organic life on Decilles a chance to thrive, to evolve and replenish itself without impact from the decillean population and its technology. A similar future awaits humanity and Earth. We have the potential to build an interstellar existence and free this planet from the detestable Anthropocene — no more devastation by wars, an end to wanton planetwide exploitation and a reversal of unprecedented extinctions."

I ran my finger over the polished stone bear. "You really believe all that, George?"

"Yes. And a fully enhanced Daniel del Oso would contribute significantly to making it happen."

"You see me persuading people to fuse with machines?"

"Eventually, perhaps, but first we must solve Earth's immediate problems. As I have said, Ursavus stands ready to implement solutions. What we lack is a popular mandate to act. We have worked for over fifty years to steer humanity away from its self-destructive path. Yes, we can alter thoughts, even change mindsets using QOT. But this is generally limited to one-on-one interactions. Overall we have failed, as evidenced by the great mass of humanity that remains unaware, apathetic, misinformed or misdirected. As a fully enhanced ursavan, you could awaken and motivate hundreds of thousands — perhaps millions — and we would see overwhelming demands for essential environmental and social changes worldwide.

"Think of it, Dan. You would have full expression of your extraordinary talents." He checked his watch. "Now, change of topic. About your son."

"My son? What else could there be, George? I don't want to hear any more about Nate's death."

"This is about your son's life, about his latent genius and the gift of his presence. Nathaniel was never a member of Ursavus, but even without enhancement, his memory nearly matched yours, and his cyberability and grasp of quantum physics were off human charts."

George pulled out his wire frames again, turned them 180 degrees and said, "These are made of clear attofibers, chiefly for appearance in the nonursavan world, and they help me phrase difficult topics, such as the aftermath of your son's fatal accident."

"What now, George? I can't take much more."

"Believe me, Dan, you want to hear the rest of this. The decilleans take their noninterference rule very seriously, and they made a rare exception years earlier when they granted our request to restore William McClun. Regettably, Ursavus was not prepared to repeat the request for Nathaniel."

"So…why are you telling me this?"

He held up four fingers. "We have Jason, Sula, Meterion and Delia to thank for what transpired. Unlike the rest of us, they refused to be bound by any rules in the case of Nathaniel Oyente, and they convinced the Decillean High Council that it was imperative — in the future interests of decilleans and humans — that Nathaniel Oyente be restored to life, that his unique gifts reach full expression."

My jaw dropped. "You're saying Nate is alive!?"

"Yes."

"Where is he, George? When will I see him?"

"That is for Nathaniel to decide, and you must hear me out on this. When your son was restored, Meterion told me, and I quote, 'Please understand, we had to be forthright with young Mr. Oyente regarding why he was under decillean care. He exhibited no fear or apprehension, only heightened interest when informed of Decilles and our inorganic existence. Indeed, Nathaniel continued to express a strong desire to remain with us and to become a member of our Pluraxial.'"

"No George! Nate's not in some kind of hyperspace."

"Call it that if you must. With Meterion's assistance your son obtained High Council approval and joined the Decillean Pluraxial. Ultimately the council's decision was based on respect for Nathaniel's right of self-determination, something that decilleans and ursavans take very seriously."

George turned abruptly to his computer and said, "Shut down, session over."

I reached out to him. "Wait — damn it — wait a minute. You can't leave me hanging like this. You said there would be more time."

"Yes, but first a reminder, if you decide against joining, I must erase all details in your mind about Ursavus and Decilles, including what you've just heard about your son."

Everything blurred — like when I pushed too hard on a steep rise. "That's a sucker punch, George! Blackmail!"

"I suppose it is, Dan, and I am sorry your situation has come down to this, but there is no alternative. Imagine being a nonursavan with knowledge of us, of Nathaniel. Inevitably you would want to confide in someone, a nonursavan friend you think you can trust. From there the story would spread, suspicions would be raised and we would be forced into wasteful self-defense. Someday perhaps, humans won't be shocked and defensive to learn that people with extraterrestrial genes and preternatural powers walk among them, but not for a while. Yes regrettably, if you do not join we must return you to your old self.

"Now, you need to catch your breath. We have one more excursion for you, a fitting end to our recruitment efforts. Thius and Delia are driving hydrogen-powered Steam Sheila and will meet you along the river below William's Place. They are twenty minutes west of there as we speak, and Riffle Stone stands ready to teleport you to Rosey's. Your bike is waiting for you, thanks to Sula, and the next time I see you there will be no quandary, only yes or no."

"What's this about, George? I need time to think!"

He pointed to the door and said, "No more thinking, Dan. Just go, and don't forget your carving."

Riffle Stone met me in the hallway and said, "Mr. Oyente, I have arranged for you to emerge from this teleport wearing ursavan-style attire. Your organic body will welcome it."

I expected diamonds for the send-off, but he said, "A classic handshake suffices for two plebeians, Mr. Oyente. I hope to see you soon."

He was gone and so was I, and this time I found myself in Rose's shed next to my bike — and dressed for a ride — damn. I tried getting my thoughts together, jumped on my bike and was down at the track when an eastbound engine came into view.

45

Out of Time

It was a local mix like the one on Bozeman Pass. I stood in a cold sidewind as the shiny black engine rolled by. Thius and Rachel were in the cab, and I waved but they kept looking straight ahead — stiff like cyborgs. Then there were gons, tank cars, flatcars, and five boxcars but no arm or shout. Was this the final bust? Had George given up on me?

I heard a voice. *Be ready for the end of the train.* Where did that come from?

A string of autoracks went by, then a bright red caboose and there was Apella leaning out from the rear platform shouting, "HAND IT UP, MY FRIEND!"

"YOU'RE HERE!" I yelled and wheeled my bike to pace the train.

She grabbed the bike, set it on the platform, reached down and pulled me up.

"Wow," I said, "you feel strong as a bear or am I just hyped from the teleport?"

"It's not hype, and I can tell you're glad to see me, Daniel." She brushed her hair aside and sniffed the air. "Hmm, I detect a few molecules of Riffle Stone's manly eau de cologne. He has good taste."

She used two fingers and a turn of her wrist to hoist my bike to a wall hook. Like Superwoman in a bike shop, I thought...dressed in tight jeans, white shirt, and at ease in the blustery chill. She tied her shirt tails loosely at her hips, leaned against the guard rail and said,

"I know about George's ultimatum, Daniel, so it's now or never and difficult for all."

The caboose wobbled as though caught in a cross wind, and she tugged on my jersey. "I like the clothes Riffle chose for your trip. So talk to me. Other than saying yes or no to George, what else is on your mind about joining Ursavus, being an ursavan?"

I braced against the railing and told her, "I think we're really different about the superhuman stuff, Apella. I've never had an urge to be more than human."

She unbuttoned the top of her shirt, put her arm around me and said, "But Daniel, I know you're intrigued with telepathy and agelessness. And tell me QOT and teleporting don't fascinate you. Besides, having a few superhuman qualities doesn't detract from being human. Do I seem different or unappealing to you?"

"No, you're as beautiful as ever, perfect, should have told you up at High Lake. How long have you been with Ursavus?"

"Since December, 1979 when my lab director called me to her office, told me about Decilla Waterbear and showed me the full set of Decilla's genes in my DNA. I was elated but sad for my mother and father. They never knew they had decillean genes, never had a chance to join. I lost my parents two years before I met you."

"I am sorry, Apella. I remember trying to get you to tell me about them but you never would."

Her arm tightened around me. "It's safe to share now," she said. "My parents were world-renowned professional climbers, a great team, died in an avalanche triggered by a helicopter crash. You read about the incident, I'm sure."

"You mean the one in the Himalayas? Reported as pilot error. I was suspicious at the time. Revar and Tine Chandigar are your parents?"

She stepped away, looked at the track behind us and said, "Yes, the unjustly accused ecoterrorists, and I would have been with them but it was final exam week. The crash was a setup, the pilot survived. My parents had so many powerful enemies — corporate and government. Years earlier they made me promise if something happened to them I would immediately change my identity, use their contacts and hidden cash to alter records, and above all, not attend their funeral. You see why I didn't want to talk about them. I didn't feel safe until I joined Ursavus."

I felt the train throttle up, and Apella tugged at my jersey again. "So, Daniel, on a lighter note, what do you think of Riffle Stone?"

"Don't know, guess I'd say he's sort of likable, funky and stiff, maybe borderline human."

She laughed. "Riffle's enjoying his fresh new existence and release from a tumultuous past. He'll soon join the Mountain Atlantic Regen's outreach program. His niece Nancy has been with MAR for eight months."

"His niece Nancy? The antler bear. I should have known. Mr. Stone is — was Andy Denton."

"Yes," she said, "Andy's special talents, like yours, were underutilized, repressed. Two neural nets had to be rebuilt, one with a neuromorphic chip enabled him to be fully enhanced as the very personable and tech-savvy Riffle Stone. Deputy Loyal Crispin disappeared the day after Andy's ceremony, his ATV found at the bottom of a long drop up Shewolf Gulch."

Her eyes burned through me. "Daniel, don't even go there. Ursavus did not kill Crispin. We are strict pacifists."

"Yes, I've been told that a lot, Apella, but I still have doubts."

"Your doubts stem from your humanity, Daniel. Virtually all nonursavan humans are capable of violence. It is a genetic mindset, a consequence of human evolution that makes it difficult to believe unconditional pacifism can be real."

I looked down at the track as the caboose rumbled onto a causeway between the river and a cattail marsh. A pair of wood ducks fluttered out of the green and veered east ahead of us. Apella looked at me and said, "Daniel, I hope you understand why I waited so long to tell you I joined Ursavus. I also hope you will understand why I waited until now to tell you I am with the Decillean Pluraxial."

KABOOM! It was like a shock wave, a brain explosion — I grabbed for the railing. "You! No, no way. You wouldn't."

I heard the voice again. *Listen to your friend. Free your mind,* and Apella said, "You and I are so close yet so very different, Daniel. When I joined Ursavus and began studying the Pluraxial, I was enthralled, eager to join, and it was a dream come true when Meterion and Delia Waterbear appeared in my lab and said they wished to sponsor my assimilation. That was March 26, 1999, and I have been working joyously as one of seven ursavans in the Pluraxial ever since."

The train entered a tight curve, and she vaulted onto the railing, balanced on it with her arms stretched up. "Daniel, this body is synthetic, capable of doing anything I ever could and so much more. I've lost nothing from my biologic years. Once again, I'll ask, Do I seem different or unappealing to you?"

I answered No and heard a raven in a dive — or was it the voice or the train?

Apella hopped down, shook her hair back and said, "Daniel, I have not been involved in your recruitment by Ursavus, but I did ask George to consider letting me help if an impasse occurred. So here we are. Your recruitment has played out, and you have a basic understanding of Ursavus, but we both know something crucial is missing. You have no real sense of what it is like to be an ursavan. My plan for you is a temporary membership. You would assimilate a set of reversible enhancements, and for part of a year be telepathic, possess teleportation ability and feel — actually be — thirty years younger. Rose, Delia and I will teleport with you to a series of meetings and mass rallies in major cities throughout the world."

Her amber earrings glittered. She looked so young and free, like when we first met. "Please consider this with care," she said.

The train slowed along a calm stretch of the river, and reflections in the glassy surface looked like — "Inverted trees," whispered Apella, "and you once told me their tips look like they are submerged in another world."

Brushy shoreline replaced the trees, then driftwood near the mouth of a stream, then rocky cliffs, then Kain's Cut, and the voice came loud and clear — *Quick, top of the cliff!*

Apella handed me binoculars. Someone was standing above the rock slide. "Erik Galen?"

"Yes, your son, and now at last the decision is yours alone, Daniel." And she turned and vanished in the wake of the train.

And I Did Not Want It To End... Ever

About the Author

Larry G Mitchell is a teacher and researcher, a student of nature. He holds a PhD and was a biology and zoology professor at the University of Montana, Iowa State University, and Iowa Lakeside Laboratory. Larry has written and produced wildlife programs for public broadcast, coauthored life science textbooks, and found time to study music history and mountain railroading, and to learn the cons and pros of hard-rock mining. Larry's research for *Apella's Turn* swept him out of academia to a life of semi-seclusion in the mountains of western Montana and northern New Mexico. When he isn't writing, you might find Dr. Mitchell out alone, climbing a steep trail on a mountain bike, snowshoeing the high country, or rock climbing and canoeing with his wife, Susan, anywhere between southern British Columbia and the Santiago Mountains of southwest Texas. He is grateful to you for taking a look at *Apella's Turn*.